Down to the Last Quarter!

by
Colin Manuel

Illustrations by
Ben Crane

PPG

Down to the Last Quarter!

E-Book ISBN: 978-0-9918604-6-3
Paperback ISBN: 978-0-9918604-7-0

Additional copies of this book may be ordered by visiting the
PPG Online Bookstore at:

🍁**PolishedPublishingGroup**

shop.polishedpublishinggroup.com
or by contacting the author at phone 403-845-4914, by fax 403-844-8482
or e-mail at colinmanuel@hotmail.com

Due to the dynamic nature of the Internet, any website addresses mentioned within this book may have been changed or discontinued since publication.

ACKNOWLEDGEMENTS

This third and likely final book about the adventures of
Aubrey and Sabine Hanlon is dedicated to some very key players…

"Doctor Mork" or Mark Bertagnolli… our friendship is hallowed.
The Bertagnolli family, Anne-Marie, Donald, Kate and Ken…
you add the spice.

The Scotts, the Mays, the Titfords…
did we really deserve to live *that* close by?

TO…
Crystal Oliver… your unwavering belief in my writing efforts is
cherished beyond measure.

AND, OF COURSE, TO MY IMMEDIATE FAMILY…
Kev, Andrew and Neil: we revel in all that you are.
Marty and Fearsome Candace Umscheid; you are inseparable from us.

AND…
My wife Felicity: Yes, we have had our ups and downs
but we endured them together.
What can I say but I'd do it all again in a heartbeat!

Contents

Whatever you might think of the folks in the farming community, we are who we are. And because we all run what amounts to our own small businesses, we tend to be highly individualistic. So it is that we are not afraid to be just who we are, to express that individuality. This is a salute to all those who struggle daily to make a living on the land, a salute to your resilience, your independence and your empathy as neighbours. We sons and daughters of the soil truly have something to celebrate…

…OURSELVES!

Chapter One
"WE'RE NOT FINISHED YET..." THE TALE OF A GARGOYLE

*T*he experts— and all of the others who know about these things—will tell you loudly that business is cyclical, that there are always highs and lows. They talk knowledgeably of boom followed by bust, of supply hitched forever to demand, of spendthrift consumers driving the economy and constantly raising the level of household debt.

"Yeah well," Aubrey Hanlon found himself thinking that day in spring, "the only cycle we get in farming these days is a picture of Farmer Joe screaming down a hill on his bicycle and shouting, 'Look Ma, no hands…oh shit!'" Ever since he and his wife Sabine went into farming, they had never actually experienced a true high, a real boom, a time when consumers couldn't get enough beef and were prepared to pay whatever it took to get it. So it is when people like farmers and fishermen have only known variations of the economic doldrums, they are compelled to search for other ways to justify what they do for a living, as long as they find themselves still on the right side of survival. They convince themselves that it's the *"lifestyle"* that makes their world go round, and there is some truth to that.

In the years of *Fancy Free in the Back Thirty,* Aubrey and Sabine Hanlon had expanded their beef operation on the farm near Rocky Mountain House, and it was clearly the larger numbers that allowed them to soldier on in agriculture. Just. Yet it wasn't economics that kept them "whole" as it were. It was the full context of farming: a lifestyle sprinkled generously with the spice of great friends and neighbours, social get-togethers and regular neighbourhood "work bees" all wrapped up in a raucous ball of fun. And as so often happens when you have gotten used to survival mode only, you don't often see that things are starting to turn for the better. Why would you when you're still on that bicycle, in headlong flight down that hill while trying to hang onto your hat?

Intuition. n. *The art or faculty of knowing without the use of rational processes; immediate cognition.* That was one of the definitions given in an old high school dictionary that Aubrey still possessed—a definition of something that Sabine seemed to exhibit in abundance. Aubrey had none, zero; hell, Sabine would be quick to vouch that he had very little imagination, either. Aubrey was the "hands-on" type, the literalist for whom imagination was an adult version of finger-painting. So it wasn't Aubrey but Sabine who came up with the suggestion straight out of the blue. "Let's keep back thirty of our best heifer calves this year and have them bred by a good bull. That way, we can either sell them next year as bred heifers or we can choose to calve them out ourselves."

"Are you nuts?" Aubrey responded.

"Has she lost her marbles?" asked Pete, their neighbour and close friend.

"My gal, you sure have prescience or spunk, one or the other," said Jeannie, Pete's wife.

But Aubrey made a point of never going against his wife's intuition, not these days anyway. She was possessed of a sixth sense that a particular moment was the right time to do something, that same "prescience" to which Jeannie had referred. Besides, Sabine was also the kind of wife who would ensure her husband would keep any really uncharitable thoughts to himself. If Aubrey truly felt the urge to give his ten cents' worth on some decision, he would go tell the cows. Moreover, and this was the best thing, they always agreed with him; at least he convinced himself this was the case. Thus it was that the Hanlons became "fully-fledged ranchers" (and hopefully not fully-fledged turkeys, Aubrey was thinking), bona fide ranchers who would be around for the foreseeable future. "What do you think, my good lady Nellie?" Aubrey asked the matriarch of the herd, the Hanlon "sacred cow". She shook her head and plopped profusely, as if to suggest he should go find someone else more amenable to all this sweet talk. Anyway, given that it was so early in the year, Sabine would likely change her mind two or three times. "It is after all a woman's prerogative, you know," she would always say demurely.

The calving season had been good to them, beneficent in fact. They had lost one calf at birth but had been able to foster a twin from another cow onto the mama, so technically at any rate they were still at one hundred percent. It was now that lull between the calving and the seeding season that gave people too much slack time, too much time to think. It was also at about this time of year that the auction bug tended to hatch. Aubrey was browsing through a Central Alberta paper when he spotted an ad for an auction not far away, a farm dispersal somewhere out near Spruce View—just one skip out of home territory, so to speak. Any auction this close was always worth a peek because you didn't have far to go home if you bought something big. He'd made up his mind to go even before he had seen what was on offer. His quick scan through the list clinched it. There was a bale mover that could carry fourteen round bales at a time. Moving bales with a clapped-out old trailer that veered from one side to the other for a quick visit with the frog that lived in the ditch or the blue bird that had its home in the fence line was a dreadful chore. With this thing, he would not even have to get off his tractor seat to get all his bales home. Not that he would be able to come close to being able to afford it because some overpaid "rig pig" would run the price out of sight. But what the heck, it would be interesting to see what it went for.

Ah, but what could he do about Sabine? This called for strategy with a big "S", a carefully calculated strategy. He rechecked the ad and there it was, "large offering of good quality household and miscellaneous." For Sabine, if he played his hand with flair, it would represent an all-you-can-eat smorgasbord too good to miss. "Items include complete English Wedgwood tea-set, exercise bike never used, china collectibles from Schmid, Johnson Brothers, Royal Doulton, and many more items too numerous to list." So the manoeuvring began.

"Honey, did you see the ad for the Rosehill auction coming up in Spruce View?" said Aubrey as casually as he could.

"No!" Sabine's "no" was flat, *way* too flat.

"Well, there's one coming up. It's got some good stuff, too."

"Huh! Like what do you call good stuff? You've got your beady little eye on something, haven't you? Our money is burning a hole right through your pocket, isn't it?" Aubrey hated it when his wife got caustic but he wasn't about to give up.

"Well, for one thing, there's supposed to be a large offering of household items. Good stuff. Quality stuff."

"How would someone like you know about quality?" Sabine huffed.

"Well, I married you now, didn't I? And don't forget who bought that antique phonograph for you that time! The dealer offered three grand for it and I only paid twenty-five bucks for both it and a stack of records." Ah, but any woman trapped by such inescapable logic usually remains in another world, by choice!

"Yes, well I said thank you then and I say thank you now. But as of today, as of this moment, we don't need a thing, not a single thing. I have everything a nice girl like me could ever wish for."

"Ah, but there's some Royal Doulton china," Aubrey was grasping at straws, and he knew it! He was flailing badly.

"Royal Doulton makes toilets, you goofball," said Sabine with a little too much gusto, knowing, however, that she would love to get her hands on some Royal Doulton collectibles. "But whatever it is on that list you want, you sure want it bad, right?"

It was time to cast out the killer bait, time to try a last troll with an iridescent lure sure to tempt any fish. "But it does say here there's a Wedgwood tea-set, complete." The reaction was instantaneous.

"Gimme that," she said snatching the paper from his hands. "Hmm, you know what? Maybe we could do with a day off the farm," she said. "Wedgwood, eh?

Complete, too. Probably go real high. But admit it, there's something you have your eye on, isn't there? What is it? Go on, tell me; I can keep a secret."

Aubrey knew his wife, knew how delicate his strategy would have to be. "Well, you know, there are a couple of things in there we could do with but they'll probably go too high for us to worry about. But you're right," he hurried on, "it's about time we had a day off the farm." God bless Josiah Wedgwood and his pottery! Furthermore, she had not cottoned onto his bale mover…yet; she was much too distracted by the thought of the Wedgwood tea-set.

So they went to the sale. Oh boy, did Sabine Hanlon ever go to that sale! Sabine Hanlon led herself totally astray! "Well, you don't get that sort of quality every day, now, do you? Not at those kinds of prices." Thus did she rationalize her purchases to herself and to anyone else who cared to listen. "I mean, we're talking genuine French crystal and real Irish linen. And what about the Norman Rockwell plates—the whole set, never opened—for a hundred bucks?" Lord bless the dear, departed old lady who must have collected for the sake of collecting. Her sad and untimely passing had left her bemused husband behind with "all this stuff" and nowhere to put it now that he was moving into an old folks' manor in Red Deer.

It wasn't that people were not bidding, they were. It was just that Sabine was bidding a little bit higher. Like a cougar hound putting yet another cat up a tree, she would corner her prey and bring that auctioneer's hammer down. The French lamp was exquisitely patterned with tiny fleurs-de-lys and crafted in a century when true works of art were created by skilled artisans. The sterling silver table set, knives, forks and spoons, again never used and made by the finest craftsmen in Sheffield, England. The original painting, in oil of course, of cows standing idly in a stream; it went so low because the frame had seen far better days. On the other hand, the frames on the two numbered Bernie Brown prints were not tatty at all, but Sabine had to have them "because we have no good agricultural art at home…those could be our cows standing out there among the poplars," she said. Okay, she need not have chased down the wide-screen TV set, but it went for only $57.50 and it worked. Or so "they" said, and she had no reason to doubt them. As if she needed an antique treadle sewing machine; but heck, Sybil, for one, would never forgive her for letting it go at $120—that is, if Sybil would ever even get to hear of it. The auctioneer, especially Jim Crawford, the man calling the honours, actually began to look her way at the outset of any bidding. She was flattered, even if he called her "Mrs. Hampton" a couple of times before she very succinctly corrected him.

In hindsight, Aubrey could've, should've stayed with his wife, but she was never one to need hubby to hold her hand. Besides, he was darn lucky he even got here. So he followed the gaggle of folk trailing the two auctioneers selling the line of machinery, Greg Sanderson and Tyler Rosehill. But before they got to the machinery itself, they had to sell the "miscellaneous" on the two trailers next to the farm shop. Fondly labelled "junk" by most farmers, it was not junk at all but buried treasure. Aubrey was cagey, though, for two very good reasons: (a) Whatever he bought, he would have to carry by himself all the way to the truck, and (b) Sabine would rake him over the coals and then not speak to him for a week if he bought yet another beaten-up ladder or a sixth pitchfork with a cracked handle, or a third tap and die set because for the life of him he could not remember where he had put the other two. He did get a real good Ridgid pipe wrench for eight dollars and an old but serviceable cattle waterer for twenty-five, both absolute steals really. Oh, and the box of mix-and-match steel cattle syringes for twelve dollars; Sabine was forever "fixing" one of theirs, usually in the middle of vaccination day with a hundred or so cows still waiting to be processed. So now at least she would have a few extra parts to play with. He swayed along with the crowd, happy to be in pastoral mode at this first auction of the year. That was when he found himself wondering how the auctioneers ever managed to remember the names of all their clients because this crew did not operate with the standard numbers system but used peoples' names. He was about to find out they didn't, remember names that is.

The crowd was now moving off to the first line of machinery when Greg, one of the auctioneers he knew, tapped Aubrey on the shoulder. "So, Osprey, how's it goin' out there in Rocky Mountain House country?"

"Oh hi, Dreg. Good, thanks."

"The name's Greg," he said, not miffed in the slightest.

"And I'm Aubrey. Osprey is a bloody bird."

"Oh I am sorry. Okay, let me get it straight. Aubrey Hampton, right?"

"No. It's Aubrey Hanlon. And you're Greg Sanderton, right?"

"Greg Sanderson with a big 'S'."

"Aubrey Hanlon with a big 'L'."

"Good deal. I'll make sure we get it right from now on," Mr. Sanderson the auctioneer grinned.

Progress through the first line of machinery was painfully slow as the auctioneers worked to whip up some enthusiasm, if not excitement. The bale mover was located at the very end of the line. In Aubrey's eyes it was an absolute monster of a machine, long enough to accommodate two rows of seven round bales and equipped with huge arms with metal wings to scoop bales off the ground and toss them onto the deck. On this particular day, Aubrey had refrained from going to look over it too closely because first, he was sure the price would climb into the stratosphere, and second, he did not want to betray his interest in it. So he had missed altogether the unsavoury-looking fellow proclaiming to all within hearing distance that there was "a bloody great crack right through the mainframe", apparently evidenced by a couple of cracked metal plates bolted thereon. On hearing this, the interest of the few potential buyers fizzled on the spot and they moved on to greener pastures while the fellow stayed on behind to continue his good deed for the day by alerting anybody else to the problem. Surprise, surprise, when the machine finally came under the hammer, there were only two interested bidders; Aubrey and Mister Scruff himself who scowled mightily at Aubrey every time Aubrey topped his bid. The price started out way below rock bottom and pretty much stayed there, going up in one hundred dollar jumps until Aubrey's final bid of $3,100, a mere fifth of what the machine would have cost new in its heyday, and a tenth of what it would have cost in today's market.

Yes, for sure the thing looked intimidating: maybe that too scared people away. The arms were reaching up high into the air, held there in transport mode by restraining chains each side. The moment Aubrey realized he was about to get it, he began to regret profoundly that he had not checked it out beforehand. Too late now, much too late! It was almost his, and at a price way too cheap, even if dear Sabine might think he had taken leave of all his senses.

"Thirty-one hundred," intoned Mr. Sanderson with the big "S", "thirty-one hundred..."

"Aw shoot, the guy can have the damn thing at that price, cracks and all," Mister Congeniality all but shouted at the auctioneer before storming off. Clearly it did not bother him that he was making an exhibition of himself but then he was too far away from his own neck of the woods to care so what did it matter?

"Sold to Aubrey Hanlon! She's all yours Mr. Hanlon at thirty-one hundred dollars," Greg Sanderson announced, not bothered by a sore loser's attitude; after all, he had seen it all before. "Good eye," he added as if it was an extra blessing.

"Why, oh why do they all say that, these auctioneers?" Aubrey was thinking. Maybe everyone else knew something about the machine that he didn't know. Maybe he would have found the problem if he had used his "good eye" to check it over beforehand. What had his opposite bidder said, "The guy can have the damn thing, cracks and all." Maybe he'd better take a look now that the crowd was moving away. Another older farmer hung back.

"You stole that thing, my friend," he said. "I paid sixteen thousand for mine when I bought it new seven years ago."

"Yeah, but that fellow bidding against me said something about a crack," responded a now very panicked Mr. Hanlon.

"Well let's you and I go take a boo," said the man as they approached the monster together. They couldn't miss it, "the patch"; metal plates not welded—as the man had been telling everyone—but clumsily bolted across the mainframe. Both plates showed signs of a crack, so Aubrey's heart went slip-sliding all the way down to his boots. A welder would charge a fortune to fix up a mess like this.

"Whoa! Whoa my friend! Hold your horses," exclaimed the man. "These goldarn plates are not doing anything. Why the bolts are not even tight. Some s-o-b has gone and bolted them on here to make it look like there was a crack. Somebody like your opposite bidder, I'm thinking. Maybe that's why he was so plumb mad when you topped his bid." The man straightened up. "Well, I'll be doggoned, I've never seen anything like it in my life."

"Me neither," said Aubrey almost compelled to kiss the man.

"The dirty rotten skunk," said the man laughing. "That's just downright dirty. Well you got yourself a hell of a deal."

It would only be the "hell of a deal" the man said it was if he could convince his dear wife it was a "hell of a deal".

"Well I thank you greatly for having spotted it," said Aubrey, not laughing so much as feeling decidedly guilty for having landed the thing somewhat under false pretences. Yes, he had trapped a rogue but how on earth was he going to break the news to Sabine that he had just blown away three thousand of their imaginary dollars? Where were they going to find three thousand real dollars without going on a begging mission to the bank? And he well knew what Sabine would have to say about that! Oh well, life was about to be a bit more entertaining, was it not?

He made his way to the front of the farm house where the household items were being sold from trailers loaned by the neighbours for the occasion. His mood should have been joyful, ecstatic even, but here he was "dragging his butt" as they say, trying to figure out the best way to tell his wife they were the proud owners of a machine she'd probably never heard of, let alone think they needed. There she was, planted squarely in front of the auctioneer, well not exactly planted for she was hopping from one foot to the other and actively bidding on— what, no, couldn't be, yes, could very well be—a fancy china doll, already up to two hundred and seventy, two eighty, two ninety, three hundred, three ten, three ten, three ten…sold! "Sold to Mrs. Sabine Hanlon. Good eye, Mrs. Hanlon."

"Good eye, good eye, my ass! I'll give you a good eye, Mister Auctioneer, black in colour," Aubrey was thinking. "A black eye, a real shiner!"

He made his way through the throng of people to his wife. There she was, standing in a field of someone else's acquisitions, a veritable collection of, well, stuff. What on earth did people do with it all?

"Oh hi, honey. Go grab me a coffee, would you? I've got one more thing I want to bid on," she smiled sweetly, much too sweetly for Sabine. Or was it guiltily? Aubrey, loyal husband that he was, decided to give her the benefit of the doubt and go with "sweetly". After all, he himself was burdened with guilt over his purchase, a purchase that Sabine would have denied him after the first call.

When he got back with the coffee, he had to give his head a good shake. Was he seeing things? No, sadly, most unfortunately he was not. She was bidding on, what the heck was it, a garden gargoyle, an enormous squatting creature with googly eyes that looked as though it was doing a slow "potty" on the trailer deck. They had not even bothered to try and move it, no doubt because it would take four men or a giant to lift it. Clearly Sabine intended it to be the "Evil Eye" to watch over her vegetable garden; no self-respecting deer would approach within fifty yards of *that* thing. But to Aubrey it was absolutely hideous, and becoming hideously expensive by the second. Worse yet, bidding enthusiastically against Sabine was the wicked Witch from Withrow, as Sabine liked to call her. She was Sabine's nemesis from previous auctions, someone Sabine loved to put down at any cost. But at three twenty, three forty, three sixty, three sixty…this was insane!

"Three sixty. Thank you once again, Mrs. Hanlon. You've been a huge help today," Jim Crawford was positively beaming at her.

"Huge help today." What was that supposed to mean? Better to tread carefully though. "People in glass houses and all that nonsense," Aubrey was thinking as he handed over her coffee. There he was, carrying his own big secret, a three thousand dollar secret, a secret just about as ugly as that gargoyle, as big too. Oh well, at least he could now mitigate her fury by pointing out how badly they needed a china doll and a gargoyle with a mouth as big as any of the day's politicians.

"Mrs. Hanlon, don't quit now." It was that pesky auctioneer. What did he think he was doing? Was he intent on bleeding their bank account dry or what? "Take a look at this beauty," he said. "It's real oak, the full nine yards."

"The beauty" was an antique tea trolley. Sure it was a beauty, but they already had one at home, didn't they? Okay, this one had beautifully crafted spoke wheels and it wasn't one of those usual "also-ran" antiques. It was the real thing as the man said, and be darned if Sabine Hanlon was going to miss out on it. But Bridget Broomstick, the Wicked Witch from Withrow wasn't going to miss out on it either. Moreover, Bridget was mad, spitting mad, all two hundred-plus pounds of her seething like a volcano about to erupt any minute, any second. Indeed, although little did she realize it at the time, she was an entertainment package all by herself the way she huffed and puffed and stomped her feet as she instantly topped Sabine's every bid. To make matters worse, the auctioneer was enjoying himself immensely, orchestrating every bid up to a new crescendo. Sure he was doing it the hard way, going up in ten dollar jumps each call, but Broomstick Bridget was on a mission, a crusade, not so much to buy the item itself but to trump her opposite bidder. That was when Aubrey caught himself actually rooting for his wife, as was most of the crowd given Bridget's formidable local reputation. Even when the bidding stopped at ten ten... hold on a minute, *ten ten*? Like one *thousand* and ten dollars? Aubrey's cheerleading suddenly gagged in his throat.

"That's enough, Big Mama!" the voice boomed over the crowd. Every eye turned to see The Wizard, the masculine version of the Wicked Witch from Withrow, same shape and all, and he was glowering. "Let 'er 'ave it kid; we ain't got that kind of money anyhow. 'Sides, you got a truckload o' crap already. Let's go!"

And as Sabine claimed her prize, everyone cheered, all except Aubrey. It was enough to put Bridget into full retreat too, into full-blown psychological retreat. No, not so much a retreat, but a "revenge psychosis". Aubrey, smart husband that he was, did the right thing and congratulated his wife for getting what she wanted, mentally aware that now they would need a loan for four thousand. The auctioneer continued with an array of smaller items but in any event they would have to wait for the sale to end and the crowd to disperse. Even the Grand Wizard and his wife would have to wait it out before anything could be moved.

"Let me buy you a burger and a coffee and we can talk about what all I got," said Sabine with a little too much mystery and a chilling emphasis on the word "all".

"…Three blankets, good shape…ten, anywhere ten?" the auctioneer was back on the hustle.

"Seven," Aubrey yelled, and nobody bid him up. "Osprey Hampton", yelled Jim Crawford to his clerk. Osprey claimed his prize without bothering to put the man right.

"Wha', what on earth are you doing?" Sabine was totally at a loss.

"We need them to wrap around your fancy trolley," said Aubrey. "We don't want it scratched up when we take it home."

"More blankets," yelled the auctioneer. "Two packages, six in a package. Take one or take them both at the same price."

"Three dollars," Sabine signalled with her fingers.

"Four dollars," yelled Aubrey not having seen her signal.

"Five dollars," responded Sabine still with the instinct of that cougar hunting down its prey. Everyone began to snigger.

"Six?" the auctioneer quizzed Aubrey, his eyes alert with a little too much humour.

"Nah. Let the other bidder have them." Why did they need that many blankets anyway?

"They're yours, Mrs. Hanlon. Five dollars. Good eye!"

Aubrey just stood there, imagining smacking that darn auctioneer one in his other eye to give him a matching pair of shiners when he would have done better to focus on precisely why his dear wife had suddenly needed to buy another twelve blankets. He should have found himself wondering if they were going into the motel business or starting up a hostel for derelict farmers. But then he still harboured his own guilty secret, the three thousand "smackeroos" he had blown on the bale mover.

So they had a burger lunch, late lunch, afternoon lunch, both of them so warm and fuzzy one towards the other, almost sickeningly lovey-dovey for a couple their age. Until…until Aubrey said, "well I guess we should go settle up our bill and head out, no?"

"I guess. I'm so glad you didn't buy anything today at least," this came out more as a hope than a statement. Then, "I don't know how you did it. You're one good boy!" This came out a little too quickly; a statement meant to fortify that hope, no doubt.

"Well, actually I bought us a bale mover."

There was a moment's silence, a long moment. This was not a computer clinically processing data, this was a highly volatile human creature with a range of emotions no computer could ever claim, and this human was desperately trying to downplay the import of what she had just heard.

"Wha'? What? How? How much did you, did we pay?" This question came out still in feminine falsetto.

"Thirty-one," said Aubrey as if trying to disguise the truth.

"Thirty-one dollars?" said Sabine still in feminine falsetto.

"No. Thirty-one hundred," Aubrey dropped the answer like a brick on her foot.

"Three thousand one hundred?" This time the question came out as no more than a squeak.

"Three thousand one hundred," said Aubrey. It was now time to be a man.

"Oh dear, oh dear," his better half whispered, not quite sure if she was the better half or the faint half at this moment in time.

"Why? Oh, I get it. How much did *you* spend?" Aubrey's question did not come out exactly as an accusation, but it did betray some of the characteristics of one.

"Well, to be totally honest, I am not sure. Let's wait and see what I have on my bill." Truth be told, Sabine had absolutely no idea. Was she just trying to delay the inevitable? Probably.

They joined the line-up to pay; or rather Sabine joined the line-up because line-ups were like gardening, they were "something Aubrey did not do". So when she had paid and received an itemized receipt much too full of writing, Aubrey was not on hand to see it. And for whatever reason, he never thought to ask when they found each other again; he was too busy thinking about what he had to load into the truck. All he said was, "so you just got yourself a couple or three pieces, right?" as they moved off. "I'll go and get the truck and we'll load up your garden thingy and the trolley and we can head on home. I'll have to bring a tractor to pull the bale mover home."

"Sure thing," said Sabine, not exactly duplicitous but verging on it by virtue of not yet saying what would soon have to be said.

By now the sale was over, and everybody was busy organizing to get their treasures out. This resulted in Aubrey having to park a little farther away from the trailers than he would have liked so as to avoid getting hemmed in. What the heck, Sabine only had a couple of pieces after all. They'd pick up the trolley first, wrap it up in blankets and load it. Then he would get the help of a couple of stout backs to help load Godzilla the Garden Gargoyle.

The trolley was a gem, no doubt about it. They took their time wrapping the blankets around it and cinching them tight with baler twine, a plentiful supply of which was always on hand in the truck because Aubrey was too lazy, er let's say too forgetful, to clean it out. Then they bungeed it into the front corner of the truck box behind the cab.

But Godzilla was something else. She was a stone and clay creation that had to weigh in at over three hundred pounds. The problem, though, was not so much finding enough strong arms to lift it; it was the fact that when the four men including Aubrey began the lift, there was a distinct ripping sound. The instant Aubrey felt that cold stab of air on the bum cheek, he knew what had happened, his worst nightmare. That morning, he had not told his wife he had run out of clean boxer shorts because he couldn't face her usual lecture about how he could never put his dirty laundry where it was supposed to go; he had simply elected to go without. But he could not now let go of the load to remedy the situation. It would have been okay if the WW from W, the Wicked Witch from Withrow, had not decided to announce this breaking bit of news to all present before turning to add her own colourful commentary on the wobbly expanse of pink exposed inadvertently to the sun. It didn't make things any easier for the other three men carrying it either; they just managed to make the tailgate before collapsing in gales of laughter at Aubrey's expense. What could Aubrey do but hold the flaps of his trousers and laugh along with them. Sabine on the other hand was both mortified and puce with embarrassment. Why was her fool husband not wearing underpants? And this was neither the time nor the place to find that out! As if to sew up the comedy routine, some enterprising young fellow appeared with a foot of electric fencing wire; the fine stuff that the cows always seem to break.

"Last time that happened to me," he said, "I sewed up my pants with this stuff; it pokes through cloth like nothing. But don't get me wrong, I ain't about to do it for you. No sir, your wife can do that."

As if Sabine wanted in on the final act, but now she had no choice. As for Aubrey, always one to make the best of a bad situation, he began hamming it up for the audience until some wise guy commented that he preferred his ham a brighter pink and without evidence of growth implants. At least that was how Sabine was to tell the story later, and what a story it was. She herself felt compelled to stab him in the pink with the wire just to keep him still, which suited Bearded Bridget just fine for she was now busy taking pictures with her cell phone—enough for every month of the calendar it seemed. Aubrey never knew how close he was to becoming Mister January-through-to-December in a "Wonders around Withrow" calendar for 2012.

Finally the men helped push Godzilla far enough back into the truck box that they could shut the tailgate. Aubrey thanked them profusely before turning to Sabine and saying, "okay, time to head home, honey." He'd had quite enough drama for one day, for one month even.

"Er, but we're not quite finished yet," she said with a hint of a tremor in her voice. "That pile over there, all that stuff on the grass, that's all mine, er, all ours."

Aubrey looked uncomprehendingly at the monster TV set, at the gaggle of framed pictures, a very distinctive fancy lamp, and all the other assorted boxes. "You mean all that, the TV and that whole pile of stuff around it?" He did well not to call it junk.

"Yes!" Abrupt and to the point. No hint of apology.

"How, how much did you spend?" Aubrey's question came out a little breathlessly.

"We'll talk about that on the way home," she said. "Just help me wrap it up and load it, will you? And don't you dare make a scene." Curt, business-like, in command.

When they were finally done, Aubrey commented that they must look like a couple of hillbilly rat-baggers, heading back to the cabin in the mountains. Sabine wisely declined to say anything, deciding not to speak unless what her husband said demanded a reply. That did not happen for a good ten miles, and then Aubrey's question came straight out of the blue. "So how many dollars do we need to find? Four thousand?"

"Let's say five," she said.

"We'd best go into the bank, then, and float a loan for five grand on the bale mover. At least we scored big time on it. They're worth way more than what we paid." It was a bit of an uncharitable statement as Aubrey came to realize later. They had in fact scored on everything. In terms of value for money, that auction was the best they ever attended, even if they did not know it at the time.

A retrospective silence ensued. It was better that way, Sabine was thinking.

Chapter Two
DIOPHOXYLENE ™

*M*urphy's Law, (The first Murphy, Irish thinker and sage preceded English Common Law by some two hundred years, at least that's what they say…), Article number 246, or thereabouts, stipulates the following:" In any and all circumstances, thou shouldst not endeavour to conduct thy business using another's conveyance unfamiliar to thine own person, especially and particularly when thy business is to be conducted upon a public artery or thoroughfare."

Now Aubrey kind of knew he should not have borrowed Pete's big Deutz 9160, all one hundred and sixty horses of it, because he always felt decidedly uncomfortable using someone else's equipment. But his own big I.H. tractor had a flat back tire, and besides, its rear duals would have made it something of an added hazard in its own right on any public highway; plus, Pete was a special friend, the sort who would do absolutely anything to help you.

"Ach man, it's just a two-wheel drive, same as most other older tractors. What can go wrong? Just steer the darn thing straight and remember you're on a public highway populated by occasional idiots and you won't have a problem. I'd bring your bale-mover home for you but I've got to be in Edmonton for the week. Just get Sabine to drive behind you with her flashers going and get Jeannie to drive ahead, same thing."

"This here Jeannie is not gonna be flashing anyone," Jeannie interrupted. "There's just not a whole lot left to be flashing anyhow."

So it was planned. Luckily the two days of heavy rain had finally eased up, so the highway was dry, even if the shoulders were slippery and the ditches full of water. Just as long as none of them had to pull off the highway, they would be fine. Yes, they would have to drive slap-bang through the village of Caroline, but big rigs went through there all the time, so what was the big deal? Better yet, it was a gorgeous day when they set out just after eight in the morning. Aubrey felt like the captain of the cruise ship the *Titanic*—no, not the *Titanic*, that name had too many negative connotations. Aubrey felt like the captain of the Q.E.II, high up there in his cab. As he would have expected of Pete, the tractor was full of all sorts of junk, but Aubrey had no need to move it or even touch it. As for the tractor itself, it was wonderful: a breeze to drive with much better all-round vision than he would have had in his own tractor with all of that glass. Why, he would be able to see absolutely everything that was happening.

It took them nearly an hour to get to the farm near Spruce View and another half-hour to hook up Aubrey's new toy, check it all out, and attach the four hydraulic hoses controlling the tilt of the deck and the bale arms. Without bothering to figure out exactly where each hose should go, Aubrey just plugged them in to get them out of the way; it wasn't as if he was going to be using the rig, after all. Furthermore, the arms were safety-chained so they could not sag or drop even if there was some hydraulic leakage in the system.

It was then that Sabine came up with her brilliant idea. "Why don't we stop at the Chinese restaurant in Caroline for lunch? You can park in that area where the logging trucks always park," she added to appease Aubrey's frown.

"Only if there's space," he said against his better judgement. "Let me repeat, only if there's space. If there are a couple of trucks in there, forget it! Okay ladies, let's stop all the cackling and get this travelling road-show mobile." As it turned out, he really should not have used those terms.

And as they had planned, Jeannie went on ahead, Sabine stayed behind. Aubrey turned onto the highway. He thought he had made allowances for the length of the trailer, but even so the one set of wheels managed to plough their way through a portion of the ditch leaving behind a huge rut. Okay, so the next time he turned, he would have to turn wider still.

Again it should be emphasized, Aubrey knew the rules; no radio when you should be concentrating. But things were going along so well, and since they only had to drive along a straight road, after all, he broke the rules to allow Pete's favourite country station to come booming in. Now psychologists or psychiatrists (whoever it is who studies these things) will surely tell you there are occasions when sound, what you hear, can be as much a distraction as sight, what you see. So there he was, in full flight with Johnny Reid, when a little Dodge Neon blasted past Sabine. Johnny Reid was just winding down when Aubrey looked in the rear-view mirror. What the heck! Where had that little flea on his tail come from? Even worse, the driver was driving like a zombie, with less than a car's length separating him from the back of the trailer. As if that wasn't enough, the guy, for guy it was, was trying to text and drive. Aubrey began a prayer as a loaded logging truck crested the brow of the hill in front of him, heading in the opposite direction. He dared not slow down for fear the little Neon would kiss his derriere but he knew, instinctively he knew, what was about to happen—and it did!

The little car pulled out to pass him, suddenly to be confronted with the full frontal of a naked Kenworth grille bearing down upon it. The driver of the Neon panicked and swerved back behind Aubrey but because he was still going too fast, he was forced to take the ditch. Aubrey watched his youthful face staring up at him through the driver's window, the eyes bulging out of their sockets. It was the expanse of the mini Abraham Lake in the ditch that prevented him from hitting a culvert full on. The little car plunged into the water and stopped dead in a cloud of steam before settling slowly down into the water like a mama fish getting ready to spawn. Aubrey slowed down, checked that Sabine had stopped to help before pushing the hand throttle back up to maximum. There was no way he was about to stop, not for some unhinged texting idiot; he just kept on going. Sabine caught up a mere ten minutes later. Okay, she would have done her Good Samaritan thing, knowing Sabine. She was such a good person.

As they pulled into Caroline, Aubrey found himself wondering about the wisdom of stopping for lunch, no matter how good the food was reputed to be. But then he was famished and Jeannie had already pulled into the parking lot. Aubrey swung into the vacant space where the big rigs usually parked and turned his own rig around so he would be ready to exit straight down the highway. Sabine pulled into the main lot alongside Jeannie and the three of them entered the restaurant looking forward to a delicious Chinese lunch. The restaurant was well known around these parts for serving up a great meal.

After they had ordered, Aubrey could contain his curiosity no longer. "Say, honey, what was the story behind the little red Neon that went for a swim?"

"You won't believe it," Sabine was still in full sail. "He passed me at a thousand miles an hour and he was bloody well texting at the same time. Unbelievable! He had a girl with him in the passenger seat, and blow me down if she wasn't working away on her own iPad or some such thing. Absolutely crazy! Anyway, I gave 'em a blast with the horn and it made not a blind bit of difference. It was soon after that he decided to pull out and pass you, and then, well, you know what happened. He landed up in Abraham Lake."

"Oh boy, what have I missed?" commented Jeannie.

"Oh, that's not the end of it. The best is yet to come. So I stop to help them and this tattooed wonder of a chick gets out, only to flop face-first into the water with her iPad floating off under the culvert. I grab onto her and pull her up and she lets loose a string of language that would have shamed a coalminer's dog. That's when her man gets out, if one could even call such a thing a man. He too is covered in tattoos, with enough ironware and chain hanging from his bits and pieces to anchor a whole darn bridge in place. He too decides he should make a speech, this one about bleep-bleep farmers being a bleep-bleep hazard and how they should all be banned from civilization. Something to that effect anyway. Well now, that didn't do a whole lot to lighten my mood, what with a gallon of water sloshing about in my boots from trying to rescue Bo-Peep from drowning. So I told the guy to try and not choke on his next hamburger, because a farmer likely had a hand in producing it. 'I don't eat meat', he says. 'I'm a vegan'. So I told him to try hard not to choke on his next dead cabbage, and I left them to it."

"You're not feeling guilty about leaving them to it, as you say, are you?" asked Jeannie.

"Guilty? No. Shocked? Yes. How can people be so ignorant?"

"You should have been a cop," said Aubrey. "It's all par for the course."

The meal was served—chow mein, chicken chop suey, ginger beef, all the usual—and it was great; a perfect and leisurely way to put some normality back into the day. But normality was not on the cards, at least not today.

The door opened, more like burst open, and a great bear of a man barged in, accompanied by a being who was fortyish and definitely all woman, judging by what all was on display. Both were expensively dressed in country dude style, or in the case of the woman, expensively under-dressed for maximum double exposure. Even their fancy leather boots had never been soiled by soil or toil. And "barged in" was the most apt of descriptions, seeing that clearly any and every appearance they made had to be dramatic. For sure, all eyes turned their way. But also for sure, was that none of the impressions were favourable. Not content to sit at a table for two, they picked themselves a table for six in the centre of the room where they would be better seen, no doubt.

This was when the command performance began, a how-to demonstration of throwing one's weight around to make the biggest splash. The waitress, brilliantly stoic under fire, handled them with a coldness reserved for "urban snots" as she later called them.

"Two coffees, two wonton soups and two chicken chow meins," the man snapped, rather than asked. "We don't need no menu; we're in a hurry. We got places to go, people to see."

The waitress, clearly a spirited young woman, didn't help things or her chances of a tip when she muttered "and trees to climb" before heading off to fill their order, which she did with the alacrity they demanded. She delivered the soup within minutes. When she came back with coffee, the man barked at her. "This here soup is cold. It's not that good either." His feminine accessory smiled sourly, undoubtedly to show her fangs.

The waitress leaned over, lifted both servings and took them away without a word. She returned a couple of minutes later with two fresh bowls which were accepted with no more than a grunt and the comment, "This coffee is no screaming hell either," from the woman who was surely trying to keep up with her Frac-Daddy. The waitress politely asked if they would care for another.

"Nah," the man snarled. "I told you we were in a hurry, didn't I? So just run along now and bring the chow mein." The man clearly had the social skills of a rig boss crossed with a porcupine.

The waitress turned on her heel, grinned widely at her audience and set off to fetch the chow mein, which she delivered with all the courtesy required of her position. But these two guests, they did not just eat the meal, they attacked it as if it was something they had just trapped, was still alive and about to get away on them. The customers in the place were mesmerized. When the waitress then produced the bill, Mr. Consultant studied it like it was some sort of Environmental Assessment before making the inevitable pronouncement. "The soup was cold, the coffee shit, and the chow mein no hell so there ain't no tip." Clearly this was a discourse aimed not solely at the waitress but at the whole dining-room, as if everybody in there had been in on some great conspiracy to sabotage their meal. But once again the waitress was brilliant. She let the man count out the exact money and hand it over. Only as they were leaving did she say "Have yourselves a better day, you urban snots." It was a pity they were out the door before they could catch the last two words. But everyone in the place heard and broke out in applause.

But the fun was far from over. Two minutes later, the door crashed open and Captain Consultant reappeared, and he was angry, boy was he angry! "Is there some dumb farmer in here who owns a tractor with some kind of big bale wagon behind it, out there in the yard?" he boomed. Okay, maybe he had a right to be angry, who knew, but this was an agricultural community, and he was not going to generate a whole lot of cooperation with an attitude like that.

"So what if there is some dumb farmer in here who owns a tractor out there in the yard?" Aubrey responded hotly. "Maybe it's mine, but then again, maybe not."

"Well you'd better hustle your butt out there right now and take a look at what that goldarn machine has done to my ve-hic-le." He wasn't about to take no guff from some dumb farmer. No sir, he was a big fish in a big pond! "And you'd better be good and ready to pay for the damage."

Having been a policeman in his first life, Aubrey had always found it hard to tolerate a rich man with a poor attitude, especially one compelled to call his car a "ve-hic-le". And this man's attitude was spilling over, so much so that half of the clients in the premises trooped out with the Hanlon crew to see what all the fuss was about. Ah, but they were not to be disappointed for it was truly a sight worth seeing: the great flailed arm on the right hand side of the bale-mover had inexplicably broken its safety chain and was now lying gently propped up by the roof of a fancy SUV, not just any fancy SUV., but a Lincoln Navigator, a shiny black Lincoln Navigator that boasted all the extras that such ve-hic-les might boast.

"Why on earth did you choose to park there?" Aubrey burst out in utter consternation.

That was when Herr Fracmeister lost any of the remaining support he might have had. "Why? Why? Cuz I didn't want no country hick smacking into me in a restaurant parking lot. That's why! Now you'll agree to pay me fifteen hundred dollars to take care of the damage, or I call the cops."

Aubrey burst out laughing, in turn prompting a general tittering among the onlookers, which did not seem too pleasing to the man. Aubrey continued. "My friend, you are way, way out of line. Furthermore you have an attitude like an alley cat with a bad case of piles. First of all, you chose not to park in the parking lot provided by the restaurant for its patrons, even though you chose to eat there, and even though there is still plenty of room. Second, you chose to park in a vacant lot right alongside an agricultural machine when there are still acres of room to park away from both cars and machines. Sadly for you, I may be one of those dumb farmers you were talking about, but I am also a retired cop so it's quite likely that I know more about the law than you do. Worse yet, seeing as I have only just purchased this baby, I don't yet know which lever I should pull in my tractor to lift the arm off your ve-hic-le as you like to call it. In fact, I could hurt it a whole lot more if I happen to push or pull one the wrong way. So you, sir, are the one with the problem, not me. If you wish to climb into this dumb farmer's tractor and determine which lever controls what, be my guest! Oh, and if you prefer, go ahead and call the cops while we go and finish our lunch which is now getting cold because of you. The cops will get a laugh out of this one for sure."

As if all this was not enough, his escort decided it was her time to get in on the act. "Don't you dare talk to my man like that!" she yelled, planting herself squarely, roundly, in front of Aubrey. With her eyes blazing in mascaraed fury and her bosom puffed up almost to spillage, enough to draw every eye in the crowd, it was Showtime at the Caroline Corral.

Aubrey's unintended response brought the whole business to a shambolic climax. "Take a deep breath, my dear, or you'll pop your buttons!"

"Pop!" went some clown in the crowd.

The man spun around to see who was that brazen, only to be met with a throng of grinning country folk. Only then did common sense finally prevail.

"Okay, okay, you've made you point. Now let's see if you can get that arm off of my ve-hic…my car so's we can get the heck outa here!"

Aubrey climbed into the tractor. There were two levers he could pull on; one would raise or lower the bale deck, the other would raise or lower the arms, provided the electric console did what it was supposed to do. But which lever should he try? That was when he discovered why the one arm had broken the safety chain; Pete's junk! A stray bolt had lodged itself between the lever and the plastic cover it came through, enough to activate the arm to go down far enough to break the chain. From there it had sagged onto the roof of Mr. Man's ve-hic-le. Huh! It wouldn't do to tell all this to "Mon Colonel" though. He gingerly removed the bolt and then got down to figuring out which lever did what. Bear in mind he was working with both a tractor and a machine that were unfamiliar to him. Brainwave! He climbed back into the tractor and checked which hydraulic hoses were supposed to go where. That was when he was struck by further brilliance; the trailer bed was already *down* so it could only go *up,* which meant the arms must be controlled by the other two hydraulic lines. But he'd had more than enough of Mr. Frac-man, so he turned to him before his next move and said, "Say yourself a little prayer, Mister, because if I pull on the wrong lever, your fancy ve-hic-le is going to have a dent in the roof big enough for a hippopotamus to wallow in." All the man could do was what he was good at, which was to scowl. The woman, on the other hand, simply held her breath, and everyone could see what too much silicone could do to a racehorse.

Aubrey started the tractor and raised the bed. Yup, he'd got that part right, and the arm stayed put. Only then did it dawn on him; if a bolt had contrived to push the lever down, causing the arm to break the chain, then all he had to do was to pull the lever up. Hey presto! It worked like a charm. Furthermore, there was still enough of a dent for the man to remember the pastoral village of Caroline. Clearly at this point in time though, Caroline was nothing more than a bad memory from which to escape; he and his "broad" had a sudden urge to go do some consulting elsewhere. Anywhere! Far away! In a hurry! They jumped into their shiny new ve-hic-le with its shiny new dent, and blasted off to a more hospitable east. West of Red Deer was clearly much too hokey for such distinguished types.

Everybody trooped back inside, and the story immediately began to take legs and to spread like wildfire among those diners who had thought better than to abandon a nice, hot lunch to watch the antics of some fool dude and his princess consort. For the first time in his life, Aubrey knew he was the talk of the hour, the topic of all conversation, a new folk hero in the making. As a plus, the management made sure they got an extra serving of hot chicken chop suey on the house, their way of saying "we appreciate you."

By the time they were ready to get back on the road, the arm had sagged further; worse yet, the clip on the safety chain was irreparable. Aubrey raised the arm and realized that from then all the way home, he would have to tug on the lever now and again to keep the hydraulic ram up. Off they went in their convoy, and once again Aubrey forgot the rules, or more likely ignored them and cranked up the radio. So ten minutes later, he could not hear Sabine leaning on the horn behind him, did not see her desperately flashing her lights to grab his attention; he was much too enamoured of Crystal Gale and "Blue Bayou". They were approaching a hill where there was a side road off to the right with the usual collection of ratty rural mailboxes, save for the one that was a classy replica of the grain elevator at Kuusamo, on the way to Red Deer. It was at that instant that Aubrey registered that the right bale arm was down, way down. Must be quite a leak someplace, he was thinking when he yanked on the lever. Too late! Pete's abandoned coffee mug got itself wedged so the lever could not activate, and Aubrey watched himself hit a home run with four mailboxes, the elevator from Kuusamo tracing a graceful arc through the air before shattering into a pile of matchwood on the other side of the fence. Frantically he pulled the cup out of the way and yanked the lever backwards. The arm responded with gusto, moving all the way back to vertical.

Now came the critical question: who had seen him? Who had seen it happen? Only Sabine it seemed, his Sabine who was either laughing or crying hysterically... but at least she was smart enough to keep on going like she did. He dared not stop, not here, not halfway up a hill with a machine the size of the *HMCS Hercules*. Ah well, everybody in life has to win some and lose a couple, even if the loss is hard to take. He held that lever back all the way home. Curiously though, neither Aubrey nor Sabine would allow the other to even think of attending an auction sale for a whole month, or almost a month. Cole's Auction, now in a new location with its own yard on the side of Highway 22, "The Cowboy Trail", was having a greenhouse plant dispersal, something that a whole team of elephants could not keep Sabine away from. Aubrey did not debate the issue; she could do with some extra shrubbery to hide that repulsive gargoyle.

Farming went on; it never stopped. The rule in the local area was to get your crops seeded by the May long-weekend if you wanted them for more than just silage or green-feed. Besides, for as long as Aubrey and Sabine had been on the farm, it always rained on the Caroline Rodeo which took place at that time of year. They had picked up an old seed drill at the auction, a year previously, for two hundred dollars, the one and only bid offered up for it. Well, it was now time to put this contraption to work. The Hanlons were going to seed forty acres of barley; only this time, they were intent on seeding it themselves rather than having a custom man do it for them.

Now every agricultural machine without exception has both its general and its individual idiosyncrasies, and by implication its own learning curve. So a seed drill would be very different to a bale-mover or a swather. But dear Aubrey, blessed by the ignorance of the blissful, could not see that a simple seed drill would present much of a challenge at all. Simple really! But Murphy's Law number 74, first translated by Brother Jonas of Weyburn Monastery intervened. "Thou shalt not assumeth thou knowest all when thou embarketh upon a new endeavour..."

It so happened, weather being as fickle as it is, that Aubrey was seeding a dry field; to put it more realistically, he was seeding in the dust. The problem was that for the life of him, he could not see where he had been on the round before. Lesson number one; it is wise to know where you are going and where you have been. Ah, well, no worries, like any and every farmer, he improvised. He tied a broken fence post on the outer side of the machine and left a visible trail even a one-eyed goblin could follow so that when he had completed a round of the field, he just lined up with the mark left by the post on the previous round. He had completed four rounds of the field when he spotted one of the seed tubes spilling grain from the top. Lesson number two: keep checking for blockages. Potentially four rounds had been seeded with a blocked seed tube...okay, so the field might have a bit of a Mohawk hairstyle when it came up. Two more rounds and now a sprocket had stopped turning. So what did this sprocket do? What was its job? Oh glory be! The main drive chain had jumped off. But where had it jumped? It was definitely still turning on round four, but this was round six. Who the heck knew? Okay, there was only one solution: reseed the last two rounds, going back over the ground he had just covered. Fine, lesson three duly noted and digested: keep checking the main drive chain is engaged.

Lesson number four (damn, this was turning into a whole darn course) was downright malevolent. For some reason, the lifters on one side of the drill got themselves out of sync with those on the other, so when Aubrey pulled on the rope to engage or disengage the seeding operation, one side of the drill would seed, the other would not. Aubrey was in full banned word mode now, swearing to the high heavens in defiance of "The Sabine Code of Ethical Agricultural Practice" that was supposed to govern all that he did. Then he had to sit down and figure out how he would address this latest problem. The mechanics were easy enough; reset the one side so both sides worked together. What was not so easy was to calculate how many rounds of the field he would have to reseed in order to fill the blank spot half a seed drill had left behind. Three rounds, he decided arbitrarily. Mohawk hairstyle, forget it! This was going to be a complete bad hair day! It was, of course, inevitable that now he would run out of seed. He had to go back to the neighbour to get some more, at more cost. And of course, the neighbour had run out of Busby but he had a bit of something else but he couldn't remember what variety that bit was. Aubrey took a bit of that "something else".

The net result of all this "spring training" so to speak was that the Hanlon barley field grew into a sight to behold. There were bald spots, lush spots, missing lines, and two very distinct varieties. Worse yet, Aubrey had neglected to take into account the cardinal rule for beginners: do not seed your first-ever barley field alongside a road because all the neighbours will see the humour in it. And laugh. Laugh for three months straight. And ask if you were drunk or simply incapacitated when you seeded it. Aha, beginner's luck came into the play though. That crop of barley grew bountifully, for this was the year things turned around.

All too often, farmers are called "next year's people". Every year starts out with great promise and high hopes, always, but there are so many variables in the farming game that even if only one of them turns contrarian, then the calving season turns into a frigid or a muddied nightmare, crops burn up in a drought or drown in a flood, and farmers' optimism just wilts and dies. But this was a year where the promise held pretty much true: markets turned for the better and for once the smiles on farmers' faces were not forced. Optimism, it turns out, is contagious. It makes for good humour, it fires up a new determination, and it begets a happier, more cooperative community. One can even listen to the politicians take all of the credit without jeering at them as they make their very own contribution to global warming with all of their hot air. Like bankers really, they convince themselves that everybody else is doing so well because of their stalwart efforts.

Humans are arguably more prone to emitting hot air—voluntary hot air coupled with high readings of idiocy—than any other animal; bovine flatulence is largely involuntary and really cannot and should not be compared to humankind's. Aubrey found that out mostly through the negative experiences the Hanlons endured with their renters. Since they had purchased old Stan Himilton's place, they had seen kids on quads ripping up their hayfields, had suffered renters' "pets" putting their stock to flight, and had survived renters giving the Hanlon name as a credit reference without their knowledge—all this and more, as fully documented in *Fancy Free in the Back Thirty*. However, they had finally got lucky in chancing across a couple of university students who needed accommodation while they conducted a research project on cougar movements in the area. They had turned out to be a real class act—cleaning up the place and keeping it as clean as it was when old Stan lived there, always paying the rent on time. They were really good people and the sort you would want for a neighbour. As so often happens however, the bureaucrats up there high in that academic wonderland where the air is thinner than in the real world decided to cut the funding for their project, and, as they say, "that was the proverbial that." So once again the Hanlons had to go looking for renters. It was not that there were no good people out there, it was that Aubrey and Sabine together had only managed to select one set of winners from a string of losers. Low-end rents attracted these people like flies no matter how hard you tried to read the tea-leaves, no matter how astute a judge of character both Aubrey and Sabine thought they were.

The latest pair of renters had been decided upon by both Hanlons together. They had shown up at the house, mobile home, well-dressed and well-groomed; both came across as well-spoken, and both were from the general area. Best yet, both were drivers for a local trucking company, so they said they would be on the road most of the time. Sometimes ninety hours a week, they said. The warning signs were there, in hindsight of course. Young bucks working these kinds of hours would naturally revel in whatever time they got for R&R. They would likely "let their hair down" somewhat. Not just occasionally but on every possible occasion. "It's party time at Big Jim's place", became a community theme song among the local youthful party crowd. There was lots of noise, music, beer and bedlam, even if there were little or no drugs, but enough rhythm and booze to stoke up any party. And whereas animals tend to have definitive mating seasons and rituals, unfortunately these young folks felt the urge to go at it whenever and wherever they felt like it, unrestrained by any natural cycle.

Things eventually came to a head over two "Wild Weekends" as they were apparently and appropriately named. The first inkling that things might be getting out of hand was the phone call from a neighbour who said there was a wild party ongoing at the Himilton place with "a bunch of crazies dancing about on the roof of the mobile home…." They would wreck it, was Aubrey's immediate response. Mobile homes didn't possess roofs that people could routinely walk on let alone do the cha-cha upon. The caller did not even get a chance to finish before Aubrey was out the door. It was a Saturday afternoon, a hot one, and Aubrey was none too pleased that his siesta had been hijacked by a bunch of jerks.

There were about thirty young people milling about outside, every one of them armed with something stronger than prune juice. Three barbecue grilles were going for those who liked to drink on a full stomach rather than an empty one. Various pieces of discarded clothing were scattered about the place as some folks became more prone to showing the world all that they were made of and how well it was put together. But it was the six fools on the roof that attracted Aubrey's immediate attention.

"Hey Jim, what the hell do you think you are doing?" Aubrey roared in his best constabulary voice. Actually, the whole thing would have been very funny had it not been for the fact that it was Aubrey's property they were wrecking. There was Big Jim, naked as a newt and hung like a carthorse, standing with a folded umbrella over his shoulder and singing "Ave Maria". The two chicks dropping off him were topless and clearly proud of their accomplishments. Another young adventurer was being held up by two mates as he puked over the side of the roof.

"Are you Big Jim's dad or something?" asked one of the girls, making no attempt to cover her considerable assets and being much more concerned about staying upright physically if not morally.

"Jim! Get your sorry ass and these people off my roof NOW!" Aubrey roared.

"Oh hi, Mister Hanlon. Where'd you come from? Look, I'm a mushroom." With that he opened up the umbrella over his head.

"A mushroom with a bloody big nodule," commented some envious fellow on the ground.

Aubrey reacted without thinking. He reached over to a nearby picnic table, latched onto an uncooked pork chop, and threw it with all his force at his renter. In all fairness, it has to be said that Aubrey had never been good at any game that called for a ball. Baseball, basketball, soccer, even ping pong, the ball never went where he intended it to go. But this time, for the first time in his life, he was on target, perhaps because a pork chop is not shaped like a ball. It caught Mister Mushroom plumb on the nodule and Big Jim went down like a ton of bricks, clutching at his transmission as a busty Mary Poppins collapsed in solidarity with him, fully prepared to administer her version of mouth-to-mouth resuscitation. The others on the roof sobered up enough to make a quick escape, unfortunately not without leaving more than one unsightly dent on the roof.

Aubrey was unapologetic; and when Aubrey got mad, really mad, people tended to listen. "You folks had better have this whole place cleaned up within half an hour or I'll call the cops. Wilful damage to private property, that sort of thing." Only then did his eyes take in the other half of the renter duo passed out in what had once been Stanley Himilton's pride and joy, his flower garden.

What the Hanlons never realized at the time, what with all the unnecessary drama, was that this episode was in fact the trigger that finally caused them to change strategy. How could they ever have hoped to see the big picture when the smaller one contrived always to fill the lens? Aubrey came back after the allotted half-hour, and the place had been amazingly transformed, well acceptably so. Okay, so the one renter was still comatose in the flower bed, while Big Jim was quietly nursing his wounds with his buxom lady friend who was, who'd have guessed it, a masseuse. Or so she claimed. But the bottles were all gone and the place was reasonably tidy even if there were those unsightly dents in the roof of the mobile home. Could Aubrey have wished for anything more?

Anything more indeed! The following weekend, the same neighbour, the same basic message, only this time the out-of-control party was down *at the dugout* at the bottom of the "hill field", as the Hanlons liked to call it, the field adjoining the rental property.

"Are you sure he means the dugout?" Sabine was incredulous. "Shoot, all we need is for some drunk to drown and we'll be on the hook forever."

"Come on, hon, it's time we cleaned house." Aubrey snatched his hat off the rack on the way out, Sabine hotfooting it after him.

When they got to the gate off the road into the field, they were both nothing short of apoplectic. Some of the cars were parked in the grass around the dugout, but three cars were actually parked in the barley. That was a red rag to a bull as far as Aubrey was concerned. It was the casual dress code that most offended his dear wife, or the optionality of it as two bare-assed males galloped into the dugout to restore their sudden newfound modesty. Other revellers already in the water submerged themselves to cover whatever they might have had on display ten minutes before. You'd have thought the Salvation Army had arrived, Aubrey was to say later.

"Oh oh! We've really pissed you off this time, I can tell." Big Jim, thankfully still fully-clothed but well on the way to Inebriation Alley, approached Aubrey. It was precisely then, at that very instant, Aubrey had his brainwave.

"You tell those folks to get out of that water right this second because I treated the water with diophoxylene two days ago to kill off both leeches and Beaver Fever. If they stay any longer than about three minutes, they'll likely lose most of their body hair and maybe quite a bit more besides." Aubrey did not just say this, he broadcasted it. The reaction was immediate. "And anyone who was in that water had better head straight home and have themselves a hot shower. That diophoxylene can be bad stuff!" he added for good measure. There was an immediate mass exit of people, a fair few of them non-adherents to any dress code, as they all scrambled for cover of a different sort.

"I could never have imagined a more motley collection of human genitalia," Sabine was to comment later.

Aubrey went on for the benefit of Big Jim. "We've also got some bad news for you, I'm afraid to say. We have decided to subdivide this place off the farm as an acreage and sell it, mobile home and all. I'll bring your notice around this evening."

"That *is* bad news," responded Jim, so thick in the skin he still had yet no real idea how far out of line had been both his behaviour and that of his friends. "We certainly can't afford to buy an acreage, that's for sure so we'll have to find ourselves another place, I guess."

"I guess," said Aubrey stolidly. "And you and your buddies had better stay the hell off any other part of my land that you don't rent because I'll prosecute you for trespass. I'm liable if some fool gets hurt. Do you understand what I'm saying?"

"Okay, I understand."

"And make sure all your water nymphs go home and shower," Aubrey added, emphasizing the word "home". "That diophoxylene is wicked stuff."

Aubrey and Sabine had never seen a party end so abruptly. Literally everyone had departed within ten minutes. Sure, they had left a few beer cans behind but one thing was for certain, they would not be back in a hurry. Hopefully a good few of them had by now developed a healthy itch given the notion of the association of ideas.

When they were alone, Sabine could not hold back her curiosity any longer. "Honey, did you really treat the water with this dio-what's-it stuff? Like what exactly is it?"

"Oh that! I made it all up. But it is good for making leeches and loose appendages shrink away though."

"You made it up? Like there's no such thing?" Sabine was incredulous.

"Yup! Made it all up!" Aubrey could not help but feel smug.

"Okay, but what's with the story about selling the mobile as part of an acreage then?"

"I made that up too, but maybe it's the only way we'll ever get ourselves a decent neighbour and a bit of spare cash in our pockets. Acreages are selling really high right now."

"There are times when you can be brilliant," said Sabine, only for once she actually meant it.

Chapter Three
"NOT ON MY TIME YOU WON'T!"

*P*ete had warned them, dear old Pete. Sometimes Aubrey felt that it was Pete's mission in life to pee on the Hanlon tires. It was inevitable, then, that when they expanded their herd, they would face more and varied veterinary problems than they ever had before. This was the kind of warning for Sabine that one would have preferred to have gone without. For her, it had a penchant to spell itself out into a full self-fulfilling prophecy. Cows were cows, bulls were bulls, and calves were everything in between. Yes, they had experienced a C-section with a cow, a broken penis with Narcissus, the bull they loved to hate, and scours among the calves, but cancer eye, this was altogether different. It was also ugly, decidedly ugly. And traumatic: doubly traumatic because it was Sabine's friend Elvira. She had become the granny of the herd when they purchased her from old Quincy Klug. But now she had to be around fifteen years old. Furthermore, she had never once given them the run-around, and every year she had consistently raised an eight hundred-pound calf.

They were doing their regular herd vaccinations at the time, with Pete and Jeannie along to help as usual. Aubrey called Pete's attention to Elvira's weeping left eye.

"Say, Pete, what do you think is going on with this girl's eye? It looks like some kind of a growth to me." Aubrey was worried but not overly so.

Pete took one look and delivered his verdict machine-gun style. "Cancer eye! Not too bad yet. But heck, this girl is older than your very own Sabine. Get rid of her. Replace her with something younger."

"What? Me get rid of Sabine for something younger? Now there's a...." Luckily he never got to finish the sentence and dig himself in any deeper.

"What? Get rid of Elvira? We could never do that, could we, honey?" A panicked Sabine had heard the conversation and needed reassurance.

Jeannie could not let this one go. "What? Get rid of Sabine?" she mimicked Sabine's voice. "Why? Sabine can still walk and talk, all by herself too, as long as she's not chewing gum."

Sabine laughed but only out of politeness before her deep concern for the cow reasserted itself. "What can you do about cancer eye? Like can you save the eye or what?" This was all uncharted territory as far as she was concerned.

"Oh, you can have the vet come out and take out the eye. It's messy but it pretty much always works. But then again, it'll cost you." Never a person to paint a pretty picture when there wasn't one to paint, Pete was a literalist like Aubrey, maybe more so.

Sabine was horrified. "You mean actually cut the eye right out? Do you put the cow to sleep or what?"

"You'll soon find out if you choose to go that route. But you know, for a girl of her age you'd be much further ahead to cull her and ship her out. It's not a cheap operation. It'll probably be around three hundred bucks."

"Maybe Pete is onto something…." That was as far as Aubrey got.

Sabine phoned the vet clinic to book the appointment. The receptionist told her to bring the cow into the clinic for the eye operation.

"Why?" asked Sabine.

"Well, it is better to do it here because," she sighed heavily as if she was explaining the obvious to a child, "for one thing, it would be way cleaner than on your farm." It was the way the woman said it that raised Sabine's hackles.

"I can understand that," she replied, "but in this instance I would prefer the vet to come out to our farm. It will put far less stress on the cow."

"It-is-more-clinically-sterile-here-than-on-your-farm." The woman seemed compelled to spell it out for this moron out there in the sticks.

"Besides, you'll have to pay mileage."

"Tell me, are you in training to be a lawyer?" Sabine asked acidly, "Or do you just think you are one?"

"Pardon me?"

"Look, my dear, I am the customer, the one who pays the vet bills and I have just told you what I as your customer want. So let me say it again slowly. I-want-the-vet-to-come-out-to-the-farm. Is there any part of that statement you do not understand?" Maybe Sabine was being a bit unfair, but she hated being talked down to by anyone.

"The vet can be out there at 10 AM." The voice was all business now.

"Why-thank-you," said Sabine and hung up.

And so it came to pass on the morrow that the vet showed up at ten o'clock on the dot. It was a lady vet, recently hired on as the clinic expanded. She was a no-nonsense, let's-get-busy type as true professionals always are.

"Hi! I'm Crystal Blingworth. And no, I didn't choose the name." The smile broke the ice; it was positively infectious. "I presume you have the cow up there in the barn? We'll need a bucket of hot water and another of cold, if that's at all possible," both things she had asked for when she had confirmed her appointment that morning.

"Water all present and correct and on parade," Aubrey gave her a mock salute. "I'm Aubrey Hanlon, by the way. I'm the tired hand, the one who does all of the work around here. And this here lady is the C-in-C, the Cowpoke-in-Chief, my wife Sabine Hanlon at your service."

"You start behaving right now," said a somewhat embarrassed Sabine.

"Hi, I'm Sabine Hanlon, this man's far better half."

At least the vet's eyes twinkled, even though the business on hand ruled the day. "Well, let's get to it, shall we? I've got another cancer eye after this one and then a calf with a broken leg to deal with." Not that the Hanlons needed organizing, not with Sabine at the helm.

Cows are funny, as in funny strange. Elvira had known from day one she was a Sabine favourite, in much the same way a soft-hearted old granny is a favourite. She sensed the humans gathered about her were there to help somehow; she also sensed that Sabine was feeling not just some of her pain but all of it. She knew something was wrong with her eye because she could barely see out of it, what with the cancer spreading and all the crud collecting around the eyelid. She went into the head-gate without undue ceremony and stood quietly while they put a halter over her head and cinched it to one side so that the malignant eye was facing outward, the approach unimpeded. Both during and after the initial series of injections required to freeze the whole area, Elvira was as stoic as any monk enduring a routine flagellation, as if willing her helpers to go ahead and get on with the job. With the very first injection, Sabine's tears started to well up so it was a manly Aubrey who needed to step up to the plate as the surgeon's assistant. Nah, this kind of thing wouldn't bother him, not with all the blood and gore he had seen during his long service as a cop. But nonetheless, it still happened! Why it happened he was never truly able to explain. Maybe it was because, via some form of psychological osmosis, he was feeling the pain his beloved Sabine was feeling, and by extension his brain told him the cow must be feeling even if she was partially sedated and her eye frozen. Maybe it was the grotesque nature of the procedure itself, the eye literally being chopped out of its socket leaving a bloody mess behind, or the sheer technical efficiency of the vet in carrying out such a messy operation. Whatever it was, Aubrey first teetered on his feet only to pass out alongside the bucket of water.

Ms. Blingworth, the vet, didn't even blink an eye, didn't stop for a second what she was doing. "Just sprinkle a little bit of that cold water on his face, would you Sabine?" she said, adding, "Men can be such wimps sometimes. He'll be all right." But she did begin to wonder what she had got herself into, both of her tough farmer helpers seemingly incapacitated, the one by grief and apparent solidarity with the cow; the other, a big strong hunk of a man keeling over at the sight of a bit of blood. However, "The Happening" as Sabine would later call it, galvanized her into action and re-awoke those nerves of steel. She quickly cupped her hands in the cold water and sprinkled some over her husband's face. He reacted not so much with gusto as with a stirring of life, the one side of his face as white as a goose's bum, the other speckled broccoli-green with fresh cow excreta.

"Clean your face!" barked Sabine helping him up. "It's full of shit…just like the rest of you, come to think of it." So much for empathy!

The vet noted Sabine's transformation and reassessed her character assassination of this farmer's wife into something a little more charitable. Aubrey did as he was told, took one look at the… well, the battlefield and withdrew as gracefully as he could to safer, higher ground—meaning he got the heck out of there. That left Sabine to look on in nothing but awe as Ms. Blingworth deftly sutured up the wound and cleaned up the cow's face. "She'll be fine now," she said. "Just keep an eye on her. I've got to get going and do the next one."

"Thank you! Thank you so very much. That was truly impressive," said Sabine. "Come by for a cup of tea any time you are out this way and have a moment, we'd love to get to know you. I'm sorry about my husband, he's never pulled a stunt like that before, and he's an ex-cop too." As for Elvira, Sabine was quite sure she was saying thank you, too, when Sabine let her out of the barn.

Spring turned seamlessly into summer and gorgeous, hot days. During the long, never-ending depths of winter, Aubrey convinced himself he was suffering from SAD, Seasonal Affective Disorder, a kind of depression prompted by the incessant darkness and the incarceration of winter. Sabine thought otherwise, suggesting he was suffering from DEI, "Deliberately Engineered Inertia". Whatever it was, long sunlight hours cured it. He could now wear little and loose, he could stop where he was working and spring a leak without fear of frozen pipes, and without having to navigate out of half a mile of coveralls and the subterranean layers of clothing that winter's cold always demanded. He could actually feel the sun warm his skin, like the old friend Mister Sunshine had always been. Okay, it was true we human fools had brought on global warming so that by the height of summer it was advisable not to get too close to your bosom buddy even with a liberal application of sun-block. Sabine, too, liked to feel Mister Sunshine's warm caress on her skin, while Aubrey naturally enough would have lobbied Mister Sunshine directly for him to get unimpeded access to her skin, the more skin the better. He always thought his wife looked her best while gardening in a billowy pair of shorts and her favourite yellow bikini top reminiscent of the days when she had been somewhat trimmer. The top, in and of itself delightful to behold, occasionally revealed more than it concealed when she was in full garden mode and bent over the carrot patch, which was all right by an Aubrey compelled to keep coming back to check how the carrots were growing. So in a way, it was inevitable the day would come when he would overplay his hand.

This was the day in question. He appeared in the garden an hour before high noon, a day of glorious sunshine and a light, westerly breeze. Aubrey had cut some hay a few days before because he wanted to try out that old temperamental square baler one more time. He had convinced himself he had found the problem that caused it to leave intermittent unstrung bales behind, but the only way to find out was to give it a try. He hooked up the ancient Farmall H, the very same that had dumped him flat on his bum some years before when bolts broke and the seat fell off the tractor, him with it, a story left to posterity in *Footloose in the Front Forty*. But he would need Sabine's help; she would do the driving while he would walk behind to see exactly what the baler was up to.

"Can you come and give me a hand, honey?" he said. "Let's see if we can make forty bales before lunch. I think I've found the problem that was causing us all the grief the last time we used it."

"Okay," said Sabine, surprisingly agreeable. "But you'll only get one full hour of my time, starting right now." She made a pretence of looking at her watch. "I'll just go on into the house and change into something more appropriate."

"Not on my time, you won't!" responded Aubrey with mock severity. "Besides, you don't really need to do that. All we are going to do is make one run up the field and one run down. Come on, you're on my time now and you're wasting it!"

"Oh, all right!" She adjusted the cloth to prevent an accidental double exposure and they set off on foot up to the tractor, which was already in the field.

By this stage in her agricultural career, Sabine could drive pretty much any of the farm machines on the place; she had made it her mission to do so. She climbed up onto the seat, with Aubrey remaining behind as they had planned. She sat down, only to jump up with an ear-splitting shriek; the metal seat had heated up almost to the boiling point in the hot sun. She would have to drive standing up, not a particularly thrilling prospect but it was something she could manage and it was for a good cause, after all. She revved up the engine to the appropriate speed, engaged the power-take-off and an enormous clatter ensued. It was so abominably loud that she would have jumped off the tractor instantly and bolted for the hills, had Aubrey not given her the thumbs-up. Or maybe he was just thanking her for twisting so far around that her magnificent physique made him forget what he was even doing there. She started into the swath and the clatter immediately dissipated as the machine was given something to chew on. The first bale came out a trifle too loose, so Aubrey adjusted the tension and they continued. Two good bales, four good bales, six, ten, twelve; they were on a roll! Was this too good to be true, or what? You bet it was!

Now the previous fall, the cows had been turned into this very hayfield after the growing season was over to eat the regrowth, a common practice in these parts. As always, bulls that had not seen each other all summer because they had all been on different pastures with their own designated herd of cows now came face to face, head to head. As is their wont in such circumstances, they had fought like Roman gladiators, vying for some fair damsel's imaginary favours, and they had scraped great big holes here and there in the earth with their hooves as they defied each other.

Sabine never even saw the massive hole she hit; why would she when she was too busy watching what was going on behind her? Indeed she was so happy that things were going along so well that she found herself whooping and hollering and carrying on like a bronco buster. She hit that hole with true panache, pizzazz, a bang. It was all she could do to hang onto the steering wheel, but the clasp, the string, the strap—whatever it is that holds such things in place—let go on her top, with just enough breeze to carry it over and drop it into the hay swath. Out of the corner of her eye, she saw it go but her hands were far too busy holding on for dear life to make any sort of grab for it. Nor could she stop in time. In seconds, her top had been gobbled up by the machine, tamped deep into a bale by the mighty steel plunger, and there she was left flopping around in distress before she brought the rig to a halt. She shut it down.

"My top went in," she yelled at Aubrey from her perch high up on the driver's seat.

"I know," he said grinning like a Cheshire cat and giving the thumbs up.

"Well, stop grinning like the randy ape that you are and help me look for it," she said, clambering down off the tractor.

"It would be a great pleasure, Madam," he said. "But I'm afraid it's long gone."

"What do you mean it's long gone?" Sabine was highly indignant, scrambling around on her hands and knees scanning the baler's pickup teeth for signs of her precious top.

"You won't find it in there, honey, it's now well inside a bale, and those pickup teeth likely holed it all to rat-shit."

"Language please, Mr. Hanlon."

"So the only way to find it, even if you still want it, is to run the bales through and see if we can spot it. Oh hello, who's this pulling into the field?"

"Ha! Ha! Aubrey Hanlon, you can't fool me!" Sabine deliberately did not turn around.

"No, really! Turn around and take a look."

Only then did she hear a vehicle approaching. Suddenly she found a burst of speed she never knew she had, finishing up in a crouch on the far side behind the tractor's rear wheel, signalling frantically to Aubrey that he should conduct his business at least some distance away from the rig. Aubrey walked towards the edge of the field, apparently succeeding in drawing the visitor some distance away from the hiding Sabine. It was the Service Manager and part owner of Hexagon Farm Supply in Red Deer, a Mr. Kevin Benelli, a man with whom Aubrey always enjoyed a verbal jousting match.

Mr. Benelli exited his truck. "Good day Mr. Ordinary Hanlon," he grinned. "How's it goin'?"

"Good day, Abu BenSmelli, Al-Quaeda Ambassador to the Republic of Canuckistan."

"Yes, yes and I am here on a trade mission for my masters. You see, Mr. Ordinary, so ordinary, it is time that you buying, a new one, tractor that is. That old heap of bones is not being up to it, not no more," he pointed at the old Farmall. "Pete suggested I come and see you," he reverted to normal parlance the better to fish for business. "I was at his place this morning sorting out a problem on his Deutz. But hey, that old Farmall is in nicer shape than you for a creature your age." He turned and started walking towards it for a closer look. "My dad had one of these things in the old days when...," when he rounded the front of the tractor to come upon a very wide-eyed Sabine squatting on the ground, her hands not quite big enough to cover a partially unveiled art exhibition.

"Well, and a good day to you too, Mrs. Far-out-of-the-Ordinary. I hope I'm not interrupting anything." He could at least have turned away when he said it but he just grinned.

"My top just got blown into the baler." It came out more of a stammer than a statement.

Mr. Benelli, well-travelled man of the world that he was, could hold it no longer. Much to Sabine's chagrin, he burst out laughing, guffawing as if there was no tomorrow while she crouched down ever more discreetly. Finally, recovering gentlemanly conduct and hoping that what he had or had not seen would not seriously impinge upon the purpose of his mission, he turned away.

"Well, it's not that important. Just a hood ornament," said Aubrey coming over. Sabine allowed that the clod of earth which connected with her husband behind the right ear merited the two second-exposure the throw demanded.

"You get yourself down to the house right now and take your horrible friend with you for a coffee," she yelled at them. "I'll walk down by myself when you are gone. I don't need any piggy eyes staring at me like they are watching some reality show called 'Grannies in the Raw'. Go on! Get out of here and leave a nice old lady in peace, why don't you?"

"Well, is that one piece or two?" Mr. Benelli had to have the last word.

No, the Hanlons did not go out then and there and buy a new tractor, but Mr. Benelli now had a talking point if not a bargaining chip that he would not be afraid to use...like at the Hexagon booth at the Red Deer Agri-Trade show where people might enjoy listening. As for Sabine, never again would she be inveigled into going on some agricultural mission clad only in beachwear with or for her husband, even if that mission was to last a mere ten minutes. Aubrey would just have to get his "jollies" some other way.

They finished the baling that afternoon, Sabine in full combat gear. And the baler missed not a bale. Oh, and they did find the top, or rather a part of it that was sticking out of a bale. But when they gave it a good yank, all they got was a single cup. The rest had to be buried deep inside. "Nellie will have to wipe her nose on it next winter," said Sabine sourly.

"Well, look at it this way. Better to have one cup with something in it rather than two cups that are empty. That's what I say," Aubrey responded, resolved to buy some sort of replacement topping for Sabine's next Christmas stocking. But if it was to match the brevity of the original, he would probably have to buy it off the juvenile rack.

Aubrey was so proud of their baling triumph, he went ahead and made another sixty bales by himself with not a single one broken. But people like Aubrey tend to forget that over time the brain matches the body in its deterioration. Square bales, when they are made without duress, are fun to make, lovely to behold, but if you don't possess a bale picker-upper, then somebody, correction, *some body,* has to pick them up one by one, load them onto a trailer, stack them on the trailer's deck, unload them from the trailer, and then stack them somewhere appropriate. Carried away as he had been while baling, he had not paid quite as much attention to how heavy he wanted his bales to be. Looking at Aubrey's body, a seasoned campaigner would have said, "Make 'em fifteen pounds going on thirty-five"; Aubrey's bales were well over sixty.

An appendix to one of Murphy's Laws stipulates that if you desire to avoid panic mode, do not listen to any weather forecast that you might actually believe in for as long as you wish that panic mode not to be present. Aubrey, the fool, phoned up the weather station. "Sixty percent chance of showers later tonight," said the male voice. Meanwhile, to add insult to injury, his strident little speeches of the past chose this moment to come back and haunt him. "Get it into your head once and for all," he had lectured his dear wife, Sabine, "this here boy doesn't do gardening, anything that even smacks of gardening, nor does this boy feed birds of any feather, either."

Now it was her turn, and she made no pretence about what she said. "Get it into your head," she said, "this here girl does not lift square bales. Ever! Slide them into position on the trailer floor, could happen with a little appropriate bribery. Stack them on a trailer bed two bales high, only blatant bribery and corruption will persuade her. Three high? A categorical NO! Lift them off the ground, not ever!"

Worse yet, much worse, Aubrey's dear wife had caught him very foolishly stating out loud that maybe he needed to jump on an exercise bike to get back into shape. Currently he was "a little too rotund" as he put it.

"Excessively rotund," she corrected him. "Bowling ball rotund." And he knew who was closer to the mark even if he did not admit it. Alas, this once innocent statement, now transformed into a meaningful conversation, had gone too far. He knew that after her next sentence his wife was going to organize him and there'd be no getting away from her.

"Look," she said oh so logically, "do twenty bales on day one, twenty-five on day two, twenty-five on day three, and thirty on day four. On day five, you start working out on that exercise bike you bought for me years ago at one of our first Cole's auctions. It's still there in the back of the garage. By September for sure you'll be more bull than ball, more meat than potato." Sabine could be horribly brutal in her own inimitable way. But what about the forecast? Sixty percent chance of showers tonight.

They began day one together, and it was going really well until Sabine contrived to fall off the back of the trailer after bale twelve. Well, perhaps not "contrived" because it was actually Aubrey's big foot that caused the problem. He would jump off the tractor, throw two bales from the ground up onto the trailer for Sabine to stack, no more than two-high. Two-high? Hell, after bale ten, Aubrey was already getting the message that square bales ought to be no more than eighteen pounds going on ten for a man with a figure like his; he would run out of steam long before Sabine had stacked the trailer two high. He was already sweating rivers and they had barely started. When Sabine was ready, Aubrey would drive forward to the next two bales lying in the field, load them and so on. Only this time, this one single stupid time, when he let the clutch out, Sabine had not quite finished putting the last bale in place and lost her balance. Off the back of the trailer she flew, shriek and all. Aubrey let loose that dread s-word and stopped. Apologies didn't work, whining never worked, pretend backache, arthritis, malaria, dengue fever and smallpox, none of them worked. He had to do the rest, all the rest, by himself. Yes, there was an element of luck in that the rain did stay away for four days. What was sad though was the fact that despite all the gallons of sweat and the accompanying pungent aroma, his perfect roundness remained exactly as it was when he had started. Indeed, it may have been worse because he had deliberately upped his calorie intake to accommodate heavy lifting. All the while, his muscles ached in places where he had never known he even had muscles. But by day four, he was into the swing of things even if he swore some of those bitching bales weighed in at a hundred pounds. On day three, Sabine deigned to help a little, but now she would have been in the way of her husband's "system" though he did not dare to tell her like it was; so she got to help anyway. On the last day, he was feeling so good, he excused his wife from jury duty, and did it all by himself. Moreover, he was feeling so exceedingly good about himself that he got on that exercise bike with grandiose plans to put it to full use for a month. How hard could it be after lifting one hundred and twenty pound bales? All he had to do was to sit in a saddle and pedal, right? There could be no comparison.

Sabine, bless her hard little heart, had spent a whole hour of her time cleaning that bike up, lubing it and generally checking it over. Clever Sabine; now he would have to contend with a huge guilt trip if he decided to abandon it after the first session. They then moved it into a spare bedroom and Aubrey stripped down to his shorts, anticipating how much he was about to perspire and picturing all those inches just slipping away from his waistline. Aubrey dressed in shorts was a sight hard on the eyes or wondrous to behold, depending on the viewer's frame of mind. But Aubrey seated on an exercise bike was much more akin to a performing chimpanzee: the same facial grimaces, the same furry features, and the same penchant to scratch where various itches took him. With all the bits that moved when he moved, he was nothing short of a spectacle, awesome and hilarious beyond words, but not beyond the lens of Sabine's camera. She got herself banned from the room, and the door was locked. She had to admit her folly and repent before he would agree to leave the door unlocked in case he should have a heart attack or fall off the bike.

Aubrey had even found the instruction booklet for the machine. The advice for beginners read as follows, complete with (in brackets) Aubrey's thoughts about what he was reading.

HOW TO FOR NOVICES…

- Follow each segment of the workout, working to find a pace/resistance that allows you to work at the suggested RPE, Rate of Perceived Exertion. *(RPE, Rate of Perceived Erosion, more like. And "perception" would be in the eye of the "peddler", the one who pedals).*
- Your legs may get tired quickly *(Yup!)* if you're not used to this bike. *(Ah, but I've just spent days on end lifting two hundred-pound bales of hay on and off trailers)*. It takes time to build endurance, so go as long as you can, *(five minutes max.)* as you can stop early *(and have a beer if you need to)*. You can go a little longer during the next workout *(and have three beers afterward)*.
- Perform this workout three times a week *(with no more than twelve beers in one week to recuperate)* with a day of rest in between. *(Make that a week)*.
- Progress by adding a few minutes each time you work out *(how about a maximum of thirty seconds?)*, until you're up to thirty minutes. *(Thirty minutes! You're joking, right?)*
- Stretch your lower body after your workout. *(That's all fine and dandy if you have a lower body that will stretch. Bowling balls are not known for their elasticity.)*

Time	Intensity/Pace	RPE
5 minutes	Warm up at a comfortable pace *(sleepwalk mode)*, and keep the resistance low *(like take the wheels off)*.	4
3 minutes	Increase resistance by 1- 4 increments, or until you're working harder than your warm-up pace *(of near death)*. You should feel you are working, but you should be able to hold a conversation *(without drooling uncontrollably)*. This is your baseline.	5
2 minutes	Increase your resistance and/or pace back to baseline *(from comatose to spasmodic movement)* until you are working slightly harder than baseline *(bedtime)*.	5 - 6
3 minutes	Decrease resistance/pace back to baseline *(almost comatose)*.	5
2 minutes	Increase your resistance and/or pace until you're working slightly harder than baseline *(but hard enough to merit a beer)*.	5 - 6
5 minutes	Decrease resistance/pace back to a comfortable level to cool down *(such that you can lie in the fetal position for the rest of the day)*.	4

Actually, that would be easy enough, Aubrey thought. What the heck, he'd set the resistance on moderate. He began pedalling, the machine communicating all sorts of useless information he would gladly have done without—like how long he had been pedalling. It said he had done only two minutes, when he knew categorically he had done ten. Like how far he had supposedly travelled; 2.8 km when he knew for certain he had cycled the equivalent of twice the three kilometers to the highway and back. And there he was, drenched in sweat pedalling at 13.8 km an hour while Sabine had said—no not said but boasted— that she was comfortable at 17.5 km an hour, and for a full twenty minutes at that. Like the machine said he had burned up a pathetic 28 calories; did this thing think he had to pedal all the way to Moose Jaw, Saskatchewan to lose a full meal deal's worth, or what? Maybe the darn thing just couldn't count!

Worse yet, far worse, after three minutes his mouth was parched, his tongue all but hanging out, while his heart was asking his head in very succinct terms whether he had gone off his rocker. At the four minute mark, he could definitely hear his knees creaking, and he could feel that his bum was at war with the seat, which in turn raised the eternal question, why could the ingenuity of man not engineer a bicycle seat that was universally comfortable? If somebody could come up with the notion of "air-ride" for a big truck, why couldn't that same somebody design a bicycle seat that didn't seek to work its way through your anus? His shoes were feeling too tight, his head ached and he was rapidly coming to the conclusion that the regimen he was following was for "very advanced beginners" and not for derelict couch potatoes and occasional bale tossers. Some time after the five minute mark, there was a humongous crash; so startling that Sabine dropped her baking and was through the door in a flash. There was Aubrey, her very own unique version of prehistoric man in shorts, lying flat out on the carpet and breathing like the little engine that could not nor ever would. His face was puce, purple, maroon, somewhere in that range of hue, and he was perspiring like the Roman emperor Nero watching Rome burn. She laughed then (some of it from relief) until the tears began to roll down her cheeks, even as she helped him to his feet—a threshold at which any and all show of sympathy ceased.

Aubrey was supremely embarrassed. His dignity had been trashed; the myth of the Indomitable Agricultural Man was shattered. So bad did he feel, he decided to devote himself to his own personal resurrection. He went at that exercise bike full bore for a month, even if full bore for a sagging bag of muscles like his meant still only being able to pedal for sixteen minutes after thirty days. So he and Sabine added walking to their daily agenda. Even then, walking could never be a "couples' thing" because he just liked to walk, amble, tread carefully, whereas dear Sabine was a "strider", one who walked with purpose, and so Aubrey inevitably fell behind after the first fifty yards. Finally Aubrey decided it was time to weigh himself.

That banned f-word resonated right through the house. It brought Sabine running. After all, that word could easily have indicated some new disaster in the making, another smashed vanity sink to Aubrey's credit. Not at all! There he was, planted squarely on the bathroom weigh-scales, completely naked and amazingly unsightly. He was squinting at the numbers between his feet.

"This bleeping (insert bad word here) machine lies like an S-O-B. (Fill in the requisite vocabulary here). This bleeping (repeat bad word here) thing says I have only lost two bleeping (and here) pounds. This bleeping (this was the sort of unimaginative repetition that truly galled Sabine, so maybe insert a different bad word) thing doesn't work. We need to buy a new one."

Sabine was very calm and collected. "I've been meaning to talk to you about your eyesight, Mister Eagle Eye. I know how much you have to squint these days in order to see anything, so let me take a look. What weight were you when you started exercising?"

Now this was a state secret if ever there was one. "Two hundred and twenty pounds," said Aubrey reluctantly, forced into revealing highly classified information and thinking at the same time that there should have been privacy of information legislation in place to protect him from having to reveal such sensitive data to just anybody. "And now I'm a lousy two hundred and eighteen. What a wasted bleeping (same old word) effort. You can put that bloody exercise bike back in the garage."

"Hmm, two hundred and eighteen pounds you say. Well, either you need glasses—and by the way, I know you do—or you need a calculator because you can't subtract. You are two hundred and eight pounds," Sabine said, straightening up. "What is more, you owe me for all the foul language you have used in public over the past month. Let's just round it up to an even twenty bucks."

"Two hundred and eight pounds? Are you sure?"

"Sure I'm sure!" She should not have said that, but then how was she to know he would hug her full frontally having just completed his sixteen and one-half minutes on the exercise bike? It was not an agreeable olfactory experience; it was like being kissed by an overripe Danish blue cheese that had been left a little too long in the sun.

"Darn it!" he was positively bubbling bonhomie now. "I'm getting so darn streamlined I'll have to start wearing sweat pants with racing stripes."

Wouldn't you know it, but Sabine came across some sweat pants with racing stripes the following week in some bargain store: "Odd sizes on sale for $14.99, this week only." "That's my Aubrey," Sabine thought at once, "Odd in size, odd in shape." She bought two pairs as a stocking stuffer, since Christmas was not that far away. By then, maybe he would be less than two hundred pounds.

In a good year, haying is always a happy time. But then what constitutes "good"? First of all, the weather must be stable enough that you can actually finish the field you started before your hay goes through the rinse cycle a couple of times. As if that is not enough, there is the machinery aspect: the haybine, the rake, the baler, and now the bale-mover. They all have to be pandered to in their own way, adjusted and serviced correctly. The tractors need servicing too, and all of this entails a significant dollar cost. Then of course there is the human element; human error inevitably occurs, with the greatest cost arising as much from the things you neglected to do, like a full service, to the things you do, like shearing off a fence post with the haybine because of your inattention, which can really leave you in that other sort of doo-doo. Yet in all of these departments, this year went particularly well, until the rake decided to jump over a gopher's holiday resort and break clean in half. Aubrey was using Fanny the Farmall at the time, that same antique Fanny of yore. He had covered many acres with this rig, this Farmall and rake combo, and had become very competent with it; he could even go faster, well not than a speeding bullet but certainly faster than a fat farmer with a pitchfork and racing stripes.

The rake was an HS II, a rake and tedder combined. The three-spiked rake wheels were attached to a frame that the operator unfolded outwards so the wheels could feed the swath into the centre of the machine, where the tedder proceeded to fluff it up. Aubrey was sailing along, his voice in full *basso profundo* while singing his dad's one-time favourite ditty, "My bonnie lies over the ocean, my bonnie lies…" when he glanced back to see one half of his bonnie lying dead in the ocean. Inexplicably, his rake had broken into two very distinct pieces, and the rake component was lying in the swath, twenty yards behind him. Oil was pulsing out of the two broken hydraulic pipes that raised and lowered the rake, so Aubrey was compelled to switch off immediately. He vented, that is he cursed, a whole string of unhealthy and unwholesome cuss words with not a soul to censor him. This was not good, though; this was not good at all! This was going to be big, big as in expensive. This stunk of money: big money for new hydraulic hoses and for a welder who would charge lawyer's fees, and then some, because he, unlike Aubrey, could do vertical and upside down seam welding without setting himself on fire. But worst of all, it would cost oodles of time, and the wind and the rain, in the meantime, would come and blow and beat upon his swaths. The monsoons would roll on in and piss upon his hay, and it would be sorely and surely soiled…. Hold on a second! One of two critical lynch pins had fallen out of its home. The split pin that held it in place was gone, and the lynch pin itself was lying there in all its shiny glory in centre-swath for him to see, even with his eyes. Now this was luck. This had to be a reward for clean living. This falling out of the pin had in turn precipitated the shearing of the two lugs holding a second pin, and the rake portion of the machine had simply dropped off. He could make new lugs himself; even he, Aubrey G.W. Hanlon, Aubrey Great Wun Hanlon, could do that. Indeed he could fix the whole thing by himself, if only he could get it home, that is. He just had to believe! He unhooked the two sections of broken pipe from his tractor so as not to lose all of the oil, and took it home with the tedder portion of the rig still attached. He came back with the loader tractor, hooked a chain around the rake, hoisted it up, and took it home, too. Six hours later, he was back in business; even his welding this day was a category above turkey shit. Oh was this ever a boost to his confidence! Two new pipes completed the picture, and it was time to get rolling.

Confidence. So much of what we do or how we act is a matter of confidence. Driving and operating farm machinery is no exception, particularly if that machinery belongs in some museum of yesteryear. Each year, for example, it takes a couple of rounds to rekindle the appropriate cerebral pathways, to recharge the brain circuits that remind you what you should be doing at any given moment. So for the John Deere 530 baler, Aubrey would read the owner's manual to remind himself to start out any bale by weaving down the swath so that Sabine did not have to ask him why all the bales he made were shaped like ice cream cones. He had to remind himself what the lights on the baler monitor were telling him, that he should STOP now and tie up the bale currently in the bale chamber before it went oversize and jammed the works or broke all the belts. He had to remember to back up and dump the bale after it had been tied. And since it was Sabine who did ninety percent of the baling, the nerve pathways were ever more fragile from lack of consistent usage, the brain cells ever more reticent to come to life.

Ah, the bale-mover was to be all his though! An exclusive! Sabine made it crystal clear she was not going to drive *that monstrosity!* "I really don't know why we ever bought it," she said using the royal "we".

"And I have no idea why we bought Godzilla the garden gnome," said Aubrey just to stay even.

But to mitigate all of this, there are occasions when as you grow older you get smarter. First Aubrey did a deal with Pete. They would share the bale-mover if Aubrey could use Pete's big Deutz, the tractor Aubrey had used to bring the bale-mover home from Spruce View that time. It was perfect for the job, given its one hundred and sixty horses of power and the all-around vision it afforded. But Aubrey was smarter still! He experimented extensively in the open field, loading and unloading, picking up bales, both side-on and end-on. In fact on this particular day, he was good, a real prodigy for a beginner. He did not wreck a single bale even if he left a fair few with tousled hairstyles. However, he was soon to discover that bale picking is a game akin to golf. There are those days when you hit the ball so perfectly you wonder why Tiger Woods is not your caddy. The next day you can't hit that ball/bale for love nor money; on those days, Tiger Woods' caddy wouldn't even let you wash his cart. More than this, some bales exhibit extreme personalities, while others are just plain friendly and cooperative. Some have a malicious streak and deliberately bounce themselves off the bale arms the instant they are touched, and sometimes even before. Others seem to think it is inordinately funny to do a sudden backward flip and stand on end. Aubrey developed a worrisome new habit because of these; he began to grind his teeth and talk to these bales, reprimanding them for their insolence, usually to no avail. Some bales made it very clear their only goal was premature self-destruction; they would quite deliberately de-string themselves before your very eyes or hook onto any jagged edge they could find. At that point, they would proceed to shed themselves in outright defiance of anything you tried to do. It wasn't too long before Aubrey discovered that on a bad bale day, the best plan was to go back home and wash the dishes or something.

Happily though, it was good old Pete who was to suffer the final indignity, through no fault of the bales, the bale-mover, or even the operator. It was the Deutz that let him down. A loaded bale wagon is big and heavy with fourteen round bales, seven to a side. Every bale came in at around thirteen hundred pounds. Fourteen times thirteen hundred calls for a calculator or an abacus. It makes even a big mama of a tractor grunt and smoke. Pete was in top gear, bombing down Township Road 37/12, one of the gravel roads that constitute the usual rural infrastructure of roads. His eyes took in the little car approaching him, a young lad at the wheel, and he slowed down. He saw the panic in the boy's eyes as they tried to make sense of this huge monster bearing down upon him. Pete saw granny in the passenger seat reach over to allay the lad's fear and to encourage him to hold his course. Pete slowed right down then because he realized this was granny teaching her grandson how to drive. What he did not see—but certainly felt—was the rim of the tractor's rear wheel give way. But he could not miss seeing the wall of "water" (the calcium ballast) from the burst tube literally soak the little car as it went past. Momentarily he saw the lad's mouth working overtime and granny hollering who knows what, all in some imperfect dream. He felt the tractor sag to one side and begin to labour mightily. He stopped. By the time he had come to a complete halt, the ballast from the tube was pretty much all gone. He got out and saw the little car stop about a half-mile down the road. He signalled to the occupants to come on back as they got out and changed places. He wanted to tell them how sorry he was and about what the calcium mix might do to their car's paint job—that it might peel away, given the caustic covering it had just received. But they took one backward look, granny gave him a royal one-finger salute, and they took off. Pete turned back to the disaster on hand. The rim had split, in turn bursting the inner tube of the tire and spraying the whole port side of the tractor with goop.

With Aubrey's help and Aubrey's tractor, they got the load home, the wounded Deutz too, and began the tedious job of finding a rim. Tedious because they sensed that everyone they phoned saw a sucker caught firmly between a rock and hard place, every one of them seeking to profit handsomely from their misfortune.

The first used-parts place Pete called wanted $900 for a used rim. The second one could get them a new rim for $1,250. A guy in Lethbridge, whose card had somehow made it to Pete's fridge door, shipped one, for sure the right one, for $575. Plus freight. It was the wrong one, plus return freight. So in desperation, Aubrey called Kevin Benelli at Hexagon Farm Supply. Oh sure, he could get one for $450 delivered—if he could deliver it himself and check out Sabine's latest baling adventure.

Ah, the woes of mechanization! It was time to go back to the era of the horse and the mule!

Chapter Four
"YOU FOLKS OWE ME A LOT OF MONEY!"

*H*alloween was a long way off on the year's horizon. Normally somebody in the local community would have staged some sort of get-together by now, but not this year. Not so far. Nobody in the entire neighbourhood had shown the slightest inclination to play host. The very same day that Sabine and Aubrey were lamenting that very fact, the invitation arrived in the mail.

"By royal decree of our reigning monarch, Queen Elizabeth II, Lord Richard Conley formerly of the English borough of Hunk-Under-Maid, Cheshire, England and lately of Farting Towers of Edmonton, Alberta, Canada, doth hereby summon the presence of…

The Downright Dishonourable Sir Aubrey and Lady Sabine Hanlon, Duke and Duchess of Dovercourt, Alberta…

…to an August 27 symposium of The Alberta Brains Trust and Research Institute to be held on the grounds of the Hanlon Estate, south and east of the urban agglomeration known as Rocky Mountain House, beginning at noon. Halloween costume shall be obligatory, beverage provision essential. Do not under any circumstances protest or RSVP; your presence is taken for granted!

> *By Royal Proclamation,*
> *The Right and Very Honourable, Lord Richard Conley,*
> *Queen's Equerry.*

"Well that's nice, 'the Hanlon Estate'," said Sabine flatly. "And from the Queen's Equerry no less!"

"What do you mean, 'well that's nice'?" retorted Aubrey. "Just the other day we were saying how we haven't had a get-together like we used to have for such a long time. Well now it'll happen. And you know what? It'll be a blast!"

"You're right," Sabine perked up. "It was just, well…it was just that the party could have been somewhere else, like at the dugout perhaps. Oh well, maybe it is our turn to host anyway."

It was so true; they all needed to shake a leg and get together for a laugh, even if the last big blast at the Hanlon place, and blast it had been, had cost them an outhouse demolished by gunfire. The fact that this time it would be a dress-up party, even if it wasn't Halloween, would add to the craziness. God bless Lord

Conley not only for coming up with the idea but also for bringing it to life in his own inimitable way.

But then a solid dose of reality hit Sabine. She had no idea how many people this Lord Conley had invited to the symposium, nor yet how the issue of food had been taken care of. She phoned him.

"Plan for thirty," he said.

"Yes, but which thirty? Like, exactly who have you invited?"

"Oh, all the usual members of the diplomatic corps. Oh, and Mavis has elected to organize who is going to bring what, food-wise. That's all you are required to know," and he hung up. Typical Dick Conley.

Mavis, Ernie's wife, eternal bookworm, and wine-taster extraordinaire, phoned up a half-hour later. After their regular "state of the union" chat, Sabine informed her that she would cook up a great big mutton biryani curry.

"Perfect," said Mavis, "because Sybil is planning on a pile of tandoori chicken, which will give us a decidedly East Indian menu. Pierette Moreau is going to make a great big Acadian ragout de boeuf, so you know what that means: we'll all be eating like the rich and famous. Siggy has put himself in charge of the wine, Ernie says he'll corral a float of beer, and Jean-Claude insists he'll bring enough French baguettes to feed the five thousand. Dick Conley has made it very clear that he and only he is in charge of the music and drama department, whatever that is supposed to mean! I'll do some phoning around now that I have talked to you and get some people lined up to bring dessert."

"Good! I feel really happy there's so much groundwork already in place, and I truly thank you. It's good to know that it's not just Lord Conley calling all the shots." Sabine knew well how the "regulars" would band together to ensure there would be more than enough of everything to go around. There'd be enough in the way of drama too, apparently, if Dick Conley was handling that aspect below the radar, as it were! And it was kind of fun not knowing who exactly might be coming, even if they had a pretty good idea.

The day arrived. First off, the weather cooperated perfectly; it was warm and sunny. Second, Dick Conley, the inspiration behind it all, turned up early, which was unusual for him at the best of times. He opened a beer early too, way too early, but that was Dick Conley for you. Lawn chairs were set out, some tables set up, that sort of thing.

"We need a small dais," Dick told Aubrey.

"A small what?" Aubrey responded.

"A dais. You know, some kind of small platform. Do you happen to have a couple of spare sheets of plywood lying around somewhere?"

"As a matter of fact, I do," Aubrey was highly suspicious. "But they're full sheets so I don't particularly want to cut them. And they're heavy too because they are three-quarter inch."

"That, my son, is perfect," Conley responded enthusiastically. "What about a few cinder blocks, by chance?"

"Why on earth would I have cinder blocks?" Again, Aubrey was highly suspicious because it paid to be suspicious when Conley was around.

"Well, tires then? Old ones will do."

"Oh, we've got loads of them, you know that. We use them to hang on the hay tarps."

"Excellent, my friend, excellent! We'll need about ten or twelve. Let's go get 'em!"

They laid the dozen tires on the ground and placed the plywood sheets on top. "Voila!" said Mr. Conley. "The dais. Or as true Thespians might say, the stage."

This was getting a bit serious, Aubrey was thinking, not daring to ask what a thespian might be when it was at home. If he had known that a thespian was connected to some Greek dude by the name of Thespis, he might have been compelled to ask! But still, who was going to be doing what on this stage? Wisely he said nothing. Truth be known, he really did not want to know.

Right at noon, folks began to arrive; everyone would have known they would probably end up missing something if they were late, what with Lord Dick Conley in sole charge. Pete and Jeannie were the first on scene, as one would have expected because Jeannie would feel honour-bound to help Sabine as a welcoming hostess. Then came Sig, the trumpet player in the ESO, the Edmonton Symphony Orchestra, and his wife Sybil, already "in costume" for the day. Of course! Sybil was dressed as the ultimate hippy girl from the days of Woodstock. She was a reincarnation of flower power, braless and bouncy and loving every minute of her 1960s liberation. Sig was dressed as he always was, seeing no reason to drive all the way down from Edmonton dressed as the tuba he planned to be. Then came Ernie, Aubrey's unofficial mechanic, and his wife Mavis. She was already gowned as Queen Victoria and as regal as that queen had ever been. Ernie was in his usual red coveralls, no explanation, no apologies, but at least they were relatively clean. Last but not least of the out-of-town regulars were Jean-Claude and Pierette Moreau who soon metamorphosed into Mr. and Mrs. Bonhomme de Neige, sorry, Monsieur et Madame Bonhomme. In no time at all, the atmosphere was alive with good cheer and flowing beer, part of Lord Conley's master plan, no doubt! Apparently those now present formed some kind of an "in-crowd", or put another way, they were those guests coming "from away". All of the other guests would be local, or so it appeared.

At two o'clock, the self-appointed Master of Ceremonies and Commander-in-Chief, Lord Richard Conley—still the only person who knew what had been planned—commanded that all present should put on "their uniforms". Soon after, Siggy appeared as the C-tuba he had always aspired to play, an orange plastic mixing bowl taped to his head to simulate the bell of the instrument and a good ten feet of vacuum cleaner hose wrapped tightly abound his torso to represent the lead pipe and four coloured containers to portray the valves. It was all quite ingenious really. Jean-Claude, it seemed, had done some kind of a deal with Ernie because he appeared in the latter's red coveralls with a large cardboard sign on his back that read "DILEMMA" in bold black lettering. Ernie, in turn, emerged as Bonhomme alongside Bonnefemme. It seemed he had chickened out of what he had planned to do and had persuaded Jean-Claude to do it in his place. And Jean-Claude had embraced the idea with great enthusiasm, his creative juices working overtime. Pete entered the fray as a "shit-shoveller extraordinaire", with a plastic kid's beach shovel taped to a hard hat and unmistakable blobs of dried cow poop on both shovel and hat. Aubrey followed him dressed as Alberta's latest premier, Alison Redford. His shape was decidedly unRedford-like, it was true, but the wig made up for any lack of realism in the shape department. Sabine trotted out as Bo-Peep, accompanied by Jeannie as her one and only baa-baaing sheep whose clear preference, if not intention, was to get herself lost. A more curious collection of humanity had never before assembled on any Albertan lawn. It was then that the other invited guests began to appear and swell the numbers, all part of the Conley master plan.

To the delight of absolutely everybody, it was Quincy Klug, redneck rancher and occasional perfect gentleman who arrived first. He stepped out of his rattletrap of a truck wearing that garish and now infamous nightgown that Jeannie had found for him the night he had made his unscheduled visit into Pete and Jeannie's swimming pool. It had gone on to attract further infamy when he and his designated driver were stopped at a police Check Stop, and dear Quincy had seen fit to step out of the passenger seat with a view to wowing the two morally upright custodians of the law. It was the latter who got the view!

He was followed by Hugo and Marta Hartford dressed as a pair of bananas proclaiming that living under a Stephen Harper government was like living in a banana republic. Then it was the turn of the Delameres, Jim and Sonya, who came not as Hansel and Gretel but as Tinsel and Pretzel, two fairies auditioning for the latest "Survivor" reality show. In the middle of all of the welcoming and greeting, Dick Conley retired to his trailer to re-emerge as Narcissus (the infamous Hanlon bull of yore) wearing a helmet with horns on his head, a furry suit from some dollar store, a garland of fake flowers around his neck and two passion fruits in a netting onion bag hanging between his legs.

"Hey Dick, maybe you've forgotten that Narcissus was the bull that broke his penis," Aubrey yelled, harking back to the story of Narcissus in *Fancy Free in the Back Thirty*.

"That's right, old son, that's right!" He reached into his pocket and pulled out an obscenely orange and decidedly bent plastic carrot that he pinned to his fly. "I hope you feel better and more fulfilled now," he said as he sat down, moving his appendages to the side.

The French, the Moreaus, would have been the first to agree to use the evocative word "ambiance" to denote a relaxed atmosphere generated by the genuine camaraderie of people who were totally at ease with and among each other. With this gathering of people, there simply could be no false pretensions; you'd be called out much too quickly. At the same time, there was an unqualified respect, each for the other, because everybody knew and acknowledged not only just how hard people worked but how much they cared for their fellow man. In this sense they were very much birds of a feather, even if on this particular day they were all in very different feathers. They ate voraciously; how could they not with such a feast provided? They interacted not with reserve but with gusto, dredging up all the wrongs in their world before putting them to rights. And they relaxed. Of course there was not a single one among them who did not wonder about the presence of Lord Conley's dais, the stage, but since none of them contemplated a new career in either acting or modelling, they deemed it better not to ask. They knew they would have gotten nothing out of the Queen's Equerry anyhow!

Finally, the great Conley got to his feet and moved onto the stage, where he proceeded to break the ice. He would have looked even more outrageous but in deference to decorum and in keeping with the image required of the queen's representative, he had removed his more obscene appendages for the time being. Clearly our Sabine retained some degree of influence over the unpredictable Mr. Conley.

He signalled for everyone's attention. "Here, folks, is a deal you cannot ignore," he boomed in his best English town-crier's voice. He reached into a nondescript brown shopping bag and withdrew not one but two magnums of champagne. "What we have here, ladies and gentlemen…and Aubrey Hanlon," he said holding up the bottles, one in each hand, "is the prize that one of our illustrious number shall claim after going on stage and representing whatever it is they are dressed as. You can do whatever comes into your tiny little brain; sing, dance, or stand on your head to prove Alberta's got talent. You will be given one hour's preparation time starting from now. There is, however, one stipulation. One bottle of the champagne appropriately chilled, shall be shared among those in the audience who have the fortitude to remain seated and endure whatever performance blights their eye. The other bottle shall be a part of the winner's take-home research project on the effects of a magnum of champagne on the brain." He paused for effect before continuing.

"Here in this envelope…"

"Five bucks," yelled Sonya Delamere, doing something she had never ever previously had the courage to do during her entire life … before then going puce with embarrassment as the realization settled in.

"There is a pair of prime seat Oilers' tickets to the Battle of Alberta on December 12, in Edmonton."

That was the announcement that by itself transformed the prevailing attitude of "I wouldn't be seen dead making a fool of myself in this get-up even for a whole magnum of champagne" to "what the hell, I might as well give this a try, I've got nothing to lose." It also served to increase "consumer spending" on everything drinkable: beer, wine, fortified water, punch with a crunch, Coke, Coke with rum, Daiquiris, Bloody Marys, all in the name of "Dutch courage". Thankfully, Aubrey, good ex-policeman that he was, had organized a couple of local lads as designated drivers to ferry people home when they so decided.

It was somewhere around 3:30 p.m. that Dick Conley stood up and made what for a few was the dreaded announcement. He took centre stage and launched into his spiel.

"Ladies and gentlemen, and those like Aubrey Hanlon who fall into neither category, I hereby call this meeting of The Brains Trust and Research Institute of Alberta into full plenary session. The order of participants this afternoon shall be decided upon by individual impulse and courage. In other words, whenever you feel you are ready, come on up to this stage and do your thing."

For a full minute nobody moved. Nobody dared. Conley said nothing and went back to his seat.

It was Pete who finally stood up, looked across at his wife Jeannie and said, "I gotta get this over with." He got up on the stage, made sure his shovel was where it was supposed to be, took a deep breath and began to gyrate as he launched into his recitation…

> "Here I stand, an old farmer who just shovels shit?
> With all this darn shovelling, you'd think I'd be fit,
> The slickers all insist it's why I smell so darn bad,
> No matter the hundreds of showers I've had…
> On the day of my wedding, my bride held her nose…
> She even stood up and said, "You stink like no rose."
> On the night of our vows, I was so full of strength,
> When she said, "No dear, we'll do it arm's length!"
> So if you are hoping to be a true man of the soil…
> Remember it's a full lifetime of never-ending toil,
> Remember you'll stink for the rest of your life,
> For that reason alone, you'll need one special wife…"

For a moment there was a profound silence as everyone took it in. Pete looked across at Jeannie and winked. She ran up and hugged him, and then held her nose while the rest of the audience cheered wildly. It was an auspicious start, and now Pete could relax. Conley too, if this was the calibre of what might come up.

It was time for Hugo and Marta to take the plunge, or rather it was time for Marta to drag Hugo on stage before the excuse he was trying to make, that he couldn't walk, actually turned out to be true. They embarked on some kind of skit about Canada being something of a banana republic with Stephen Harper being "The Big Banana"… only Hugo could not remember for the life of him why he was even up there. Naturally Marta was furious with him, but the only thing she could think of doing was to launch into the "Banana Boat" song they had planned in hopes that Hugo's lame brain might suddenly decide to kick in. The thing was, Hugo's brain was one of those that turned extremely creative when both hop and grape in combination had worked their magic. So picture this: a man and a woman banana dancing opposite each other, the man version being at least two and a half beats behind the music, with the lyrics being sung *forto tassimo* by the female version. The act might have come out a little more seemly had the male banana not decided (a) to incorporate the mating antics of a previously undiscovered Jamaican primate into the routine and (b) to echo the lyrics of his mate, *porto presto* with his own contrived variations. If you add the necessary pelvic to-ing and fro-ing, you will assuredly get the picture!

Marta: "Day-o, day-ay-ay-o…
Echo: *Play-oh, play-eh-eh-oh…*
Marta: Daylight come and me wanna go home…
Echo: *Twilight come and me wanna go home…*
Marta: Day me say day, me say day, me say day
　　　Me say day, me say day-ay-ay-ay-o…
　　　Daylight come and me wanna go home…
Echo: *Play, me say play, me say play, me say oi-vey…*
　　　Me say play, me say play-eh-eh-eh-oh…
　　　Twilight come and me wanna go home…
Marta: Work all night on a drink o' rum…
　　　Daylight come an me wanna go home…
Echo: *Play all de day, chasin' your bum…*
　　　Twilight come and me wanna go home…
Marta: Stack banana till the morning come…
　　　Daylight come an me wanna go home…
Echo: *Chase that bum till in de night she come…*
　　　Twilight come an' me wanna go home…
Marta: Come, Mister tally man, tally me banana…
　　　Daylight come and me wanna go home…
Echo: *Come Miss Jellybean look at me banana…*

> *Daylight come an' me wanna go home…*
> **Marta**: Lift six foot, seven foot, eight foot bunch…
> *Daylight come and me wanna go home…*
> **Echo**: *It's a six foot, seven foot, eight foot crunch…*
> *Twilight come and me wanna go home…*
> **Marta**: Six foot, seven foot, eight foot bunch,
> *Daylight come and me wanna go hoooommmme…!"*
> **Echo**: *Six foot, seven foot, eight foot crunch,*
> *Twilight's here, take me and my banana hoooommmme!*

By the end of it all, both partners were totally into it, Marta and her Echo. Indeed, Hugo seemed to think he had been cruelly deprived when it suddenly ended, especially since his raunchy gyrations had the audience howling for… an encore, or maybe it was mercy? Marta led him to the edge of the stage to take a bow, and he promptly fell off. She left him where he fell, took the bow by herself, and returned to her fan club. Hugo was rescued by Quincy who assisted in administering additional strong medicine to resuscitate him.

Mavis went up by herself and started into her speech. "As Queen Victoria, may I now call this court to order? Lords and ladies, courtiers and courtesans, knaves and damsels of ill repute, noble and not-so-noble citizens of my realm, be good enough to lend me your ears." Her accent was perfect Oxford English, upper-class, and as they say in the more exotic English circles, so "twee". "I have been asked today by the Royal Academy of Splendid Genetic Achievement to show you all what to look for in a cutting-edge, fruit-of-the-loom, breeding bull. Lord Conley, would you be good enough to pass me my pointer." Conley rose and passed over a yellow metre rule, with everyone in the audience quite sure he was to be the bull. But alas no! He was allowed to resume his seat.

"I now call on Mister Aubrey Hanlon, proprietor and resident stud bull of the Hanlon Estates to please step forward."

Aubrey was taken by complete surprise. He quickly shed the Redford skirt and blouse and was now reduced to a comfortable pair of shorts and a UFA tee shirt. He put his flip-flops back onto his feet and climbed up onto the stage.

"Please stand there, sideways to the people so that they can appreciate a fine example of profile. Thank you." No sign of friendship; she was stiff upper-lip regal; she was She-who-must-be-obeyed.

"Now the first thing to look for in, um, a breeding bull is a clean line, a clean profile. Now what you have before you is a wondrous example of a breeding bull, one with a curvature that our scientific classification system would describe as 'unbelievably lumpy'; a curvature that sets one to wondering who but good Lady Sabine could have purchased such an ill-shapen animal. Note first, if you will," the metre rule pointed, "the sling of the belly. This is a belly that clearly converts fodder well, with a very high feed-to-flesh ratio." She paused for Aubrey to exaggerate his profile, one that manifestly had just consumed all it could eat.

"Now take a look at the legs. If spindly is what you want, spindly is what we get. If a Louis XIV chair can be regarded with shock and awe, so too can a bull with legs such as this. Yes, it is true that these legs are somewhat on the pallid side and a trifle lacking in hair cover but on this particular Hanlon blood-line, the farmer's wife will willingly tell you there's more than enough of a hair coat elsewhere to keep this beast warm in winter." Aubrey was now playing his part, preening about like a show bull.

"Hold still, you abominable animal or I shall be compelled to get your regular handler to put a halter on you!" Again, a regal pause. "So as you can see, my lords and ladies, this specimen is truly halter-broken, a fully domesticated bovine, even if one must never assume that the male of any species can be domesticated. Nor trusted, I hasten to add!"

"Now take a more focused look here." The metre rule indicated Aubrey's expansive derriere. "This is what we call Triple-A: lots of marbling, double, even triple-muscled in places. As you can see, this particular specimen is so well muscled there is a pronounced overhang here, and here. Simmental and Angus would be put to shame. They would not even make it to the menu."

"Two other factors that ought to be taken into account are basic disposition and libido. Now this specific specimen can become a bit wild, especially if he gets into a herd. He is known for two unique traits, his mellow bellow when he is displeased and his tendency to add to global warming by way of methane expulsion. As for libido, why just last week he was spotted lusting in the hayfield when he saw his intended target toss her halter top wantonly into the wind. Sadly, it was not a meeting of the minds, however, for while the damsel made it clear that she was indisposed, the squire thought it to be a message that she was predisposed. Thus it did not end in connubial bliss, but not for lack of libido on the part of the bull. Thank you for both your time and your patience, dear citizens. You may now retire, Mr. Hanlon, and go talk some more bull." She gave Aubrey a dismissive wave and swept off the stage with great majesty.

Jeannie and Sabine's Bo-Peep routine was creditable but definitely not memorable. They were nonetheless heroic enough to get all the way through it before making a graceful retreat.

Then all went kind of dead for a few minutes before Quincy, yes, good ol' Quincy Klug got up. But he did not go straight to the stage, he walked over to Sig who was debating with his wife Sybil whether she was fired up enough to go and do her act.

"Say old son, could you borrow me that there guitar of yours for a minute or two? Like, I know she's likely your baby an' all, but see I didn't have the gumption to bring mine along with me."

Sig was initially at a loss. His guitar was absolutely his baby, so much so that nobody had ever got their hands on it. But these were his friends, Aubrey and Sabine and the whole crew, and if Quincy was one of them no matter how wayward he might look, why he was Quincy's friend too, no questions asked. No, these people were not just "friends", they were family. As he handed it over, he noted with satisfaction that Quincy handled it like the baby it was. At that point, Quincy got Jim Delamere to put a chair on stage for him. He sat down, strummed the guitar a bit to get the feel and then in the most mellifluous country baritone voice anyone had ever heard, he began to sing...

> "I'm a broken-down rancher,
> I've lost all my class,
> My neighbours keep sayin'
> I'm a pain in the ass.
> Sabine bought most of my critters,
> Cut me off at the pass,
> Soon she'll be sayin'
> I should be put out to grass.
> Now my life was so happy,
> I can hardly explain,
> We shared all the hardships,
> With no-one to complain,
> Then after the roundup,
> It's whoop time again,
> Me and Dick Conley,
> But man he's some pain.
> So all you young hoodlums,
> Take a warning today...
> Stay away from Dick Conley,
> He'll lead you astray.
> Stay away from Mrs. Hanlon,
> She can drink like a boot,
> Look what she married...
> Now there's some galoot!"

Silence. Deep silence, then applause. Wild, unrestrained applause. Quincy was suddenly no longer some cowboy curiosity from somewhere out west; with that one performance, he had earned a lifetime membership in the club. Still with the reverence of a priest bearing some priceless religious relic, he made his way back over to Sig, lifted his hat and returned his guitar. Sig could not speak he was so moved. Lord be! He had not heard a voice like that in years, and this was no audition, this was impromptu. He had just seen the act that would likely claim his beloved Oilers' tickets, but he almost did not care. "You'll have to have something up your sleeve to top that," he whispered to Sybil.

"As long as you play along, it's in the bag," she said with that knowing smile of hers. Oh well, at least she was wearing some kind of skimpy yellow creation beneath her too transparent blouse, assuredly for the sake of decency Sig surmised. And that was all to the good; there was no point in offending anyone, not if it cost them the prize.

Two minutes later, she turned to her husband. "Let's do it!" she said. He latched onto the bale of straw they had fetched specially for the occasion and tossed it onto the stage, making a point of leaving Quincy's chair right where it was. Now it was Sybil's turn to shine, Sybil with flowers in her hair, Sybil of flower power and Woodstock. Sig sat down on the chair and began to strum his guitar, losing himself almost immediately. And suddenly there was Sybil carrying the Farmall tractor seat that she had persuaded Ernie to remove from mama tractor earlier in the day. She dropped the seat on the bale and stopped, making a point of having a slow look around, the audience now quiet and highly expectant. After all, Sybil was famously quirky, so heaven alone knew what might transpire. Meanwhile Sig was focused, intensely so; there was a lot riding on the outcome after all, two Oilers' tickets.

Sybil began to gyrate sensuously as Sig played the lead-in to a rendition of that old Beatles' favourite, "Hey Jude". The sight and sound already held the audience entranced. Sybil was, well, visibly and physically well-endowed, and she certainly had a sense of rhythm, the slow gentle rhythm of the seasoned flower child. And then she began to sing. As with Quincy, nobody except Sig had ever heard her sing; nobody had ever asked her nor expected her to sing, nobody had ever given it a thought.

> "Hay nude, don't be afraid…
> To take a baler song and make it better…
> Remember to tie it at the end…
> Then you'll start to feel much better, much better, much better…"

She swayed gracefully around the tractor seat before finally settling and sitting on it.

> "Hay nude, don't be afraid…
> To take your socks off and make it better…
> Remember to show the sun…
> All you have to make it better, much better, much better…"

As she sang she removed first one white sock and then the other and then, oh joy of all joys for all of the boys, she took off her blouse. Everybody there had heard about Sabine's haying mishap so the laughter was raucous. There was an air of expectation too, but nobody in their wildest dreams could have predicted what came next. Sybil rose to her feet and began to sashay around the bale to the accompaniment of her husband's guitar.

> "And any time you hay in the sun, don't refrain…
> Don't think to cover up your pretty shoulder…
> For well you know it's so good to be cool…
> Just let it go and make it colder, colder, colder…"

As she hit that last line, off flew her bikini top, that yellow scrap of cloth à la Sabine, to be caught by one bemused Quincy Klug. And there she swayed, a full ten seconds of topless glory. She then snatched up her clothes and bolted, Siggy strumming the refrain one last time as if to mourn her absence.

"How can anyone top that?" Only Conley could have put the question in that fashion.

As Alison Redford, first female premier of Alberta, Aubrey Hanlon tried but he could not come close, largely because when it came right down to it, he couldn't read the writing in his notes. So he/she resorted to every modern party leader's favorite theme and promised "no new taxes" at least fifteen times, likely not a record for these things. He realized how his effort had been somewhat flat so to deflect attention away from the fact, he called for Jean-Claude.

"Hey Jean-Claude, what are you going to do? It's your turn. You're up next!"

"Moi? Rien! Nutting!" he said, ducking into his native tongue as he always did when he felt under pressure.

"Come on everybody, join me in my call. All together now, we want Jean-the-clod, we want Jean-the-clod…"

"We want Jean-the-clod," shouted the crowd with great enthusiasm. "We want Jean-the-clod…"

"Deux minutes," he said, still dressed in Ernie's red coveralls with the cardboard sign reading "DILEMMA" on his back. "I'ave to do me some consultancy work first." Jean-Claude had always been bashful, but here he was *tout en famille*, the nearest he ever got to people who he thought of as his kinfolk. He could not let them down, nor would he. He had quite a few hurried words with Sybil and then with Quincy, both of whom then disappeared only to reappear three minutes later wearing raincoats and carrying a couple of large bedcovers, a couple of pillows and two more bales. The bales were placed alongside each other apparently to simulate a double bed. The pillows and the covers were placed thereon and Sybil and Quincy made a show of climbing into bed, one on one side, one on the other leaving a space in the middle for Jean-Claude. Both seemed to be heavily into adjusting themselves beneath the covers before finally settling down. That was when Jean-Claude began.

"Messieurs et Mesdames, Ladies and Gentlemens, in the complicated lives we are living, we are all 'aving the dilemmas, you know, les choix, the choices that we are all 'aving to make. Eh bien, moi, me, I never understood dis word 'dilemma', what it is really meaning, so I ask mon ami, my friend Ernie, what does dis word 'dilemma' mean? Let me tell you what dis Ernie say. 'E say, you cannot comprend, 'ow you say, comprehend dis word without an exemple, example. I am now going to show you 'ow to define dis word using Ernie's exemple."

Jean-Claude climbed into the "bed" between Sybil and Quincy, and all went still and quiet. First a diminutive hand appeared to the left, and then another hairier claw appeared from the right, both then appearing to grope at the sleeping Jean-Claude in the centre. Finally he came to life as if he had suddenly woken up. He looked at the audience and said, "Mes amis, my friends, I 'ave a big probleme, a big dilemma, and it is this. Who do I turn my back on?" He lay back down and Sybil and Quincy both sat up in unison, letting the cover fall away, Sybil with her arms across her naked upper torso, Quincy wearing that hideous night gown he had arrived in, his hairy chest exposed for the maximum ape-like effect. While Sybil smiled oh so seductively, Quincy sported an alarmingly lascivious leer that would have sent the female of any species racing for protection and/or cover. They dropped back down and Jean-Claude popped back up. "Dat, Messieurs et Mesdames, is my dilemma. You see, I 'ave a choice, yes? But then again, I 'ave no choice. Merci beaucoup," and he was done. The three actors then retreated without more ado.

If anybody had planned on following that act, their resolve melted away. Everybody was pretty content, anyway, until it dawned on Aubrey that Mister Conley himself had not done anything. Aubrey led the new chant. "We call upon Conley to sing us a song. We call upon Conley to sing us a song…" Most of the crowd knew he had both the voice and the repertoire if only they could get him to show some inclination.

"Conley has lost his courage," Dick proclaimed flatly.

"Conley is a cow-ard, Conley is a cow-ard," sang Aubrey undeterred, determined not to let his good friend off lightly.

"Conley might be a whole lot of things," retorted Dick, "but cow-ard isn't one of them. Make me a challenge and I'll prove to you I am no cow-ard. But I'm not singing you a song, not after what you've heard already." In hindsight, this was the stupidest thing he could have said. Aubrey had a small herd of cows grazing in the adjoining front field. One of these was the notorious Nellie, and as Aubrey well knew, she had never shown any love for one Dick Conley.

"Okay, here's the deal," said Aubrey setting up something he should never ever have considered, something he was later quite ashamed of. "Here you are, not only full of bull but dressed like one as well. So I'll give you ten bucks if you dare to cross that field west to east dressed in your full get-up. But you've got to bawl like a bull, and you've got to cross the field in no less than four zigzags, not in a straight line."

"Ten more!" yelled Ernie.

"Forty," yelled Quincy, convinced that Conley needed some cowboy's adjustment.

"Ten each," yelled the Hogarths.

"Ten each," yelled the Delameres.

"Twenty," said Sig, sadly disappointed that Conley refused to sing.

"You're all on," said Conley coming alive. "All proceeds to go to Pete and Jeannie's World Vision Chicken Supply Fund."

"A hundred bucks from each of us then," said Pete, which in turn led to the doubling and tripling of all the other pledges.

Sabine was the lone voice of reason, and she was drowned out. "Is this really a good idea?" she asked Aubrey. "Like what if the cows charge him?"

"Then we'll all get to see how fast Dick Conley can run," responded Aubrey, way too flippantly and much too lubricated with brown ale to think clearly.

So the die was cast. Aubrey took Conley up to the far fence by quad so all he had to do was to make his way back to the plank fence separating the pasture from the garden where the festivities were being held. He was to await Aubrey's signal from the garden before he embarked on his journey, a distance of about two hundred and fifty yards.

Aubrey finally gave the signal, whereupon Conley climbed through the fence, adjusted his headgear, and began bawling and carrying on like a mad bull as he started out. The cows' heads perked up at once but they made no move as they tried to make sense of what they were seeing. That was when Dick made his first mistake; he zigged away from them when he should have zagged towards them. And because he was now heading away from them, this only served to pique the curiosity of some younger cows. They rushed towards him to get a better look at the weirdest-looking bull they had ever set eyes on, coming to an uncertain halt about thirty feet away from him. At that moment Conley zagged, straight towards them. Huh! What was all this about? Was this bull threatening them? Whatever he was trying to say was certainly not in any bovine vocabulary! They decided not to hang around to find out; they high-tailed it back to the comfortable security of the herd and the bull whose sweet talk they were intimate with. That unfortunately did not put a stop to Conley's noisy performance of a bull in rut; he zagged for a second time, heading away from them once again. This was the signal of a bevy of younger ones to come on back and take a second look at him. Clearly they remained unconvinced that this bull was their kind of stud. They studied him closely as they edged nearer. Then he zigged. This time they let him come within about fifteen feet before they made the decision to head for the far gate, taking the whole herd and their own pansy bull with them in a headlong stampede. All but Nellie! She objected to having her afternoon Pastoral Symphony in B Minor interrupted by some scrub-looking bull so gaunt that it had actually climbed through a five-wire fence. She began her run. So did Dick Conley, one second too late. He actually did make it to the plank fence, had even placed his hand on the top plank to heave himself over when Nellie's head took him right between the buttocks and catapulted him way over into the garden. Then she shook her head in evident satisfaction and trotted off, no doubt to tell the story to her cohorts.

"Oh God, are you all right?" called out an almost hysterical Sabine, rushing over to an inert Mr. Conley. In response he began to laugh uncontrollably, or was it hysterically? Nobody could decide until he rose unsteadily to his feet, a wide grin of triumph creasing his face. "You folks all owe me money," he said. "Lots of money."

Nonetheless, such a close call slowed things right down. It was inevitable. But Conley had yet to deal with the last order of business, who had won the champagne and the hockey tickets. It was a toss-up between Quincy and Sybil until Quincy stated loudly that he would rather learn to knit than watch an entire hockey game. Siggy was ecstatic. Sybil was ecstatic for Siggy. As for the champagne, that all vanished in a series of toasts "to us and all who sail with us."

Chapter Five
THE ANTICS OF KONG THE KING

People don't generally realize this, but one of the great things about owning a farm is that you have the space to dig a hole. Any size. Anywhere. You can fill it up again if that is what you choose to do… but this is by way of digression.

Aubrey and Sabine had an acquaintance who, because he had the appropriate qualifications, occasionally conducted appraisals for real estate companies in town. A nice man, Wesley Hodgins was quiet and soft-spoken, a nerdy type who preferred to stay so far out of people's way nobody knew he was even there. One afternoon, stinking hot it was, he showed up at the Hanlon place on foot, visibly distressed. Aubrey was puttering about in the yard when he arrived. The look of relief on Wesley's face when he saw Aubrey was priceless.

"Mr. Hanlon, Orberry, I wonder if you can help me?" he stammered.

"I can sure try," said Aubrey genially. "What do you need?"

"Somehow I got my truck stuck in a mud-hole down by the river. We were going fishing, you understand. My wife is still down there looking after the vehicle." Aubrey visualized Mrs. Hodgins; a formidable character on a par with the Wicked Witch from Withrow, and a lady with whom you would never want to tango or tangle. "I wonder if you would come down and pull me out."

"Oh, for sure! You'd be surprised at how often we end up doing this. We'll just grab us a chain and then we'll head on down."

"Maybe, maybe we, er, we should take your tractor. I'm afraid I've really gone and buried it. I don't think your truck would even pull me out. My Susan is rather upset about it, let me tell you!" An image of "my Susan" feathered all in black, sitting up in the heights of a swamp spruce and cawing like a demented crow at her cowering mate flashed through Aubrey's mind. He couldn't help it, he smiled.

"Okay, no problem, we'll go in the tractor. If we get *that* stuck, then we really will be in trouble with your Susan. But it's not as if we're going to try and cross the river or anything." The attempt to lighten up poor Wesley's mood died in stillbirth.

In a heavy silence now, Aubrey threw a chain into the tractor bucket and both men climbed into the cab. On the way there was some desultory conversation about the weather, with dear Wesley (not Wes, never Wes) muttering something about the fact that dear Susan (not Sue or, heaven forbid, Susie) would ever accompany him fishing again. "She's not very happy with me, my Susan."

When they arrived on site, Aubrey saw instantly why Susan would be mighty unhappy. She was standing beside their baby blue, of course, two-wheel drive pickup which was mired up to the axles in thick, gooey mud. This was actually what Aubrey had anticipated. What he had not anticipated was the precise visual version of Mrs. Susan Hodgins. The only thing left unsoiled was the floppy straw hat affair on her head. Otherwise, she was streaked and muddied from head to toe. Clearly even with her stout frame pushing the truck from the back, the only reward she had been blessed with was an inglorious mud-bath. If the sight of her in such condition was not arresting enough, the face more than made up for it. She had the demeanour of Mount Trudeau about to explode in a "fuddle-duddle" eruption. Her face was akin to a prairie thunderstorm rolling in from the west. It was enough to make Aubrey double up with laughter, but nobody, repeat nobody, ever laughed at Mrs. Hodgins, Susan—not ever! Not even Aubrey Hanlon, who as a policeman had learned to control his emotions long ago, however difficult that proved to be.

This is the trouble when you are saddled with too lively an imagination; on occasion it gets a little too lively! As the two men dismounted from the tractor, with Wesley demonstrating abject subservience, Aubrey could not help but get a closer look at the indomitable Mrs. H. Immediately his creative mind began to wonder if the very substantial under-armour showing through her pastel skirt and muslin blouse was constructed of Kevlar and boasted bullet-proof properties.

"Hi, Mrs. Hodgins," he said in greeting and trying to be as friendly as he could.

"Good day to you Mr. Hanlon. Thank you for coming to our help. Old Wesley Wobbly here decided he was some kind of hotshot rally-car driver and thought he could cross a major tributary of the Clearwater River. Look at the horrid mess he has got me into." Aubrey was now compelled to look and was immediately convinced that if this lady ever went to war, the other side would need armour-piercing rockets to make any impression on this formidable woman-of-war, a veritable *HMCS Invincible*. Or, if she was ever seconded by the military to assist the Canadian effort in Afghanistan, why, the Taliban would quit in a second and scurry off to their caves high in the hills, never to be heard from again.

Banishing such uncharitable thoughts from his mind, he turned to the task at hand. At once he realized she was not angry because her klutz of a husband had got them stuck, but because she had gotten so abominably filthy for no good cause and now there was a relative stranger looking on. Who knew what he might be looking at? This was good for neither her dignity nor her ego, and nobody trifled with Susan's ego, nobody. Wesley, by contrast, was still a picture of laundered cleanliness, with his blue corduroy pants tucked neatly into the top of his gumboots. Yup, Aubrey could see it all so clearly, as any man in his circumstances would. Yup, dear Wesley had cajoled his wife into pushing because he, her husband and alpha male, was the only person around competent enough to get into the driver's seat and know what he was doing. Nerdy as he was, cleanliness was next to godliness as far as he was concerned. Which is why, being a fastidious type, he asked Aubrey if he wouldn't mind attaching the chain to the truck "because I'm not exactly sure where I should put it."

"Yeah right," Aubrey was thinking, "like I have no real desire to grovel under my truck because I might get as dirty as my dear Susan."

"Sure thing," said Aubrey, digging enough of a hole in the mud so that he could attach the chain around a spring shackle. Thank God he'd thought to put on his coveralls.

"Okay Wesley, here's what we do. Start up the truck and leave her in neutral. Let the tractor do the work. I'll just take the strain and then I'll ease you slowly out. Got it?"

"Got it," said Wesley adjusting his beige fedora, the one with the fishing fly, a Royal Coachman by the look of it, stuck in the band. Then he climbed into the truck, still immaculate inside, caked with mud on the outside. He started up and slipped it into first gear. Aubrey naturally enough did not see him do that, and had made the wrong assumption that Wesley could follow a simple set of instructions. It never occurred to Aubrey that Wesley might think he knew better; so Aubrey, now in his tractor, inched forward until the tow chain was taut. Then in the lowest possible gear, he let the clutch out. It was a piece of cake for the tractor. The truck hesitated a split-second only to surge forward like a blood-doped rabbit and connect with the rear tire of the tractor. The truck's front bumper had just enough time to sniff the solid tread of the left-hand side wheel before bending downwards, curling almost as symmetrically as a mountain sheep's horn. Thankfully, the truck duly stalled.

Aubrey got out of the tractor to see what had happened. The sound emanating from Mrs. Hodgins was almost primordial, a throwback to the era of warring dinosaurs in mortal conflict. It was nothing short of bone-chilling. And there she was, banging so furiously on Wesley's door that she actually succeeded in putting her own dent in it. Sensibly he simply refused to come out; he just stared straight ahead in utter consternation. Aubrey, unwilling to risk life and limb in a one-sided combat with this unhinged version of Tyrannosaurus Rex, got back into his tractor, pulled forward a couple of feet, and waited until some of the noise tailed off. Only then did he risk emerging and detaching the chain from the truck. By this time, the "sound" emanating from Mrs. Hodgins, Wesley's Susan, had subsided enough that Wesley was persuaded to roll down his window. And that was also when he did the bravest thing he had ever done in his life; he suggested that dear Susan might like to climb into the back of the cab because she was "a little too grubby" to join him in the cab. This launched another round of prehistoric wailing before her husband's logic had penetrated far enough for her to accept the practicality of the proposal. Telling the world that even "Willy Wonka has more in his chocolate-coated cranium than my brain-challenged husband," she hitched up her skirt and climbed over the tailgate.

Aubrey walked over to Wesley's door.

"How much do I owe you?" Wesley asked weakly. "I've got a toonie here."

"Actually, nothing. But it's my turn to ask you a favour."

"Oh," said Wesley almost cowering beneath the dash.

"You occasionally assess properties for realtors, right?"

"Well, yes I do but then I do have the qualifications you know." It was as if he had to duck the prospect of some form of criminal investigation.

"That's what I have been told. You see, I have seven acres with a mobile home that I want to subdivide off my farm and put on the market. My problem is I have no idea what I should be asking for it. Would you be willing to come out and take a look at it? Maybe you could give me a realistic idea of what it might be worth?"

"Oh I can do that," said a clearly relieved Wesley Hodgins. "I'll just go and dump, er drop, Susan off at home and we can do it right away if you want. I can be back at your place in fifteen minutes."

"Darn right you can do it," added the ghoul in the back of the truck. "It'll get the old fool out of my hair while I clean up," she muttered through clenched teeth at Aubrey.

And so it transpired that Wes, Wesley, was as good as his word; he was back at the Hanlons' within fifteen minutes. Aubrey and Sabine jumped into their own truck and Wesley followed them up to Stanley Himilton's old place. There they had a general walkabout before Aubrey got down to explaining where he planned to put the boundary fence. Wesley was nothing if not focused; this was his territory after all.

"No," he said shortly. "Put the one corner over there, the second over by that clump in the hayfield and square it up with the existing road fence. The other two corners will draw from that. That will balance your property nicely, even if you lose an acre or two from your hayfield. You've got to put something together that people are looking for. What you've got here is a place where someone can keep a couple of horses for example." His logic was inescapable.

"Oh, and that ratty old greenhouse and tumbledown shed over there? Knock 'em down. Dig a hole some place and bury them. Either that or take them to the dump." Wesley Hodgins may not have been much of a mud-bogger, but he was all business when it came to looking at property.

"And this is what I'd ask in dollars." He mentioned a figure a full one-third more that the Hanlons had figured on asking. "Advertise in the local paper at that price for a full month. Don't drop your price whatever you do. Acreages are selling like hotcakes right now. Get the place properly surveyed so you're in county limits for acreages and so you can get a separate land title. That's what I'd do anyway. Now I'd best be getting back to my Susan to see if she's okay."

"As if," thought Aubrey to himself. "No doubt she'll be waiting on the porch seated in the old rocking chair, the ancient family blunderbuss cradled across her knees with the express intention of seeing how fast her idiot husband could run." *[**Blunderbuss:** n. A short musket of wide bore and flaring muzzle, formerly used to scatter shot at close range.]*

So now the Hanlons had a plan, a genuine down-home plan. All they had to do was to go ahead and execute it. The professional part was easy; they just delegated the surveying and so forth to the professionals. The amateur part called for some creative thinking.

"Say Pete," Aubrey asked when Pete and Jeannie came round for their weekly visit, "who do you know around here who can dig a great big hole now that Ed Tilley has gone?"

"What the heck do you want a great big hole for? I thought you had rebuilt the outhouse that Jean-Claude blasted all to hell."

"I want to bury a couple of buildings."

"Don't tell me. You're going to bury your whole house in some kind of time capsule. Anybody digging up something like that will surely be impressed with the supreme level of your sophistication."

"No, we need to bury a couple of the old buildings on Stan's place." He went on to explain their plan.

"Well, our buddy Jim Delamere has a backhoe now. Why don't you ask him? He rents it out with himself as the driver. Ask him."

"Well there you go. I'd no idea he had such a beast."

"Well he does. And for you, he'll likely do it cheap—unless I get to him first!"

He did, do it cheap that is, and he did it the very next day. A week later, and the two eye-sores were gone: deconstructed and dumped in "Jim's pit", as it came to be known.

These days on any farm where margins are high and money is owned by bankers, inevitably it is the farm house that ends up being among the lowest priority item that gets attention because something else, some other emergency, always conspires to put itself at the head of the queue. But the day came when Pete happened to look up at the curled and broken shingles on the Hanlon roof and commented, "You'll be darn lucky to get yourselves another year out of that roof of yours. And let me tell you right now as someone who has been there, you don't want to get to the point where it starts to leak."

"Well, how much would it cost to get it done, do you think?" said Sabine now breathless with a new panic.

"Oh, a roof that size done professionally? Nine to fifteen grand," said Pete who knew about these things.

"You mean nine to fifteen *thousand?*" Sabine was almost gagging now.

"Yup, nine to fifteen big ones," Pete was never one to beat about the bush.

"Where on earth are we going to find money like that?" Sabine's face was white.

"Calm down, dear lady, calm down! Don't go twisting your knickers into a fishing line." (Aubrey made a point of trying to remember that one.) Pete was always at his best when he was in his "keep-it-cool mode".

"Here's what we do. We put a weekend together for the usual crew. No beer, no wine before sundown but a great big curry for lunch. We all set to and strip your roof. I'll bring over my Ford one-ton because it has a hoist. We toss all the old shingles into it and take them to the dump; that's if the dump will take them. You might have to dig yourself a great big hole to bury them in."

"Hey! We got ourselves a great big hole already," said Aubrey ecstatically. "All ready to go. Remember? Jim came over and dug it with his backhoe."

"Great. That's one problem solved. On the Sunday, we'll start putting on the new shingles that you, Mr. Hanlon, are going to purchase this coming week. Twenty-five year warranty, no less. What we don't finish on the Sunday, you and I, Mr. Hanlon, will finish during the week. It'll save you a bundle even if it costs you a bit extra in groceries."

When that same old work crew assembled that September Saturday, they were all ready to rumble. Using the special metal shingle-removers that Pete came up with, Conley and Siggy, Jean-Claude, Pete and Aubrey went at it like a Louisiana chain-gang. By three in the afternoon, the truck was full of shingles and nails, and the plywood roof was laid bare. Sabine said it was kind of like losing one's top. Of course she would be the one to know, commented Dick Conley.

"But what if it rains?" Sabine had to ask the obvious question. It didn't. In fact, it remained dry for the full week.

"So which two of you bunch is going to take the truck up to the hole?"

"A hole, a hole, have you ever seen a big black bull with a white asshole?" Conley let loose in his fine tenor voice. The man just didn't care!

"Okay," said Pete. "I'll take that as you volunteering to be one of the two. I'd rather you were let loose up there, than have you singing loud, lewd, loony tunes from the rooftops down here. We have our dignity to consider. Get Sig to go up with you. He'd love to drive that beast."

Sig of course needed no encouragement. Now Aubrey needed to get in on the act, legitimately. "Listen up guys! This is a Pete truck so the brakes won't be good, the hoist will have a hard time getting up, and there'll be more junk in the cab than Conley has in his whole house. What I'm saying is, don't reverse right up to the hole because you might not stop. We can always push any pile on the lip into the pit with the loader. Think you can handle that, Mister Tuba?"

"He's right, you know," said Pete contritely, for he knew that what Aubrey had said was true. "Got all that?" he added.

"Got it, Mrs. Redford, Premier of my province. Got it Mr. Poop Shoveller Extraordinaire," Sig responded.

"With Pete a-poopin' here, Pete a-poopin' there, here a-poopin', there a-poopin', a-poopin' every bloody where…" sang Conley up on the roof, reducing Old Man Macdonald to a new and lower level.

"Off with you, boys," barked Pete the unofficial foreman. "And hurry up because we need you back here for some real macho horse muscle to hoist all these new shingles up onto the roof."

Off they went like a pair of schoolboys who have suddenly been given the plum job of the day. Ah well, Siggy would likely know what he was doing, while Dick Conley would undoubtedly provide the entertainment.

Four o'clock came and went with no sign of Sig or Conley. Same thing at 4:30. "Maybe I should take a spin up there with the quad to see if they're all right," said Aubrey, growing apprehensive and fearing the worst. That was the very moment they heard Conley's whistling. There he was, strolling through the front field with apparently not a care in the world. He could just as well have been out for a Saturday afternoon ramble for all the urgency he showed. The men watched him from the roof as he climbed over the fence and approached the house.

"They probably ran out of gas," said Pete, getting ready to deflect any criticism coming his way. "There wasn't that much in it."

"Probably they forgot what it was they were supposed to be putting in that hole," said Jean-Claude, a little unkindly.

"Hey Dick, what have you done with Sig and the truck?" Aubrey yelled down at him.

"Oh them, let's just say the whole project is a little up in the air right now."

"Oh merde!" said Jean-Claude. "They 'ave gone an' did it. They 'ave backed le truck into le trou, the 'ole."

"Don't panic, oh ye of so little faith. But we do need the tractor and a chain."

"Et voila!" said Jean-Claude, totally ready to confirm the worst. "Complètement in the merde, 'ow you say en Anglais, completely stuck in le poop."

"Pete, you go on up on the quad with Conley. Jean-Claude and I will come up in the tractor and we'll bring a chain along with us," Aubrey directed. It was best not to ask questions, especially of someone as devious as Dick Conley.

Pete had to know the answer though. "What have you guys gone and done?" he asked Dick as he descended the ladder.

"Oh you'll see for yourself soon enough, old son. But you might want to bring a camera. You might not ever see something quite like this ever again," he added enigmatically. He certainly showed no sign of panic mode, but then maybe he was too dumb or too impractical to panic, Pete was thinking.

And yes, they saw soon enough, and none of them could believe their eyes. Oh well, all was recorded for posterity on Pete's camera. There was the truck about ten feet from the hole, exactly where it should have been. The hoist was up too, as one would have expected. But the nose of the vehicle was also up: way up in the sky, like a leaping buffalo sniffing the wind. There staring foolishly out of the driver's window, was Siggy who, for the last thirty minutes, had dared not move for fear of shifting the balance and toppling the truck. Pete could see at once what had happened.

Asphalt shingles are by nature both very sticky and very heavy, so they would not slide readily off the back. With Sig in the cab, Conley had raised the box by pulling on the outside trip lever located just behind the cab. The box had responded with zest for someone who thought all he had to do was pull on a lever and magic would ensue: the shingles would all leap out of the box, and they could go home. But the load, sticky and heavy as it was, refused to budge; it was the whole front end of the truck that budged instead. Siggy was immediately a captive up there in the cab, not master of all that he surveyed, as he would have liked, but an unwitting and precariously balanced prisoner of circumstance. But at least he had an uninterrupted view of the mountains. Conley being Conley saw no real danger in the situation; as one would have expected, he saw only comedy and humour.

Pete took charge. They chained the front end of the truck to the loader of the tractor and Aubrey slowly lowered it, the nose following the chain downwards. They could then have gently pushed in the lever, thereby lowering the truck box; but Pete figured the box might as well stay up or be raised even higher to dump the load. What he failed to anticipate was the behaviour of their very own Howler monkey, Dick Conley. Before anyone could make a move, he had climbed up over the load into the top of the box.

"Nooo!" yelled Pete, frantically signalling to Dick to come down.

Too late! Conley's stomping up and down on the top of the load was enough to trigger its release and issue him with an express ticket off the truck, together with the load. But of all the helpers who would likely bounce rather than be buried, Conley was the one. Nonetheless, it was a salutary lesson because he bounced hard on his rump on very coarse shingles, giving himself acute BBR, "burned bum rash," to remind him of his foolhardiness and his impetuosity. Even when his momentum bounced him right into the hole like a golfer's hole-in-one, he still survived—as always!

They all returned home in a convoy, the day now essentially eaten up. Even though the ladies had prepared a sumptuous meal and there was no shortage of wine, they all retired early. All of them knew in their heart of hearts that down on the farm, you ought not to tempt fate too many times.

The roofing itself went very well with so many hands making light work under Pete's ever watchful eye. Better yet, nobody fell off the roof, however many times Conley came close, and nobody contrived to staple their thumb to their shoe, or that sort of thing.

So a week later saw the Hanlons delivering the kind of country thank-you gift that gives the whole issue of neighbourliness its genuine meaning. They went round to Pete and Jeannie's with a leg of lamb that Jeannie would love to prepare in true cordon bleu style, along with a couple of bottles of vintage red that Pete would be a connoisseur at drinking. The joy of farmers' gifts to one of their own is that they invariably end up being shared with the donors, a notion expressed in that old adage, "quality of life resides in the company you keep." So the next day it was leg of lamb for supper.

They had literally just arrived when the Delameres drove in right behind them. Sonya explained that she needed to get her husband out of the house so that he could cool off a bit. It turned out that the invitation for a lamb supper played no small part in achieving this objective.

"But what do you mean, Jim needs to cool off?" asked Jeannie. "Our Jim never gets mad, do you Jim?" Jeannie was always so solicitous of her neighbours but even so, nobody had ever seen Jim get really mad.

"You tell them the story," Sonya insisted, a merry twinkle in her eye.

"Well," Jim began, "we went to Red Deer for the day so we left the girls to do chores, thinking to keep them busy. I very stupidly said they could go quadding after they had dug up the potatoes. So we take them over to the potato patch, give them a fork each and show them exactly what we wanted done. Okay, so in hindsight it was quite a lot, enough to keep them busy for four or five hours.

There were about ten lines, enough spuds to get us through all of winter. We also gave them twenty pails to put them in, telling them that if the pails were filled before they finished, they could leave the rest. After telling them not to let us down, we headed for the big city." Jim paused as if to let his audience digest the story's background.

"So they get themselves busy. It seems they hadn't even done half a line before dear little Candace, she's the wild one of the twins as you know, turns to her sister and says 'you know there's a better way of doing this, don't you?'"

"'Yeah right!' says Chloe. 'Get Mom and Dad to do it.'"

"'No, we just get Dad's backhoe,' sings sweet little Candace. 'I know how to drive it. We can be done in an hour.'" Jim could mimic Candace's voice to a tee. "So Chloe looks over at all those empty buckets, then looks at all those lines they still have to dig and tells her sister what a great idea it was."

"Does Candace really know how to drive that thing?" Sabine interrupted, half in dread at what might be coming.

"Oh, for sure! That girl can drive anything on the farm and she's only fourteen. So like the fool I am, I gave her a couple of lessons on the backhoe a couple of weeks ago. She was pretty good at it, too. So to pick up on the story, Candace goes off and fetches the hoe. They get busy, and within the hour decide they're all done. So off they go on their quads and have a rare old time messing about down by the river. You tell the rest," Jim said turning to his wife.

Sonya continued on. "So we get back from Red Deer, thinking that maybe we had been a bit unfair giving the girls all ten lines to do. Six or seven would have been much fairer. But the place is as quiet as a morgue. Not a sound. Obviously there's nobody home. So we head over to take a look at the potato patch. Four and a half buckets of potatoes, with a whole bunch of them really scarred. We normally get twenty plus. And the ground is really well dug over. 'The little buggers' says Jim. 'They used my hoe. Oh man, they buried more potatoes than they ever dug up.'"

Pete burst out laughing. He could not help it. The others followed suit. "You know" he said, "you'd better get those two interested in working for our government, and then we'd really get things done."

"So how did the girls explain themselves?" asked Sabine.

"Oh, the pair of them breezed back into the yard an hour later. 'So how did you girls get on with the potatoes?' says Dad here, not letting on that we already knew the answer. 'Oh, it went pretty good' says Candace, 'but we didn't get near as many as you said we would. We only got four and a half buckets. Must be a bad year for potatoes.' She's got an answer for everything, that one.' Actually,' says her dad, 'it was a real good year for potatoes. The problem is that you went and buried most of them with the backhoe.'"

It was dad's turn to carry the story. "Well, you should have seen their faces. But then Candace gets this grin like a chimpanzee and says 'You never thought we were that smart, did you?' That's when I explained the facts of life to them both. I told them they were going to buy whatever potatoes we needed that winter out of their allowances, emphasizing that we Delameres are good, solid peasants who like their spuds. Then I informed them that with their grubbing forks they were going to go back over all the ground they had dug up, and they were going to stay there until they had at least filled another two buckets. Until that was done, I told them, their quads were off-limits. I reminded them just how much effort their mother puts into the garden and they needed to respect that. Then I told them how they had blown a whole lot of that effort to smithereens."

"'Well I guess we were not quite as smart as we thought,' says Candace."

"Did they get their two buckets more?" asked Jeannie.

"Actually they felt so darn bad about it all they really worked hard and got another four," said Jim. "But still, what scared the heck out of me was they used that machine when nobody else was around. Like what would have happened if one of them had gotten hurt? But farm kids are great though. I didn't have to spell it out any further. They twigged right away. That—more than anything—was why I needed time out. Kids can sure drive you crazy, God love 'em!"

Sometimes, more often than not in fact, farming involves warming a number of irons in the fire all at the same time. The original "iron in the fire" likely refers to the blacksmith of olden days. Agriculturally, it would be more in context to think of branding irons in the rancher's fire. Most brands call for three different irons if you brand in the traditional manner. And if you do happen to brand in the traditional western manner, you know how incredibly tricky it is to keep all three irons evenly heated to the right temperature for a perfect application. So it is with the wider aspects of farming. For example, the weather that is good for your haying might well be burning up your pasture faster than you would like. The rain that's good for the longevity of that same pasture might be decidedly unfavourable for the ripening of your barley. That unexpected dump of snow in September may flatten that same barley, even if it brings needed moisture for something else. That's the nature of agricultural reality.

But this particular year was smiling on the Hanlons' fortunes and on the Hanlon spread in general. The barley was turning from a fading green to a sunny yellow and it would not be long now for the heads to start drooping. "Six weeks from ear to shear," said the old-timers. That was if the GWC, the Great White Combine, did not arrive on the scene first, bringing with it those instant storms of thunder and lightning and hail that could shred the ears of any crop of grain in mere minutes. They had already paid a visit to the general neighbourhood, those storms; oh yes, they'd been around all right. Old George Cruikshank said he lost 85 acres of barley in less than five minutes: one hundred percent wipeout, and he had no insurance. He was fanatical old-school though. "You get your crop or you don't, that's it. Don't need no new-fangled insurance to tell me if I got me a crop or not!" One could expect the same sort of story from that old rascal Len Bloscoe, but then with dear Len, you were never sure if he was remembering this week or the last week of August 1972.

So with the barley turning colour, Aubrey decided to pull old Mama Swather out of the shed and get her running again. She seemed pretty mad at being woken up from her extended hibernation, but that was only to be expected. After all, she was a temperamental old bitch anyway. But this particular year, she made it abundantly clear that she had no intention of running any longer than a minute and thirty seconds, all the while farting blue smoke and carrying on like a severely lung-damaged chain-smoker. (He should not have thought of her in terms of that B-word - not "Butch" the other one- Aubrey was thinking). What if she had read his thoughts? But it was too late now to start calling her Sweet Lulubelle. No problem, he would phone Ernie and pick his brains; better still, he might persuade him to come on down from Edmonton to take a look at the machine.

No, Ernie couldn't make it down but he advised Aubrey to go buy some carb-cleaner, "the heavy-duty stuff" and to disassemble the carb as far as he could, or dared, before soaking all of the constituent parts in this solvent brew.

"Oh yeah," said the parts man at the local automotive store when Aubrey explained his problem. "For sure your carb is all gummed up. Old gas is terrible stuff because it is so full of additives and other good stuff these days. This will clean it right up for you. But let me give you a word of advice for free. There is a gallon of the stuff in this can. Go ahead and use it but don't leave any in the can when you're done. Put it in a glass container. Over time, this stuff will actually burn through the bottom of the can." Aubrey would have been wise to give a little more consideration to that statement, but then what did he know?

He went to work on that swather. He detached the throttle and choke cables and unbolted the carburettor from the old, industrial, Chrysler slant-six motor. He dissected it into three or four basic component parts before dropping them all into a bowl of virgin yellow solution from the can. He left them to soak not just for twenty-four hours but for a full forty-eight. "Double whammy" was his line of thinking.

So two days later he psyched himself up to "go for it". Because it was so stinking hot, thirty-four degrees Celsius, he stripped naked and then donned his coveralls before setting out to put the carb together. Using a pair of long-nosed needle pliers, he gingerly lifted the various bits from out of the now black, crud-filled fluid and laid them out on his workbench. Seeing as he hated working with gloves, even the fancy mechanic's gloves he got from Santa this past Christmas, he put the carburettor together with his bare hands which after all were sufficiently calloused to take the heat, as it were. But wouldn't you know it? This was the precise moment when nature suddenly called: not just softly as in a whisper but loudly as in a shout, like "You'd best be relieving me now old man or I'll do it myself." He undid the zip on his coveralls, pulled out his "fire hose" as he liked to call it, and in the manner of all juvenile males he proceeded to write his name in the dust. What happened next started simply as a tickle, but it quickly morphed into a fiery, red-hot furnace that consumed his nether regions and propelled him pell-mell to find the garden hose. At the same time, his mind had just made the intellectual connection; if heavy-duty carb cleaner could burn its way right through the bottom of a tin can, what could it or would it do to a gentleman's transmission? This was the intellectual Eureka moment. The physical Eureka moment expressed itself very differently. It formulated itself into a decidedly modern variation of the Cossack Polka, a merry little jig danced upon the sward beside the fire hydrant. The picture was worth ten thousand words: There was Mr. Aubrey Hanlon, his coveralls now down around his ankles, prancing up and down as much as his coveralls would permit while spraying his lower regions with the garden hose on full. Even at the height of summer, water that comes from a well one hundred and twenty feet deep becomes one degree above frigid within a minute of being turned on. So it was either the sheer volume of water or its frigidity that maintained the level of the poor man's hollering.

It would have been good luck if it had only been Sabine who then happened on the scene. Naturally she was concerned enough to come barreling out of the house to see what all the hullaballoo was about. However, it was downright bad luck that the lady enumerator registering voters for the next provincial election also happened to drive into the yard. And neither woman could turn away, mesmerized as they were by this hairy version of King Kong leaping about the place and chanting incomprehensibly in high falsetto, as if embarking on the mother of all fertility dances.

And then Aubrey's eyes took them in. His reaction was pure instinct. He dropped the hose, pulled up his sopping coveralls, and yanked up the zip. Yes, well. Any male may legitimately flinch at this point. Aubrey caught his thingy in the zip, really caught it. And it hurt like hell, oh how it hurt! The zip wouldn't go down. And the pitch of the whine rose higher!

Sabine bolted for the house and sanctuary; this was a problem for a man to sort out!

The enumerator rammed her car into reverse, thinking first that with a whine so painful, this fellow would surely vote for the NDP, and thinking also that perhaps it was time for the federal government to tighten up its immigration policy to stop all these weird foreign nationals from getting into the country. How could she have known that Aubrey was originally from Winnipeg, even if he was born on the right side of the tracks?

Chapter Six

SUE THE SQUIRREL

*W*hen people say of a man, "he's focused", it is usually meant as a compliment, a sign of respect. The problem with agriculture down on the family farm is that there are so many skills, not so much to master but that require a level of competence at least a couple of degrees above that of an idiot, so the usual understanding of the word doesn't apply to farming. The essence of being focused implies the ability to exclude everything that does not pertain to the task at hand. But on the farm, everything somehow conspires to have a bearing on everything else. Furthermore, most hands-on knowledge has to be acquired both through practice and experience. It is akin to picking yourself up by your own bootstraps. Oh yes, particularly with machinery, you can help the learning process along by reading the owner's manual. But this is always so clinical and dry. The pictures, too, presumably cropped as tightly as they are to save on valuable printer's ink, are too often like a puzzle—until it dawns on you that the specific picture you are looking at was taken by the photographer lying *under* the machine or perhaps flying above it like a purposeful mosquito. Furthermore, this machine already so apparently unlike yours, is both factory-clean and unbent, and without all the oil leaks and the gathering of chaff that makes your beast bear no resemblance to the much prettier one in the book.

After Aubrey followed the instructions for putting the carb back into the swather, he connected first the choke cable and then the throttle cable in such a way he thought they looked about right. Maybe this represented a lack of focus; you don't put things back in such a way that they just "look right". The moment of truth had finally arrived. He worked the hand fuel pump until he knew the carb would be primed with gas before he climbed up into the cab.

By way of digression, Sabine had been assiduously nurturing a lilac hedge along the driveway; anything that helped screen them from the road and assured their privacy was a plus as far as she was concerned. The plants were now a good four feet high and very robust. This year the blossoms had been bountiful, prompting a glorious visitation on the part of a variety of butterflies. But now the plants were retrenching in early anticipation of winter. Sabine was really proud of that hedge, and justifiably so. The trouble was, (a) Aubrey was facing that hedge when he started up Mama Swather; (b) Aubrey had incorrectly reattached the throttle cable so that it was permanently on full bore; and (c) Aubrey had always been an eternal pessimist. He never ever expected anything to work right after he had fixed it, least of all anything as complicated as a carburettor, so no worries—this beast would likely not run anyway. Only this time was an exception. Old Mama Swather fired right up, giving Aubrey such a fright that he inadvertently pushed the control column which in turn engaged forward motion. Mama Swather needed no further urging; she surged forward like a racehorse at the starting gate, ploughing straight through that lilac hedge like a knife ploughing through butter.

"Focus!" said Aubrey's mind in the first few milliseconds.

"Focus on what?" He tried pulling back on the throttle. Nothing.

"Focus some more!" said his mind, using up further precious milliseconds. He stomped on the left brake, missing the oncoming water hydrant sticking up out of the ground by mere inches.

"Focus! How do I stop then?"

"You turn off the switch key, you fool!" Mama Swather obligingly lurched to an immediate halt, a halt made even more sudden because the right side of the table had conveniently hooked up with what, until now, had been a perfectly symmetrical, thirty-foot tall Colorado Spruce. A number of the wooden fingers on the reel had also decided it would be a good idea to crack themselves up, leaving the right side of the reel sagging onto the canvas below. If Mama Swather was in no position to care about the fourteen-foot hole in the hedge, that was to be expected, but Mama Hanlon sure cared! She had seen it all, everything—all her hard work flattened in three seconds. The spruce tree didn't look quite as good as it had either, with a few of the lower branches either lopped clean off or lying cracked sorrowfully across the machine.

Mama Sabine did what all mamas would do in the circumstances; she vented mightily. It was a noise akin to the Chipmunk Choir singing the "Hallelujah Chorus" inside an empty steel barrel. In any normal course of events, that would have been enough to hold centre stage, but not this time. No Ma'am. This time there was serious competition emanating from the cab of the swather: not a "Hallelujah Chorus", exactly, but a modern day version of the "Dinosaur Dirge" in a heavy metal format. The lyrics were clearly not penned by Elton John either, for they seemed to be in some lowbrow Canuckian dialect. Sabine's effort in descant simply could not compete; it tailed off into a subsiding wail as she realized she had never ever seen her mate for life so angry. Wisely, she slunk off to the house to wait it out.

Aubrey howled on for another three minutes before he realized first that he was running short of compressed air, and second that his effort was wasted given that there was no audience to care. So he climbed off his machine, circled his way around it, and swore at least a dozen more times before deciding to take a closer look at the throttle connection. Focus…or lack thereof! He spotted right away what he had done wrong. He readjusted the cable and climbed back into his cab. With his legs quaking like a jellyfish in labour, he restarted the swather. She purred like a kitten. He inched his way backwards and she cooperated. But now the only way out was a dipsy-doo to the right to avoid the water hydrant, and then back over the bedraggled hedge. Please Lord, let Sabine be far away (like in Muddy Valley, Saskatchewan) he was thinking, praying that she would not arrive on the scene until he had rescued both himself and Mama S. One step forward, two steps to the side, two steps back over the hedge and he was back where he had started. Maybe he and Sabine should have taken up square-dancing years ago! So now he had the reel to repair. He could have set to, could have focused and made new wooden fingers to replace the old ones, but Aubrey and wood had never been made for each other. Yeah, but they were just simple bits of wood, right? The dealer would have some on hand for sure.

"Oh, we might be able to get some," said the parts-man, "take it or leave it at forty-six dollars and seventy-two cents apiece."

Aubrey left it. Once again it was dear old Pete who came galloping to the rescue. He made twelve of what Aubrey needed at a cost of "three beers for each one and unlimited abuse amortized over the next twenty-five years." The beers could be amortized too "if need be" said Pete.

Aubrey very carefully rebuilt the reel, making sure the whole thing turned by hand before he pushed his luck too far. He replaced two knife sections wrecked by the tree, or by the bouncing reel or by the unfocussed operator. Yes, the reel still looked a bit saggy, but a check of the tensioners seemed to indicate they were tight.

It was time to set off up to the field to give Mama Swather a run. Sabine made the strategic decision to remain indoors. Aubrey's mood would have been best described as "tentative" when he got into that swather and headed down the drive. When he arrived at the field, he stopped for a minute and gave thanks to the Almighty for giving him Sabine, whom he knew wanted to strangle him but had not yet done so; for giving him Pete, a man who could work wonders with wood; and for His (the Almighty's?) part in cajoling Mama Swather to get her act together in readiness to lay down that grain. He concentrated his mind, focused his attention, engaged the machine and covered forty yards or so to the first corner of the field. There it was, a beautiful swath of barley laid out behind him. But he dared not whistle, not yet. He turned Mama Swather into the first four hundred-yard run up the length of the field. Ah, true perfection is its own attraction and sets a pattern all of its own, Aubrey was thinking.

Another corner. Straighten out, hit a hole but bounce on regardless. A great skiff of barley gets tossed up, not onto the table but over it. What the hell? But now it's fine—or wait a sec, is it? Why does the knife seem to jam sporadically? Aubrey stops, disengages the cutting operation, backs up a mite from the swath, and jumps down to take a look. Two knife sections are not just broken but gone. Huh! Okay, count up to ten, turn the machine around, and head back to the shop and that riveter he loved to hate: the one that always caused him to curse an inventor who could design a tool more appropriate for a lemur that peed on its digits than for a fine-skinned gentleman with two fat thumbs. Must have struck a rock in that hole he hit, Aubrey decided.

Twenty minutes later he was back in the field. Forty yards later and it was the same darn thing all over again. The two new knife sections were still there, but two neighbours must have joined the same trade union and commenced their own job action, or they had simply gone AWOL. Okay, okay, count all the way up to twenty-one and head back to the shop and the hated riveter. "Patience, my son," Aubrey lectured himself, "speak not unkindly about the tools of thy trade." And so he completed the repair and returned to the field.

This time however, probably owing to a much heavier part of the crop, Aubrey found it necessary to raise the reel and then gradually lower it, as would any competent swather-man coping with such a variant crop. And this time the reel contrived to send enough barley up over the table that for a second or five, Aubrey thought he was being showered with sheaves of grain at some way-out Greek wedding or something. He stopped, pulled out of the crop and . . . FOCUSED. Basic psychology for beginners likely teaches that extreme caution tends to block true focus, to block the capacity of the mind to think clearly. Whatever the reason, Aubrey's mind was roiling; his affection for Mama Swather now having turned to extreme hatred. Two more knife sections GONZO! How could this be? He studied the reel itself. FOCUS, AUB! THINK! Why? Why would the reel play such silly games?

This was to be another moment of truth, although Aubrey did not appreciate it at the time. The concept of "focus" can have both a mental and a physical dimension, and in this particular instance it was the physical capacity that was lacking. Sabine was absolutely right: Aubrey badly needed glasses. He could not **see** the two broken bolts that controlled the reel setting. This meant that whenever Mama Swather bounced like a Playboy bunny, the reel would pivot downwards. This occurred most readily when the reel was under pressure from a heavy crop, or when the operator boingy-boinged through a dip in the terrain or a hole. At that moment, a couple of pickup fingers would play kissy-kissy with the knife and then bounce back to base as if nothing had happened and all was well in the Hesston world. Disconsolate now, Aubrey headed home, parked Temperamental Mama, and decided it was high time for a cold one. But alas, this was not to be his day! Sabine appeared on the scene as if to confront him about his hedge-hopping folly, but no, she had a puzzled look on the face.

"Honey, I just went for a walk up to where the cows are. We seem to have an extra twenty-five animals in the herd. I have no idea where they could have come from."

"That's all I bloody well need," growled Aubrey. Actually he could have dropped the growling part because this was exactly what he did need to distract him from all his other problems. Ten cold beers would have done little to generate perspective. He accompanied Sabine back to the field. Sure enough there was a whole bunch of other animals in the Hanlon's pasture: not twenty-five though, more like fifty, a mix of yearling steers and heifers. But where on earth had they come from? He glanced over towards the patch of thick bush and willow to the south, just as another group of about ten or so animals appeared. Aha! So they had to be Bill Stott's. They must have broken out of his pasture and then proceeded to break through two more intervening fences to get to where the Hanlon cattle were. Well dear old Bill Stott would have to get his butt in gear and come on over to do some good old-fashioned running, like real running, because Bill Stott's quad could never work its way through the scrub and muskeg unless it had wings. Or unless Bill Stott had wings, which was unlikely since Bill Stott had always been a long way from being an angel. But then again, maybe Bill's wife Marie just needed to stand up and holler and those critters would surely turn tail and head home, or to Dog Pound, Alberta; any and all creatures would run if Marie got mad!

So Aubrey and Sabine went back to the house and phoned Mr. Stott on his cell phone.

"They're ours for sure," he said a little too smugly, "but we're more than halfway to the Ponoka Stampede and we ain't turning back. You'll have to call my dad. He'll sort it all out for you. Two of the seventy head are his, after all. Besides, he's the guy that supposedly fixed the fence in the first place, before we even put 'em out there." At that, he hung up. Smart man that he was, he wasn't about to give himself any kind of a guilt complex, not if he was to enjoy the Ponoka Stampede. Maybe he knew Aubrey was an expert in begging and cajoling, at staking out all of the high moral ground so that there was no place for his adversary to stand. He had been a cop after all. Maybe he knew Sabine was the type who could overreact and impound them all, impound his old dad, too, if he showed up with a bad attitude.

If Bill was not interested, his dad Stewart was everything and more; he was very contrite. As one would expect from a man of the old school, he was ready for action. "I'll jump in my truck and come on over to see where them buggers got out," he said.

"I'll see you up there," said Aubrey.

A half-hour later saw the two men at the main gate of the next-door quarter section. As was generally the case with rented quarters, the fence was only a fence if you saw it as a fence or willed it to be a fence, no matter how many times the landlord might insist how good a fence it was. The northern half of the land was comprised of a large slice of heavy woodland on the west side and a field of barley on the east. The southern portion, where they were now headed, was comprised of one large chunk of pasture. There in a low spot, a stretch of fencing lay flat with at least ten posts embracing the bosom of Mother Earth.

"Some darn thing spooked 'em, I'll bet," said Stewart who knew about such things. "Probably a bleep-bleeping moose."

At that point, a black form with a white face appeared in the bush followed by fourteen more. "Aha! So them buggers didn't all go to your place for a visit." But as soon as the two men made an attempt to count them, the cattle turned and bolted, crashing away through the bush. "Them buggers are something jumpy, that's for sure," Stewart added in explanation.

What was extraordinary was that the animals which had gotten out had not entered the barley, but instead had charged their way north along the edge of the field between the cultivated part and the woodland. When they had reached the northern boundary fence, they had simply kept on going, taking the Hanlon fence down and making their way to the cows they had seen grazing beyond. While Stewart began to sort out wire and to remove the staples from the dead posts, Aubrey went back home on his quad. He threw a dozen new posts and some wire into the loader of the tractor and was back to Stewart within twenty minutes. With Stewart holding the posts upright where he wanted them, Aubrey pressed them into the ground with the loader bucket. Re-stapling the wire was a ten minute chore.

It was then that the usual ritual between farmers began. The old country code of yore, the same that says you should be able to seal any and all deals with a simple handshake, stipulates that "I'll do for you what you have done for me, and a bit more."

Now anyone with any number of livestock knows that at some point in time you are going to have dealings with your neighbour; that is a given. Yes, Stewart Stott was only a distant neighbour geographically in terms of where he lived, but still he rented the place next door. The thing was, Stewart was a gentleman of the old school. True he didn't look like no gentleman in his suspendered jeans and his faded, checkered shirt. And he didn't walk like no gentleman, either. How could he when he had ridden a few too many cayuses (a cayuse is a sad-looking nag of a horse) in his time, cayuses that had given him a little too much saddle-burn to leave him with anything resembling an aristocratic posture. He certainly did not talk like no gentleman, not with his lingo peppered so generously with all sorts of words from Sabine's banned list. If you had asked his wife Ruby, she would have told you he danced like no known gentleman either, "more like some Emperor penguin that sees no difference between a waltz and Mexican poker." Anyhow,

Stewart being the definitive country gentleman he was, insisted on paying for the posts, for Aubrey's time and the use of Aubrey's tractor. Aubrey almost literally had to stamp his feet when he refused payment. Besides, they had yet to finish the job and take the animals home; and although both left it unsaid, both knew what chaos that particular exercise could turn out to be. Yearlings are like teenagers: overflowing with sass and raging hormones, and generally unaware of where they have just come from or where they need to go. Hell, Aubrey himself sometimes felt like that even at his age—not the hormones part though, for they had long since left a body that could not have made it to the ninth tee without an injection of oxygen or a golf cart.

"I'll be over there tomorr'er with my stock trailer if it works for you," said Stewart. "Can't be in the morning mind, I've got me an appointment with the quack. But we gotta get 'em tomorr'er or them critters'll be eating up all your bleeping pasture, them bleepers."

As alluded to, a mix of yearling steers and heifers can be spooky at the best of times. If they have endured a bit of do-sa-do with a moose or a wolf, they are liable to stampede right through you, especially if you're a stranger they have never seen before. So Aubrey sat down to do some serious thinking. He had to forget about Sabine's precious hedge, he had to dismiss the memories of Mama Swather and FOCUS; he had to figure out how he could play a long enough line to get all the foreign critters into a corral without undue stress.

It was nigh on dusk when he took the tractor and dropped a couple of fresh hay bales into the feeders in the big corral. Then he took four pails of chop up to the main gate and called. Of course his cows had to come and check out his message, ready to bolt in a second if this was some new form of skulduggery, ready to cooperate warily if it sort of turned out not to be… The thing was, they brought at least a half of the illegal immigrants with them. And who was it who led them in? Why, Nellie of course. Who was it who sensed at once that this was an unexpected treat? Nellie. She led a whole mob of them into the corral where Aubrey was dispensing the chop into the wooden feeders with the generosity of a government bailing out its bankers. Then he left without making any play to shut them all in.

Early the next morning, he repeated the process. This time, to an animal, they charged on through the holding area and into the corral. All Sabine had to do was to shut the outer gate and they were trapped. Aubrey hooked up the trailer and by lunchtime the foreigners had all been deported back home—no muss, no fuss.

At noon the phone rang. It was Stewart and he was all business. "Say Aubrey, I'll be on my way over to your place in half an hour. I've just got to go hook up my trailer."

Aubrey couldn't help it; he had a right to be smug. "Don't sweat it, my boy. We took 'em all back this morning."

"Eh? What's that? Who took 'em all out this morning?"

"Me and the missus. They're all back home."

"Eh? What d'ya mean you got 'em all home? Who else helped you? You mean all of 'em? There should have been around sixty you know."

"Sixty-one."

"So who did you say helped you?" Stewart could not believe what he was hearing.

"Just me and my old lady."

"Wow! You guys must be darn good at cow-whispering or something. So now I really owe you, big time!"

"Okay, then seeing as you owe me so darn much, why don't you come on over and help me figure out what's going on with my swather. I can't get that old girl to work worth a hoot."

"Oh bleep! Don't you go bleeping around with that! I'll bring my old one over for you to use. She's a fourteen-footer and runs real sweet. Needs a workout, too. It'll do your little patch of grain in a day. I'll bring it on over this afternoon."

Well that could not have worked out any better for the Hanlons. They knew Stewart's machine would be more likely to stay the course than their old clunker, unless of course Aubrey contrived to drive it up a tree or something, a thought wisely left unspoken in case it should amount to a self-fulfilling prophecy.

There is something that farmers have to learn, usually sooner rather than later. "Focus" and "familiarity" do not come from the same stable, so to speak. Aubrey's Hesston swather was a very different beast from Stewart's Massey-Ferguson. For one thing, with the Massey you didn't have to push and pull on the steering column to get the machine to go forwards or backwards, you had a lever. For another thing— a serious "other thing"—on the Hesston, Aubrey had a hand lever to raise and lower the reel and a foot pedal that you stomped on to raise or lower the table. On the other hand, for these two functions the Massey had two foot pedals side by side. The outer one raised and lowered the reel, the inner one raised and lowered the table. Or was it the other way around?

Stewart drove the Stott swather off his trailer and signalled Aubrey to "come aboard". Now familiarity with any machine does not come from a two minute lecture on which lever works what, what happens when, and most of all why you should do this and not that. Ah, but Stewart was smarter than that! "Look," he said, "I'll come with you on the first round, like to show you what all's going wrong kind of deal. That way you should have it all figured out pretty quick, eh."

Yeah, right!

Aubrey put on his headphones, the ones Sabine (sorry, Santa) gave him last Christmas, and the ones the Commander-in-Chief ordained that he never work without "because I don't want to spend the rest of my life trying to communicate with a deaf old crow croaking 'wha'? whaa'? whaaa'?' every time I have something to say."

They set off, Aubrey driving. "Honest to God," Aubrey found himself thinking, with Stewart hanging off the step, "this is like going to work with my pet chimpanzee." Yet inasmuch as Stewart was familiar with his machine, he was decidedly unfamiliar with the layout of the Hanlon family farm. So they headed across the now harvested hayfield to the gate at the bottom of the hill, the one that opened into the twenty-five acre field of barley. Aubrey knew the gate was (a) open because he himself had opened it, (b) wide enough for the swather because he had built it that way. Yes, Stewart saw (a) that the gate was open, but (b) that it was not wide enough, nowhere near wide enough!

"This dang machine ain't gonna fit through that there gate," he yelled at Aubrey, thinking for a second that Aubrey would immediately moderate his speed. Not a chance; Aubrey was on a mission. He speeded up!

"Hey Aub, man, this bleeping machine ain't gonna make it through that there bleeping gate of yours," this time the warning screamed out at the top of Stewart's lungs. ("Oh, so it's going to be one of those F-and-F days," Sabine would have said, had she been there.)

None of it, not the antics of the chimpanzee, nor its shouting made the slightest bit of difference. Aubrey sailed through that gate with mere inches to spare on each side, his pet chimp cavorting about on the platform-step clearly in two minds about going down with the ship or jumping off and making a run for the trees.

"Well bleep me!" was all he could manage by way of strangled commentary when it registered that he wasn't up a tree and his ship had not sunk.

Aubrey stopped at the grain's edge and grinned at a still shaking Stewart. "Keep your hair on, Dad!" he said with a smile. "This boy is a maestro with machinery." Stupid! Stupid thing to say, for now he had something to prove. He engaged the operating mode and set off tentatively, "as slow as a one-eyed snail" Stewart was to say later. But Aubrey still had a major problem to deal with; his advisory chimp still hanging off the step. A camp counselor who was not simply content to yell out intermittent instructions but also prone to physically intervening when those instructions were apparently being deliberately or overtly ignored.

"Lift up your reel!" the chimp would screech. Down would go Aubrey's foot and up would go not the reel but the entire cutting table, up to a height where it merely nipped the heads off the plant.

"Not the *bleeping table,* the *bleeping reel!*" But there was no way Aubrey could react quickly enough in the 0.975 seconds before the chimp's leg would shoot out and stomp on the correct pedal, first to bring down the table, second to raise the reel. So Aubrey's leg, both late and misguided, would end up in an intimate two-step with the chimp. This haphazard performance, for that was the only way to describe it, lasted a good hundred yards, with the swather's vital parts alternately bobbing up and down like a rutting mallard drake and leaving behind a field that looked as if it was being shorn by a drunken or demented barber. Finally poor Stewart could stand it no longer. He tapped Aubrey on the shoulder, signalling him to stop.

Remember, Stewart was a gentleman of the old school so he kept certain things unsaid. "Look," he said. "I think (even) you (might) will get the hang of it (by tomorrow if we're lucky). You just need to figure out your pedals, (like all two of them with a brain that seems to have a twenty-eight second lag time). I got other stuff to do (like not supervising the village idiot), so I'll leave you to it. Good luck eh!" He could have said more, especially something pertaining to the concept of "focus" but he was a gentleman. "When you're done, (if that is ever going to happen), call me," (hopefully with the machine in not more than seven pieces). With that he jumped off the swather, but the real message lay in the manner of his parting. He did not just walk away, he slunk away: loped off like the cheated chimp he might have been, his hands gesticulating wildly, his head shaking vigorously from side to side. Aubrey did what the incompetent always do in such circumstances, he looked away.

When Stewart was safely out of sight, Aubrey changed tactics. Remaining stationary, he practised all that he had felt unable to practise with a monkey on his back. Within five hours the field was done, and within two hours more so was the small field adjoining it. And apart from the part at the very beginning where the Hesston had played its silly Greek wedding games, both represented a perfect barber's brush cut. Better yet, when Stewart came back to retrieve his swather, he was so impressed that Aubrey (here read Sabine) had actually washed it down, he offered then and there to see if he could find the problem plaguing Aubrey's machine. He may have been over eighty years old, but he was spry…and he could see a whole lot better than Aubrey. It took him less than a minute.

"You know them two bolts are busted, don't you? Them two that control your reel adjustment? So your reel's gonna bounce around like that there chick on 'Babewatch' and them fingers are gonna keep breaking your knife sections. So you'll have to jack up the right-hand side to get the busted bolts out and new ones in. Then you'll be fine. Oh, and thanks a ton for washing my old girl, eh! She's not been washed like that since she was new," and he was gone, conversation taking up too much of his day. Aubrey duly carried out the repairs and then tested out his machine on a patch of long grass. Yep, she was all set to go…into hibernation, ready for next season.

Combining the crop turned out to be its own story, short and sweet and to the point. It went, well; as well as one might expect with a custom operator, and given that Dick Conley appeared on the scene and promptly designated himself as lead-driver of Pete's borrowed one-ton Ford, the one with occasional brakes and a hole in the floor. Aubrey was allowed to be swamper and commander-in-chief of auger operations. It was through Bud Perkins, his old RCMP buddy, that Aubrey met a young cop who said his dad always did a bit of combining on the side and he was based only about ten miles from the Hanlon spread. What the young man failed to mention was that his dad was a German from the old country with a reverence for a greatly misunderstood Adolf Hitler and a temper like a Teutonic wolverine. It was only when Aubrey had set it all up that the young cop decided to call Aubrey and give him "the heads-up" on his father's tendency for aberrant and irate behaviour.

"Look," he said, "I need to warn you that my dad has a real bad temper, which is the reason me and my two brothers never went farming. So when you drive up to the combine with your grain truck, make darn sure you put yourself right under the unloading spout because if you're not exactly where he wants you to be, he's quite liable to go ballistic and let go a hundred bushels on your head. He can be one crazy dude when he gets going! Sorry about that, I should have told you before."

Of course Aubrey alerted Conley to the situation, knowing in his heart of hearts that Conley would handle it in a way none of his other friends would… Oh well, let the chips fall where they may!

Old Hermann Kreutzer was not your average friendly farmer for sure. How many wars he had lost in his life was not exactly clear, but he was one of those angry men who made it plain how much they hated the world and most of the people in it. Yes, it was great that he showed up with a shiny red M-F 750 combine, but right from the get-go he was all vinegar and no pleasure, all unnecessary haste without a second to spare. Aubrey would actually have sent him away if he could have found someone else to do the job, but it wasn't to be. So when Herr Kreutzer arrived without so much as a "Guten morgen mein herren," he launched into a rambling tirade, the gist of which was that he would brook no delays, that he had set aside only one day "to be doink zis piddling little bit of crop zat is hardly worth of mein time but I'm doink it because I have ze big heart." Aubrey bit his tongue because he wanted his grain in the bin. But Dick Conley had heard and seen enough of this fellow— "this sausage-muncher with attitude" was how he described the man later to Sabine. No doubt about it, this fellow needed to be taught that the world did not function according to the whims of one Hermann Kreutzer. But now was not the right time to straighten him out, not yet. Pete knew of Hermann too, said he was famous for driving his combine so fast that half of any customer's crop floated out of the back. People, he said, had taken to calling him "Kreutzer the German Hot-air Seeder" because, they said, you didn't have to worry about seeding the next year's crop if you got Hermann to work for you because he did it all for you!

Sure enough, as soon as he was in the field, Hermann set off like a blood-doped racehorse. When Aubrey and Dick got up there, he was already three-quarters of the way around the field, so this gave them time to check out the chaff and the straw left behind by the combine. Sure enough there was more than a liberal amount of grain that had not made it to the tank.

"I'll have to stop him and have a little talk," said Aubrey grimly anticipating a Gothic fireworks display.

"No, my son, I'm the one who's going to stop him and have a little chat because I think I have a little bit more to say than you do," Dick said quietly. "You sit tight, keep your gob shut, and don't even get out of the truck."

Aubrey knew his friend well; this would be either triumph or disaster. There would be no middle ground. Aubrey was fine with that too because he knew that whatever happened, there would be no going back to the status quo. They watched silently as the combine approached, Hermann already activating the unloading spout outward in readiness to dump the first load into the truck. Dick allowed him to pass then drove into the field to come up behind and line up with the spout, or so dear Mr. Kreutzer thought. Aubrey, too. But Dick very deliberately overshot the mark and very deliberately parked markedly off-centre. Hermann's hands had already come to life and were gesticulating wildly; his eyes were already blazing, with his face nearly as red as his combine. Dick very slowly got out of the truck and stood at the bottom of the combine steps. This in turn caused Hermann to disengage the machine's threshing mode and throttle back before switching off. He flung open the cab door ready to blast off and give this Pommy hillbilly "ein guten piece of his schadenfreude."

Conley beat him to it. "Say, Hermann old chap…it is Hermann isn't it?" said Conley all bright and breezy.

"Ja, my name is Hermann."

"Well, say old chum, two things we need to clean up, you and I, you know, among friends, that sort of thing." Conley ploughed on making sure Hermann didn't have time to interrupt. "The first is that if I don't park in quite the right spot for you to unload into my truck, if you start carrying on and swearing at me, I'll climb up into that combine of yours and deck you. Got that, Hermann? You know, just an understanding between friends." Dick paused for his message to sink in. The look on Hermann's face was worth a thousand beers. His belligerence abandoned him at once, leaving his body slack and him standing there speechlessly like an unmasked class bully.

"Second, my son, you will drop down at least one full gear if you expect to be paid in full for what you do. You're leaving a pile of grain behind in the field which my friend Mr. Hanlon would prefer to see in his grain bin. He's not paying you for seeding his field. Either that or you can, as they say, *fungula!*"

(That was Conley's way of suggesting to the fellow that he consider a journey involving…, well you get the picture!)

"Oh ja, no problem! I vas goink to do zat anyhows. I knowed I was goink a bit fast, yes. And you, who are you?"

"Me? Richard Conley, Emperor of Shawinigan."

"Ist gut, Mr. Shawinigan," barked Mr. K. "You now line up und I load you, ja?"

"Ja, das ist gut," said Dick heading back to Aubrey and the truck. He got in and looked across at Aub. "He's cool," he said. "No more Bavarian toe-tapping."

And so it was. The combining was now done with both dignity and style, thanks in large part to Richard Conley. The one bin was filled to the top and the second one up to half-way, even if barley was not worth a whole hell of a lot this year! "If you can't sell it, maybe we should think about making our own malt whiskey." Conley would assuredly make a great Prime Minister; he had a solution for absolutely everything.

But it was Pete who was to set out the lay of the land as it were. "You know, if you insist on planting a bit of grain every year, then you really cannot afford not to own your own combine. Doesn't matter if it's a museum piece as long as everything goes round and round as it is supposed to."

"Yes," said Sabine a little too sarcastically. "Aubrey just needs to go out to the money tree in the back forty, give it a good shake and pick up a fistful of thousand dollar bills as they come fluttering down. And hey presto, the Hanlons will get themselves a new combine."

But this time Jeannie sided with her husband. "He's right, you know, and I don't say that very often about my husband. But relying on some guy like Hermann Kreutzer is not good for the soul. Think about how lucky you were with the weather this year. It won't be like that again for the next fifteen years, trust me!" And that was where they dropped the subject.

It was late in that October when Sabine—yes, Sabine—offered up that there was an ad for a combine up for sale in the paper. "Let me read it to you," she said to Aubrey, who was somewhere in Never-Never-Land picking his teeth with a paper clip. "Retired from farming. Older line of machinery. Case 1070 tractor. Massey 510 combine, gas, 3-sieve. I.H. seed drill. Will consider any and all offers." There was, of course, a phone number.

"Hey woman, I thought there was no money out there on that money tree." Clearly Aubrey had been in this territory before, more than a few times, and he wasn't about to get all gung-ho and excited only to have the *HMCS Sicamous* torpedo him below the water line.

"Well, how much grain are we planning on seeding this coming year?" Sabine asked, continuing with her offensive.

"Fifty acres," said Aubrey, now scratching his back with the fork from the lunch plate he had neglected to put in the dishwasher. Boy, men could be such utter slobs, Sabine was thinking. "We can sell a bit and feed the cows a bit," Aubrey went on. "At least that's the plan."

"I'll phone the man and find out how much he wants. We can always say no, and knowing how cheap we are, we almost certainly will." She dialled the number. A lady answered.

"Hello. Mabel Etherington speaking."

"Oh hi! You folks are advertising a combine for sale in the paper."

"Oh yes! Please hold on. You'll have to talk to my husband, Gumboot."

"Excuse me! Did you say 'Gumboot'?"

"Yes, that's right. That's what folks call him around here."

A man's voice came on the line. "Hello, hello."

"Hello", said Sabine. "Is this, is this er, Gumboot?"

"Yes ma'am. This is the old boot himself talking. How can I help you?"

"Well, you do still have a combine for sale, right?"

"Yep. She's still sitting here. Damn good machine she was in her prime, too. Haven't used her for a couple of years though."

"How much are you asking for this combine may I ask?"

"Well, you'd best come on over and take a look at her. Then we can talk. I can't hear worth a hoot most of the time."

"Whereabouts do you live?" Sabine had already pretty much written him off.

"Oh, just north of Caroline. If you're not busy tomorrow, why not come on down and have a cup of coffee with us. My wife makes the best blueberry muffins in the West Country. How about eleven o'clock?"

"Okay, it's a deal." She took down the instructions to find the place. Aubrey was sideswiped. This was Sabine. This was The Great She who always insisted they had no money unless it was for a Wedgworth doll, or an antique oak trolley, or a hideous garden gargoyle. Well blow me down, does she have her own private money tree, he was thinking.

"We have nothing to lose, honey. And for heaven's sake stop scratching yourself with that fork. It's disgusting!"

At eleven o'clock precisely, the Hanlons drove into the Etheringtons' yard. It was one of those places so symptomatic of agriculture these days. The corrals were empty and crumbling, the house needed a paint job, the pickup outside was a vintage rust-bucket Chevy. Even the tired old dog could barely muster up more than enough energy for a single whimpering bark. The whole place was downright sad. But the couple who answered the door was anything but sad; they were joviality itself and very hospitable. They were the sort of folk whose happiness emanated from within, the sort who could be quite content with what they had rather than hankering for something more. In many ways, farming forces you to think like that, to be thankful for what you actually *did* harvest, not for what you *could* have, *might* have, or *ought* to have. In other words, farming taught you that true happiness was predicated on other things, most of them intangible.

After the pleasantries they were invited in and talk turned to the combine. "Oh, she was his baby," cooed dear old Mabel. "We bought her near new, you know. Now she's so out of date, nobody wants her. And we so want her to go to a good home, where she'll be used and cared for like we used to care for her, right Gum?"

"That's right, dear," said Gum, his reedy voice wavering somewhat. "But I never got to drive her a whole lot. I wasn't allowed. Mabe here drove her at harvest time, didn't you dear? I was the gopher. All I got to drive was the old grain truck, lucky old me," he paused. "Truth be known, women are better with them machines than men are. We're too darn ham-fisted while women folk have a much lighter touch. Yes, I have to tell you Mr. Hanlon, combining is women's work."

"Not this woman," Sabine was thinking.

"Boy, there are a whole lot of macho men and boys out there who would roast your onions if they heard you talk like that," Aubrey felt compelled to say. Gum just laughed.

"Anyhows, it's time we got our rotting old carcasses out there to look her over," old Gum resumed. "I got her started up this morning. I make a point of doing that once a month to keep her sweet, that sort of thing. Goldarn squirrel sure came out of there in a hurry though. Heh, heh!"

Although covered in that fine layer of dust that comes from prolonged disuse, the machine ran well, and to Aubrey's unschooled eye, everything seemed to shake, rattle and roll as it was supposed to. So it came down to the issue of dollars and cents, the fewer, the better, but these people had been so gracious, it was a hard subject to approach. So Aubrey tackled it head on, not with a view to haggling them down but with a determination not to go over the budget they did not really have. What he failed to appreciate was the fact that this was how the Etheringtons had conducted their business all of their lives. They knew what was going on and played the game accordingly.

"Here's where we're at," said Aubrey, hoping his voice was not too assertive. "After this year's performance with a custom man, we realized we never want to rely on those folks ever again. But we haven't got a whole lot of spare cash lying around either. So our hope is to find something older but good in our price range. If we don't find anything, no worries, we'll just hold off until we do."

"Makes perfect sense," said Gumboot inscrutably, and who was therefore no help at all.

"So we know what we can pay and what we can't pay is what my husband is trying to say," Sabine added diplomatically.

"Well, we were hoping for four thousand," said Mabel boldly. "But we too have to be realistic."

"See, I want to take my honey on a better holiday than a two-night stay at the Fleabag Motel in Bowden," said Gumboot laughing.

"We're all being so nice to each other, this is like pulling porcupine quills from a cow's face," Aubrey could not help thinking.

"Well, you're going to hate me for saying this but we'd figured on two thousand dollars, tops. Simply because that is all that we can afford," Sabine had taken over the director's chair.

"Deal," snapped Mabel.

"You heard her," said old Gumboot when both Hanlons looked to him for confirmation.

And so it came to pass that the Hanlons got a combine, a Massey 510 with a gas engine and three sieves. And Pete, thank heavens it was Pete and not Siggy or, Lord forbid, Dick Conley, got the honour of driving it home to the Hanlon estate. Aubrey escorted him from behind in Pete's pickup.

One of the most ancient of Murphy's Laws, one that must have been cobbled together with the help of Methuselah himself, proposes the following: "If thou art prevailed upon to tempt Fate in all her glory, then gird thy loins about thee for Fate shall surely and artfully intervene and smite thy impertinence upon the rocks of happenstance."

There they were, the combine just turning the corner, not just onto Main Street, Caroline, but onto Highway 22, "The Cowboy Trail" when Aubrey spotted it, couldn't miss the healthy plume of smoke coming from somewhere within the engine compartment. Pete must have smelled it for he stopped right there in the street, almost opposite a small café, thereby giving the regulars something new and exciting to talk about. God bless Pete, three or four times over! He actually had a fire extinguisher in his truck, one that was fully charged, no less! Aubrey grabbed it and handed it up to Pete who scrambled over to the engine area and began spraying it with foam. Aubrey was in consternation; why, why oh why had the motor caught fire?

The answer of course was provided by Mrs. Squirrel. Squirrels have nests. This particular squirrel had been a real worker; she had had the time and the resources to construct not just a simple abode but a whole condominium complex in the engine compartment. While Gumboot had started up the machine on a regular basis in winter, all he had done was provide a bit of central heating. As the days had got hotter, he had not seen any need to run it for very long, never making it hot enough for Mrs. Squirrel to hightail it out of there. Unfortunately, this time she was forced to seek safety. As she hit the ground, there were just not that many options as to where she could go. So she ran straight through that open door and into the coffee shop.

A terrified squirrel loose in a coffee shop is cause enough for alarm. When that same café is half-full of women and children chomping on a pre-lunchtime snack, then the cause for alarm multiplies, particularly in terms of the decibel level. Four complete circuits of the café did that squirrel make, sending shrieking kids to the tops of the tables, marooning a bevy of heavy mamas standing on their chairs, and leaving behind a trail of considerable devastation, crockery and such, as she leapt from point to point in frantic flight. Finally she spotted the open door and made her exit, first looking right and then left and then right again as if she had been properly schooled in roadside etiquette. Only then did she choose to bolt straight up Mrs. Smithson's dress, that same Mrs. Smithson who was on her way to check out other people's business. Now normally this Mrs. Smithson was a formidable presence who carried, or so she thought, a lot of weight in the village. She was an officer of the "Maids of the British Empire", a holder of the Queen Elizabeth II Plate, (awarded not for how fast she could gallop but to those who didn't qualify for the Jubilee Medal), and a force not to be ignored in the conduct of her mayoral duties. Well, such trappings of office made no impression on Mrs. Squirrel whose quick trip around and through the mayor's foundation garments left the august lady flat on the ground, her legs in the air and offering more of a grand spectacle than simply a sight to mesmerize any wandering eye. Everybody had heard of "layering", this was Canada after all, but layering to this degree? Happily, Mrs. Squirrel found an alleyway, and she was gone.

If Pete had been even a minute later, there would have been a burnt-out hulk of a combine on Caroline's main street. Luckily for all, it was a smouldering piece of chewed-up rag that had given off most of the smoke. Yes, there was flame and plenty of heat but nothing that the foam from the fire extinguisher could not handle. With vehicles now backed up, some enterprising fellow took a hand at traffic control while Aubrey and Pete cleaned out as much of Mrs. Squirrel's resort as they could get their hands on, stuffing the large amount of debris into the old mineral bags Aubrey found in Pete's truck. As if in some kind of apology, the combine fired up, no "fired" would be the wrong word here, started right up, Pete slipped it into gear and off he went.

Aubrey was about to follow suit when he was accosted by the more than somewhat dishevelled mayor. "Not so fast, Mister," she barked. "Do you have any idea who I am?"

Taken cleanly by surprise, Aubrey could only stammer an attempt at a response. "Why, you er, you must be er, must be the lady who er, who had the altercation with the squirrel. I am sorry," he added lamely, in a last-gasp effort at a friendly gesture.

"Are you the registered owner of that monstrosity of a machine that just left?" Clearly she saw an Aubrey snagged and hooked on her line.

"As a matter of fact I am," he said.

"Well you'd better give me your name and address as I intend to seek legal redress for damages to my person."

"Ma'am, you really need to understand that it wasn't the machine but the squirrel that caused the 'damages to your person' as you choose to call them. So take it from an ex-policeman and get the squirrel's name and address because you definitely have no claim against me. Don't worry about suing me; sue the squirrel and have a good day."

Chapter Seven
"I AM THE LORD OF ALL YOU SURVEY"

*O*ne thing that farming teaches you very quickly is that you are not the only creature to lay claim to your sacred patch of land, particularly in the area that they call "The West Country" around Rocky Mountain House. For many, if not most farmers this becomes a lesson in humility. Despite how many men might think otherwise, man is not omniscient, not all-powerful— no matter if he has a title deed in his pocket and a rifle over his shoulder. Coyotes and moose, wolves and cougars have no regard for your property rights any more than the elk that pees on your bales to mark his territory. Skunks and porcupines, mule deer and whitetail, the common raven and the Canada goose have no call to heed your property lines. The squirrels that insisted on colonizing Aubrey's shop, and Gumboot's combine if it came to that, felt no great compunction to maintain a human style of order with all the stuff on Aubrey's shelves; indeed, it seemed to work best for them if they dumped all of it on the floor. They could not see that Aubrey's roll of paper towel on the dispenser had not been put there for them to make their nests a little more luxurious. The two pigeons that made a comfortable rain-free home to raise their young up in the rafters of the shop roof felt no compulsion to curb their prolific crapping on whatever Aubrey might choose to work on beneath. And, bless his soft mushy heart, he could not bring himself to summarily execute them as so many others would have done; perhaps he could envision himself coming back as a squirrel or a pigeon in his next life.

It wasn't just the animals. The insects too seemed to have little reservation about using a person's private property for their own ends. Hornets deliberately built nests under the eaves of granaries. Bumble bees found suitable crannies in the siding of the house. A whole squadron of yellow jackets of the family *vespidae* saw fit to build an unobtrusive pad deep inside one of "Loosie Goosey's" rear seats, "Loosie Goosey" being of course the Hanlon's boat. For one reason or another, they (the Hanlons, not the wasps) had failed to take the opportunity to go boating all summer, but that one balmy last Saturday before fall they decided a leisurely picnic cruise around nearby Cow Lake might clear the cobwebs out of their ears, and it would give the outboard motor a much-needed run. Besides, it was still hot enough for the beachwear of high summer, a kind of a last hurrah for the shorts and the sandals and whatnot, at least for a welcome few hours

When Aubrey hooked the boat onto the truck, nobody noticed the tiny wasps winging their way in and out of the boat, basically because nobody thought to look for them, let alone check out the boat's interior. They put the boat's fuel tank and the battery into the box of the truck, ready to install when they got to the lake. Sig and Sybil were down for the weekend, so a leisurely picnic on the water would be a delightful way to bid a final goodbye to a summer that had been good to them.

They got to the lake in short order. Aubrey backed the trailer down the slipway and they then proceeded to stack their gear into the open prow of the boat. Oh gosh but those ladies were to wish they hadn't stripped off as much as they did to give their bikinis one last bit of fun in the sun, particularly Sybil who had a penchant for trying to contain too much with too little. But then how were they to know what a juicy target they were to present to squadrons of kamikaze wasps? They were finally all aboard when Sig and Aubrey poled the craft away from the shore with their oars; at about forty feet out it was time to lower the motor and connect up both the battery and the fuel tank. However, oh dear however, the constant rocking of the boat had riled up the illegal squatters beneath the left-hand seat, and they were none too happy. A few scouts emerged first, circled around a couple of times on reconnaissance and flew back to base to call forth the troops. The entire warrior class immediately poured out ready to take on the foreign invaders. And take on they did! The first one to zoom in found Sybil's delightful cleavage. Seconds later two more homed in on the undefended pink expanse of her right buttock. She was overboard instantly and surging mightily towards the shore; which left Aubrey, Sig and Sabine still on board. Maybe it was because of all their fur, the hair on their legs and arms and chests but whatever it was, the Stuka pilots were deflected from the two males of the species to the more tempting target of a Sabine still trying to make sense of what was going on, her largely unclad body in the bow of the boat. She suffered three searingly sharp stings on her derriere: so searingly sharp that she, too, jumped overboard without more ado, the pain in her outboard motor propelling her to shore with significant speed.

That left two manly heroes behind to defend the ship, swatting madly at the swarm of very angry wasps whose secretive lifestyle had been so rudely interrupted. But no matter how manly they may have felt, manliness was no option; to be courageous in the face of grave danger did not mean they should be foolhardy along with it! Both followed their mates overboard with unseemly haste, both getting well "peppered" by the wasps before they could immerse themselves in the water. Ah, but this was the one day Aubrey found focus; he tossed the anchor overboard as he made his getaway, even though it cost a couple of extra stings. Both men then made their way ashore. No, there was nothing else they could do; either they would have to wait for nightfall or somebody would have to drive the seven or so miles into town and buy a can of hornet spray at the local "Crap in the Tire" store. But who would have thought that looks would play such an inordinate part in the discussion?

Aubrey's left eye was swollen almost shut within minutes, which of course excused him. Sig, though, was the star of his very own horror show. Stung once on the nose and twice on the bottom lip, he would have prompted a stampede for the door had he ventured into any department store, particularly insofar as he was now drooling heavily. That left the two ladies to pick up the slack, Sabine now with a decidedly lopsided derriere, and Sybil brimming over in a location where the swelling had already been ample. But their imbalances and their swellings could easily be covered up without being a hazard to their driving. So while Sig and Aubrey settled in for the wait in a couple of lawn chairs, Sabine and Sybil went to town.

Sig was the one who noticed it first, about four minutes after the ladies had departed. "Say, Aub, that boat looks to be a lot further out than when and where we left it."

"Nah!" said Aubrey having to squint even to see it. "It's pretty much where we left it. I tossed the anchor out, you know."

"It sure as hell is further out," Sig insisted. "Anchor or no anchor, that baby is floating away. Besides, if you threw the anchor out and it was holding, would the boat not be facing into the wind?"

That forced Aubrey to take a more studied look. He even lifted up his one fat eyelid with his finger to make sure. "Shit and corruption," surely a more poetic way to avoid saying something stronger, Aubrey exploded. "I put a new rope on her this spring but I forgot to tie it on the boat itself. Son of a gun, I'd better swim on out there and catch our girl before she gets a mind to head south with the geese." Ordinarily, Sig was the nicest guy, but he had always maintained that if the Creator had truly wanted him to swim, He would have given him fins and a tail and dispensed with the buoyancy tank out front, his way of saying swimming was something he could absolutely do without. Quite apart from that, no matter how warm the air, the water itself was already disagreeably cold for frolicking about. He stayed stubbornly and stolidly put and slobbered, "you'd best get yourself going then, before she leaves without you." He could not have been more final than that.

Ah, but he was not that dumb, not our Aubrey! As he made his way out to the boat, which had now caught a light current and was fifty yards from the shore, he came across the anchor rope. Smart fellow, master mariner that he was, he had purchased floating anchor rope so the loose end was lying limp on the surface. He hauled up the anchor and coiled up the rope, thankful that the water was only up to his chest at this point. By the time he got out to the boat, the water was up to his neck, which gave him a new problem for which the frigidity of the water was urging a quick solution. The anchor eye was out of reach. There was nothing else for it but to toss the complete anchor up over the prow before climbing into the boat and tying the anchor from there. Okay, so he succeeded in tying the anchor, but this was not to be his day. A wasp fighter patrolling in the sky above swooped down on this trespasser and stung him just above the other eye, his good eye. He and the anchor went back overboard instantly, but at least the anchor was now tied. He headed for shore, swimming under water for the first twenty yards to avoid any further aggression. Finally he made it to the shore, his language not the stuff of classical literature. His second eye was well on the way to closing so that he, like Sig, was beginning to resemble Teddy the Tremulous Toad. By the time the ladies got back, the expedition was clearly over, the moral of the story being that summer activities should be scheduled for the height of summer, not when the season is on the wane.

Abandoning the expedition was the easy decision. Deciding who was to go out to the boat, hoist the anchor and toss it into the bow before pulling the craft back to shore was not, at least for Sabine. Clearly Aubrey was now out of the running. Clearly Sig was out of the running too, especially after he had given an Oscar-winning performance as Erik, the Phantom of the Opera.

"My chest really, *really* hurts," said Sybil showing Sig and Sabine how ridiculously voluminous it had become, so much so that she removed her top to ease the pressure. Aubrey missed out on this though; his view of the world was currently reduced to two mere slits of light.

"Okay, I guess I'll do it," said Sabine with far more resignation than grace. She removed her outerwear to reveal a rump remarkably saggy on the one side.

"You'f got yourthelf a fwat back tire," said Sig before he realized he had better shut up before he got dragged into the operation.

"I'll give you a fwat back tire, Mister," retorted Sabine before setting off. Ah, but she was so clever, was our Sabine. She wore that floppy hat which to any patrolling wasp must have resembled some gaudy form of lily pad with a severe case of weed pox floating on by. She dragged up the anchor, struggled mightily to lug it up into the boat, whereupon an all-out wasp assault was launched upon that hat. It was like Iwo Jima all over again. The fighters came in waves as Sabine resolutely towed Loosie Goosey back to land. The cowards, those dastardly cowards on shore, they took one look and bolted for the security of the truck the moment they realized Sabine was exposing them to a direct line of fire. She ran the boat aground only to be stung again, this time on the unaffected buttock as she sprinted for the truck; clearly those wasps had an eye for balance. Ah, but she was transformed: she was now Savage Sabine the Invincible whose unrequited anger would far exceed that of many thousands of wasps. She arrived at Aubrey's window accompanied by a trio of the more aggressive of the fighter pilots. Aubrey, the fool, refused her admission of any sort until it occurred to him via his distorted view of the world that all she wanted was the can of hornet spray. He let the window down just far enough to get the can out and allow two suicide bombers in. Poetic justice perhaps, but it inaugurated the most turbulent free-for-all in the cab as three pairs of hands sought to annihilate one pair of highly aerobatic wasps. Finally it was Sig who made his first valid contribution of the day when he swatted not one but both beasties as they zoomed down on him in formation. To hear him seek the accolades of his peers was to think he had just won the Battle of Britain all by himself. As for Sabine, she sped back to the boat, climbed aboard with steel in her soul and a verve that ignored all pain, and she soaked that nest and anything by it that flew, crawled or walked anywhere near her. This was not just pest control, this was overkill. Only then did she sit down, not just to cry but to howl in a manner that hearkened back to primitive man/woman. Yet even then, a last dying wasp managed to penetrate her defences and launch one final mission way down into Happy Valley. Oh well, now the men could legitimately say their wives were something of a matched pair...or a bulging foursome!

So to return to the initial point; farming can force you to respect the fact that all the fowls of the air, the insects on the wing, the creatures of soil and slough, plus all of the creepy-crawlies have their entitlement to space in the universal scheme of things. Humans have to learn and accept that the encroachment of these creatures on human tenure of land and property is both incidental and legitimate. The other thing worth remembering is that inasmuch as you regard yourself as tame and predictable, these creatures are wild and therefore highly unpredictable. Sabine was to find that out in the fall when a magnificent bull moose shambled through the front field not fifty yards from her sitting-room window.

A large bull moose, standing statuesque in the muskeg, is a true monarch of the north and likely the only genuine Canadian monarch you are likely to encounter. He is big, he is muscled, and he is the ultimate in alpha males. He doesn't have to train to be so, to pump iron and watch his carbs and all of that, he comes by what he is naturally. Sure, like every male of any species, he has to project an image, but that's a whole other biological story. For Sabine, the crux of the matter was that she could take her very own photograph which in turn could be enlarged to make a stunning picture, which, in the right frame of course (a sort of dark carved oak) could dominate one entire wall. Better yet, that moose would be "their moose", one that was familiar with "their place", and they had not felt compelled to shoot it dead as so many others would have done. The picture itself would be trophy enough.

So she donned her heavy winter boots and her parka, and armed with her trusty Nikon, she set out to get that picture of all pictures. The problem with photographing all wildlife is invariably the same; what you visualize and what you ultimately get is rarely compatible. Furthermore, in her quest for pictorial glory, Sabine was decidedly handicapped. She had no wings, no webbed feet, no heron-style legs to stride over all of the obstacles, and she was wearing a pair of heavy winter boots, great for comfort but not for speed. Nonetheless, she struck out after that moose, trailing him up to the patch of tamarack and muskeg that bisected their home quarter and began just beyond the corrals. She caught her breath when she saw him. He was just as magnificent as she could ever have wished for. He looked casually across at her as if to say, "I am he, the Great One. I am the ultimate alpha male. Come, take my picture." At least in her naiveté that's how she interpreted it. So she took his picture, and then another and another, eventually not even having to use the zoom lens to fill the viewfinder. But when you have confined yourself to looking through a lens, a zoom lens at that, you can quickly lose all sense of perspective; you can lose a true understanding of the actual distance between yourself and your subject. Suddenly the king shook his massive head. Was he threatening her? Or just telling her something? She looked over the top of her camera. Oh yes, he was threatening her all right, not only telling her to stay the hell out of his way but also making a move towards her. But her leaden boots were not made for hiking, let alone sprinting through soggy muskeg. Maybe that moose had a sense of humour, but how was she to know that? He stopped. What she had just discovered was that he could take one stride to her six. She turned and headed for home. Twice she fell down, with her hands holding that precious camera—and the even more precious pictures—above the pools of water trapped by the muskeg. All the while, she was expecting to be trampled into her very own patch of wilderness, hers and dear Aubrey's. Twice she stood up, her heart threatening to beat its way clean out of her chest and abandon that decrepit old body for higher ground. Only when she had finally made it to the edge of the muskeg did she turn around. She was sure, she swore ever afterwards, that she could hear the moose laughing at her, could almost hear him announcing to the world, "You don't own this land. I do!"

Aubrey arrived back from town just as she had made it back down to the house. "What the heck have you been up to? Were you having a little paddle up there in the muskeg, or what? Look at you. Have you gone and forgotten that the Hanlon Hotel has a bathroom with hot water and a jetted tub? And we even have soap!"

"If you must know, I was having a bath with a big hairy male far better endowed than you'll ever be." He could wait a while before he got to see the pictures.

That picture in its frame of dark carved oak looked spectacular when it was hung above the fireplace. But it was the little brass plaque affixed to the bottom that said it all: "I am lord of all you survey." There was a message in that, especially for Sabine.

So, during their time on the farm, the Hanlons found their attitudes changing. Where so many on the land saw coyotes and cougars as predators, and regarded porcupines, squirrels, and skunks as vermin, Aubrey and Sabine found themselves preferring to leave these creatures alone as long as they went about their own business. To take a life, any life, gratuitously is in essence to play God, and that in turn entails its own set of implications and responsibilities. Implicit in this more evolved attitude is the notion that in their own way, all animals are sentient beings. Whether they are wild or domesticated, within their own biological context they should be free to express themselves. So it was, for instance, that when it came to the Hanlon cows, they all demonstrated their own individual social traits. And so it is that the breeders of bulls make a gentle disposition a centrepiece of their breeding program.

Anyone who has raised livestock will likely tell you that the happiest and most productive animal is the one that is best taken care of. Yes, we end up killing many of our own animals for our own needs, but that does not give us cause or licence not to respect them. Besides, the animal that has suffered indignities at the hands of humans is the one that fears humanity, and fear so quickly begets aggression. Inasmuch as people may have a violent temper, so too may many animals. Likewise, inasmuch as people may also have a sense of humour, so too may many animals. You could almost hear Nellie's laughter when she boosted Dick Conley over the garden fence that time. And as much as any person, animals can have a good day or a bad day. They may be traumatized through no fault of their own. Two incidents occurred that fall going into winter that proved the point.

The first took place when the Hanlons decided to de-louse the cows prior to those long winter months. It was enough that the cows had to feed themselves without having to feed the human equivalent of lawyers and bankers—the parasites that would suck them dry if they were so permitted. The usual cowpoke team was on hand; Aubrey and Sabine, Pete and Jeannie, and Master of All Ceremonies, The Right Irreverent Dick Conley.

"Dick," said Aubrey, "are you okay to go fetch the big bull in the far corral and bring him up into the alleyway? We'll be ready for him by the time you get here, that's if you're not too darn scaredy-pants to fetch one big bull all by your little self!" Because of Nellie's overt dislike of the man, impugning Conley's manhood was a favorite sport of Aubrey's, even if it might spell later retribution. But to all of the other bovines on the place, Conley was just one more "babbilicious" human, a mouthy representative of the authorities, so to speak. But then don't all representatives of government have too much to say? Dick was back in a couple of minutes, without the bull.

"Where's the bull?" asked Aubrey, ready to cuss at Conley for letting him out or to laugh at him for being too chicken.

"He made it very clear to me that he's a mite indisposed," Conley said enigmatically.

"What do you mean he's a mite indisposed? Go on, admit it, he put you on the run, didn't he?" This last was truly a dumb thing to say because Conley's response was so obvious.

"You go get him then, Superman," Dick winked at Pete, alerting him to the fact that some unscheduled entertainment was about to begin.

"Fine, I will!" said Aubrey without any sober second thought; he was jousting with that rogue Conley after all. "I can go and get one lousy, big, fat bull into one little alleyway without having to stage a full bloody parade over it."

When he got to the corral, he could see the bull with his head in the round bale feeder, facing him from the centre of the corral. Aubrey should have noted that the feeder was pretty much empty, save for a skiff of hay in the middle; obviously what the bull had been chewing on. The animal watched him come through the gate, simultaneously communicating his wish to Aubrey that he had no desire to go anywhere in a hurry. Aubrey took two steps in. The bull, with the unlikely name "Willy Wonka" (some breeders cannot restrain their wayward humour when they register their progeny), took one look at him and charged. For some reason he and the bale feeder seemed inseparable; they came at him together at full bore. Aubrey only just managed to step out of the corral and chain the gate before Willy and his heavy, metal necklace crashed into it, changing the shape of a once circular heavy-duty bale feeder to curiously elliptical. Being brought to a dead stop, almost a little too literally, did nothing to improve Willy's mood. He reversed at full speed, dragging his hood ornament with him. Then he charged forward again, and there was that pesky feeder still with him. What had happened was that in reaching for the last skiff of hay, Willy Wonka had forced his head through the bars. When it came time to withdraw, the feeder came along too. Judging by the sweat on his flanks, he had been trying to divest himself of this unwanted fashion accessory for quite some time. He was exhausted. He was angry, irate even. And he would have liked to have killed someone, anyone.

Conley's voice now floated across Aubrey's consciousness, "So where' this big, fat, lousy bull, Mister Hanlon? You shouldn't keep your crew waiting!" Dick was merciless as he and Pete appeared on the scene. The sound of voices and, worse yet, laughter, only served to enrage Willy further, and one more time the feeder came crashing into the gate.

"We'll have to free him with your loader tractor," said Pete, always a cool head in a crisis situation. And this was a crisis, even if Dick Conley could not recognize it. "Aub, I'll let you in with the tractor, you grab the feeder with the grapple to anchor it, and hopefully Mr. Congeniality will be smart enough to pull his head out. But whatever you do, don't be getting out of your tractor because what we have here is one very unhappy boy."

The procedure, simple as it was, went like clockwork. Not that Willy Wonka was in any mood to give thanks. He already had a monstrous headache. When he yanked back on that feeder, he did so with such force that he fell hard on his rump on frozen ground. Instantly he was on his feet and charging the tractor, ready to pin the blame for all his woes on this noisy beast that was encroaching on his beat. Now when two thousand-plus pounds of over-stimulated rump steak connects with a stationary object with four wheels designed to dig deep, it is the moving object that will experience the pain. Willy stopped, backed up in total incomprehension, then snorted a couple of times before leaping clean over the gate where Dick and Pete were standing. The entertainment value of the spectacle that had been unfolding before the two humans was converted instantly into an adrenalin-filled race for self-preservation. As usual, Dick Conley had to have the last word. Perched up there on his post, he let loose a couple of wild "Olés" to help Willy Wonka find his destiny.

Not too long after that, it was dear old Sabine who suffered through the second incident: an event for which she was never forgiven by the aggrieved player. When the Hanlons had weaned their calves, they had selected fifteen of their very best heifer calves with a view to keeping them as replacements to accommodate the natural attrition that every herd experiences. Old cows, like old people, get sick and die. Others fail to conceive in the breeding season, others, again, simply "run out of bullets" and get old before their time. In order to keep these heifer calves sweet-tempered, they were segregated into their own corral and fed their own dedicated feed throughout late fall and winter, with Sabine supplementing the ration daily with pails of barley/oat chop. Every day, as she poured the grain into the wooden feeders Aubrey had built for the purpose, she would endeavour to pet "my babies" as she called them. Pails of chop are heavy enough that if you can find an easier way to handle them, that is to your advantage, particularly on snow-covered ground where taking a tumble can cause you injury. And besides all of that, you don't want arms longer than those of an orangutan by spring. Sabine hit upon the brilliant idea of using the big, green plastic calving sled. She would load up her three buckets, pull the sled over to the corral with the tow-rope provided, open the gate, and slide the sled in before commencing the feeding, always making sure to fold the tow-rope back into the sled so it could not get caught on some animal's foot.

This particular day, "her babies" crowded around her as they were wont to do. They were becoming really friendly, especially a deep red Gelbvieh cross that Sabine was grooming to be her best friend. Curious Ginny, as she was named, was the equivalent of a boisterous teenager, always nudging Sabine to tell her to hurry up with the room service. This particular day for some reason, assuredly because of her unbridled curiosity, Curious Ginny picked up the rope with her teeth and began to chew on it, lifting her head at the last second as another animal bumped into her. Instinctively she lunged forward and the rope slipped down around her neck. The attached sled naturally came with her, making a loud clatter as it bumped against her back legs. The combination of this alien noise and this foreign green object chasing her with such gusto only served to instil pure panic into a young "lady". She took off, sending Sabine flying as she did so. The faster she went, the more that sled clattered against her. The more it clattered against her, the faster she went. The outcome was inevitable; she slammed up against the plank fence at one of its weaker points. Two planks splintered into pieces and the sled itself broke in half as Miss Ginny surged through that fence. But the front half of the sled was still hanging in there determined to continue the torment until it got caught on a straggly willow bush on the edge of the muskeg and fell off. The rope had been pulled right out of it.

Well now for the other fourteen young bovine adolescents, here was unexpected freedom, and they were not about to miss a minute of it, not when their mamas were right there in the adjoining pasture... And hey, look, what do you know, there were a couple of big, double-muscled bovine studs out there with them! Talk about stirring up the hormones; this was like fresh nectar for the bees! Studs are studs, not steers for good reason; and these girls wasted no time in checking out this unexpected bonus, their version of a walk on the wild side. So, as they say, the initial problem compounded itself. Trying to persuade big Willy Wonka from taking an unseemly interest in Princess and Curly and Mellow Yellow was like trying to keep an Irish Paddy away from his Guinness. Trying to keep Princess and Curly and Mellow Yellow away from big Willy was akin to trying to stop an ecstatic bevy of female groupies from seeking Justin Bieber's autograph, an autograph big Willy was only too happy to give.

For Mrs. Hanlon, it was a full Emergency Code Red. Aubrey was sought out and dragged away from his precious CBC radio program, his appointed hour with Stewart McLean and his *Vinyl Café*. From the outset, it was clear they would never get cows, heifers, and bulls separated out there in the open field. The heifers after all were teeny-boppers on the razzle, with absolutely no intention of cooperating with *Genius Humanitas*. A bit of sex, rap, rock and roll at their age, why, that was what it was all about, wasn't it? Aubrey and Sabine had to bring the whole herd into the corral so that the heifers could be separated out more easily, which was fine except that big Willy and a young bull called Yes Man both had a very definitive crush on a very willing Sassy Pie. Aubrey finally had to dampen their desire with his trusty length of two-by-four to deter their lust from spilling over completely.

"Teenage pregnancy" among bovines is never a good thing. She who has her first fun in the sun before she is mature can end up permanently stunted because while still growing, she is yet too young to bear progeny, and the issue of that fun in the sun, the calf, is more often than not a weakling prone to every virus and bacterium going. So Aubrey and Sabine had to resort to an extra injection to induce early abortion in those heifers that had been over-lascivious, "the heavy petters and flirters" of the group. As for Curious Ginny, never again did she demonstrate curiosity, preferring instead to keep her distance from anything in human pink or plastic green. Ah, that was okay because Mellow Yellow stepped in to take her place, and she and Sabine became fast friends.

When it comes to the nature of farmers' relationships with the cows they raise, there are essentially three basic camps. There are the "Molly-Coddlers" or the "Empathists": those bovine huggers who embrace the petting zoo approach of the "Titford Technique" described in *Fancy Free in the Back Thirty*. But these are a special group. They seem to have an unusual and uncanny affinity with their animals that most people simply do not possess. Whereas a cow would have absolutely no qualms about giving Aubrey a couple of solid, cracking kicks to the kneecaps, she would show inexplicable restraint if there was one of these "cow whisperers" breathing sweet nothings in her ear and coaxing her where she has no desire to go. In the middle are the "Neutralists": those who refuse to get mad or gooey, preferring an even, cool, calm and collected manner in getting their business done. Finally there are the "Latinist Firecrackers": those with the oft-described Latin temperament, or those with the tendency to explode and use strings of Pig Latin as their preferred mode of communication, usually at maximum volume. For them, their yelling and screaming is as much a technique as cow-whispering is for "The Empathists". One thing is certain however; the Latinist Firecrackers' techniques induce rapid movement and reaction. No cow will hang around for a last sloppy defecation in response to a cusser and a shouter. Then again, more often than not, this method can also be counter-productive and may lead the practitioner's intentions wildly astray, generally because bovine logic under pressure involves more of a straight line west than a circular one chasing the tail. In addition, it can be fun to watch because the more *tremens agitato* the practitioner exhibits, the more of a surreal aura they add to the language, any language.

In all of this, however, Aubrey was a sub-species, a "Vacillator". He had moved away from being strictly a Neutralist to a Firecracker, depending on the prevailing wind, how good the past week had been, whether he had a hangover or the flu, whether his knee, knuckle or head was sore, whether his co-workers were doing what he expected of them, or if Dick Conley was in "idiot mode". If the cows showed cooperation, why he could even veer towards being an Empathist, but all it took was a single cow to sneeze, or heaven forbid, crap in his pocket or his boot, then the tenor version of the "Whiner's Aria" would begin. It has to be said that the notion of self-control is very much of an abstract concept, something readily discussed in Psychology 201 but not necessarily wired into someone's personality. There is a direct connection between a "heads-up" cow and a farmer's own self-control. The "Beginner's Manual for Uninspired Herdpersons" defines a heads-up cow as "a female bovine with an instinctive inclination to go any way but the one chosen for her by her attendant herdsperson." Good old Matata was such a cow.

Matata did not care for Aubrey, did not care much for humanity in general, and after hanging around with Nellie too long, she adopted Nellie's pathological hatred of Dick Conley. She only needed to hear the man's voice and her nostrils would flare, her tits would tingle, and whatever equanimity she possessed at that moment would abandon her altogether. Matata, as Aubrey and Sabine fans will already know, means "trouble" in Swahili. Those same fans will also know the Hanlons stopped calling their cows by names that might morph into a negative self-fulfilling prophecy.

"The accident" actually happened the previous spring when the cows were being herded into the main corral for some procedure or other, at a time when the terrain was exceedingly soggy from spring run-off. For a very explicable reason (even if explicability and reason were foreign notions in her tiny mind anyway), Matata decided to make a run for it, likely because she heard Dick Conley singing his own made-up version of the "Cowpoke" song. In the meantime, Aubrey had long ago decided that he, Aubrey Hanlon, had never been designed for running, jumping, climbing or swimming, or for anything that called for any degree of athleticism after the age of forty-two. That was why he had invested in a quad. And right this minute he had to prevent Matata streaking through the bottom gate which he, the fool, had left open because he was sure no cow would turn back on the posse escorting them towards the corral. Double fool. He jumped onto his quad and took off after her. When the quad hit that really soft spot, its front wheels got sucked deep into the goo causing it to come to an "arrêt, toute bleeping suite," as Conley was to tell it later. However, unfortunately, Aubrey's face continued onwards, led by his large (some would call it "bulbous") nose. But the nose, in turn, was not going fast enough to unseat an ass of such generous proportions, so all that the nose could do was to arc downwards and smack itself into the steel carrying-rack on the front of the quad. It must have been seismically traumatic because even Matata stopped and hesitated for a second before immediately turning back to join the others. She must have thought that this would surely make daddy go look for his gun.

But daddy, poor daddy, was momentarily out cold. Sabine, mommy, poor dear mommy, instantly convinced herself that her partner for life had expired. On the other hand, Pete was thinking Aubrey would have to be one strong man to get up after a crash like that while Conley was surmising that this was one helluva way to get a nose job. It was then that Aubrey contrived to wobble his way upright, blood streaming from both of his crushed nostrils. Yet even that was not the most dramatically colourful part of the spectacle, it was what Aubrey could do with the English language. It wasn't poetry, it wasn't prose, and it certainly was not literary, but it was rivetingly creative with expressions juxtaposed together in a way that no English speaker had heard before, a kind of oral tapestry burnished with fire and brimstone. When Matata heard her master, she pretty much begged mommy Sabine to let her into the corral with the others. Sabine obliged because she too was thinking that daddy might go and get his gun. Okay, so even if Aubrey was not athletic any more, he was still tough. He found a grimy shop towel in his pocket, went over on foot to the nearby cattle waterer, soaked the towel in the frigid water, and placed it over his hooter. He was definitely not a pretty sight.

"Let's do it folks!" he announced…and so they did. By the end of it all, Conley had already given Aubrey a new nickname, "Papa Smurf". But even then the name did not quite do justice to the grotesque visage that Aubrey was forced to wear for the whole week.

"Even Papa Smurf could not match *that* proboscis," commented Mr. Conley.

Stranger still, Matata never again saw fit to take on her lord and master. Maybe she knew that from then on she was on borrowed time.

Over coffee at the end of the day, it was perhaps Pete who put it most succinctly in a comment intended for Sabine, maybe with a hint of premonition. "Cows are like people. By all means trust 'em as much as you dare, but be very careful if you invade their space. Doesn't matter how nice they are."

"I had a girlfriend like that once..." Dick Conley began, before Sabine shut him down.

But it was nonetheless a comment that Aubrey was to recall in the upcoming calving season. When he went to check on his cows at night, he always went armed with a cane that afforded protection of the person, a flashlight that enhanced vision, and a knife to slit the birthing sack of a newly arrived calf if need be.

The incident happened at around two o'clock in the morning. The cows close to calving were sequestered in a deep bed of straw. It had snowed some and it was one of those pitch black nights, eerily silent and as still as a cemetery. There was not a star in the sky thanks to the thick, heavy clouds hanging so low it was as if they were trying to stop Mother Earth from breathing. The air itself was very oppressive; indeed it was one of those nights where you could easily imagine you were the only human being alive on the planet.

Aubrey switched on the corral lights. Talking softly to his ladies, he made a tour of the smaller corral. Some cows were at the feeder, others were lying comfortably in the bedding. Most did not bother to move; they just blinked sleepily in the light. They knew who he was and what he was doing. Fine. Nothing happening in this particular corral. He moved across the alley to the big corral.

Maybe the problem was that there were only two floodlights to illuminate the whole corral which inevitably left some areas in more shadow than others. Maybe it was because the heavy darkness felt so uncanny to both man and beast, but Aubrey felt somehow uneasy. How could he not? But he made a point of standing at the gate and shining his spotlight into the nooks and crannies from there. Aha! That was Snowflake in the far corner, and she had definitely just done something. Quietly he slipped into the corral and closed the gate behind him. Talking quietly all the time, he made his way over to Snowflake who, up to now, he and Sabine had rated as perhaps the gentlest cow in the herd. About fifteen feet from her, and between Aubrey and the cow, lay the inert form of a newborn calf. It was hard to tell which end was which, it being all Charolais white like its mama. Instinctively Aubrey rushed forward to see what was going on. He got down on his haunches and gently lifted the calf's head. It was alive, for sure, but appeared somewhat stunned, likely because his mother had dropped him into this world from a standing position. Aubrey had no time to react before Snowflake— dear, gentle Snowflake— came barreling in and floored him. He rolled over with barely time to squat before she turned and came in a second time. He had no choice. With all his force, Aubrey hurled that spotlight at her in a last defiant act of defence. He had never been an ace with a ball but this time he sure hit the mark.

It was a shot that in all probability saved his life. The light was heavy and caught her on that sensitive spot on the end of a cow's nose. She stopped dead in her tracks. Maybe it was his attire that had spooked her, he being dressed in the same black as the night: black toque, black coveralls, and black boots. But none of the others had spooked when he came in. Okay, so maybe in terms of his timing he had invaded her space at a moment when she least expected him. Whatever it was, this was not the best time to find out. Talking softly and leaving his spotlight behind, Aubrey backed his way up to the nearest fence, with Snowflake eyeing him all the way. Only when he had actually climbed over it and was safely on the other side did the cow move over to her new baby and begin to mother it. Aubrey spotted baby's head pop up out of the straw, saw the ears wiggle, and he knew then that Snowflake would do her thing. She would have done her thing even if he had never shown up.

Was Aubrey surprised the next morning when Snowflake showed not the slightest bit of aggression when he went up to the corrals to check on her? If she could have talked, he was sure she would have told him all about her new baby, a little bull, and how this past night she had sent packing a great big black bullfrog that had tried to steal her baby the moment it was born. He retrieved his flashlight, none the worse for wear for having been used as a guided missile, and then quietly moved mom and baby into the barn. Mom got her bowl of chop, baby got his shots and tags, and the calving season rolled on.

Beyond all of this though, there were all of the "what-if" implications of the incident. What might have happened if Aubrey had not been able to get up when Snowflake first bowled him over? What if she had continued her attack as she clearly intended to do, and stomped him into the ground? What if all the other cows had gotten all spooked up too; would they have joined in the attack? What if Aubrey had been injured badly enough that he had had to lay where he was until the morning? It is always the "what-ifs" that encourage you to modify your behaviour, that tell you to learn your lesson from any and every dangerous situation you find yourself in. Because Aubrey had looked so unfamiliar and threatening to Snowflake and because his timing had invaded what should have been a very private moment between a mother and her offspring, she had done what any mother would do: she had vigorously defended her baby. Any normal mother of any species would have done the same.

Chapter Eight
"NO TRUCE!"

*O*ver a single century, the grand march of civilization has morphed into a headlong rush to be the first with the latest scientific breakthrough or the latest technological innovation. But there was a downside for types like Aubrey who, himself, would have been a natural Luddite because he saw technology as too often diminishing the intrinsic value of work. He was one of those types who often lamented that the forces of government and change never seemed content to leave him alone as a traditional peasant farmer doing things the way his forefathers always did. Only none of his forefathers had ever been in agriculture. Among his forefathers were a baker, a cabinet maker, a dentist, a banker, and even one who had found fame as Scotland's first-ever serial killer in the nineteenth century, but no Hanlon had ever worked the land. The same thing went for Sabine's side of the family tree; nobody had ever farmed. She often opined that the Hanlons were making their way down the ladder of social mobility when so many were heading the other way. At any rate, for both Hanlons there was no soil in their genes, no implicit "agricultural understandings" from having been raised on the land, whether from eating dirt as a kid or dancing with the latest bout of weather rather than perpetually whining about its perfidy. This meant they had to come by all of their agricultural knowledge the hard way, that everything, absolutely everything, had been one long and arduous process and would continue to be so as long as they farmed. As if that was not enough, neither science nor technology ever stood still. The machines and the techniques of the day could be so easily rendered redundant by tomorrow.

For example, to a non-scientist like Aubrey, science seemed to run in circles with the disciples of the latest fad broadcasting, always broadcasting as loudly as they could, that if you didn't hurry up and see the light their way, at best you were an unenlightened hillbilly, and at worst you were, oh dread of all dread, "regressive". Practitioners of sustainable this, or holistic that, or organic-the-other, all claimed to have found the key not just to survival but to wealth and prosperity. So it was that western Canada had witnessed the rise and fall of Boer goats, bison, ostriches, llamas, yaks and elk, plus other related exotic animals. In the arena of livestock feeding, those who championed bale grazing, swath grazing, feeding silage, pasture stock-piling, or protein supplementation could be heard insisting that only they had the answer. And like any convert or any snake-oil salesman who has stumbled upon true understanding, they really got to believe their own preaching. Aubrey and Sabine could not miss reading in the supposedly prestigious agricultural publications and journals which somehow found their way into the Hanlon mailbox that the way they chose to feed their cows in winter— using a balebuster to shred a bale of hay and lay it out in a line— wasted anywhere from 11.65% to 22.78% of the hay: data that were less likely the consequence of how well the machine was operated and more likely due to the research methodology used and maybe even the eyesight of the researcher himself. Aubrey just could not help it; he invariably ended up with this image of the nutty professor on his hands and knees in the field, peering down through his Coke-bottle glasses and counting up and then weighing all the uneaten sprigs of hay before plugging this precious mass of data into his portable laptop. He would then press a magic button and hey presto, that mysterious program called "Bits and Bytes Wrapped in Baloney" would come to life and spit out reams of important scientific facts about protein levels, palatability, moisture retention, composting potential and, yes, levels of wastage. Aubrey had a lively imagination for a modern-day Luddite, it had to be said. He also knew that if you had invested your hard-earned dollars on a machine commonly called a balebuster, then naturally you would be loath to then turn around and invest in a totally different line of machinery because some new guru had arrived on the scene preaching a revolutionary new gospel.

In thinking about the issue further, the Hanlons knew that laying out the food in one long line for their cows meant that whether they were big or small, domineering "bitches" or timorous waifs, all got equal access to the groceries. Moreover, if they planned it effectively and laid the line out in a different place each day, the cows did the manure-spreading all by themselves. When the Hanlons finally reverted to bale feeders as they did when they confined the cows just prior to calving, you could be sure that Nellie and her cohorts would dominate the feeders until they had gorged themselves. That was why the Hanlons put the more aggressive cows in one corral and the more timid ones in another. But then the fanatical bale-grazer would likely interject with his traditional refrain. "Oh, oh, but you guys still have to start your tractors every day in winter." The logic of their righteousness was indisputable. "You use up fuel that we don't use. You have running costs we don't have. You contribute more to global warming than we do." And so it is that the righteous shall inherit the earth for they shall have the high moral ground, and they and their tractors don't fart in the wind.

For Aubrey the problem was that both science and logic are reductionist, but there were always many other variables in the equation: variables that reductionist science underplayed in order to get its uninterrupted view. So he just shrugged his shoulders. He and Sabine had jumped on enough bandwagons in their day, and they had fallen off one or two of them as they went.

It simply did not matter what branch of farming you were involved in, the science was there to intimidate you, to torment and cajole you, to bite you when you weren't paying enough attention. When cattle breeders talk about gene pools and genetics, they talk in reverential tones about EPDs (Expected Progeny Differences), performance data that can supposedly tell you what a specific specimen of a particular cattle breed might do for you. Of course Dick Conley had to come up with his own take on EPDs: "EPDs referred to the 'Expectations of hot Party Dates'. You know, how well that sizzling party girl with the big…."

"Enough of that, Mister Conley!" Sabine would halt the flow.

But the EPD discussion did not stop there. There were the homozygous, horned and scurred and polled bovines; there were full-bloods, purebreds, and hybrids, "guppies" and "balancers"; there were all sorts of musings about red factor and pigmentation, about calving ease and carcass traits, with added predictions about "cutability", longevity and heritability. The list went on and on, and for Aubrey, on some more yet. So he did what any scientific neophyte would do; he turned the whole story around in his head in order to give himself the peace of mind to carry on with the little he knew. Whatever he did not understand about the science and needed to know, rather than weigh himself down with the baggage of useless knowledge, why he would pick someone else's brains as required. If the Hanlons wanted to assure themselves of a good buy at a bull sale, they would take their friend Pete along. He could talk about things like outcross and line breeding with the best of them, but the one thing he was not hard-wired to do was to double-cross like some of the "wide boys" out there!

Machinery, the development thereof, the use thereof and the sourcing thereof went on in much the same way. Even if you had the coin to ride the techno-wave, the new hot machine you had just been so proud to acquire was obsolete within six months. The model with the self-levelling this, the air-ride that, and the auto-sense the other must have been nothing more than the prototype if the latest ad for the line was to be believed. "Totally re-engineered from stem to stern," the ad would shout in your face. "Most improved tractor of the year," would proclaim the endorsement from some glossy publication that nobody had ever heard of: "The Tractorperson's Companion". Really? Like the prototypes had been *that bad* they needed to be totally re-engineered and improved upon? The hyperbole was laughable. Surely it would not be long before some engineering prodigy could figure out how to attach NASA's Canadarm to the loader of the latest tractor so that the company could charge another twenty thousand dollars for a new "basic necessity". Or maybe they could come up with a tanning salon inside the cab so you could do your summer bronzing as you worked. And Lord knows how these folks ever came up with their model numbers. Maybe the model number 6180 for Massey-Ferguson referred to the number of failed prototypes that preceded it or to the number of miles, oh pardon me, the number of kilometres of wiring that lay beneath the hood. Maybe the John Deere 5200 used that many gallons, pardon me, litres per day in fuel. Perhaps the Case I.H. Puma 125 had that number of techno-sensors hidden deep within its entrails so that some specially trained digital whiz-kid mechanic could go play a game of hide-and-go-seek when the on-board computer told the operator not to pass "Go" and not to collect two hundred dollars. Whatever had happened to those good old days when any old son of the soil could go out and fix what it was that ailed his sweetheart? That was another thing Aubrey Hanlon, ex-cop, had a hard time getting his head around, that somebody's tractor could even lay claim to being their sweetheart. But then again, there were plenty of fruitcakes out there who worshipped their Dodge, pardon me, their Dodge *Ram* with all its "guts and glory".

Go into any large John Deere dealership and you'll see not only the requisite lineup of replica toys to brainwash the little folks when they are most vulnerable; you will also find the full array of golf balls, tea towels, toques and bed sheets, toothpicks and, yes, toilet seats and gas barbeques all sporting that iconic leaping deer logo. Was this indicative of just a simple love affair or did it denote something more psychologically sinister: a personality disorder of some sort, an infatuation or an obsession? Why didn't John Deere have a wife yet, a Mrs. Deere? Surely the marketing department was asleep at the wheel. There was plenty of room in the family for a Jenny Deere or a Jemimah Deere to keep poor old lonesome Johnny company, wasn't there? Better yet, the corporation could then launch a whole line of women's foundation garments with that frolicsome deer leaping its way around the trails of paradise. It was amazing how people took this stuff so seriously, their seeing green paint as better than red, red paint as better than orange or blue or yellow. Okay, so yes, blue could be the colour of a baboon's ass and orange could be the colour of envy. And if you had anything in the colour orange, such as the Agco line for example, presumably you would envy someone who had the same concept in magenta or deep purple. Aubrey took this to the extreme that day he drove with Pete all the way out to the John Deere dealership in Unity, Saskatchewan, to look over a used 567 baler. The day started out badly for Aubrey because, despite the verbal agreement he had concluded with his friend, all the way there Pete contrived not to stop at a single Tim Horton's for Aubrey's favourite Caramel latte and a "dog-nut" as Pete chose to call them. Then the salesman proved to be as brash as he looked; he was entirely what one would have expected of a modern-day machinery salesman. Partly in revenge, Aubrey livened up the proceedings by playing the devil's advocate and he landed some great jibes at both Pete's and the salesman's expense. But the baler was fundamentally in good shape and at a fair price, and besides, the experienced salesman knew he had a prize fish on the line in spite of the fish's prattling companion. Pete bought it. While the salesman and Pete went off into the man's office to draw up an "Agreement to Purchase" that looked about long enough to be the baler's last Will and Testament, Aubrey felt compelled to sashay around the showroom where he was totally unable to avoid all of the John Deere bric-a-brac—the rows of overpriced John Deere ball caps, the utility knives and cigarette lighters, and all of the things a cult member might want but never need—all made in the Great Peoples' Republic over the broad, blue sea. Finally, bored out of his skull, he chose to go into the office and take the vacant chair alongside Pete. Just then an attractive lady walked into the office, ostensibly to pick up some papers. Maybe because Aubrey had razzed him so aggressively about the imperfections of John Deere balers, Mr. Salesman decided to address himself directly to his tormentor.

"Now you can talk about baler imperfections all you like but *that*," he said nodding at the woman, "represents the nearest thing to perfection you'll ever see on this earth."

The comment took Aubrey totally by surprise. What did the words "that" and "thing" refer to? The lady? Was that any way to talk about a lady, any lady? "You're pathetic!" he said to the salesman, a smile on his face.

The woman, (Aubrey was to discover from Pete later that she was in fact the man's fiancé), turned and fixed Aubrey with a beady eye before turning back to the salesman and saying, "He's right, you're pathetic!" She then walked out. Aubrey now had the man on the run, so to speak, so he thought one more shot across the guy's bows might be fun.

"Besides, it seems clear to me that you people run a pretty crappy outfit here," he said.

"Oh? What d'ya mean we run a pretty crappy outfit?" the salesman responded belligerently.

"Well, I've seen three or four guys walk in here and not a single one of them was wearing a John Deere cap. I've seen an M.F. cap, a Cat cap, and Agco-Allis cap, and mine is a New Holland cap while my friend Pete's here was stolen from a Wetaskiwin body shop. Now that tells me that your hats are as over-priced as your machinery."

"Gimme that damn cap," the man said. Pete aided and abetted by snatching it off Aubrey's head and handing it over.

"Now you have my permission to choose any John Deere cap you see in that showroom cuz you ain't getting this one back!" With that he deliberately placed it on the floor, stomped on it until it was good and dirty, and then tossed it into the garbage can. This only succeeded in convincing Aubrey that brand loyalty was more than a simple marketing strategy; it was a contagious disease or some weird obsession for sure. Maybe there was an obsessive gene as opposed to a recessive one?

What was so ironic about all of this wondrous machinery available to North American farmers was that the jobs to make a lot of it and its components had been outsourced to the Republic of Elsewhere, presumably to the lowest bidder in some place like Mexico, Ireland, or Indonesia. So when all was said and done, many of the tractors were really a potpourri, the literal French for a mixed stew or a dog's breakfast. Yet it was inevitable really; the day came when the Hanlons had to find themselves a better, more up-to-date, chore tractor, something a little—no, a lot—more reliable than what they currently had. Sure it would have to be second-hand. They had no desire to remortgage the house or the farm to pay for a shiny, new John Deere, nor to liquidate their RRSPs to buy a new Massey-Ferguson or a Case I.H., all of which would likely wear out quicker than their own bodies.

Aubrey had forgotten what the world of machinery was like when it came to dealers, not that he had ever been that familiar with it in the first place. But right from the start, he knew it was going to be a world of smoke and mirrors, of agro-spin and techno-babble, of tough-talk about this brand and trash-talk about that one. The salesmen, too, seemed to come in as many variations as the products they were selling. "Shop local!" screamed the local agents. "We know you, you know us, and we'll take care of you!"

"We'll take care of your money, more like it," Aubrey found himself thinking cynically when he encountered the first of the salesmen.

"What have you got for a trade?" asked the next one. When he heard Aubrey's response, he made no effort to mitigate his laughter. "Did they make that thing before the Model-T Ford or after?" he added as his interest expired.

The next fellow at some outfit in Red Deer was clearly tired, very tired, jaded, very busy or almost dead. "You folks go on out into the yard and take a look," he told Aubrey and Sabine, moving his butt no more than an inch, pardon me, millimetre, and then only to scratch it. "If you find something you feel you might like to talk about, just come on back in and we'll deal." He yawned and went back to ogling the Sunshine Girl in the day's *Calgary Sun*. The Hanlons walked their way out, and kept on walking.

The agent next-door was no better. "Look, can you folks come back in say, an hour? Our computers are down and the other salesman has our only printed list of inventory. Sorry about that!" He too yawned and went back to his game of pocket solitaire.

The final stop was a very gung-ho salesman type, clearly very much at the top of his game, his inventory, and his ego. His bulging eyes were all over Sabine. He claimed he had a range of tractors in the right price bracket too but Sabine insisted on cutting short the chase just so she could get some air and some space away from the man's incessant leering.

"Why don't we go and talk to your friend after we have had some lunch?" she said to Aubrey. " I need time to calm down after that revolting man."

"Everybody and their dog seem to want to be my bloody friend right now," growled Aubrey. "So which friend are you talking about?"

"You know, that fellow you call Abu Bin Smelly or something, the one who showed up in the field when we were haying that day."

"Oh, you mean Kevin Benelli. But he's the Service Manager of the place. I doubt that he will know anything about what they have for sale, although he was trying to flog us a tractor that day, wasn't he?"

"Yes, but better yet, he probably works on all the makes. He can surely advise us about what we should stay away from, no?" Her logic was inescapable. "Besides, you seem to have a good rapport with him."

But then why wouldn't I, Aubrey was thinking, when he's seen my playmate for life half-naked?

The upshot of that conversation was that they drove out to Hexagon Farm Supply, just outside of Red Deer's city limits. As soon as they were in the door, they knew this was going to be different, maybe not good or exhilarating, just different.

"Now you behave!" Sabine hissed at her husband as they entered. "And no silly references to my haying accident either!" So Aubrey switched into "Passive Mode" which called for exemplary behaviour in a public gathering place. Mr. Benelli emerged from an office on one side of a large showroom.

"Well hellooo, hello! This is a great surprise. The Hanlons both! What brings you to our humble store, may I ask? Haven't seen you folks for such a long time, even though I did see most of one of you sometime back." He grinned that sardonic grin of his to which one could never take offence. Sabine turned scarlet; Aubrey in Passive Mode could only snigger.

"Hey! Gimme that hat, right now!" Mr. Benelli did not wait to be given it; he took it off Aubrey's head. Mr. Hanlon's fancy-schmancy John Deere cap from Unity, Saskatchewan, was about to be history. "If you wear that sort of thing around here, you'll have to answer to obscenity charges. If we don't find you something different, and quickly, somebody might want to charge you for indecent exposure. Karmen," he yelled at the lady manning the parts counter, "would you bring this very important lady customer and her sleazy partner a new cap each. We can't let them just swan about our premises with their heads in such a state of undress. And you sir, if you ever wear another piece of clothing with that logo in here, I shall burn both you and the offending piece of clothing in our incinerator out back."

Karmen the parts lady clearly possessed the same zany sense of humour as her boss. She reappeared with a bright yellow and black Cat Challenger cap for Sabine and a thoroughly boring black one with a tiny M-F logo for her prince consort.

"Swap you," Aubrey immediately said to his wife.

"Get lost, Mister!" she retorted. "Now, explain our problem to this nice man."

"I'm not really a trained sex therapist," responded the man. "But I can sure try."

"Do you want our business or not?" Sabine snapped back with mock severity.

"See, Kevin," said Aubrey suddenly serious, "we're looking for a new tractor." The word "new" triggered a very, well, professional response.

"Let's go to my office," Mr. Benelli said. At that moment, a young mechanic emerged from the back somewhere and interrupted them with a technical question for the Service Manager. Kevin answered him and then said, "Hey Justin, give me your hat." Somewhat bemused, Justin took off this really filthy Agco-Allis cap and handed it over to his boss. "Now take this one and get it as filthy as you got the other one. Get it dirty, filthy dirty!" With that, the Service Manager gave his mechanic Aubrey's John Deere hat and threw the other one into the garbage can. If it had been worth retrieving, Aubrey would have retrieved it, but it looked so revolting it could have harboured enough bacteria to start the world's next pandemic. They all trooped into the office and sat down. "Okay, let's talk business," said a now very focused Mr. Benelli.

For sure, Mr. Benelli's smile seemed to wilt a bit when he discovered the tractor the Hanlons were looking for was not going to be "new-new" but new/second-hand. It wilted a good deal more when he heard they wanted to trade in their old one. It positively died when he heard the make and model of the tractor they intended to use in the trade.

"But you see, Mr. Bensmelly, we need to know what we should buy so we can avoid getting caught with a clunker," Sabine interjected so earnestly she had no idea how she had said the man's name. "Then we can talk to all these wise-guy salesmen with a little more understanding."

"So how come someone as smart as you got herself caught up with this clunker?" said Mr. Benelli with a straight face. "And by the way, my name is Benelli. Only retarded types call me anything else," he finished, pointing at Aubrey. "But hold on! You don't have to buy from a wise guy salesman when you can buy what you want through me." Sabine didn't miss that; Aubrey of course did because he was figuring out a suitable insult for his would-be friend.

"Sheesh, and she keeps telling me to behave!" he said lamely.

"Actually, I have just signed a deal on a tractor that might just suit you folks right down to the ground," continued Mr. Benelli earnestly, not forgetting his primary purpose in business was to make money. "It's a Massey. But here's something you need to understand, though. When we trade in a tractor as dealers, we have to trade in good faith. Believe me, there are lots of really honest, good people out there but there are more than a couple who are not. So in the final analysis, we never really quite know what we're getting either. Just so you know. So dealers like us try to cover themselves by adding to the price. That's life, the cost of doing business, you might say."

"Okay," said Sabine a little dubiously.

"Okay," echoed Aubrey. So what you are saying out loud is that this Massey tractor you're talking about might have a problem that you don't know about, so you're going to charge us double so you can cover your ass."

"Precisely! That's exactly what I'm telling you. But here's what we can do. We can give you a six-month warranty on everything. We should find out over the next six months if anything is not functioning the way it should, right?"

"I guess," said Sabine even more dubious than she was before.

"O-kay," said Aubrey. "So where exactly does that put us?"

"Where? I'll get Karmen to give you a much nicer hat if we do a deal. How about that?" Mr. Benelli had that evil grin again. "But seriously, the Massey should arrive in the shop tomorrow. We'll clean it up, check it over, and then call you. But feel free to hunt around. After all, I might be a wolf in sheep's clothing."

"More like a goat in clown's clothing," said Aubrey coming up with his version of a Dick Conley comment.

"I might also have a guy who'll take a look at your tractor, as long as you don't expect any more than five g's for it."

"You can't be any fairer than that," said Sabine wishing that she believed implicitly in what he had said so far.

"If we do happen to do a deal, it'll cost you a little more than a newer fancier cap, I'll expect a pair of monogrammed Massey long-johns," Aubrey had to finish.

"Oh, for you guys we can go one better. We can throw in a quick-release top for the wife."

"You're all unmitigated chauvinist bastards!" said the only lady in on the conversation. "Come on, Aub, let's get out of here. There's got to be a better-looking salesman down at that fancy dealership to the north, someone who might even talk nicely to me. He couldn't be any worse than this fellow."

They actually did go on to one more place, a place that sent its own unique message. The salesman was decidedly un-good-looking, had severe halitosis, and was of that greasy genre of salesmen that tend to stick to you like the maple syrup you spilled at breakfast. But he did have a used Massey of the same model and vintage as the one that Hexagon Farm Supply was offering. "Come and take a look," he wheezed over a wilting Sabine.

They took a look. At the big dent in the grille. At the exhaust stack slightly askew. At the one cracked fender, at a broken back light. Worse yet though, far worse, they could not ignore the reek of stale cigarette smoke in the grubbiest cab either of them had ever seen but, well, what was that *other* smell, that undefinable *stink?*

"Pig shit," said the salesman helpfully. "Came from a pig man, out there in Delburne country. Here. Let's jump in. You and I could take it for a quick spin," he said hopefully, looking at Sabine as he said it.

"Nah," said Aubrey not missing where the man's biological impulses were directed. "Nah, I think we'll head on home. This baby's been in one too many demolition derbies by the looks of her. Come on, honey, let's scoot!"

"Right you are," responded a Sabine whose feet were already making the very move she had wanted to make at the outset.

"Suit yourselves, folks!" the salesman endeavoured to get the final say. "Thanks for not wasting too much of my time!"

So it came down to seeing what Hexagon Farm Supply might cough up. Trust is one of those things so quick and easy to lose, so hard to build up, and even harder to maintain. Yet the Hanlons trusted Mr. Benelli more than all of the others combined because he didn't try to be someone other than who he was. Perhaps too many career salespeople try too hard to project a certain image without ever realizing what a poor job of acting they are doing. Others of course, don't try to project an image at all, forgetting that their lack of interest sends its own message. Mr. Benelli was primarily a Service Manager and a technician, and as it turned out, a primary shareholder in the company. So yes he was familiar with the sales protocols for the machinery his company sold, but he was also familiar with the "guts" of what he was selling. The issue therefore came down to just how extensively he might choose to "bullshit", as they say in good agricultural parlance. Would he say the engine was good when he could hear a knock? Would he say the transmission was sound when he could hear it whining? At the same time as their dealings with Mr. Benelli (soon to be known simply as "Kevin") were going on, the Hanlons came to really appreciate how the world of agricultural technology itself was moving so rapidly. They could see how it might be nigh impossible for practising mechanics to keep up to date leave alone stay on top of technological innovation. Aubrey understood this from his own limited exposure to the mechanical world, so he was much more understanding than his wife of tradesmen and journeymen when their repairs did not quite work out as they were supposed to. Sabine had no patience whatsoever with that perspective. "If you're asked to pay someone what they ask for an hour of their time, then there should be no excuse!" she would insist. And in her world she was right, that same ordered world as the house where everything had its own place and its own logic.

A week later they drove back to Hexagon Farm Supply to see the tractor, by this time having convinced themselves it was likely to have lived life to the full as much as the last one they had seen, the one with the twisted stack and the broken light. To give it full title, it was a Massey-Ferguson 6180 Dynashift complete with FEL, front-end loader. Okay, so it would be red—not hallowed green or rusted orange or Swiss cheese blue—but when they saw it, wow! It was as shiny as a new nickel, even if it already had sixteen hundred hours on it and had been traded in by a construction company that decided it needed something bigger. And yet more wow because of all the bells and whistles, although the only thing dear Aubrey felt the need to check out was the radio with its patented "sound-surround" speakers. Sabine was a little less beguiled, asking Mr. Benelli, Kevin, all sorts of questions he would never have expected from a china-doll type. He finished up with a whole new respect for a lady who clearly would brook no nonsense in her business dealings.

"So the tractor looks okay," she said. Sabine never made a point of waxing enthusiastic over anything she was paying for because inevitably she would be let down if she did so. "Where do we go from here?"

"Well, if you can get your pet ape out of the cab, we can go to my office and throw around the numbers."

Sabine signalled Aubrey back to planet Earth. "What do you think, honey?" she said as he climbed down from the cab.

"Awesome!" he gushed. "It sure has awesome sound." Evidently he had made it no further than sound.

"But shouldn't we start it up, and you know, check out the controls, that sort of thing?" She felt compelled to refocus his child-like brain.

Of course she would be the one asking, the Service Manager wisely kept his thoughts to himself. Aubrey was a boy with a toy. "Let me show you," Kevin stepped up to the plate. He had no desire to see a ham-fisted Aubrey Hanlon repeating the disaster of a month ago when a seventy-year old rancher had contrived to raise the loader bucket of the tractor they were dealing on right through the shop roof. He went through all the basic operations first for Sabine and then for Aubrey, the tractor purring serenely through it all.

"The throwing around of the numbers" actually amounted to the throwing about of one number. It was to be a straight up-front deal, take it or leave it. "First off, I'll have to come out to your place, the Hanlon Beach and Spa," said Kevin mercilessly. "I'll need to look your old beast over. If it looks like I think it should, there will be no problem with my other customer taking it. I'm assuming that clothing is still somewhat optional out there?" he finished with a totally straight face so that Sabine almost missed it. Oh, but how little did he know what peril he was courting; Sabine had a memory longer than that of any elephant. "So on the numbers front," he continued, "here's what I can offer, no haggling, just plain old bottom-line." The figure was in the acceptable range, not the great range, and far more palatable than the astronomical figure Mr. Halitosis had floated for his scrap metal collection. Mr. Benelli came out to the farm the very next day, the deal was sealed over a cup of tea, and the Hanlons had confirmed a new friend in one Kevin Benelli ("that bloody Kevin", from now on), a friend, who, like Dick Conley never tired of verbal jousting and practical jokes. The day after that, the Hexagon truck drove into their yard with their shiny new toy aboard. To Sabine's utter consternation, the trucker suggested that since it was now their tractor, Aubrey should be the one to drive it off the truck. Aubrey would have done so too, until the man calmed Sabine down by telling her he was just joking. Apparently joking was a systemic problem in the Hexagon organization.

She picked up his line of thinking by saying, "Yeah right! My husband would drive it off all right, in three pieces, one piece for you, one piece for me, while he would take the cab with the radio. So you get up there and take it off right now before you go giving him any more crazy ideas." She had that Sabine granite-face now, the one that announced the end of playtime.

"What the hell is that hanging across the front window?" asked Aubrey squinting up from the ground.

"Oh that! Kevin said you'd understand," said the trucker, climbing onto the trailer deck. Aubrey was compelled to climb up with him and then into the tractor cab. There they were: a pair of scarlet long-johns with a Massey logo sewn into centre-rear, with a shiny new hat on the seat. Oh did Sabine ever have fun at her husband's expense, now seeing the need to inform the bemused trucker how Aubrey's back forty got so easily chilled in winter.

To begin with, the Hanlons were very tentative with their new machine. It was, after all, the centrepiece of their entire machinery line; it was the one machine that had to remain absolutely reliable. It had also cost more than anything else they had ever bought. It took Pete to put it into some sort of perspective. "Remember that a tractor is just another tractor, and a new used one is one that's already grown old. You'll have to keep it busy and soon enough the problems will show. Make a point of experimenting with everything. Get yourselves used to all of the functions. And," directed to Aubrey now, "make sure the radio works. Besides, if this beast came from a construction company, it likely got driven by all sorts of hot-footed operators, most of whom will have driven it like a backwoods cowboy on a borrowed horse. It was never theirs and they never had to pay for it."

It was a few days later that saw Sabine by herself in the cab trying to familiarize herself with everything. She checked out the lights and the lighter, the joystick for the loader and the grapple, the switches that activated the various aspects of the three-point hitch (both the ones inside and those on the rear fenders) and engaged and ran the power take-off. Yep, she could handle all of this, no problem! She looked up. There was a storage compartment above her head to one side of the radio with an obviously new add-on label affixed to the door proclaiming "TOP STORAGE". Why on earth did someone feel the need to put a label on something that was so obvious? Did they think old Joe the Yokel, or Aubrey the Tired Cop would think there was a popcorn dispenser or a coffee machine up there, or what? She opened it up and a hideous mauve bikini top fell out into her lap. There was a typed label stuck on it, "Peavey Mart hay tarp : $4.99."

"Oh Mister Abu Bensmelli, thou shalt pay for this. More than once shalt thou pay," Sabine muttered, so glad her husband was not around.

The first oil leak appeared after two weeks; it was not serious, but not very pretty, either, just niggling. Then one day Sabine was heading up the road to go and pick up a bale from their bale yard, when all by itself the tractor automatically dropped through three gears, giving her both a nasty shock and an unpleasant skirmish with whiplash. Then all was fine, which convinced a disbelieving Aubrey that his wife was hallucinating or something. Two days later the tractor did it again, this time shifting a range of four gears at high revs, and this time poetic justice! This time it was the unbeliever himself whose head nearly got taken off its mountings. Hexagon sent out their senior mechanic who was smart enough only to say that his name was "Jon"; he must have known that Sabine was the type who would want to know name, rank, date of birth, credit history, health record, name of his dog, all the man's pertinent information. Besides, he made it clear didn't want to be much associated with computers that did what they liked when they liked, or so it seemed. He was greeted by one very anxious Aubrey who was by this time thinking that it would be just their luck to have invested in a lemon. "I'll take it for a spin," said Jon. He too came back with WHS, Wobbly Head Syndrome. "I'm afraid we'll have to get our man with his laptop out here," he said shortly. "I am certain it's your computer. Welcome to our world of high technology."

"Yeah," said Aubrey, "they call the transmission 'dynashift'. They should have called it 'dynamite-shift.'"

Days later, Jon reappeared, this time accompanied by "this nerdy little fellow with a laptop," was how Sabine was to tell it afterwards. Maybe it was because he was the absolute image of the bespectacled, archetypal nerd, or maybe it was because he was so deeply embedded in his binary code and his gigabytes, but whatever the reason was, he communicated in unintelligible grunts or with nods rather than in any recognizable language as he tapped away on his keyboard. It was a strange experience to witness, the real, live, hands-on mechanic, Jon, awaiting the judge's verdict by the back wheel. It arrived in minutes, stripped of any extraneous verbiage and in likely the only complete sentence nerd man offered up that day. "Yup, the computer is shot; you'll have to change it." With that, he packed up all his wires and retreated back into the air-conditioned cab of the truck presumably to plug in and play "Advanced Computerized Tiddly-Winks for Nerdy Folk." It was now Jon's turn to go to work, not to *repair*, you must understand, but to *replace*, this being the era of the throw-away society. But evidently he had to get something off his chest before he started.

"Here's the deal," he said a little apprehensively, not at Aubrey whom he knew would be a pushover, but at Sabine whom he knew might baulk at the proposition. "It would be smart to put in the latest upgrade." For Aubrey it would have been an immediate "Go ahead"; for Sabine this was doublespeak for "This is now going to hurt because it will cost you money, a lot of money, all because of that one little word, 'upgrade.'"

"The problem is that because it is an upgrade and supposedly an improvement on the original, it'll cost you an extra seven hundred dollars installed." Yup, just like going to the dentist to have your teeth cleaned and coming away with the unpalatable information that you need three full root canals and a shot of laughing gas to ease the pain.

"Kevin told me to bring an upgrade with me if you want to go that route. We don't have a replacement for the computer that's in there, but we think we still might be able to get one from Nebraska or some place."

Oh there is so much poetry, such hidden meaning in words like "still" and "upgrade" and "might". Aubrey got to thinking uselessly. When caught between a rock and a hard place, wiggling the toes invariably saw you digging yourself deeper and giving yourself a rash on the tail. In such circumstances, the family farmer just does not have a whole lot of choice; especially the Hanlons if they wanted to remain confident that their heads would remain somewhere in the proximity of their shoulders. So seven hundred dollars later, their tractor was cured of its sudden "urgent surging", its very own version of *delirium tremens*. The rest of the bill, thankfully, was covered by warranty, all twenty-one hundred or so that Jon threw out—no doubt to get Sabine to understand what a hell of a deal they were getting. The trouble is, was, a deal is only a deal if you have the money to pay for the deal; otherwise, a deal can be akin to a burning tire around your neck.

Two weeks later saw the Hanlons back in the Hexagon dealership picking up some parts for their plow. While Aubrey was talking shop with the parts lady, Karmen (shears and heels and such), Sabine was wandering around the showroom looking at what was on display on the shelves. Oil, grease (how exciting), grease guns, replica toys of course, packets of air freshener, gasket cement, utility … hold on a minute! Air freshener! Packets and packets of it!

"Where's Mr. Benelli today?" Sabine called out to Karmen.

"Oh, I'm afraid he'll be quite a while. He's out back with some guy, looking at his very sick combine."

"Oh good!" Sabine responded with enthusiasm. She went back to the shelves and picked up an armful of air freshener packets and placed them all around Mr. B's office. Then she "borrowed" a piece of cardboard and made up a sign with Karmen's marker pen. "DO YOUR PART TO STOP GLOBAL STINKING! USE HYPOID DEODORANT!" She hung it over a picture of some fancy yellow combine. Karmen seemed to want to say something but clearly opted not to, and the Hanlons left without ever seeing the Service Manager.

When Mr. Benelli finally made an appearance a half hour later, he was not in a good mood. The farmer with whom he had been dealing was one of those rich types who had made his fortune investing in gold or something, certainly never in farming; he also happened to be one of those who believe the workers of the world were put on this planet to keep him in the manner to which he felt entitled. Spending an hour with such a man was akin to spending an hour in Purgatory, if not in Hell. The man had left in a huff, loudly telling the Service Manager and the rest of the world who should have been listening even if they weren't, that "this damn combine better be ready in three days or there'd be big trouble." Mr. Benelli strode into his office, saw the sign, saw all the air freshener hanging from everywhere anything could hang, and exploded.

"Kaaarrrmmmeeennn," he yelled. "Are you bloody well responsible for this mess?" he shouted as she came running.

"As a matter of fact, no," she said sweetly. "I've had a parade of customers coming in all morning. It's been nonstop." Oh but she could keep a straight face with the best of them. Anyone would want to keep a straight face when Mr. Benelli was beating his war drum.

"Fine," he said. "We'll soon find out if it was you!" He was spitting mad.

Sabine took the call the next day. "Mrs. Hanlon?" said a man's voice. "How are you doing today?"

"Fine," she said noncommittally, ready to tell this bleeping telemarketer that his call amounted to nothing less than an invasion of her privacy.

"Say, do you think I smell bad or what?" said the voice.

"Pardon me?" Mrs. Hanlon was now caught totally off her guard. "Who is this?"

"Do you think I smell bad?" the question was repeated.

"What *are* you talking about?" She thought she recognized the voice now but still could not put a face to it.

"I'm talking about the fact we have a security camera in our showroom and it clearly shows you helping yourself to packets and packets of air freshener, all of which somehow finished hanging up in my office."

"Oh shoot!" Actually, Sabine used the other word, the one she never used. "I never even thought. All right, I confess and I'll be nice to you next time, I promise. Oh and by the way, thanks for asking, the tractor is working fine. And the top fits too, that is when I bother to wear it. Have a good day, Kevin." And she hung up. What else could you say to a man who sent you bikini components by courier?

It was at the regular Cole's Auction a couple of weeks later that she picked up about one hundred and fifty dog-eared plastic flowers all the colours of the rainbow, and then some, all for a dollar.

"Good eye!" said Clayton Cole when everyone else in the place was wondering where in fact Sabine's good eyes had gone.

When she and Aubrey were inevitably back one more time at Hexagon Fart Supply, as everyone local tended to call the place, one more time Sabine popped the question to Karmen at the parts desk. "Where's Mr. B?"

"Oh you can go do what you like, he won't be in this afternoon."

"Goody! Goody! Come on Aub, you too Karmen, there's nobody waiting. Oh, and switch the camera off too."

They hung those hideous plastic flowers from anything they could hang from in that office. Then they put them on all of the brand new machines in the showroom. They stuffed them into the filing cabinets, packed them into the drawers of the desk, had them springing gaudily from the wastepaper basket, even had them blossoming out of the spare pair of shoes Kevin kept in his office, and being plastic they would be unlikely to wilt no matter the aroma from there.

When he returned that afternoon, Mr. Benelli repressed the urge to go ballistic, really struggled with himself to contain his ire. He didn't have time for this, this tomfoolery. Wait a sec! Of course! Of course he knew exactly who was responsible. He phoned the Hanlon number. A lady's voice answered with the sweetest of hellos.

"Truce!" he said.

"No truce!" she replied.

"You win!" he said and hung up. "Kaaarrrmmmeeennn!..."

Chapter Nine
AMONG OTHER THINGS, A VISIT TO THE THEATRE

*N*o matter how much and how fast tractors and machinery in general might change technologically, biologically the human body stays much the same as when you arrived with it in this world. Yes, it may grow like a plant, or in some cases a weed, it may blossom like a flower, or it may be given to smelling like a decomposing onion, but fundamentally you cannot change it. Oh for sure, as with any car or truck, you can affix all the fancy hood ornaments you desire, you can paste your very own stickers on it by giving yourself a tattoo, you can even paint or stain it different colours as folks do with their hair, lips and skins. But in the last analysis, you pretty well have to stick with the same chassis and transmission that you first arrived with. This is not to say that science has not taken great leaps and strides when it comes to ministering unto the body, and repairing it too. It has: so much so that even the most complicated and sensitive of organ transplants have become routine. Knees and hips are regularly replaced, hearts and kidneys transplanted, prosthetic limbs are used to supplant damaged hands or feet, stomachs can be stapled so they don't get bigger, and breasts and chests can be inflated with silicone to ensure they do. While the service managers of the medical industry— the GPs, the surgeons and the dentists—work their magic, there is a whole other elective industry that exists in its own right, the glamour and cosmetics industry. This has grown exponentially in humanity's bid to add style to the drab, curvature to the flat, lift to the sunken, and so on. But to most any farmer, this represents little more than unnecessary frivolity. The bearer is darn lucky to have the disposable income to alter those looks the Creator saw fit to endow him or her with in the first place. What other animal, a farmer might ask, gets to change its appearance on a whim, or would even want to change its appearance? Can you imagine Mr. Porky Pig going to the tattoo parlor for instance?

For farmers, the body is primarily a tool. If they abuse it as they might abuse, say their tractor, it will soon fall apart. Like government spending, aging is an inexorable and inevitable process. But the body is more complicated yet. For example, the diet you maintained in your teens and your twenties is not the diet that you should continue in your forties. For men in general and for Aubrey in particular, the wrong diet can quickly give new meaning to the concept of "downloading". It is all very well to proclaim that the man with the biggest hammer needs the biggest roof over his tool shed, but it doesn't do him any good if the only way he can ever find that hammer is by feel or with a global positioning instrument. They say of the farming lifestyle that at least you get your daily exercise naturally, but even here technology has intervened. It has replaced your horse and your legs with your quad. You don't have to walk pretty much anywhere; let your Honda, your Kawasaki or your Suzuki do the walking. This is all a long way of saying that Aubrey was beginning to show distinct symptoms of sag, heavy sag. As with any loader tractor, too much weight in the bucket puts too much pressure on the wheels, the primary means of locomotion. So it goes with the body; knees begin to creak and complain, hips begin to telegraph anxiety, fingers and toes decide to freeze way quicker than they ever did in youth because of too many near misses with frostbite. Luckily the body is not quite as prone as the tractor to spring an oil leak, but it does happen.

Other things start to go wrong too. Hearing is one, with wives never really connecting impairment to their husband's hearing per se because of hubby's penchant for selective hearing. Only one day when she is feeling romantic and says to her spouse, "C'mon honey, let's go play with Slinky," and he replies, "Hold on now dear, we lost the dice for that game years ago," does she know that either it is the hearing or the mind that has finally gone.

When you are exposed to machinery on and off all year, when you ignore all of the education out there and fail to wear your headphones when you should, or if you're simply so untidy you can never put a hand on a pair when you need them—even though you purchased seven pairs and placed them strategically around the farm—you as a farmer put your hearing in jeopardy. Worse yet, farmers and hearing aids are not a comfortable match. Ever! You can't leave them in if you are jumping in and out of tractors or if you're trying to stay still while restraining a two hundred-pound calf. And then there's that apocryphal story of the old dirt-digger whose one hearing aid fell out unnoticed into a bowl of mixed nuts he was grazing on, and he finished up eating it along with the cashews; a two thousand dollar snack you might say.

Eyesight was another of those things that deteriorated until finally came the day you knew, or more likely someone close to you knew, you were not seeing things quite the way you once did. Sabine could see it happening in her husband, could see that he couldn't see the way he was supposed to see. One half of the trick is getting the sufferer to admit that what he or she is seeing is in fact only half of the story, the other half being hidden in myopia, macular degeneration or nascent cataracts. Aubrey finally acquiesced to an eye exam, largely in a desperate bid to convince himself it wasn't as bad as all that, and certainly not as bad as Sabine would have him believe. Besides, it had always been serious anathema to him to spend money on himself without his wife accruing at least some of the benefit; farm couples tend to think like that! "But I can see perfectly well," Aubrey would insist.

"You can't. Truth be known, you probably couldn't tell the difference between a tennis ball and a mushroom." That was the jibe that achieved what all of her bleating and cajoling had so far failed to do.

"Fine!" he said in a mumble, "book me in." Mumble or not, Sabine was not about to miss her opportunity; she booked him in to the local eye clinic right then. She had lived with her husband long enough to know he would have changed his mind by supper time.

The best way to characterize the various tests was to say that Aubrey was a terrible patient when it came to any medical procedure; he hated every minute of every test. It was made worse because he knew his vision was fine, a little ragged perhaps, but fine nonetheless. His confidence was however gradually dismantled test by test, until the point when the optician informed him very bluntly that he needed glasses, absolutely needed glasses if he proposed to continue driving on the highway. "As you now are, you are a hazard to yourself and everybody else on the road," he said, not afraid to mince his words. "So you need to sit down with one of the ladies out front and get things in motion. You'll be amazed at the difference glasses will make, I promise you." The optician had been here before, many times!

Now Aubrey was one of those who always sought out an ally in every critical field of endeavour in which he was involved. Maybe it was because he had been a policeman and knew the value of a support network. He had Kevin Benelli in the world of machinery, Pete in the livestock world, Quincy on the cowboy scene, and Dr. Green in the medical field. Now he needed an ally in the visual world. A lady who introduced herself simply as Celeste took him under her wing, immediately sensing this bumbling country bumpkin would need all the help he could get, despite an obviously solicitous wife. Farmers tended to be like that: great in the field and in the barn, but like babes in diapers in a world like hers.

"Nothing to be ashamed of," said this Celeste, trying her best to put him at ease. "After this you'll be able to see how beautiful your wife really is." She winked at Sabine.

"God forbid!" retorted Sabine. "It's taken me all these years to deflect his unwanted attentions. But now he'll probably go looking for greener pastures when he sees all the wrinkles I really have." She laughed.

"Listen chick, you ain't the only creature around here with wrinkles," said Aubrey. "Now what happens next?"

"Well, we need to decide exactly what you need. A lot of farmers like bi-focals so they can use the bottom half of the lens to see little things up close when they're fixing something small. The rest of the lens gives them the longer perspective. Then of course we need to decide on frames. You also need to decide if you want or need transition lenses, though they are more money." This was all said, well, so nicely; Aubrey wasn't getting his usual cynical impression that here was the company's obedient servant trying to fill the company's bank account to bursting.

"Transition lenses?" he said. "So what do they do? Get me a bus ticket to Nanaimo for free?" Aubrey was off on his funny train.

Celeste laughed along so graciously. Sabine on the other hand told her man to behave himself and listen to the lady. This wasn't something simple like buying a screwdriver, she said.

"Transition lenses are the ones that go dark in bright sunlight and with glaring snow. Lots of folks really like them."

"Pete has them," Sabine felt compelled to tell "her child".

"Pete hates them," said Aubrey. "He says they take so long to get back to normal after you come in from the sunshine."

"Does he have the grey lenses or the brown ones?" Celeste asked.

"The grey," said Sabine, the fount of all knowledge.

"If you like to use sunglasses, then I'd recommend them. And I'd choose brown. They tend to be a lot softer. But again, it is a question of budget."

"How much more are they?" Aubrey was starting to panic now.

"Do it!" interrupted his lawyer. "He's always squinting in bright sunshine or when there's a pile of snow around. Honestly, sometimes he puts me in mind of a Canada goose that has lost its way."

"With a comment like that, my dear, you shouldn't assume that all Canada geese mate for life." Again it was Celeste who laughed graciously as this couple jousted on her time.

"Well, let's go for brown. Now let's talk frames then, so we can get a handle on the full picture. Come on over here to our frame section and take a look."

The "cosmetic look" and the farmer are surely a contradiction of someone's terms. As Celeste handed him one frame after another to try on and check out in the mirror, Aubrey started to giggle. "Darn it!" he said. "Now I'm beginning to understand why it's so difficult for a woman to choose a pair of earrings. Boy, do I ever look cool in these. What do you think, hon, should I go with these?"

"These" were Buddy Holly glasses with thick, heavy black frames which would certainly have made Aubrey into something far cooler than he had ever been—if he were thirty years younger and a 1960s wastrel or musician. Sabine told him to grow up and stop wasting everybody's time.

"But seriously though, haven't you got a frame that's like, virtually indestructible. I am a dumb farmer who has a tendency to walk into things, fall over things and fall off things. I am a man who can barely walk a mile in winter boots without falling over them at least twice."

If Celeste was wondering whether she was dealing with Captain Klutz himself, she wisely refrained from saying so. "Aha, so you need these!" she said, taking what at first glance appeared to be a flimsy wire frame whose arm she twisted into the shape of a question mark before it sprang back into its original shape. Then came the telling moment, the one that Aubrey knew was his opening. "I have a brother-in-law up north who is a farmer too," Celeste continued. "He's always doing dumb things like leaving his glasses on the wheel of the tractor while he crawls under some machine or other. Then he forgets about them and two minutes later he finds out he just ran them over."

"I don't do dumb things," said Aubrey severely.

"Oh, oh, please get that in writing and get it stamped by a Commissioner of Oaths, why don't you?" interceded his advocate. "So your brother-in-law wrecked his glasses?"

"Well, the last time he went and did it, he brought them in to me and I managed to straighten them out enough that they were usable. You won't be able to do that with your Buddy Holly frames, that's for sure. But once again, you're looking at more money."

"How much more?" Anyone would have thought Aubrey was the manager of a thrift shop.

"Do it!" said Sabine, now lawyer, Justice of the Peace, and Alberta's Attorney-General all rolled into one. "When you drive over them, as I know you will, you can bring them into our new friend Celeste who can straighten them out for you." Was she an unwitting part of his "alliance strategy" or what?

"You bet," said Celeste. "Now that we have decided, I have to tell you it'll take about ten days before they will be in, but I'll put a rush on them because the doctor says you shouldn't be driving the way you are. And then, as I said, you can see how truly beautiful your wife is."

"Yeah, and how unbelievably ugly her husband is when he first looks in the mirror. But you'd better be here for me next month when I walk in with them all bent to, to heck." Aubrey should have known better than to utter that last statement. Murphy's Book of Modern Laws, upgraded second edition, stresses something to the effect that if you knowingly and wilfully set yourself up for a self-fulfilling prophecy, it will happen; very likely on your birthday if the planets are in alignment, and even if they're not. Sabine simply said nothing, but she knew right then that some form of disaster was surely in the offing.

The glasses duly came in. Celeste did her duty and fitted them on Aubrey's odd-shaped skull. And best of all, she reminded him to come on back at any time if he ran into a lamp post or a problem. He studied the result in the mirror. Wow! These things almost put him among the ranks of the intelligent! But the split lens was going to take some getting used to.

"Wear them in before you try driving," warned his new ally.

Actually it wasn't the first accident that caused him to go back and see Celeste, and even though in hindsight it was the more traumatic, Sabine still knew this wasn't the one.

At the time, Aubrey was realigning the downspout that fed the rain water from the gutter of the roof into their prized three hundred gallon water storage tank on the ground. The aluminum downpipe had somehow detached itself from the end of the gutter and was waving merrily in the wind. With a few pop rivets, he was intent on attaching it to the wall bracket he had just made. Being too lazy to go and get the fancy ladder that he, or was it she, had bought at an auction way back in the mists of agri-time, he settled for a wooden monstrosity lying against the wall, ready to be carted away on the next trip to the landfill. He propped it against the house in such a way that he had to climb up over the tank to reach the top of the wall, deliberately, oh so delicately skipping rung number seven because it was badly cracked. There was no fear of debris getting into the water because the tank had a hard blue plastic cover over it.

He had just finished mounting the bracket at the top of the wall when a car bearing the logo of the Wildrose Party of Alberta drove into the yard. Now for Aubrey, politics was nothing more than a blood sport, the more blood about it the better. For him, jousting with any party flunky or would-be politician was akin to that fairground game of gopher-bashing where you tried to thump the gopher with a mallet the moment he stuck his head up out of a hole. The politico would pop his head up out of some policy hole, say something exceedingly wise, provocative or dumb, and whammo, Aubrey would smack him down. The more extreme they were, left or right, the more sport was to be had. He remained perched atop his ladder as an older man and a younger woman got out of the car.

"Hi! I'm Heinzel Luden-something-or-other, the Wildrose candidate for your riding, and this is my campaign manager, Rosa Gumdrop," he said as he approached. "How are you doing today?" The plastic smile was absolutely in keeping with the artificiality of a perfect set of dentures. All Aubrey could think of though, was what an unfortunate set of names these two had to go through life with, let alone the next provincial election. But he did manage an "I'm fine thanks," and an "I'm Aubrey Hanlon."

"Can we count on your vote in the upcoming provincial election?"

"Depends," said Aubrey, hunkering down on the tenth rung. "Are you deniers of climate change, for a start?"

"Well, there's no such thing as global warming if that's what you mean," said Rosa Gumdrop launching herself like a hunting terrier on a dopey rabbit. "That's all one big myth."

"Oh, is it now?" said Aubrey getting set to pounce. "Now would you mind explaining to this old son of the soil how come you folks figure it's a myth when most scientists seem to think otherwise?"

"Let's not go there, Rosa. Let's just say the jury is still out on that one," said Mr. Whatsit, trying to steer the conversation to safer ground at the same time as endeavouring to silence his second line of artillery. "So, Mr. Hamden, what do you think about governments deliberately getting into deficit?"

Now Aubrey had no intention of miring himself in some ultra-serious discussion with such people, not because he was anti-Wildrose Party or anybody else for that matter. It was just that there was so much more potential for entertainment here, and he felt it could not be left to pass him by. In his book, people who took themselves too seriously usually deserved all they got, he concluded. "Well now, it depends if they're spending the money on themselves or on me."

"We would outlaw government deficits." That second line of artillery was not to be silenced.

"So John Maynard Keynes was just a scoundrel and a fool?" said a grinning Aubrey.

"Who?" said Miss Gumdrop.

"No," said *Heinz 57*. "It's just that his type of thinking is not really applicable to our current fiscal reality." He approached a little closer to fire his big bazooka, his pet lecture on basic economics for backwoods bozos.

Aubrey was revelling in his height advantage because he could look down on his adversaries. But the next salvo brought him down a rung.

"We wouldn't bail anybody out," said Rosa Firebrand. "No sir, not bankers, not car companies, not businesses, not even farmers." She wasn't just vehement, she was a crusader, a champion of all that is right and good and libertarian.

"What if the farmers you just mentioned were all about to go under because of a BSE crisis like the one we had or because of a drought like we had in when was it, '02 or thereabouts?" Aubrey asked acidly. "Even if the crisis, any crisis," he moved down another rung to get his point across, "even if the drought, say, was no fault of theirs? Even if the drought might have been the result of global warming?" Aubrey had now made it to the seventh rung, the one with a crack in it, and he was slowly resting his full weight upon it ready to intercept any incoming rockets with his Patriot Missile System.

BANG!

He went through that ladder in a single blur, right through the lid covering the tank, shattering the lid into multiple shards of blue plastic, and clean through into the ice-cold water in the tank. It was so cold, so utterly frigid, that when he hit bottom he surged upward like a porpoise on multivitamins for the old and infirm, partially losing his baggy sweatpants as he emerged to swing gamely onto the bottom rung of the ladder. Would you not know it? That was the very same moment Sabine chose to come out of the house. Her eyes took in the car and the logo first, then the two people standing there with eyes bulging unnaturally, and finally her soaked husband hanging onto the bottom of the ladder, with his pants around his knees.

"Aubrey Hanlon, I see you're not wearing any underwear, again!"

Aubrey Hanlon was the one who, up to this point, was unaware that the two spectators below him (a) could not have missed that inescapable fact and (b) could not for the life of them tear their eyes away.

But Sabine was not done yet, for she had absolutely no time for anyone even remotely connected with politics of any stripe. "You need to know that my husband here is a card-carrying member of the Canadian Communist Party which is why he reads Karl Marx every day and can't afford underpants. As for me, I'm an anarchist. So please have yourselves a good day and allow my husband to regain some semblance of dignity."

What else could they have done but leave?

Aubrey then did what any sodden, freezing, logical soul would have done in the circumstances; he shed his footwear and all of his clothes. That was when the question of the day came in, dropping on him like a grenade dead on target.

"Aubrey Hanlon, where are your glasses?" this from one very agitated better half.

"Ugh! My glasses? Oh, where are my glasses? I don't know where my glasses are."

"They have to be in the water tank." That statement would have been perfectly innocuous had it come from anybody else other than the great She-Dictator. "You'll have to climb back in and find them."

"Have you any idea how cold it is in there?" That question was the full extent of a rather pathetic defence.

"Have you any idea how cold it will be if I lock you out of the house tonight without your underwear? We didn't just spend hundreds of dollars on a pair of glasses for you to throw into a tank and then write them off because you can't be bothered to get off your cold duffer to go and look for them. Now get back in there and find them. Please!"

Aubrey had been a fearless policeman for many years. The pride of the force, he had faced many ugly situations, had resolved many a nasty crisis. He had even been involved in a couple of shoot-outs, had endured armed standoffs, had been assaulted, cursed, spat upon and kicked. But this, this was something else. No way, no how did you gainsay the voice of *this* authority. He had been trained to obey his senior officers, and as he had been trained, he obeyed and dropped himself meekly back into the tank. It took less than a minute to find his glasses by using his toes, and that was frigidly bad enough. But then he had to bend down and dunk his whole body into the water to retrieve them. By then his heart was thumping like the engine of a diesel locomotive climbing its way into the Rocky Mountains, his skin was a pallid blue, and to add insult to injury, the frame on his glasses was bent. Trust Sabine, though; without any fuss, she straightened them out Sabine-style so that they were relatively close to what they once were, save for the fact that Aubrey seemed to resemble an owl with an off-kilter eye. Oh well!

The second accident was, well, still an accident but less preventable. When you choose to move cattle, you have to have your wits about you, especially when there are calves in the mix. Matata's calf, of course, was excessively wild even when it was first born, actually managing a chew on Sabine's plump rump while she and Aubrey were tagging and vaccinating it. Now it was running amok. Aubrey tried to block it with his cane and his bountiful girth to stop it heading north down the alleyway, but this little dogey had visions of the true north strong and free—and this slow-witted, slow-moving country porpoise in his way would have to move itself or be moved. It came down by default to the latter option, a skinful of *genius humanitas* being dumped unceremoniously into a tangle of legs and arms and tasseled toque, spectacles going one way, stock cane the other. Not surprisingly, this same heap of personhood, sounding much like Mars the Roman god of war must have sounded, rose up in some fury, only to be upended one more time by a calf that was now highly concerned that mama was heading south without him. And in the manner of his going down this second time, Mr. Hanlon managed to tread upon those sacred lenses, twisting the frame into a shape likely never seen before by any dispenser of artificial eyesight. Worse yet, he gained an excessively fat lip for all his efforts.

So when the good Celeste saw him walk through the door at the eye clinic, she knew. Right there she knew, and burst out laughing. She just could not help it. There he was, her newest customer, with a bottom lip hanging so low it resembled the ramp of the Horseshoe Bay to Nanaimo ferry about to disgorge its load, and with a pair of wretched-looking all bent-up glasses clutched in his hand. Sabine could not help herself either, laughter being contagious and all. She too crumpled up in hysterics, the two of them causing the other customers in the establishment to look on in wonderment at the poor unfortunate individual who seemed to have prompted such merriment. They too exploded when, after the two ladies had scaled it down enough, Aubrey popped his question.

"Pleath Mith, can you pleath try and fix thith?" Fat lips were not made for talkin' any more than fat ankles were made for walkin'.

Both Celeste and Sabine had to sit down before they fell down. So did a few other people it seemed. Finally Celeste, professional that she was, took a look at the glasses. In her time she had restored quite a few pairs back to utility but these, these were a challenge. Of course, as if it had a bearing on how the glasses were to turn out, she had to hear the story of how it had happened. Good old Sabine, not content to recount just the calf story, she had to tell—and embellish at Aubrey's expense—how he had fallen off his ladder and into the water tank. The only thing she left out, thankfully, was the absence of underwear. That would have been too much.

"You know what, I'm gonna be a sit-down comic in my next life," Aubrey was thinking. "Standing up is something I don't seem able to do for very long."

With the human body, though, when it tends to rain, it also tends to pour. It's almost as if the other parts of the system that are not ailing today suddenly see the need to vie for daddy's attention tomorrow. "What about us? What about us?" the arthritic knees start to scream. Feeling left out, an ankle might decide on a twist and a shout so that it can be wrapped in swaddling clothes for a week or two. That's what happens when men like Aubrey get old: the decaying body betrays the virile mind. And that's natural aging. Throw the dangers of farming, the so-called occupational hazards, into the equation with all of the quad busting and calf butting, all of the cuts and the sprains and the bruises, all of the excrement, the spores and the dust, it's a wonder the agricultural body survives at all.

The next thing to really trouble Aubrey over time was his feet. The initial round of pain started over an attack of gout. Where it came from and where it subsequently went, Aubrey had no idea. Truly, heroically even, Aubrey tried not to be a wimp; but when your big toe feels like it's clamped between the jaws of an unyielding alligator, and you have to do something ordinary like walk not only is your progress painfully slow, but you are also prone to uttering phrases not usually heard in polite circles. Okay, so a regimen of pills prescribed by Dr. Green took care of that.

But his feet were not done yet, not by a long shot. He began to get more exercise by walking whenever and wherever he could (he and Sabine together), in his case with the added incentive of preventing his stomach from colonizing the rest of his body. And then the pain began, first throughout one foot and then the other; first just niggling but then excruciating until the day came when a further trip to the doctor was called for. The trouble was that Aubrey always had a "thing" about going to the doctor, any doctor. This was something he understood, however, because in his first life he had encountered plenty of people who had a "thing" about cops. It was not that he distrusted doctors; it was just that they were called upon to know so much, a lot of it unknowable. And even then, a good deal of knowledge these days had such a short shelf life; you had to keep abreast of all developments if you wanted to stay on top of things. Only when he was in dire straits would Aubrey even consider going to a doctor, and then only with his lawyer for life by his side, goading him on. Doctors always made him feel like some kind of specimen in a jar that someone had brought in after dredging the pond in the backyard. But at least with Dr. Green you could attempt a joke and not have him look at you as if you had just passed gas in his examination room. Doctors took themselves seriously. They had to given what they were asked to deal with, the whole gamut of society from bleating hypochondriacs to the walking dead. Illness and disease are no cause for humour, so of course doctors take themselves seriously.

Dr. Green, though, could always be relied upon to be blunt. "You need to exercise," he told Aubrey.

"I do," said Aubrey.

"Then a lot more," said the doctor. "Walk five kilometers a day."

"I do," said Aubrey.

"You do not," said his moral custodian. "Two clicks a day if we're lucky. And it takes a whole half day to do that!"

"Well, it would take you half a day too if you had sore feet like I do," Aubrey pouted indignantly.

"Well, if the pain is that bad, maybe you should go and see a podiatrist and have him take a look at your feet. They're not particularly good-looking feet, by the way, so you can put your socks back on. And when you go, make a point of putting a clean pair of socks on!" said Dr. Green mercilessly as he got up and pointedly scrubbed his hands.

So they paid a visit to the foot doctor, who, to Aubrey's great surprise, they got in to see right away. They were ushered into his office, Aubrey accompanied by his lawyer/accountant/moral guardian, and the doctor sat him down before asking him what the problem was. As one would have expected, the good doctor wrote it all down. Then he asked Aubrey to remove his shoes and socks. The sudden, sharp intake of breath had Sabine thinking for one awful moment that Aubrey had ignored her directive to put on clean socks. But the doctor's first utterance told her it wasn't an issue of socks at all.

"Those things are not feet," he said looking down in apparent astonishment at these, these, call them prehensile toes that poked way up into the air like a well-travelled monkey's. "No, nobody could ever call those things feet, least of all a practising podiatrist. I don't rightly know what I'd call them, but certainly not feet. You must have had trouble all your life, no? I mean walking, running and jumping, and so forth."

"No, not ever," said Aubrey unwilling to go further and suggest that this was maybe why he had always been such a clumsy athlete.

"Did you wear socks that were too tight for you when you were a kid?"

"Well, maybe a bit," he said grudgingly. He did not want to go further and confess how his mother had a thing about knitting bullet-proof socks so unyielding to the feet that those same feet were essentially bound and gagged for as long as he wore the socks.

"Well, let's take a look and see what my computer has to say. We'll take a stride profile of your feet. The computer will tell us how you distribute your weight when you walk. Then we'll see if it's even possible to come up with an insert to put in your shoes."

So Aubrey was duly assessed by the wonders of technology as he walked across some special kind of sensor pad.

"Huh!" said the doctor. "Would you look at that now? Even my computer doesn't think those things are feet. Look at the pattern on the screen. That profile could have been made by a magpie walking across a hot tin roof. But if you wish, we could try and put together an insert using the information we have. I'm sure whatever we come up with will be something that will help."

"What will it cost?" said Aubrey.

"Just do it!" barked the Auditor-General. "I can't go on listening to his constant whining anymore."

"Joy and goodwill to you too, Madam," said Aubrey sourly.

It all ended well. The new inserts worked. The pain went away. The constant whining was no more. Soon enough, Aubrey could not even remember in which pair of boots he had last seen the inserts.

To return to the basic theme of the general fragility of the human body, and of Aubrey Hanlon's body in particular (both of them in a strictly agricultural setting), when your tractor dies, either you fix it or get another one. But when your body wants to flake out, your choices are far more limited. Can you go on doing what you have always done? Should you even try to keep doing it? Is there a point in time when your disconnected mind finally has to listen up to what your body is telling it: that chasing cows on your two little fat legs is no longer an option, that holding down a bucking, three hundred-pound critter while "wife-y" gives it a shot for coccidiosis or pneumonia is actually putting both of you in danger because of your enfeebled body? It gets to be downright embarrassing when the calf you are restraining gets right on up and walks through the barn door as if you're an overgrown flea riding on its back. And what about those organs: your organs, the ones you cannot see, the heart, the lungs, and all of the plumbing? It all came to a head when Dr. Green first opined that at Aubrey's, advancing age, he ought to have a full "physical". The word "physical" was enough to put Aubrey instantly on his guard; he had heard the apocryphal stories of the doctor giving you the finger while checking out your prostate gland. But the doctor's recommendation, one endorsed wholeheartedly by Aubrey's gendarme for life, was an even more unpleasant brush with reality. The doctor said that Aubrey should get himself booked in for a routine colonoscopy.

"For a what?" asked Aubrey, incredulously. It was, for him anyway, the wrong question to ask. He should have asked something along the lines of, "What does a routine colonoscopy involve?" but he didn't.

"Because you are now at *that* age," said the doctor unsympathetically. "I'm younger than you and I've had it done."

"Do it!" thundered the Commissioner of Police.

"What does it cost?" Aubrey was now clutching at straws.

"Nothing," said the doctor, "at least nothing but a little bit of your precious dignity."

"Do it! Twice!" The Commissioner of Police was clearly an ardent believer in corporal punishment.

The booking was made and Aubrey was consigned to the meat market on a Thursday morning, the first carcass on the day's "ass-embly line", as Aubrey was to put it later.

"I'm a little worried about you," said Sabine as they were driving into town.

"Why?" asked Aubrey.

"Well, you do know that you will have to wear one of those hospital gowns, don't you?"

"What hospital gowns?"

"Those back-to-front hospital gowns that never quite do the job of covering you up."

"If you had told me that," said Aubrey slowly, "if you had told me that before, I would never have agreed to go ahead with this." He meant every word of it; he would never have gone through with it.

"I know," said Sabine smugly. "That's why I didn't tell you until now."

"So you betrayed me?"

"Yes, I betrayed you and I'm really sorry. And unless they have an extra-extra large, you're going to need a 'wide load' sign." Sabine was making it a little too obvious how much enjoyment she was getting out of the situation.

"Well, dear lady, one of these days you'll be old too. Like next week. Then you too might have to get the plumbing checked, and you'll be whining at me for not holding your tiny little hand."

"Oh don't I know it! That's why I am razzing you now, my dearest." They had arrived at the hospital. Sabine watched her man all the way to the door, and then waited an extra minute just to be sure he didn't sneak back out.

Aubrey and hospitals had never been a good match. He was sweating with dread as soon as he got inside. But the nurse in charge was great; they darn well had to be, thought Aubrey, because they were dealing with bums like him. They were a far cry from cops, too, that was for sure. "Please take off all your clothes and get into this gown," she directed.

"The last time a nice lady said that to me, I was playing Thor, the god of thunder in the Bolshoi Ballet," he said. The lady knew at once she was talking to a farmer and a clown, if not an ex-cop.

"Oh and how good you must have looked in your tutu," she offered. "You know you put these gowns on backwards, don't you?"

"But what if my tail lights stick out?" said Aubrey, not quite done with clowning.

"Well at least I'll be able to tell if you're about to stop, or turn left or right for that matter," she responded without missing a beat. "To us, a body is just that, another body. A pound of flab is a pound of flab. As for flashing tail lights, big or small, we've seen them all."

"Are you trying to tell me something?" said Aubrey.

"Yes," she said. "Hurry up and do what you're supposed to do, or I'll have to go find a smaller gown!" So much for decorum, Aubrey was thinking.

Aubrey entered the curtained-off cubicle, put his expansive body into its own barely-curtained wrap-around and lay down on the bed to wait. He didn't have to wait long before he was summarily wheeled off to some joker's idea of a "theatre". God how he wished it was real live theatre with real live make-believe. Hell, he would even have settled for *The Sound of Music* rather than this performance. A nurse took his vital signs, and she didn't look remotely like a youthful Julie Andrews dancing across the meadow.

"Look," Aubrey said to her. "I'm not one of those easy-going, happy-go-lucky folks who will lie here contentedly watching a horse doctor stick a fire hose up...."

"Give him a shot right where you'd give it to a horse," said a doctor's voice with a distinctly Irish twang.

He woke up an hour later. The same older nurse who had received him initially was there to greet him again.

"Well, did they find a pot of gold at the end of the rainbow?" he asked.

"Nah, just a pile of tired old bones like you'd expect to find in an elephants' graveyard. But they did find a polyp, along with a half-digested mouse. They sent the polyp to the lab to be analyzed, as they usually do. They're most always benign."

"What did they do with the mouse?"

"Oh, they gave it to the doctor's cat."

Just at that moment Sabine arrived. The nurse and Sabine apparently knew each other. "He's good to go," said the nurse. "But you'll have to bring him back next week because there's two feet of vacuum cleaner hose we couldn't get out."

Aubrey was not the only joker around the place.

Chapter Ten
THE HEAD WADDLER

Government represents the "they" people love to hate, those faceless bureaucrats who have so much impact on all that we do, and on what we neglect to do. Try not filing your taxes on time, for example! Yet government in all its aspects is what stands between us and chaos. One only has to take a look at all the failed states in the world to realize how incredibly fortunate those of us who live in the western democracies actually are. People are dying daily to achieve what we ourselves take for granted. Yet governments, like people, depend upon those intangible qualities like credibility and trust, transparency and integrity, if they are to function well. Even then, given the volatile nature of humanity itself, government policies can be, and are too often, crafted to benefit insiders; this, in turn, detracts from people's overall belief in democracy and in their own system. Every democracy the world over ends up in a struggle with itself. Apathy, cynicism, marginalization, crony capitalism; all do their bit to erode the process and render it meaningless. What's good for a company or a corporation is not necessarily good for the public good, and so it goes!

What of government's place in agriculture, then? How do farm folks actually perceive government and its role in the agricultural sector? Farm folk tend to be a different breed, as the Hanlons found out in all their years on the land. Furthermore, the longer they were on the farm, the more like their friends and neighbours they became: independent, sometimes a little too fiercely; ornery like the skunk that demands and expects right of way; forthright like few politicians could ever be; and generally honest, although every grocery store has its share of bad apples. When it came down to dealing with government and its officials and functionaries, these qualities could all too easily work against country folk. Caught in a supposedly free enterprise system, oftentimes the only thing that seemed free about it was the labour expended by farmers to bring their products to the market. Inevitably over time, family farmers became in some measure wards of the state, and that could never sit well with such people. Like so many, Aubrey and Sabine hated having to avail themselves of what was on offer through a variety of government programs, but like so many small Canadian farmers, they had little choice if they wanted to be around for the long term. So yes, when it came right down to it, they were dependent to some degree on the goodwill of the taxpayer. All too often though, the other side of the coin never came into view: the one where it was the taxpayers and the consumers who were dependent on the farmer for cheap groceries. And if the truth was to be emphasized, those same taxpayers and consumers were getting away with a hell of a deal; the problem was that the only time they might recognize the bargain they were getting would be when food itself became scarce for some reason.

So the question bears repeating: Should government even have a place in agriculture? But then again, maybe a better question might be, do those men and women down there on the traditional family farm, people just like the Hanlons, know where and even if the family farm fits into the hierarchy of government priorities? Do we in Canada have a long-term, non-partisan agricultural national strategy? Or a national food policy? If the answers are yes and yes, then why do the frontline food producers not know about it and where they fit? If the answers are both no, heaven forbid, then the question becomes, why is this so? Why do so many people of the soil ask why government policy is so consistently aimed at tilting the rules in the interests of the big players, those corporate entities with deep enough pockets to lobby the political elites, with enough funds to divert to the political war chests of their preferred political party, with the spare coin to fund university research that will ultimately advance their own bottom line because they will patent the knowledge? Like so many of the bit players on the land, the Hanlons became increasingly cynical. Why wouldn't they when no matter what they did, they still ended up essentially as price-takers at their own farm gate? In the final analysis, was and is the family farm now an anachronism, or was and is there a viable role for it in the GST, the Great Scheme of Things? With a measly two percent of the voting electorate, were farmers' votes even worth counting? With the levels of political posturing and partisanship in the corridors of power, was and is there any point in seeking to develop an ongoing conversation when any allegiances are likely tied more to the latest polls than to any principles?

Of course like everybody else, Aubrey and Sabine could see the need for basic regulation because that was common sense. But regulation for the sake of regulation could so easily become a hollow shell inside of which all sorts of irregular activities might go on. And so it was that in 2013, European consumers could not tell whether the hamburgers they were chewing on were bovine or equine. It could even evolve to a point where the following appeared in *Beef Illustrated*, February 2013: "According to a UPI article, suppliers in Hungary have been dyeing cuts of pork to make them look like beef, and exporting the product to Sweden. Over the past two years, Sweden has imported ninety-five tons of the disguised pork, which was labelled as 'Argentinian tenderloin.'" So yes, it would be nice to know the "beef" you were chowing down was in fact the genuine thing and not a recycled mattress. Of course certain farming practices and protocols have to be regulated because after all, farmers still produce much of the food we all eat. It's just that when the regulatory process becomes a free-standing, self-administering, and self-evaluating empire in its own right, problems will arise.

So to the Hanlons and many other tillers of the dirt and chasers of hoof and feather, the role of government could easily assume too heavy a hand, could so easily become misguided. Aubrey had seen up close in his other life how bureaucracy and red tape could all but strangle a policy or a process that was worth promoting. So at this juncture, it is perhaps instructional to understand how so many in the farming community perceived the rise of the now prevailing malaise they called B.S.

No, B.S. is not what you're thinking! B.S. refers to "Bureaucratic Syndrome". The big, old, high school dictionary Aubrey still possessed defined the word "syndrome" thus:

"**syndrome**: 1. A group of signs and symptoms that collectively indicate or characterize a disease, psychological disorder, or other abnormal condition. 2. Any complex of symptoms of the existence of an undesirable condition or quality."

It was sad, then, that so many on the land saw government as some form of malevolent fungus, or worse still, some sort of malignant disease. Yet the old adage that "one's perception is one's reality" holds true wherever you are, in whatever you do. At the tail-end of the twentieth century and the outset of the twenty-first, government was suddenly *THE* place to work. You were assured of a suite of benefits, a pay scale commensurate with or above that of the private sector, and an indexed pension if you made it to Nirvana. If you didn't and were made redundant, a generous severance package would help you refocus.

Here's how ex-cop Aubrey Hanlon came to see it all, experienced as he was in such things. If you were young, bright, and had the "right stuff", you should head off to some hothouse university and pick up a grab-bag of courses, some useful, some not so useful, but all with high-falutin' names like "Numerological Schematics and Statistics in Agricultural Architecture". You would then march forth into the big wide world and represent these courses not as something so banal as your education, but as your "portfolio" or your "skill set". You would make certain that you cried out, shouted from the rooftops, what a brilliant "multi-tasker" you were: how you could tie your shoelaces while driving down Highway 2; how you could chew gum while walking and dancing and scuba diving; and how you could balance chubby chicken in one hand and knit socks with the other. Your first goal in this era of goals and objectives is to spin the mirage that you are utterly indispensable. The aim is to get the message out there; the whole office, department, team or company will collapse without you. You work on building up your own empire with your own hand-picked, preferably sycophantic underlings who will remain loyal to you because you have convinced them they owe it all to you primarily because you were the one smart enough to hire them in the first place. Naturally it is important to ensure that you have your very own "Director of Communications" who can broadcast the news about all the stellar work you are doing to keep the world unfolding as it should. You must also educate "your people", those same underlings, to believe that they, like you, are knights in shining armour, mounted upon majestic white chargers coming to rescue civilization as we know it from "Apocalypse Now", Mad Cow Disease, and Bird Flu. Have them take ownership of their jurisdiction to the degree that only they can know the truth, the whole truth and nothing but the truth, for they are the truth! Have them wrap it all up in an artfully embroidered Mission Statement together with the requisite "Summary of Goals and Objectives" and a "Statement of Performance Parameters and Indicators". Revise these annually as you expand your reach, and ensure that the importance of your own function keeps up with the times. Above all, since you are an Obedient Public Servant, be obliging but not fawning. Bill Hockenhammer was given a demonstration of this approach a long time ago, in the days when Coles Auction Mart was still where it used to be on the edge of town and when it was still in the cattle business.

Bill was the man who sorted the animals that came into the auction into uniform groups, packaged in such a way as to appeal to the buyers. It was a taxing job, one that really did call for a good eye and a deep knowledge of cattle in all their variations. On this particular day, there were scores of calves to sort through. And would you not know it, the man from CFIA, the Canada Food Inspection Agency, was there. As government officials occasionally do, he appeared on the scene as if he had dropped inexplicably out of the sky. He parked his broad beam atop the plank fence along the main alleyway, and presumably because he thought he had to make his worthy presence felt and raise the government flag, he launched into a colourful commentary on all that was going on. Naturally, as all government officials must, he had to demonstrate his considerable expertise. Now when you are the one tasked to sort through fifteen hundred calves in a clean two hours, you are unlikely to take too kindly to a self-anointed sports commentator adding his opinion to the mix. And this was craggy Bill Hammerhead as he was known, not some easygoing laid-back cowboy on hand to help out. It was not long before Bill had had enough.

"Hey you!" said this mean-looking s.o.b cowman that nobody in his right mind would want to do the "Tangerine Tango" with, "Who the bleep do you think you are anyhow?"

Well of course as the government representative of the GST, the Great Scheme of Things, he came up with a reply something along the lines of "I de man!" Totally unintimidated, he jumped down from the fence and shook Bill's hand. "Pete Simmons, Canada Food Inspection Agency. Here's my card."

"I don't need no bleeping card any more than I need your bleeping chatter. I need you to shut the bleep up. I need you to get off that bleeping fence and give me a bleep-bleep hand, or I need you to get the bleep outa here. Your choice!" To Bill's utter astonishment, the man offered to help.

"I'm your man," he said. Smart fellow that he was, he was sending the message, "I'm one of us."

The less enlightened bureaucrats, on the other hand, inevitably contrive to send the wrong message. They let you know quite clearly that if anything, you were put on this earth so you could be told what to do and when to do it by the likes of them and their ilk in the governing class. Sabine ran into the clutches of one of these when she responded to an ad in the paper suggesting farmers call this particular government number to explain any problems they might have encountered with the newly mandated ear-tags ranchers were required to use. The tags were a great idea—if only they would stay in place. Traceability was assured, identification was certain, and all things would fall into place in a Foodie Empire where order was paramount. If only the tags stayed put. Trouble was, they didn't. The G&GPUT folks, the Great & Glorious People Up-There people, the scientists and government apparatchiks, had made certain false suppositions about where a cow was likely to put her head. But nobody had told the cows that they were to follow this government line of thinking, so those same stupid cows put their heads wherever they felt like it: into willow bushes and between the steel bars of bale feeders, between strands of barb wire that snagged ears and tags on barbs, all with the result of pulling out the owner's fancy label. Of the first one hundred and thirty animals they tagged, the Hanlons lost at least ten tags within six weeks. Dear Sabine, always one to do her bit in the name of government research and so forth, called up the number and found herself toe-to-toe, voice-to-voice with a male empire-builder of the arrogant sort: some elevated keeper of the keys, files, and other obscure state secrets.

"Good morning to you," Sabine said brightly. "I'm calling to tell you about our experience with your newly mandated ear-tags. I'm responding to your ad in the paper calling on farmers to discuss any problems they have had."

"Good morning and thank you for calling. Have you had a couple of problems?" Okay, this was starting out on the right foot at least.

"Well yes. These tags don't seem to stay in as well as they are meant to. We've lost about ten out of a hundred and thirty in the first six weeks of using them."

"Well clearly you have a problem. And when I say you, I mean you. The tags do stay in place when they are properly inserted, that I can tell you. Our research makes that part very clear. You must be doing something wrong." The man was not about to be gainsaid.

"I see. Something wrong, you say. What do you mean by 'doing something wrong'?"

"Well, are you absolutely sure you know what you are doing? Are you putting the tags in as per the manufacturer's instructions? Are you reading the instructions correctly?"

"Hold on a second now. I hope you're not implying that we don't know how to use a tagger or worse still, that we don't know how to read, are you?" Sabine was very put off by the man's suggestion and she wanted him to know it.

"Madam, it's entirely up to you to decide what I'm implying. If the hat fits, then maybe you should wear it." It was not so much what he said as the sigh of exasperation at the end of his statement that set Sabine off.

"Look Mister, you're darn lucky you're on the end of a phone line or I'd come right down there and put a tag in your ear with the name 'L-O-S-E-R' written on it! Oh, and thank you for not taking due diligence, that's D-I-L-I-G-E-N-C-E in listening to my concerns. Please be sure and have a better day after I'm gone." She hung up with pizzazz, took a deep breath, and started to laugh.

Then came that awful day they attended the meeting at the district agricultural office, the day that a couple of government technocrats came to deliver the great good news about all that the federal and provincial governments were doing on behalf of farmers, (you farmers), so they could keep their heads just above water provided there was no wind. Under the masthead of "Growing Forward"(was this something along the lines of Chairman Mao's "Great Leap Forward", the one that turned out to be a great leap backward?), farmers were assured that they had not been forgotten by their surrogate mamas up there in government heaven. The thing is, the presenters were good people, very nice people, and people of obvious integrity and goodwill who manifestly believed in all that they were doing. Well of course, Aubrey found himself thinking, when you are swanning around dispensing government charity to the needy, it is bound to be a great feeling. But such "feel-good" meetings are only feel-good if your audience is sufficiently clued in to know what you are talking about and, furthermore, whether they can see the direct and unimpeded benefit without wondering about all the hidden implications. The key word was "unimpeded". "Why must government technocrats craft these programs to be so incredibly cumbersome and convoluted," both Aubrey and Sabine found themselves thinking. Cynicism and deep suspicion tend to generate parallel lines of thought, sometimes humorous, sometimes not so darn funny.

The meeting was ostensibly an update on all of the BRM programs on offer. "BRM," explained the technocrat meant "Business Risk Management."

"BRM, BRM," Aubrey was thinking a little uncharitably, "Boggles Rustic Minds." It was just as well his partner-for-life didn't know what was bouncing around in his tiny mind, or she would have been ordering him to "behave" and "focus". But trying to focus on something that would hardly have mesmerized a career accountant was akin to watch a boring game of hockey through the bottom end of a half-full bottle of Molson Canadian. So when the lady presenter launched into a wonderfully articulate spiel about "reference margins" in the so-called AgriStability program, an income assurance program for farmers, Aubrey's mind immediately took to fooling around with the concept in his mind. Your "Reference Margin" might refer to your optimum weight if you were to be selected as some hot number's male partner in "Dancing with the Stars". A "Positive Margin", one that he clearly did not possess, would mean that you could actually reach your partner without the encumbrance of too much girth and good living getting between the two of you. It would certainly not encapsulate how replete you might feel after having just consumed five beers and a twelve ounce New York steak. A "Negative Margin", on the other hand, probably meant that you had just survived a week of no beer and Dick Conley's cooking. Okay, so the "Olympic Average" the man went on to talk about was akin to a gaggle of figure-skating judges offering a score out of six on both your profile and sex appeal when you were paraded before them clad only in your "New Age Speedos": 1.8; 1.6; 5.1; 2.3; 1.4.

Okay, as they have always said, "beauty is in the eye of the beholder", except for the one judge who must have been seeing double negatives because clearly she had something in both her eyes. Aubrey wouldn't have got a score of 5.1 even at the height of his youth!

Then there was the issue of "Allowable Expenses", expenses that could be deducted from income to show some very wondrous thing that was pertinent to the "Analyst II" in charge of your file. It was all so logical said the presenter.

"So 'Feed Expenses' would include both hay and pasture?" offered one obviously very attentive farm lady. "So 'Pasture Rent' would come under feed because it is primarily a feed expense, right?"

"Well, actually no. Rented pasture is excluded from feed expenses because it's not technically feed but...blah! Blah! Bleugh!" Aubrey for one, and he was not alone, had a hard time with this. If "Pasture Rent" was not categorized as "Feed Expenses", then maybe he should categorize it as "Entertainment" or "Vicarious Living Expenses" or maybe "Condo Rental".

Then there was the issue of the 'valuation of commodities'. "How do you guys go about valuing hay?" asked another voice of deep thunder. "Are my best bales valued at the same price as the ones I call my 'smokies' because them ones got rained on about five times before I could get 'em up?"

"Well, as you can probably understand, we can't discriminate...blah! Blah! Bleugh!"

By this time, Aubrey, like most of the farmers there, had concluded this was primarily a JFOP program (a Jobs for Other People program): a part of governments' efforts to keep crime down, undesirables off the street, and unemployment statistics artificially low. The bureaucracy required to administer these programs had to be both enormous and growing. So what did it actually cost the government to get a dollar into the farmer's pocket?

Now here was a state secret if ever there was one, better yet it was an OSS, an Obfuscatory State Secret, because officialdom at every level would find a way not to tell you regardless of FOIP, the *Freedom of Information and Protection of Privacy Act*, regardless of whether you hired the services of the best weasel-hound reporter ever to seek the truth. As somebody else, a true pragmatist, pointed out, none of these government programs were necessary if the farmer could count on a realistic price for the product of his or her toil. Worse yet, as the technocrats made abundantly plain, most farmers had to hire the services of a professional accountant, so the JFOP concept was surreptitiously expanded to benefit the private professional sector too. Accountants, like lawyers and dentists and shoplifters, don't come cheap. But the very idea of having to contract a financial professional to navigate the rules was in and of itself an indictment of the whole policy as far as Aubrey was concerned. The implication was serious; you as Joe and Jane Small Farmer would unlikely have the expertise to access all the government aid that you might deserve, let alone all that you might be entitled to, and this in a business where profit and loss were roller coasters all of their own making.

In general business, the same broad principles apply because you use a basic business model with widely recognized teachable principles. You know what you have to put in and at what cost in order to get your end product out the door at a modicum of profit. By contrast, small-scale farming is more of a crap shoot in every sense of the word. The costs of inputs like fertilizer can show staggering variances from year to year. Your start-up date can be a month earlier than you anticipated, two months later, or sometimes not at all depending on silly little things like weather. The start-up date affects the quality of the product and its best-delivered-by date. When you actually seed or start calving or lambing naturally affects your harvest date. Then there are all of the things that can happen in between. What amounts to a cut-and-dried process in the factory, might on the farm amount to a waltz with the weather, a rumba with a plague of grasshoppers and other assorted pests, a tango with time, and a two-step with the soil and everything it produces including the weeds. So the farm business model is all too often not a model at all but a haphazard development of whatever it is you are producing. The oft-bandied concept of "sustainability" becomes the ultimate yardstick of what you achieve on your land, with your very own sustainability being paramount.

The Hanlons saw all of this firsthand and absorbed the lessons readily because they had to, they had no other choice. When you are forced to cut back on fertilizer, you are likely not only cutting back on this year's harvest and production, but also on the nutritive capacity of the land to sustain next year's crop. Refuse to cut back and both your banker and your bank account start wheezing horribly with neither one of them fitting the sustainability concept. If the fundamental economics are not sustainable, then the lifestyle isn't either!

People who wax enthusiastic about the agricultural lifestyle often take for granted that it involves life cycles, most of them much shorter than that of a human unless you're into raising elephants or tortoises. A cow with real longevity might make it to seventeen years old, whereas a bull might be lucky to make it to six or eight years old before he is deemed no longer "on top of his game". A mama sheep, sorry, a ewe, might actually produce progeny until she's ten. Chickens, well laying hens, might give you eggs for a couple of seasons or three, while Jimmy the rooster will strut his stuff until about five or six years of age, but by then he'll be way too strung-out to put in the pot for *Coq au Vin;* that would be like marinating your old suede boots in red wine and oregano before attempting to eat them. Now let's factor into all of this the farmer's life cycle, with perhaps not too much emphasis on "cycle". Most farmers when they are sixty-two do not walk, run or jump like they did when they were twenty-five. (Getting smartly out of the way of an unhappy charging bovine does not count here because it's the adrenalin doing the work, kind of like the devil's pitchfork urging on a reluctant body.) So for farmers, especially those who are male as most tend to be, there comes a stage in life where they could be seen as kindred spirits with that old rooster, too much crow and not enough cock; or like that old cow or ewe, long past being this or any season's honey. Therefore, it becomes incumbent on them to plan for the tail end of their life cycle, to decide in what manner they want to be put out to pasture. It is always better if they plan for themselves rather than having another, likely less sympathetic herdsperson to oversee the job. In looking at their place in the GST, the Great Scheme of Things, insignificant; in looking at their contribution to the country's national food strategy, deemed insignificant; in assessing how well their bodies are coping with the "physicalities" of farming, bold no more; and in acknowledging that their minds are now prone to the asking of existential questions like why the hell are we doing this, the Hanlons were forced into long-term planning. They were pushed into asking themselves the key question: At the end of our own life cycle, where do we want to be? Back in the city? Or out here in the country, probably on our own acreage with, God forbid, someone else farming our beloved land?

For many farmers there is an unqualified answer. Only when they face up to the stark reality of losing their precious dirt, their trees, their creek, and yes their coyotes and their moose, do many farmers start to feel pain, a spiritual angst, with some even getting the sense of being ready to be given back to their Creator. Ashes unto ashes, dust unto dust. Sure there are those who see only the dollar signs of a real estate transaction, likely because they never actually bonded with the land or because in today's hothouse culture, the dollar exerts too great a hold over them.

It was that government-sponsored meeting that essentially kick-started the Hanlons into focusing a little less on where they were at the time and a lot more on where they wanted to be. Down there on the farm, the realities of day-to-day agriculture have to be confronted continuously. Even when one is on holiday, one's mind is reluctant to let go. What if the cows get out? What if they finish up on the highway? What if a tornado, hailstorm, windstorm, tsunami or the local weed inspector comes barrelling through and you are not around to pick up the pieces because you are on your ninety-fifth stroke of a nine-hole-round of golf in Vernon, B.C.? Like any coyote, skunk or porcupine, the farmer is bent on survival. As for the coyote and the skunk, so for the farmer: there are always bigger and tougher predators out there. Bankers foreclose "with regret" because they are forced to do so by bank policy. Insurance adjusters refuse to make disaster payments, also citing policy, while everyone the farmer deals with "up-line" is entitled to their legitimate dollar. The small-time farmer takes only what is left, hopefully with some dignity intact.

So both Aubrey and Sabine were thinking hard, each in their own way, not yet ready to broach the subject together. The trouble is, thinking like this, thinking about things like life cycles and the dignity of life tends to fill you with too much empathy—not that dear Sabine ever lacked empathy!

The ad in the "Freebies" section of the *Western Star* went like this: "Help! Happy farm home wanted for Morton the Muscovy drake. We can no longer keep him as we are moving abroad. Please phone this number and ask for Iris."

"Let's do it for Morton!" yelled Sabine, looking up from her part of the paper over morning coffee.

"Yeah, let's!" said Aubrey, not even bothering to look up. "Morty all the way, that's what I say! Who the hell is Morton anyway?"

"If you must know, Morton is a Muscovy duck who needs a happy farm home. We could throw him in with our ducks."

"Yeah right, until he's fattened up enough to eat. Why not?" Aubrey was either not listening or he was not taking this at all seriously.

"I'm serious, honey. There's an ad in the paper looking for someone to take Morton home to their farm. Let's do it. After all, he is free." Sabine positively trumpeted that clinch line; not that it had any great impact because Aubrey well knew how his wife could never pass up anything that was free. If you ever accompanied her to a trade show, you simply could not avoid walking out of there loaded to the gunwales with free pencils, metre rules, samples of every sort, and fifty-five free writing implements.

"Sure, if that's what you want." Most married men have in their minds a "Partial Engagement Mode" mechanism that they can switch into and conduct not so much meaningless as semi-detached conversations with their spouses. Aubrey should have listened more attentively, and then he should have been more forceful in rejecting the very idea. Who would name a duck "Morton" anyway?

So it came to pass that Aubrey and Sabine found themselves on the doorstep of an address in town that afternoon. There they were met by Iris, Morton's foster-mother. Yes she was named for a flower and was maybe once in blossom forty years ago in her hippy days, but clearly the bloom was long gone, probably choked by too much weed, or something. Anyway, looking back in hindsight, the Hanlons should have been suspicious for they never made it beyond the doorstep.

To one side there was a plastic tote with holes drilled through the top for air. It was tied tightly with twine.

"Morton is inside the tote, which by the way you may keep," said Mother Duck pointing at the tote. Ominously, not a sound emanated from it, not even the faintest scratching. "You *will* look after him, won't you? He was a very special pet."

"Must be one fat pet too," said Aubrey picking up the tote. "Got to be twelve pounds, at least!"

"Yes, well I do admit we rather spoiled him," responded this now Mrs. Get-out-of-my-face-people person. "Have a great day and thank you for taking our Morty." With that she spun on her heel and was gone; Sabine could hear her after she shut the door in their faces. Either she was harrumphing around in there with great joy, or she was crying her eyes out over Morty's final departure. Nobody would ever know.

"Well, home we go with Morty!" said Sabine perhaps a little too heartily. When they got home, Sabine made the very practical suggestion of driving straight alongside the duck-pen, opening the rear door of the station wagon, whipping the lid off the tote and hey presto, Aubrey would grab a hold of dear Morton and launch him over the chain link fence into his new home.

Aubrey did not know it yet but he was about to learn a whole lot more than he ever wanted to know about ducks. Like ducks can bite and can give a really severe nip. Like ducks can crap more copiously that anybody would ever give them credit for, especially if they had been as well fed as Morton. Like ducks can rotate the cannon on their poop deck quicker than any machine gun. That they can move just as fast as any grapeshot they are in the process of "loosing" off, "loose" being the operative word. That they can be as fast as greased lightning, despite clipped wings, webbed feet and a twelve-pound under-slung bomb bay.

Aubrey was so far out of it, he was even whistling when he lifted the car's rear door; heck, it was a gorgeous sunny day so why not whistle and show appreciation? Sabine positioned herself so she could get her first unobstructed view of the newest citizen of their republic, Sir Morty Morton of Muscovy Wallow. Off came the lid and out shot one very angry Muscovy projectile with a guidance system that was very clearly malfunctioning. It smacked Aubrey plumb on the nose, instigating a massive nosebleed and a banned word expressing major disapproval of the duck's uncalled for behaviour. The now somewhat pulpy immovable object in Morton's way, Aubrey's snout, deflected the duck's trajectory first to the side and then the front of the wagon. Mistake number one: Aubrey lunged to catch the duck, thus putting his entire body into the car. Sabine made the logical move and slammed the door shut. Her mate was now trapped in a confined space with the ugliest specimen of *Carina moschata* the world had ever seen, and that duck was hissing mad. He came for Aubrey and bit him on the neck, his feathers beating the daylights out of what he saw as the source of all that unwarranted noise and foul language, Aubrey's visage. Then he high-tailed it, literally, firing off a fetid stream of recycled cannon fodder as if to add colour and spice to the mix. No doubt about it, Morty was on a roll. He landed on the dash, left his full signature all the way across it, spun around, and came at Goliath one more time. Goliath's action was not classic offense; it was defence in the guise of offence. He threw himself headlong onto that bird, pinning Morton with a two hundred and twenty-pound splat and yelling in triumph as he did so before screaming at Sabine to open the bleeping door.

Well, poor Sabine. Poor Morty too, but he had long since forfeited any prospect of sympathy, let alone love. As for Sabine though, never would she be allowed to forget the sheer sacrifices Aubrey was making and had made in the interests of dear sweet Morton having a happy farm home. What emerged out of the back of that vehicle was one very flattened and subdued dumpy duck, the word "dumpy" now very aptly describing Aubrey's once very nice going-to-town clothes. To Sabine standing there, that duck had to be the most grotesque winged, well maybe half-winged creature she had ever set eyes upon. But her husband was an equally arresting sight, more of a total spectacle really. There was blood and shit from the top of his head to the tips of his shoes. The soundtrack emanating from his voice box was just as arresting, volume on maximum, any comprehensible word in bleep mode—those few words that even made it out between the blood, the spittle and the excreta. That duck, poor darling Morton, was quarter-back tossed into the duck-pen with not a receiver in sight. He landed hard on hard ground and lay still, dead still.

"You just killed him!" said Sabine, careful not to sound too reproachful as she had no wish to rekindle Aubrey's bleep mode of communication.

"Good!" said her husband shortly and panting like a mastodon that has just run a marathon.

That was the moment when the regular residents of the pen, mostly Rouens and a few more Muscovies, arrived on the scene to check out their new cell mate. The dominant Rouen drake, seeing a new rival on the scene, one that was apparently at death's door, made the mistake of seeking to administer the *coup de grâce*. Morton would surely graduate this day, all the way to "Quacky Heaven".

That poor old Rouen never knew what hit him, something of a webbed wallop that left him lying there gasping on his back. All of his fair maidens and the few young squires abandoned him to take refuge in the duck house, there to watch Morton rise up and limp around the joint checking out his new surroundings. Apparently satisfied, he lay down in the long grass to recuperate.

He never did care much for Aubrey though, never; Morton started hissing like a demented thing whenever Aubrey came closer than fifty feet. The feeling was entirely mutual; Aubrey never did care for Morton either, cursing him like he would the perpetrator of any kind of bird flu pandemic. Besides, that really classy Mark's Work Wearhouse sweater, the striped one he got from Santa that past Christmas, now had to be relegated to "farm-wear" because the stains, like Morton, never opted to come out. The car too, the old station wagon in which Miss Piggy had first left her calling cards some years ago, now stunk worse than ever. On even a mildly warm day, nobody could even think of getting into it without risking life and limb. Maybe it would not have been so bad if either of the Hanlons had gotten around to cleaning it out right away, but both of them were too busy playing the blame game in a bid to get their opposite number to do it. To a point, Aubrey held the moral high ground because he was the one who got shut in with the creature, he was the one who had endured the creature, and he was the one who had to have a "scrubathon" in the tub to get rid of all the evidence of his victorious defeat at the tail end of a duck. By the time they had seen fit to compromise, both agreed to do it, the stains and the stench were well-baked throughout the car's entire hospitality suite. As a postscript to the affair and in order to somehow exact some measure of revenge on the bird, Aubrey suggested to Pierrette Moreau, the true *chef des chefs,* that Morton could be executed for terrorist activity on behalf of Al-Quaeda and then be rendered into a meal of Peking Duck.

"'Ow old is this *canard,* this duck?" she asked.

"The lady said he was at least five."

"Well, at 'is age, 'e will be, 'ow you say, *une boule de suif,* a ball of lard, yes? 'E will be *deguellasse,* disgusting!"

However, the incident with Morton segued into the Hanlon's new line of thinking. Did they truly want to go on raising ducks purely for ornamental purposes, which was the reason that Sabine bought them in the first place? And just how ornamental were they, cooped up away from view in a half acre of pond and muskeg? However beautiful they might be, how "ornamental" would they be if they ever got into Sabine's veggie garden and pooped all over her immaculate lawn? Perhaps this was why it was Sabine who got the ball rolling.

"I'm not really sure why we're keeping the ducks anymore," she said. "When we get old, we certainly won't have any need to be feeding ducks that we rarely even see."

"We are old," said Aubrey.

"Well, I think we should get rid of them next year," said Sabine. "Just so as we can say we did the right thing for Morton."

"I'll do the right thing for Morton right now if you want!" growled her husband.

"Oh honey, don't hold a grudge so bad! Morton was simply displaying the survival instinct any animal might display when it feels cornered."

"Yeah well, I'm an animal too and I would love to demonstrate my killer instinct to dear little Morton."

The next spring came around, as it always does, and although the ducks were advertised in the paper, there were no takers. The Hanlons' chance meeting with Bill Stott solved the problem, albeit not in a manner to salve Sabine's conscience.

"Oh, I buy anything that breathes, walks and flies," he told Aubrey and Sabine. "Chickens, ducks, turkeys, goats, you name it, I'll buy them. I sell 'em all to a Chinese gentleman who comes up to Olds on auction day. We meet on the street, he buys my critters and goes home, and I go to the auction."

"Oh, and what does the Chinese gentleman do with them?" Sabine asked naively. "Does he have some kind of oriental garden or something?"

"Well no, he sells them to the restaurants in Calgary. City folk eat anything, don't you know?"

"Oh no, we can't do that!" Sabine was genuinely horrified.

"Oh yes we sure can!" Aubrey was not about to grant any sort of amnesty to Morton, not about to extend his life cycle another day if he could possibly avoid it. So what if he held a grudge; he had really liked that striped sweater.

"I'll drop by your place tomorrow on my way down to Olds," said Bill when they talked next on the phone. "Oh, and I have wire cages to put them all in."

"Tomorrow it is," said Aubrey with a finality not to be ignored.

"Oh honey, how…?"

"Tomorrow it shall be; no ifs, buts or maybes. I've got the hammer," he cut his wife off at the pass, leaving before she got to the valley of unstoppable sentimentality.

Tomorrow arrived inexorably, only to find Sabine decidedly uncomfortable about the fact she had now lost control of events. Aubrey was resolute: the ducks were going, together with the hated Morty. But without the attendant entertainment? What was he thinking? Why did everyone even think that dear Morty would surrender quietly when he had arrived with such panache?

All of the ducks were easily shepherded into the main duck house, all but dear Morton. With Bill and Marie Stott, Aubrey and Sabine, it took a mere twenty minutes to catch the seventeen ducks whose life cycles were about to be shortened by the capricious exigencies of the Hanlons' retirement planning. Evidently Morton did not consider he should be part and parcel of any such package because he had established himself as Head Waddler with all the official privileges of that office. He side-stepped the whole sordid business by taking refuge beneath an old truck canopy that Aubrey had dumped into the duck pen years ago as an additional storm shelter.

So the whole issue of Morton's continued existence came down to two very portly, very plump men discussing who should be the first to do battle with a deranged duck. Bill held all the cards. "I can easily leave him here, you know." It was the clinching argument; Aubrey knew it, Bill knew it. "Besides, I'm wearing my town clothes," added Bill as if to slam the door. Aubrey dismissed him as having no morals.

"No bloody way does that duck stay," said Aubrey dropping to his hands and knees and crawling under the canopy after Morton. To begin with, it was more a problem of physics than it was a military offensive. Inserting himself under that topper was akin to trying to squeeze a large, semi-inflated pliable object into a non-pliable, very compact container, like trying to squeeze a beluga into a sardine can. But it went far beyond basic physics because the dynamics for propulsion were generated by passion and energy and will, with the semi-pliable invader "uttering dire threats" as a police report might say.

There comes a point when, if there is really nowhere else to go, you are forced to confront danger head on. Morton, so savvy for a duck, kept his powder dry and conserved his ammunition until he could see the whites of his adversary's eyes, and then he went for it. It was lucky that Aubrey was wearing his glasses or he would have taken the first salvo in the eye. As it was, he got it full in the mouth, which in turn immediately ceased uttering dire threats of any sort. And he got it on the head and shoulders: a green and pungent scattering of glorious and unadulterated duck excreta as Morton flew over him toward the exit and sunlight. Bill was there with a fishing-net. He trapped that duck the instant he emerged, and he did not even take one sharp breath doing so. Aubrey wiggled his way back out on his belly, while the audience very diplomatically held its breath as he rose unsteadily to his feet, covered in dirt, bits of grass and twig, and with gobs of duck shit trickling down his glasses.

"Oh no," said Sabine. "You've twisted your glasses again, pretty badly too. Celeste will have to hear this story." That's when the dam burst and Aubrey found himself once again the source of considerable merriment.

Chapter Eleven

THE CAT THAT THOUGHT SHE WAS SOMETHING ELSE!

Someone, somewhere, has likely done some kind of research project on working farm couples. One thing is for certain, they are different from most normal couples because both partners are compelled to work together as much as they play together; that after all is the essence of the family farm. The *faux pas* of the day, the crisis of the week, these are both inevitable and expected. Yes, farm folks play the blame game just as well as anybody else, but the pickup's tailgate that one half of the partnership just "modified" is not going to get any better or any worse because spouse number two cannot let it go and keeps haranguing spouse number one. On the farm, everyone, but absolutely everyone, shows flashes of brilliant even creative foolishness; reality asserts itself and either you look for a replacement tailgate or your pickup wears the one you bent so artistically. Besides, if you yourself happened to be the culprit, you have to regard yourself as something of a community health expert in that you can promote unbridled laughter, such laughter being good for people's mental health and all that. To take the tailgate issue a step further, if ever you do come across a suitable used one, you can guarantee it will be somewhere far away, like the other side of Medicine Hat, and it will be a hideous purple when your own pickup is ivory. It will also be the only one in the entire province... Oh hang on a sec, here's one on Kijiji; oh, but it turns out it's actually in Woodstock, Ontario. No, don't get your hopes up. It was neither Aubrey nor Sabine who smacked the tailgate; it was Jeannie of Pete and Jeannie fame, and Pete knew enough to keep his big mouth shut because the boo-boo ledger already showed an unhealthy balance on his debit side. Moreover, truth be known, Jeannie had every right to be distracted the day she smacked the power pole/yard light combination because she had just learned she was about to be a granny times two because there were twins in the package. Better yet, the power pole did not react nor show resentment, it just stood there.

When it came to Aubrey and Sabine, because their skills on the farm had evolved together, they had also learned largely together. One of Aubrey's former police colleagues, a well-respected policewoman, had asked him how he thought he would cope when he retired. After all, she said, there would be no co-workers or associates, no comrades-in-arms to consult with or to razz, just a wife whom he would have to see and work with from the moment he got up in the morning to the moment he went to bed at night. Most other spouses are never blessed with each other's company for twenty-four hours a day, seven days a week.

"How are you ever going to stand it?" asked Mrs. Cop, clearly concerned for her associate's mental equilibrium. "Besides, now you won't even have a chain of command, you'll have yourself a Commanding Officer. You won't even have a subordinate to whom you can delegate tasks or who can shoulder some of the responsibility when things go wrong. It'll be just little old you, the only one with the rank of constable."

Yes, there was a great deal of truth in all that she said, but only to the extent that one looked at a marriage as some unitary form of business management. On the farm though, a marriage is something far greater and more complex than mere management; it is a system of communication that transcends any model of management. Sometimes it actually works on the level of telepathy. At other times, it unfolds like a high-wire circus act without a safety net; and on occasion, it is a wild and intimate two-step with both partners knowing exactly what the other is doing and will do next.

Like a pair of Canada geese, Aubrey and Sabine had become mates for life. All they did on the farm, they did together—even if there were times when one of the geese was left wondering what the hell the other was doing, circling aimlessly around and flapping its wings with no apparent destination. As they matured as farmers, so they split the load and the responsibilities as most farm couples do. Sabine, for example, took charge of the herd health program; she was tasked—correction, she tasked herself—to purchase and administer all drugs. If a calf or a cow needed a shot, Aubrey was the catcher; he had to be, for he was the one with all the ballast in the slip-tank, so to speak. Even then, he could easily be transported expressly into a tree or through a fence if he failed to read his animal well. It was Sabine, then, who knew which drug had to be used when and for what, while in that specific department, Aubrey found it far easier to defer to his wife. On the rare occasions that he stumbled upon a sick animal, he didn't have a clue what drug to use, leave alone the dosage. Okay, that amounted to a "systems failure", but they had never lost an animal because of it. Bottom line, it was obvious that when it came to livestock, there had to certain jobs that were Aubrey's, such as the EIC (Enforcer-in-Chief), CHL (Carrier of Heavy Loads), COB (Chaser of the Bull), that sort of thing. In other words, he was the one assigned to the more mundane and physically taxing chores; whereas, china-doll Sabine tended to do the more cerebral ones, except of course the calculation of the fertilizer budget; Aubrey had always been an artist at spreading fertilizer.

So, too, on the wider farm, the tasks seemed to delegate themselves to one or the other of the duo, and thus their system evolved. Most, if not all, of the round baling was done by Sabine, disking too. Ploughing was Aubrey's baby because it required "certain finesse", he said. Women could never keep a straight line, he said; and for sure, the only time Sabine ever tried it, she ploughed the most exquisite of "bent banana furrows", one that would have left any competitor in the World Ploughing Competition in Olds, Alberta, absolutely speechless. Indeed, not one competitor among them would have been able to emulate that curve, but then again, not one of them would have been able to recognize the art in it either. For them, ploughing was science disguised as art: straight lines were mandatory, parallel furrows, the perfectly turned sod, the ultimate setting of the plough to turn the perfect sod, and so on. Not that Aubrey's furrows could be termed immaculate. How could they be when he had ADHD (Agriculturally Discombobulated Agricultural Disorder): a condition that could be brought on by something as simple or innocuous as a country baritone on the radio, or, conversely, by some fool DJ's over-enthusiastic welcome of "another gorgeous, hot, sunny day, eighty-seven now and counting," whereupon Aubrey would be screaming at him to "go look up the bloody word drought" and to get himself a "real job." Aubrey could be easily distracted by such things!

Of course, many of the chores on the farm were necessarily shared. Both Hanlons had to know how to operate the bale shredder to feed the cows in fall and winter, the discbine to cut hay in summer, the rake to dry it out, and so forth. Naturally there was a drawback to this system. The spouse that did not regularly do a specific procedure lost touch with the intricacies of how to do it; such as knowing where to look when, and remembering the basic sequence of operations. This was evidenced that one day in the summer when foolishly Aubrey took over the round baling from Sabine while she went back to the house to make a couple of phone calls and grab some lunch. Stupid old Aubrey, he figured he could do it all.

"Now you're sure you remember what all you have to do?" the Great She said, as she climbed aboard his quad.

"Poof, it's not exactly rocket science. I dunno what you think is so bloody difficult about driving a baler round and round a field making bales," said HM Aubrey—Her Man not His Majesty, for there was nothing majestic about him.

"Well do remember to weave at the beginning of every bale, won't you?" she hastened to add. "We don't want any of your famous wine-glass shaped bales, okay?" With that she was gone.

"Great!" Aubrey said to himself. "We don't want any of your famous wine-glass shaped bales," he continued, mimicking his Commander-in-Chief in a high-pitched voice. "Do remember to weave, won't you. Son of a bleeping chicken plucker, I've been weaving all of my bloody life!"

Then he got down to business, serious business. He FOCUSED by picking up the baler manual that Sabine always carried with her in the cab and read through the section entitled "Baler Operation"—just to refresh himself, you must understand. In the meantime, the radio personality was blabbing on about pruning lilac bushes on some Calgary gardening show. So Aubrey un-focused; instead of shutting the radio out of an operation for which he desired, nay required, maximum concentration, he changed the station and cranked up the volume to bring in Tim McGraw's baleful lament about this hurtful world. Aha! Now he was gonna have real baling tunes, real down-home cowtown music! And off he went, weaving along better than any drunk anyone had ever seen. The monitor, God bless modern technology, would tell him when to hold 'em and when to string 'em, so he duly stopped when he was told to, backed up and kicked the bale out when he was supposed to, and continued on with his musical ride, serenaded by the likes of Terri Clark, Garth Brooks, George Canyon, and of course Crystal Gale. It was just as Crystal was ebbing far away into the Blue Bayou that Sabine reappeared on the scene, and oh oh, she was gesticulating like a mad thing. Aubrey, recognizing this as likely to be one of those "oh shit" moments, did the logical thing and shut down before hauling himself out of the tractor. Oh the fool, the obvious fool, he had left the radio full on and nothing was able to compete with k.d. lang's rendition of "Allelujah", which from that moment and forever more became the battle hymn of disaster. He loved that voice, loved the utter soulful intensity of it, but Sabine Hanlon cut through it like a knife through butter.

"Shouldn't we be using twine on our bales?" she shouted. "Like every single bale you made while I was gone has no twine."

Aubrey responded as expected. "Oh shit!" he said as he scratched his nether regions in bewilderment, a deep frown creasing his face. Then he walked to the back of the rig to see this greatest of calamities for himself. "Oh shit!" he announced one more time; it was not as if any more descriptive vocabulary would have summed it up any better. There they all were: a line of seven unstrung bales all with a bouffant hairdo akin to Jackie Kennedy at her finest. Aubrey had never even thought to take a look at what kind of a bale he was leaving behind him. Why would he when he was immersed in the songs of all his favourite country and western crooners in full "sound-surround"?

He was further mortified when Sabine, his dear sweet Sabine, strode purposely over to the baler's twine arm and gave the twine a quick yank to free it from where it had been hung up before climbing into the tractor. Once there, she switched back to her Calgary station for the world to hear more about the advantages of "wet composting" at full bore before she adjusted the volume down to a tolerable level. Without even a dismissive glance at poor Aubrey, she resumed her baling ways, and he was left standing there in the field like a little boy who has just kicked his ball through the neighbour's sitting room window.

"Allelujah! Allelujah! Allebloodylujah!" he sang in a strained homage to k.d. lang and "sound-surround". Then he did the only thing he could do; he jumped on the quad and went on home, all the while racking his brains to remember some Sabine-type failure that could be used as a counter-weight to the story his wife would now surely spin any time she had an audience. But he couldn't think of one.

Then again, most couples in the world have their own particular idiosyncrasies. The Hanlons were no exception. Sabine never mentioned Aubrey's baling boo-boo, not once! Maybe it was her version of reverse psychology or possibly high diplomacy: get her husband to smarten up simply by leaving the threat of idiocy exposure hanging above his head. Heaven only knows, Aubrey expected to be laughed at and ridiculed because of her revelations. What's more, he had steeled himself for the occasion, even if he had only the flimsiest defence imaginable: that he had other things on his mind. Yeah right! And when all was said and done, he was very grateful to Mother Goose.

What really made him sit up and think, though, was that when it came time for him to move those bouffant bales with his bale mover, they weren't there; they were gone from the field! For a fleeting moment, he wondered who on earth would be brazen enough to steal them, to steal seven unstrung bales with all their "hair" falling out. Only then did it dawn on him; Sabine! Not only had she dismissed his incompetence that day, she had rectified it! She had erased those seven blots on her baling landscape; they would have been attributed to her by all the neighbours because they knew who did the baling. Perfectionist that she was, she could not stand to see those bales shedding a bit more every hour, so she had unrolled them with the front-end loader and re-baled them all, and this time they were tied. Nothing was said. Aubrey could think what he liked for that, after all, was his business.

Idiosyncrasy. One of the meanings given for the word in Aubrey's treasured dictionary was the following : "a physiological or temperamental peculiarity." We all have them, Sabine too, which is largely how Smokey the cat assumed her rightful pride of place in the Hanlon sun. As a general rule, farmers are not inclined to pamper or over-indulge their pets. The three dogs the Hanlons owned have not even garnered a mention in this book because they were part of the homogeneity of the Hanlon farm animals. Chippy, the Red Heeler, and Kali and Mtata, the pair of Jack Russell terriers, were often seen and more often heard, but they were as much a part of the outside landscape as every other animal on the place. On the other hand, cats, especially house cats, had become taboo ever since the day Sabine watched her own very special Pixie stroll nonchalantly over to one of the heating vents in the sitting room where she proceeded to urinate profusely, all the while seeming to look at her mistress for applause. Unfortunately for her, she got a whole lot more than she bargained for; she was exiled from the house forthwith and forever, especially since Mr. and Mrs. Hanlon had searched unsuccessfully so many times during the previous winter for the source of the sour vinegar smell that seemed to grow stronger and more pernicious every time the heating came on. No, no, forget it! No cat on the farm needed to be sent for a psychological analysis and a detailed Learning Plan of corrective measures designed by some animal psychologist cum vet specializing in feline psychiatry, not when it would amount to the cost of two cows and a horse. No, Pixie had earned her legitimate place as a farm animal, and like every other farm animal, her basic nutritional needs would be met outside. Beyond that, she would have to learn to fend for herself and catch mice of which there were no end. As for Sabine, a lady who was an open and bleeding heart when it came to showing empathy, in this instance she was forced to go contrary to her nature and harden her heart to granite. But not so with Smokey.

Right about now is an appropriate time to explain that once Aubrey discovered both his air supply and his winter heating had been contaminated by cat pee, he decided that all cats without exception were incorrigibly heathen. He became a cat xenophobe telling anyone who had a mind to listen what filthy, fur-licking creatures they were. How any sane person could even entertain the presence of such a flea-bitten creature in their house was quite beyond him; why they might as well bring in the chickens and the goats too, while they were about it, and keep them all warm and cuddly in winter. Gather from this that Aubrey found it hard to forgive, harder still to forget, and absolutely impossible to stay neutral on any issue that got under his skin—which is possibly why he had been a policeman in his first life and not a campaigner for animal rights.

It was as they were lurching their way into fall that Sabine went up to her chicken house one day to feed her laying hens. She was surprised by a mangy cat bolting out of the feed room when she opened the door. "All power to you and yours, my dear," she intoned. "Just keep the mice down and you'll be my very welcome guest." It was a perfectly legitimate arrangement given the ratty-looking walls with bits of fibreglass insulation poking out of the assorted holes in the particle board. She fed her "grannies", the chickens, and left.

The next day when she took her daily walk to collect the eggs, she found that same cat up there, but this time it was stone dead and stretched out on the floor. More distressing still was that it was very evident she must have been nursing kittens somewhere and had succumbed to starvation, as so many feral cats do. Carefully Sabine picked up the cadaver and placed it into an empty feed bag with a view to cremating the remains in one of the autumn deadfall fires they lit at that time of year. That was when she thought she heard the very faintest of meows, so faint that she decided she must have been deluding herself. It came again. She began to search. Nothing. She was on the point of leaving when it sounded one more time, but on this occasion there was a rustling with it. There, peering out of a hole in the inner wall was the tiniest grey face just staring at her, the two burnished yellow eyes literally beseeching for its life. Sabine made a move towards it and it vanished instantly, with nary a hope of catching it. So she did the only thing she could think of in the circumstances; she hurried back down to the house, put some milk and raw hamburger in a dish and returned to the chicken house. She glimpsed those two yellow eyes only for a split second before they were gone. She put the dish down close to the hole in the wall and left. How many more kittens might there be? In what shape were they, given the horrendous shape of the mother? Would they, could they, survive by themselves when they were that tiny? She was about to find out!

That evening, just on dark, Sabine slipped up to the chicken house. You could never have entered without a sound because if the door didn't creak, one of the granny hens would always cluck a warning to the others that something was around. She opened the door, endured its agonizing creak and saw…nothing! If the kitty had been there, it had gone. The milk was still there though, untouched. However, the meat had disappeared. Was this a cause for celebration? Maybe, maybe not! Mice eat meat, weasels eat meat, even skunks eat meat. Okay, she thought hard before deciding to give the benefit of the doubt to the kitten. Twice a day for the next while, Sabine took meat up to the mice, the weasel, the skunk or the kitten, and twice a day that meat disappeared with no sign of whatever was feeding on it. But Sabine was intrigued, and Sabine was stubborn; she was determined to see what it was that was getting fat on her largesse. On the ninth day she opened the door, and there was a kitten, the tiniest, plump kitty, grey in colour with a white dimple on head and chest. That was all she got to see though; that kitty showed not the slightest inclination to hang around and make a formal introduction.

Whenever it is said of men that they have an uncanny ability to listen with just one ear, it's because, like a driver selecting cruise control on a boring highway, they go into PEM, Partial Engage Mode, wherein they go through the motions of listening without actually doing so, or worse yet, not even connecting to all they are being told. That's a dangerous situation because all too easily they might discover they have agreed to something they had never truly heard, let alone endorsed.

"You know what, honey, I found out what's eating the meat," said Sabine. "It's a tiny little kitten."

"That's nice," said Aubrey, his nose buried in the weekly paper. She might just as well have told him she had discovered what the ingredients were in carrot soup.

But Sabine was excited. "Yes, and it's eating all of the meat too."

"That's great!" said Aubrey turning to the sports page.

"I hope there's only one of them," Sabine struggled on gamely. Trying to ignite this conversation was like trying to start a fire with damp kindling.

"Me too!" murmured Aubrey, more interested in a story about his beloved Edmonton Oilers getting a new coach.

"Yes, well I'll keep trying anyway. I want to be able to actually touch that little kitty."

"Me too!" muttered Aubrey, which told Sabine the fire had spluttered and died.

So Sabine did the only thing she could do when she knew she could count on so little support from a husband who just wasn't interested; she persisted. Aubrey knew she would because the word "persistence" defined his wife; and she had always been stubborn in defeat.

On day fifteen it happened. Kitty, Smokey, lingered long enough for Sabine to touch him/her/it. Then it bolted. The next day, same thing. Day seventeen came and the "it" stayed long enough for Sabine to actually touch it once. By day twenty-two, Sabine picked it up but it refused to be cuddled. It took a wild jump and disappeared.

"I had a girlfriend like that once," said Aubrey still not getting the message that he was missing out on the story.

After one full month, it came time to take stock. They had partially tamed, correction, Sabine had partially tamed, one tiny kitten. It turned out to be a female. There was no sign of any others. The kitten was an orphan; Sabine was her surrogate mother. Surrogate mothers have to make decisions about their adopted offspring's health and welfare. Okay, so seeing as Smokey lived right next door to the cow barn, she would be a barn cat, her job to keep the mice in check. But then again, mama cats tend to have babies, lots of them. They come on heat and encourage all sorts of undesirables to hang around and lower the tone of the neighbourhood, just like people. Well, she could be spayed, but what would that cost? And why would you go out and spend a full hundred dollars spaying a barn cat that would likely take off, never to be seen again. More to the point, what would dear Aubrey have to say, that same Aubrey who knew the cat existed, who had heard every turn and twist of Smokey's story but had never registered any of it?

So Sabine called the vet clinic. The basic fee to spay a cat was around one hundred and ninety dollars, said the receptionist brightly. And that was if there were no complications. Why did she have to add that bit about complications, Sabine was thinking. That was almost an invitation to trouble. Okay, so she would have to consult her partner goose for life; the same one who currently had his nose buried in *The Globe and Mail*.

"Honey, we need to decide what to do about Smokey," she said.

"What's to decide?" He said it without even looking up. "She's a barn cat. She'll have to live and die like any other barn cat on any farm in the country."

"Yes but Smokey is a she-cat. She's liable to have babies, lots of them."

"Well, give her away," he said dismissively.

That was when finally she decided to get his full attention. She tossed a cushion that crumpled that bloody newspaper across his lap. "Now you listen to me!" she said. "And I mean LISTEN! I know you could care less about cats, but this little kitty means a lot to me."

"Oh yeah! I take it this is the same little kitty that you haven't got a hope in hell of catching, let alone taming." He made a show of straightening up his badly crumpled newspaper, not realizing the extent to which he had betrayed himself.

"I knew it!" shouted Sabine almost triumphantly and snatched the paper out of his hands. "I knew you hadn't been paying any attention to what I was saying all along. I might just as well have been talking to the wall all of this time. I told you only yesterday that I can pick her up and pet her, and she even starts purring."

What could he say? Nothing! His only move, if you could call it a move, was to shut up and wait. And be diplomatic because a Sabine all riled up was about as intense as one-half of the Middle East about to declare war on the other half. So he did what she would have wanted; *he focused!*

"So here's our problem, not my problem by the way, *our* problem. Do we have this cat spayed or what do we do? We cannot have a female cat constantly coming on heat up at the barn. For one thing, every tomcat in the neighbourhood will be around here. For another, the dogs will go wild."

"Well if this cat is that important to you, to us, then let's get her spayed. It shouldn't cost much more than fifty bucks."

"How about one hundred and ninety dollars?" Sabine replied. "I phoned the vet clinic."

Had she told him this already? Had he heard it before and not reacted? Had he already tacitly agreed to pay a full one hundred and ninety dollars to spay a bloody barn cat? "I see," he said. "Well, it's your call. If you want to keep that cat around, do it. For my part, I admit I haven't been involved with it so it's not up to me to say."

She had him now; the fish was on the end of the line. All she had to do was "set the hook" and reel him in. "Come up with me and meet our cat," she said.

"Now?" he wriggled, but the hook was set perfectly.

"Yes now," she said. "She's your cat too, you know."

What could he say? He knew from that moment on that he, they, had acquired a "barn cat" with all the trimmings. Well the bloody thing could stay up at the barn with all its shedding fur and its wandering fleas. He did not want to show reluctance, for that would be churlish, so he stumbled off to find a pair of boots and a hat.

Falling in love is both magical and mysterious. Why did Aubrey fall in love with Sabine? How the heck would he know? Why ever did Sabine fall in love with him? Sabine would probably tell him all sorts of things about science and hormones and useless things like that. Why and how did Aubrey fall in love with Smokey? Was it the cutest little face he had ever seen? Was it her initial rejection of all his advances? Sabine, too, had initially rejected him. Was it his body odour? Sabine, too, had once rejected him on those grounds. Why does, did, rejection make the attraction all the more strong? Aubrey had no answer. All he knew was he loved that cat. It was a fighter and a survivor. It had been brought into this world unwanted, had been left with less than nothing, and his dear wife had shown not just kindness but a dogged persistence not so much to save it as to give it a chance. Every time she went to find the cat, Aubrey tagged along and soon she greeted him as fondly as she did Sabine. She was quite the sight too, the cat not Sabine, for she seemed to be growing fatter in all the wrong places. But she was way too young to be pregnant, wasn't she? Then again, she had never had her mother's milk; maybe her predilection for meat, not milk, put weight on in all the wrong places.

The day of Smokey's appointment with the vet duly arrived. Aubrey resurrected the Morton tote, the plastic box that had holes drilled in the lid. Smokey was incarcerated, the lid tied up, and off to town they went. The cat was to stay there for the day so Aubrey and Sabine headed off for a day in Red Deer: Sabine with specific business to do such as pick up some parts, salt blocks, and that sort of thing; Aubrey to have lunch, an eight ounce steak with blue cheese brulé and jalapeno peppers, or maybe baked Alaska cod with fresh asparagus and new potatoes. These days he considered himself something of a gourmand. With Sabine looking constantly both over his shoulder and his waistline, and like many descending the stairs into senior citizenship, he was compelled to substitute quality in place of quantity. They arrived back at the vet's at three in the afternoon.

"I'm afraid we were unable to spay the cat," said the lady vet, clearly as enamoured with Smokey as they were. "She's precious though, one of a kind. But I'm afraid we found she has a bladder infection which is why she looks kind of fat in the wrong places. So we need to put her on a course of antibiotics to clear it up before we can do anything else. I'm very sorry."

"How much will that all cost?" asked a very hesitant Sabine in the company of a husband who would surely be adding up the score.

"Do it!" said the husband. "How long will it take for the infection to clear up?"

"Oh we can try again in about ten days if you want to book her in for that."

"Do it!" said Aubrey, and it was done.

Ten days later, the same scene more or less played out. They dropped the cat off at the clinic. They headed off to Red Deer to see their financial advisor, and for Aubrey to score lunch again: shrimp linguini with pears and apples, or maybe pulled pork and goat cheese on French baguette. Hey, you only live once! This time they drove back home first before going into Rocky Mountain House to the vet's. There on the caller ID was the evidence that the vet had called at 9:30 a.m., but since nobody had left a message there seemed to be no cause for alarm. So they drove in to town to pick up the cat as they had planned.

The receptionist gravely asked the Hanlons to step into a small consulting room because she said the vet would like to have a talk with them. Sabine started to panic some but did her best to control it; she still felt she could not afford too much of a display of misplaced affection for what was, after all, to be a barn cat. The vet came in, a delightful young woman carrying an iPad. The smile allayed some of Sabine's deepest fears, while Aubrey had not yet seen any need to be fearful.

"Your kitty is something else!" she began. "Both in personality and, it seems, biologically. We phoned you because we had to go a lot further than we expected. Her bladder problem was the result of a rare malformation, one that I personally have never seen before. Here, let me show you these pictures." She flicked through four photos of the kitten's inside plumbing. "So basically we had to do a whole lot more than just spay her. We phoned you to ask permission, but there was nobody home so we took the chance and went ahead because we had already opened her up. We hope you won't object to the extra cost." Clearly the lady was concerned she had overstepped the mark, which was why she was looking at Sabine when she said it.

"How, how much…?" Sabine began to ask before being interrupted by her husband.

"No problem," said Aubrey the cat lover. Sabine could not believe what she was hearing. Here was her husband in an entirely new light.

"Well, Smokey is a bit sore, so I hope you have somewhere clean and warm to shut her in for the night?" the vet was looking at Aubrey now.

"Well, well, er, we do have a calf hotbox in the cow barn," said Sabine hesitantly. "She is a barn cat, you understand?"

"We'll put her in the laundry room," said Aubrey quickly. "That'll be clean and warm."

"But, but you're bringing her into the house?" Sabine was floundering at what she was hearing.

"Sure. Why not, unless you don't want her in the house? Or do you know someone who wants to adopt a cat?" he looked at the vet and winked. This time it was Aubrey who had set the hook, and this time it was Aubrey reeling in the prize.

"She'll have to be our new house cat," said Sabine breathlessly, almost bursting into tears.

"Well, be good and sure she takes the full course of antibiotics; that's very important. Now I'll go and fetch your new house cat," the vet said with a smile and shut the door.

Sabine took one look at her Aubrey and…hugged him! "Thank you!" she whispered. "Thank you so very much!" she lingered long enough that when the vet bringing Smokey in opened the door, she thought she had interrupted some sort of, ahem, romantic interlude. She was embarrassed, Sabine was embarrassed; while Aubrey (what did you expect) almost preened like a rooster. And he was focused, oh yes he was focused, on untying the twine and seeing how Smokey had fared. There she was, not ready to hotfoot it to any-place-else as one might have expected, but sitting there as if to say, "This is one heck of a way to fix my bellyache."

Right from the very beginning, both Aubrey and Sabine realized this was to be no ordinary house cat. Their first worry was how she would take to the dogs, or rather how the dogs would take to her—especially the two Jack Russell terriers who saw cats as having been put on this earth for them to chase. It took only two swipes of her paw, with an attendant raking of claws resulting in a copious cascade of blood from Kali's nose, for the message to get out. Mtata and Chippy must have both felt the pain vicariously for they never went near her again in an aggressive way. Kali, probably because he felt he had lost face, quite a bit of face actually, tried one more sneak attack only to come out with a whole face full of pain. From then on the message morphed into something like Smokey has been appointed an honorary dog with full military privileges.

Perhaps it was because she had been a single orphan, or perhaps because she had bonded first to humans and then to dogs that she never did behave like any normal cat. If Aubrey and Sabine took the dogs for a walk, the cat came too. If they went up to pet and talk to Sabine's replacement heifers, there was Smokey perched on the fence, endeavouring to pat them on the nose. But it was not all roses. She took to staying out at night, which was fine and dandy given that cats were nocturnal animals. But she had a chance encounter with a skunk, the only conclusion that could be drawn when she ran into the house the next morning and proceeded to make the house almost uninhabitable for a while. That was the problem; like Aubrey as a boy, she played with anyone until she discovered too late who her real friends should be. And she played whenever she felt like it, with a zest and a passion that had her aging human companions struggling to keep up with her antics. She even landed on Aubrey's face, claws out to get a grip, one afternoon when he had laid down for an afternoon nap on the chesterfield in the sitting room, suddenly to draw forth an explosion of sound and colour as he came to life. She thought it was great sport to scatter the pieces of Sabine's half-composed jigsaw puzzle on the floor. She was the cat who thought she was something else…and she was something else!

Chapter Twelve
NOTHING BUT A CATASTROPHE!

*W*hen the Hanlons arrived home late one Friday night, they found a message on their answering machine. It was abrupt to the point of downright rudeness, but maybe the fellow had every right to be mad, who knew? "This is Burt Reynolds," the voice positively growled. "I rent the land south of Hobson's place, which I am given to understand you rent for pasture. I'm the guy with the purebred Texas Longhorns. Your cows and your bull broke the fence today, Saturday, and they're now all mixed up with mine. I need them out of there pronto! Here's my number."

"That's a Red Deer number," said Sabine.

"Well, we'll call the fellow in the morning," said Aubrey, not unduly perturbed. If you had cattle out and about, you always expected at least one such call during the summer.

They never did get to call him. Dick Conley had just shown up for Sunday breakfast, telling Aubrey and Sabine how he had come down from Edmonton the previous day and finding nobody home, had gone out to have a whiskey, or seven, with Quincy Klug. Needless to say, he had finished up on Quincy's chesterfield that night. He had just finished his announcement that he required bacon and eggs, hash brown, and lots of coffee but that he had to take a shower first, when the phone rang.

"Hello! Aubrey Hanlon here."

"Mr. Hanlon? Burt Reynolds from Red Deer. Did you get my message?" Clearly the man had little time for preliminaries!

"Yes. I gather your cows are now mixed up with mine."

"No sir. It's your cows that are mixed up with mine, and I'm not too happy about it. Mine are all purebred Texas Longhorns." No doubt about it, this man had attitude, lots of it. "So I'm wondering what you intend to do about it." Aubrey kept cool even though he did not care at all for the man's high-handed tone.

"Well, if you don't mind meeting us out there at 10:30, we can get them sorted out. Shouldn't be too much of a problem."

"See you at 10:30 then, and don't be late!" barked this voice of great authority before hanging up. Aubrey made no comment. Why would he? He was in low-key mode, and besides the Hanlons would be accompanied by Dick Conley, their own secret weapon or loose cannon, depending on where exactly the stars were in their alignment.

Wishing to avoid a whole lot of unnecessary fuss, the three musketeers, Sabine and Aubrey Hanlon and Dick Conley, made their way out to the Hobson place at 9:30. It was eerily quiet for there was not one single animal on the place. They looked over the southern boundary fence and there they were, the Hanlon cows in with the man's Longhorns, just as the man had said. But what was also notable was that apart from the two bulls, the cows had split up into their two distinct herds. Maybe purebred Texas Longhorns were racist. Maybe the Hanlon cows were intimidated by the magnificent twisty horns of their counterparts, especially when there was not a single horn among their own. Maybe the Longhorns were just too darn snooty and talked funny. The two bulls though were doing their business, or endeavouring to do so without reaching any satisfactory conclusion. The Longhorn bull was truly a magnificent animal, a deep, brindled red with a set of horns fully four feet across from tip to tip. He was solid but he was young so he did not have the weight of Willy Wonka, who was built like a Sherman tank. Indeed, Willy too looked magnificent. But as much as he carried the weight, he was light on the weapons and had to rely on the thick boss of his head to act as a battering ram.

So there they were, standing in a patch of low ground and literally leaning into each other for support because their negotiations had been so taxing. Well, that was where they could darn well stay until the Hanlon crew had checked out the fence where the animals had broken through. It was the usual performance, it seemed. The bulls had been calling each other names over the fence until one had overstepped his authority; no fence is designed to stop a two thousand-pound bull on an emergency military mission. Evidence of the ensuing confrontation abounded: the ground was all ploughed up along with six broken posts and hanging wire. The crew could only do their best with the tools they had on hand, and they had to pound the six new posts into the ground by hand, which did not do much for Dick Conley's hangover or his mood, while the restapling of the wire took all of ten minutes. Then they drove into the man's pasture through the connecting gate that someone, God bless their soul, had installed between the two quarters anticipating just this kind of eventuality. They left the gate open so they could chase their cows through and made their way to the holding corral. Right on 10:30, a shiny new Chevy Avalanche arrived. A man and, well let's say it like Dick Conley would have seen it, a man and his floozy got out.

Now a middle-aged gent, a rotund city boy dressed in what he must have thought were a working dude's clothes, was inevitably going to be a spectacle in his own right; this man was no exception. In reality, he was so much a caricature of the Wild West, his attire itself so wildly outrageous, it was all Conley could do not to burst out laughing. His military escort on the other hand, was more in a state of undress than battle dress. Everything about her was, well, inappropriate for patrol: her fancy high-heeled cowgirl boots; her leather skirt too short, more of an all-round mini-apron than a skirt; a top that wasn't designed for discretion; and a neigh that would have put a rutting bull moose to instant flight. The surfeit of peroxide in her locks didn't much help either, Conley was thinking.

Then the man began. "Glad to see you've made the effort and fixed the fence," he barked without so much as the slightest hey-ho of a greeting. "Sure hope you've done a job. It's not in great shape is it, that fence?" he continued, adding "maybe you'll have to put in a bit more time" as if to ram the message home.

"So tell me, Mr. Reynolds, did you ever check the fence when you brought your critters in? Just asking," said Aubrey so coolly.

The man, more of a Humpty Dumpty clone in leather actually, pulled himself up to his inconsiderable height and said, "I don't do fences. I rent the land, not the fence. I expect the fence to be in shape when I rent it. Put it this way, the fence is a part of what I am paying for." He was no-nonsense, this man, a man who made it very clear he was used to being in charge.

"I see," said Aubrey, shifting his weight to the other foot. "So you see no responsibility for maintaining any of the fence, then? How familiar with the law are you?"

That was the statement that was the trigger to something bigger. "Have you any idea who I am?" said the man. Dick Conley could not desist any longer.

"Oh yes," he gushed. "You're Burt Reynolds the great fill-um star. You're the guy who played Darville in *Smokey and the Bandit*, right? You were great, really great." Ah, but that wicked smile filled his eyes, while what he had just said destroyed whatever was left of the man's tiresome sanctimony.

"As a matter of fact, that was Burton Reynolds. I am Bertram Reynolds and I am a judge in Red Deer."

"A judge of what?" responded Dick Conley. "Red Deer's Got Talent?" Why was he looking so pointedly at the lady when he said it?

"Look," Aubrey felt he had to intervene. "You may be a judge, but do you know the accepted customs out here when it comes to dealing with fencing?"

"Tell me," the man scowled at Dick Conley who was still leering at what he thought was a finalist of "Red Deer's got Talent or Something". The good judge was not about to show ignorance either; no judge could ever afford to do that no matter if he was a pretend-cowboy during his time off.

"Well, if we go by what is customary around these parts, if you stand in the centre of your quarter section, you are responsible for any part of the boundary fence to your right as you face it, which, incidentally, means that you, sir, are actually responsible for the stretch of fence that we have just now repaired. So maybe you should just get down off your high horse …"

"Rocking horse," said Conley snidely, grinning like Hobbes of Calvin and Hobbes fame.

"… and thank us for being so darn neighbourly and fulfilling what under law is really your responsibility. And perhaps you would do well to remember this while we are at it; out here in the country, we like to take care of each other no matter who we are."

Evidently his princess had never seen her legal honey addressed like this. As with all of the other prominent parts of her anatomy, her eyes were bulging in anticipation, no doubt, of the hellfire her very own queen's representative would cause to rain down on such saucy knaves. But Aubrey's speech must have put the fire out. Of course! Judges are smart, like lawyers, politicians and con men. They can almost smell where they need to put their feet in order to avoid the biggest cow pies.

"My understanding is that it is the landlord who is responsible for the fence. After all, when it comes down to it, all I'm renting is the pasture." Nonetheless the judge came across as somewhat chastened.

"Whose cows are going to be getting out? His or yours?" Aubrey was not to be denied.

"Well in the event, I would say yours," said Judge Reynolds, reluctant to cede any ground.

"Have you got an agreement, verbal or written, with your landlord where he specifically agrees he is responsible for the fence?" Aubrey was relentless.

"Well not in writing. But I pay twenty dollars a pair per month for this pasture, so I am sure he will be fixing the fence at that price." The judge was on the defensive now.

"I see." It was Aubrey's turn to be a bit smug. Sabine it has to be said, really enjoyed her husband when he was at the top of his verbal game, especially when dealing with such an unmitigated prig. "Well, perhaps you need to know that twenty dollars a pair per month is at the very bottom of the scale; but then again, it's way more than this particular piece of pasture is worth on the open market. The place wasn't even rented last year."

"Well, in my book I'm paying more than enough," the good judge retorted.

"Oh you are, you are…in your own mind," said Aubrey. "But let's take it a step further. How did you come to the conclusion it was my cows and not yours that smashed the fence? You're the judge so you'd be the one to know, right? At least that's what I'm thinking."

By now the judge was downright contrite, while his female consort, long past caring about the intricacies of any *Line Fence Act*, was now busy filing her nails. "Why did nobody think to tell me all of this when I bought my cows?" he said, now shifting to a different tack. "And as you can see, they are purebred Texas Longhorn so I don't want them 'er, contaminated by somebody else's scrub bull."

"My, for a judge you sure have an unfortunate way of putting things," said Conley determined to get his share of the sport. "Willy Wonka…"

"Who the hell are you calling Willy Wonka?" roared the judge.

"Why, that's the name of Mr. Hanlon's bull. And by the way, Willy is a purebred Gelbvieh, so you could even end up with a couple of calves that can carry a little more flesh on them than a spotted clothes rack." Conley was always merciless in attack.

There was no doubt about it, if the judge tolerated Aubrey, he could not abide Dick Conley, especially now that his escort was giving him, Dick Conley, too much of a "glad eye". So he turned his back on the man and proceeded to address Aubrey.

"Look, I would like to thank you very much for fixing the fence, no matter whose responsibility it turns out to be. Can I pay you something? Better yet, are you still willing to help me get our two herds separated?" This last was actually a city boy's code for "Can you help me get these damn cows back to where they are meant to be because I will be totally incompetent at doing so, and I want to go home."

"No problem, Bert. Just as long as you understand that we are neighbours, not judge and serf. I'll even stick a solar fencer in tomorrow along the stretch where they are most likely to get out. I don't need any further hassles any more than you do. Oh, and there's no need to pay me money today but if they do happen to smash things up again, I'll be asking for a contribution. Fair enough?"

"Fair enough." The man even managed a smile, an event that Dick Conley would have congratulated him for if Sabine had not interrupted him.

"C'mon Dick," she said. "Grab a bucket of chop and follow me. Our cows will come because they don't ever say no to a mouthful of grain." With that, she went over to the truck and grabbed one bucket for Dick and one for herself before striding off towards the connecting gate, calling shrilly as she went. Ah, of course those cows would come for Mama's voice, would know that they were in for an extra treat, so they and their calves trotted after her. While the judge was mesmerized, his consort was uncomfortable. What might she be asked to do? Willy Wonka would have gone too if he had not feared a two-foot length of horn penetrating his behind the moment he turned around.

"Well, let's you and I deal with the bulls," said Aubrey. "You, Bert, go stand over there and start yelling when I tell you, and you, Ma'am, go stand right about there, where that tuft of grass is sticking up. Your job is to scream and holler and carry on if either bull comes your way. Now whatever you do, don't run!" If the judge was wary of the whole arrangement, the madam was highly dubious. But then again, she was now so far out of her depth, all she could do was suppress her misgivings.

"I'll go split 'em up, then, and see if I can get your bull to go south and my bull to go north. But both of you be aware of that little crick over there where the grass is so green. Don't go running into it if either of the bulls comes directly this way!" As if the judge was going to run! As if his flight attendant could run with heels as high as a blacksmith's anvil!

Aubrey grabbed his favourite rattle cane and made his way over to where the two bulls were still leaning into each other. He got to within about ten feet of them when suddenly he launched himself forward howling like a banshee and waving his cane over his head. Which of the bulls got the biggest fright was unknowable: what was knowable was that they parted from each other as if each had received a ten thousand volt shock from the other. The Longhorn knew his harem was somewhere to the south, so thankfully that was where he headed. Willy Wonka had already seen Mama Sabine go north, but he was obviously unsure (a) if he had been invited, and (b) whether he should leave his other newfound crumpet behind. Moreover, Willy's compass was obviously spinning wildly which is why he made a beeline straight towards the woman. Now this poor lady had never been in the path of any bull, a four-legged one that is, so she took off at a wobbly clop, that being the only gait allowed by her fashionable footwear. She made unerringly for that crick, looking over her shoulder as she did so. The trouble was, her outer packaging had never been designed for or by Canada Post, had not been designed to cope with or absorb either undue stress or a full-frontal tumble into a crick. It was inevitable; the crash released most of the contents of the parcel. But while she was busy doing her floundering, Willy Wonka simply veered away from all this inexplicable noise and headed north, attracted as he was by the sweeter sound of Mama Sabine's hollering. Wonder Woman, not at all aware that she had exited most of her Wonder Bra, rose unsteadily to her feet. What had her two male onlookers in awe, however, was not so much the sight but the sound—a high-pitched keening that reached into the very heavens of descant, an incredibly soulful sound that didn't seem to call for the taking of a single breath. Finally it tailed off and tears began to flow.

"You'd better take her home," Aubrey said. "And you'd best do it now before my buddy gets here because he'll be nothing but a catastrophe."

For the first time in many years, the judge took someone else's advice. "Thank you," he said taking El Nina's tiny hand. "I owe you big time, not so much for fixing the fence and dealing with the cows but for giving me a whole new understanding about respect for our fellow human beings."

"You're very welcome," said Aubrey.

It should be obvious to most people; all ranchers are not cowboys, and all cowboys are not ranchers. Moreover, a visit to any Calgary Stampede breakfast will likely convince you that the cowboy is all make-believe. About the only thing any of those Calgary cowboys could lasso would be the pint of suds at the end of their arm or the dipsy cowgirl that stumbled into their corral. Put those same dudes astride a horse or arm them with a genuine branding iron and you'd have a reality show that would make *Survivor* seem like a fraud. Not that Aubrey Hanlon would be any good on a horse either, but then he classed horses with exercise bikes; you had to have a designer ass to ride either one of them. No, his short legs and his plum bum were far more at home on a Honda quad; besides, the Honda never groaned or rolled its eyes when you climbed aboard.

Once, a long time ago, the Hanlons had attended the Caroline May long-weekend rodeo, although few memories remained of it save the heat and the spectacle of "Mutton-bustin'." There was the still vital recollection of the fat kid who came out of the chute riding a mama sheep that made it a mere five yards into the ring before collapsing with the weight of Fat Freddy on her back. "That would be me on a 'hoss'," Aubrey was thinking at the time. It would not have been fair to the hoss, any hoss. That and the incredible wonderment at the tsunami of beer that folks were knocking back was what they recalled; although it had to be said that the dress code, too, was something of an eye-popper—the kind where what you couldn't pack in you just let hang out kind of deal, which must have left some folks confused about what they had come to see. So it was that the Hanlons had forsaken that world for the more natural one of the wildlife in the mountains, the sheep, the bears and the elk.

Then the day came when Tim the Co-Op man arrived with a load of diesel fuel for them. Now Tim and Aubrey had always had a raucous relationship, both constantly castigating the other for a whole range of character defects. Razzing each other became a matter of course, as was Aubrey's one-fingered salute… until the day when they sent a different driver and Aubrey had to apologize profusely to him for sending the wrong message. So when Tim climbed out of the cab that day and said, "Aub, do you and that fine lady of yours ever go to the rodeo?" Aubrey was instantly on his guard. He had to be. Was Tim Wonderbread setting him up for something? He'd better be careful, so he let out some line.

"What if we do Wonderboy, what's it to you?"

"Whoa! Whoa there, old man! Here I am on a be-nice-to-scumbags mission and you pop a question like that! Stop being a darn porcupine with all of its quills sticking up and answer my question. Do you and your old lady ever go to the rodeo?"

"We've been a time or two, why?" Aubrey was not about to give anything away, not yet.

"Well, I've got a couple of tickets for a Saturday evening at the C.F.R. up in Edmonton to give away. But maybe I should give 'em to someone who's a whole lot nicer to me than you ever are."

"Hold on a sec, what's the C.F.R.?" Aubrey knew the answer as soon as he said it; now he would appear like some guy who thought a ram was a Dodge.

"The Canadian Rodeo Finals. But then maybe a ticket would be wasted on you even if I'm certain your dear wife would enjoy going."

"She would love it," said the sing-song voice behind the truck. "She even has her very own cowgirl hat that she would proudly wear for such an occasion." Sabine swung into view.

"Good," said Tim. "Co-Op is giving out a bunch of free tickets to our long-time fuel customers, even to some with a condition called 'Viagra of the Finger'. You'll get a call from the office to tell you to come on in and pick them up. It'll do your old man good to see just how tough real cowboys are."

Why did it surprise Sabine that her husband's middle finger twitched uncontrollably? "Behave yourself!" she said. "This man has just been very nice to us." She turned to Tim. "Is there anybody else going from around here?"

"As a matter of fact, Steve and Marie Day, just down the road, are going. But at least Steve has known the difference between a cow and a bull since he was six years old. Your man here only knows bull."

This time Sabine was compelled to whack her husband's finger.

Sabine set it up so that they would travel up to Edmonton with Steve and Marie, seeing that they were experienced with the C.F.R. and knew the routine. That was when they heard about what was, to them, the perfect bonus. Farmfair with its beef breeders' show was on at the same time, together with a great big, glorified Farmers' Market. So now it wasn't just an evening of "Running of the Bulls" and "Bucking of the Broncos"; it was also going to be educational (Aubrey), and consumer-oriented (Sabine). Aubrey would get to see more of Alberta's beef breeds turned out to be the best they could be, while Sabine would get to spend money on all sorts of likely useless exotica. Because of all this, for her at any rate, Tim was right up there at the level of hero worship, along with Sid the Kid Crosbie,

Wayne Gretzky, Shania "Twang" and some foul-mouthed chef on TV named Fred or Gordon, or something. Aubrey did not qualify; he could swear with gusto, but he could not cook worth a hoot.

The whole thing turned out to be more than just a day off the farm; it was an adventure. Aubrey had always endorsed the mantra that says quality of life resides in the company you keep, and Steve and Marie were nothing short of a hoot. Better yet, much better, Steve was able to navigate all the way to Edmonton's Rexall Centre without getting lost, whereas Aubrey and Sabine would probably have got there via Hinton and Grande Cache, got lost eighteen times and yelled at each other at least six before sinking into a stony silence. The crowds were off-putting for sure, with Aubrey thinking how far humanity seemed to adopt the characteristics and the instincts of the herd. There were all sorts of alpha-male wanna-be's and look-alikes, while dude chicks were a dime a dozen. The Days and the Hanlons looked positively ordinary, anonymous even. Nobody gave them a second glance. Ah, but Aubrey was close to Hockey Heaven too, close to where his beloved Oilers continued to enjoy yet another losing streak. All they really needed was an ex-cop like him to take over the coaching duties. He would have it turned around in a hurry. Yessir! None of this sports psychology stuff, just plain old discipline and hard work. Like so many Oilers fanatics, Aubrey had all the answers.

They took a quick look around the cavernous hall where all sorts of booths were peddling all sorts of wares, and Sabine's appetite was properly whetted. The place was already full of people traipsing around looking for that hidden treasure or elusive bargain that you wouldn't find any place else. But then again, you had to be ready to be hustled by all kinds of dubious characters set to pounce on any stray dollars that came their way. The noise level from the general hustle and bustle made it obvious that this was a trading floor as lively as any stock exchange, which of course it was in its own way. The livestock barn where they headed next was, by complete contrast, quiet and low-key. Row upon row of tethered cattle were standing quietly chewing the cud or lying passively on beds of fresh straw, their every whim attended to, their every poop whisked away so no dude or dudette got their going-to-town footwear soiled or their stone-washed jeans splotched with a glob or two of cow shit. The atmosphere was positively pastoral with attendants alternately chatting up potential customers or primping up their animals for the next round in the judging ring. Sabine especially was astounded at how much effort went into the cosmetic process, what with the use of the fanciest hairdryers and hoof polish and so forth. Heck, these folks spent far more time on the appearance of their animals than Sabine ever spent on her own appearance. It had to be remembered though, those showing their animals were not only representing their own farm but also their chosen breed. Yet sadly, reflective of the general dynamics in the beef industry, the Hanlons and the Days were told and could actually see how much the number of exhibitors had declined given all of the empty space. The Hanlons' favourite breed, Blonde d'Aquitaine, was not even represented. It was nothing short of an eye-opener for Aubrey and Sabine to tag along with Steve and Marie because the latter knew so many of the faces they were talking to. All of them hinted something far bigger was going on in their beef world than the regular cyclical downturn.

In retrospect, too, their jaunt around the livestock barns was highly illuminating if not instructive. In one sense, it was more like a visit to a fashionable ladies' hair parlour; all these lady cows and fancy bulls being pampered for hours on end in hopes of wearing a rosette to denote "Best of the Breed". And maybe if you lucked out to be the "Supreme Grand Champion", you'd win a truck complete with a stock trailer to go with it. But in other ways, these animals were not at all representative of their particular breeds as Steve was quick to point out. "Where would you see an Angus or a Gelbvieh bull as fancy as these?" he would say, pointing out a couple of stellar examples of what a bull was supposed to be all about. "They are pushed so darn hard to gain weight, they look like a bovine version of Tarzan put together by a breeders' committee. The problem is, these bulls rarely last very long when they're put out to work, and oftentimes they're too darn fat to be active breeders." Beyond that, as the Hanlons and so many other cow-chasers knew, it was the ugliest cow in the herd that often produced the best-looking calf, like Nellie the "Hanlon Sacred Cow". If Nellie was to be entered in any such competition, she would have had the judges laughing their britches off she was so ugly; that's if she didn't have one of them hanging from the rafters after the very first day.

As Steve intimated and Aubrey had realized, the show-ring was a culture all of its own. So it was incomprehensible to most outsiders as to how the judges ever arrived at a decision; it was almost as if these same outsiders were uninitiated in some way. It was like going to an art show; sometimes you only knew what was good if you had been properly schooled in the genre. Aubrey and Sabine had their own little competition to pick the winners as the champions of the various breeds were selected. Sabine picked a full five winners; Aubrey, much to his chagrin, picked none, if you must know!

By the time they got to the concession hall with all the booths, the place was like an ants' nest that has just been kicked over. While a farmer's trip to town ranks as an occasion, a farmer's trip to the city is often a spectacle, sometimes even two-way. Country folk come across sights and hear sounds and observe behaviours that leave them in shock. How can people even consider going out in public plumed like peacocks in the mating season? How much did it cost that chick for the dragon tattoo so big it encircles her back and her arm before disappearing between Twin Peaks? She might think she looks fetching, but most ordinary folk are probably thinking she looks downright bizarre. As for the regular old Canadian dirt farmer, he's more at home in his well-worn Co-Op cap than in a fancy Stetson that resembles a Martian spaceship alighting on some dude's shiny dome. Aubrey felt refreshingly normal, ordinary, even nondescript, which quite frankly was the way he liked it to be. This projecting some form of cool image had become too much of a social fetish in his book. But then again, if you are the one mammal on the planet that has the capacity to constantly adjust its looks, why not? Turkeys strut, peacocks preen, and Muscovies like Morton swagger. Horses mince, monkeys groom, and hippos waddle. Humanity does it all, extending everything into an art form with hoops in appendages, dyes in hair, studs in ears, lips and eyebrows, and with colours to outshine any Santa Claus parade.

Then there were the stands, booths, boutiques and stalls, call them what you will. Some were staid, some laid-back; some were "come-on-in-and-spend" for we will bother you if you don't. Others again were manned by hustlers determined not to let you by if you happened to be in the target audience of whatever they were selling. They were good at it too, had the sales patter down to such an art form you felt like a complete loser if you didn't up and buy a volume-pack of the particular magic potion they were peddling. Aubrey and Sabine nearly died laughing watching a very attractive, well let's just say "a chick", reeling folks, mostly men, into a massage booth where an eighty-year-old granny with more wrinkles than a tortoise of the same age was doing the massaging. Many of them, mostly the men, obviously felt it wasn't right to ask for their money back. "So Canadian," said Aubrey.

As if, as if the Days and the Hanlons were immune! They made the mistake of stopping by a heavy-duty footwear booth. A smooth-talking salesman was onto them like a cat pouncing on mice; sometimes it can be as unfortunate to be a mouse as to be a farmer. "Take a good look, boys, these are the best boots there are for a farm in winter, that I can guarantee you. You guys need nothing but the best when it's minus thirty out there in calving season, when we city folks are lying in bed fast asleep. I know how hard you people work because my dad was a farmer from way-back-when. I was the smart one in the family; I got out while the going was good. But if it wasn't for folks like you, we'd all go hungry. That's why we've got a special on these here boots at seventy dollars off." What he neglected to say was that they were still priced at a breath-taking one hundred and sixty dollars. Aubrey meantime had never bought a pair of boots for more than thirty dollars on sale at Canadian Tire, but then maybe that was why Aubrey was perpetually whining that he had cold feet.

Okay, okay, they looked like real good boots and had a great-looking sole. And they were pliable with thick uppers. "We get 'em from the good ol' USA," said the man, keeping up the attack as Aubrey took a closer look.

"Yeah, but it says here, 'Made in China,'" said Aubrey shooting him down some. "What do they know about cold feet in Shanghai?" The man put himself on pause.

Aubrey then glanced over at Steve, deciding that he could be impressed if Steve was impressed.

"Take your time, boys. Take a good look. Your feet deserve to be warm and these babies are good to minus seventy. We've had nothing but good reports about 'em."

"Yeah, but my feet are only good to minus eighteen and my blood to minus six," said Aubrey again trying to stem the flow.

"Get yourself a pair," snapped his Arbiter of All Things.

"Get a pair!" said Steve's Arbiter of All Things.

The salesman knew he had reeled them in when he saw the women join the offensive. The rest was mere formality.

Not that the ladies had been idle. Oh no, far from. They had done more than their fair share for a depressed economy by buying all sorts of Christmas presents for the lucky and the deserving. And now they were some way ahead, beckoning their menfolk to join them at a large "country clothing" display that would have made any Hutterite proud. That was the moment when a swarthy individual, a big man as big men go, accosted Steve. How could he have misread the passing flow of humanity so badly that he pounced on Steve of all people, Aubrey was thinking. The man was flogging some miracle oil product for the skin, something from an emu or a camel or a whale, presumably long since dead. "Veryee goodh for de skinh", the man said. Could he not see that Steve's dermatological composition was more leather than skin?

Yes, well Steve was a big man too, but farm-big, low centre of gravity and farm-strong big. One flex in anger of those biceps and the man would be calling for mama, the Southside gang, the Edmonton police, or all of the above, all in a language that nobody hereabouts had ever heard. Strangely enough, the man did not see fit to simply talk to Steve. The same instant Aubrey was smart enough to beat a swift retreat, the fellow forced Steve to *physically* stop and listen to his sales pitch. Steve, humble fellow that he was, remained courteous enough; but for some reason the man then decided to assert himself a bit more and literally invade Steve's space. Worse yet, he was fanatical to the point of smearing some of his wonder-oil on Steve's cheek before pressing the rest of the bottle into his hand and demanding twenty bucks. That's "demanded", not "asked for". Well Steve's dome light started to signal extreme danger. Aubrey was about to go back and intervene on the side of justice and common sense when he saw Steve grab the lapel of the man's coat while forcing the bottle into the man's pocket. He then proceeded to make a pronouncement in Agricultural English which immediately encouraged the man to detach himself in a great hurry. Steve's dome light was still flashing brightly when he rejoined Aubrey.

"What did you tell him?" asked Aubrey, greatly impressed.

"Ugh? Tell him? Why I told him I didn't need any of his bleeping snake oil so he should take a hike because I had Bovine Spongiform Encephalitis and it's highly contagious. That's when he said it wasn't oil from snakes but from male Muscovies."

"Morton oil," said Aubrey.

"Come again?" said Steve. And so the story of Morton the duck became a local legend.

The rodeo! What could one say about the rodeo? A rodeo was not something the Hanlons would ordinarily attend. Many said of rodeos that once you had seen one you had seen them all. But that was unfair. It was like saying once you had seen one game of hockey you had seen them all. The C.F.R. was special; it was the Grey Cup of rodeo. To Aubrey and Sabine, just as it took a certain type of fan to attend a hockey or a football game, so it took a certain type of fan to enjoy a rodeo. Moreover, for anybody with beef in their background, it hearkened back to something elemental in the relationship between man and beast. It wasn't, after all, anything like the "Running of the Bulls" in Pamplona, Spain: All that seemed to call for was a healthy dose of idiocy rather than anything closely resembling a skill. Even the Mexican Poker game at the small-town-smack-down in Caroline called for more grit than idiocy as you played a hand of poker while waiting for an exceedingly large and rank bull hopefully to take out your opponents and leave you still at the table, and sitting on the jackpot. These bronco-busters and barrel-riders, these calf-ropers and steer-wrestlers, and last but not least these crazy bull-riders, they had to be athletes first and foremost, with bodies that could rise above the extreme. On top of that, they had to be if not fearless then able to control fear with an iron fist. They could not be fearless and no athlete, nor the other way round. Only then did the skills come in, skills that were learned more through experience and immersion in their sport than from the teachings of another. It was all of this and then some that made a rider's style unique; everything had to be tailored down to your own particular body.

The whole experience of going to that rodeo got Aubrey thinking about his and Sabine's own special relationship to their animals. They were at ease with their cows, had learned to respect them and their space. So it was for a bull-rider or a bronco-buster; they too respected the animals that provided them with an excitingly exclusive lifestyle. They respected them at their own level. They, the animals were sentient beings, yes, but not sentimental beings; sentimentality is a human trait as demonstrated by those who would ban rodeo because it is "cruel and inhuman".

For sure, in rodeo as in any other field, there were those who could never relate to any creature, but then people like these could never relate very well to the human animal either. For the Hanlons, their cows actually grew into their names and established their own individual identities through that name. Nellie, for example, was everything you would expect from a heads-up suffragette. You could never take her for granted any more than the good old politico boys could have taken Nellie McClung for granted. If you endeavoured to show Nellie the cow your sentimental side, she would likely bunt you up there where the moon shines brightly. Respect, then, is a fragile thing. Betray respect with an animal and the chances are that it will never forgive let alone forget, not you, nor all of humanity. Animals remember, maybe not in quite the same way as humans, but they have memory nevertheless!

⊢— Chapter Thirteen —⊣
SIMPLY PASSING FIGURES
ON A LANDSCAPE

*I*t was not some sort of epiphany that gave rise to the Hanlon decision to hang up their shovels and their boots. Nor was it that somehow their story needed to come to an end. It was not about some terminal ailment or condition nor a sudden understanding that none of what they did made any economic sense. Like many of their past major decisions, it was arrived at in very small steps, prompted in turn by a host of small signals. The trip to the Canadian Rodeo Finals, for instance, convinced the Hanlons there was a whole wide world out there that they had never seen nor thought about; it deserved some further exploration. The fact that the Farmfair showed such a decline in livestock exhibitor numbers also sent a message that the Hanlons chose to interpret in a negative light; that in the G.S.T, the Great Scheme of Things, they were utterly insignificant. The government-sponsored meeting they had attended also left a sour after-taste, one that suggested that they could become either indentured wards of the welfare state or they could become vassals of big agri-corporations like Cargill, Monsanto or Novartis. The no-holds barred meeting with their Financial Advisor in Red Deer that day in the fall had further convinced them that when it came time for the ultimate liquidation of their assets, good timing was of the essence; you got out when things were good and people wanted your land and your inventory and would pay a good dollar to get it. Then of course there was Dr. Green who was relentless in telling them both that not only were they well over the agricultural hill, but they were also slip-sliding so fast down the back slope that they risked a crash, a spout-over-teakettle crash if they didn't slow down, he said.

"Yeah, and knowing my luck, I'd probably break both my own spout and the sound barrier at the same time," added Aubrey unnecessarily.

As if to add substance to this pessimistic line of thought, winter that year decided to come early so everyone in the beef business had to begin feeding their herds three weeks earlier than usual. Naturally the price of hay soared as those farmers who refused to bank on an early spring the following year sought to supplement their stocks. Neither of the Hanlons wanted to spend that kind of money, even if they could both see the logic. But it was a topic that nonetheless called for some discussion, and it was that discussion that coughed up the dreaded decision, the decision to pretty much quit farming while they were still ahead. Sort of. The more Aubrey and Sabine talked, the more they saw the decision as right for whom and where they were. They had watched too many older farmers succumb prematurely because they kept on telling themselves they could not stop. For them, "next year" was always the story. They had seen others struggle right to the end, much too proud to admit not that they couldn't do the work but that they shouldn't. There were those again who had succeeded in boxing themselves in by borrowing too heavily in the lean years only to discover that those bankers who had clamoured to lend them money in the first place now felt little pain in abandoning them. At the microlevel, the bankers' world was one where they, the bankers, were always largely in control; perhaps unfortunately, they, the bankers never experienced a serious scours epidemic among the calves, a hailstorm that dropped the entire crop, or the wresting of their market control by much bigger players. They could always stay within the comforting confines of bank policy. All of the Hanlons' experience, all the Hanlon thinking fed into this one transformative decision, transformative because it affected the very essence of who they were. They had to put themselves in charge of their own destiny. And so they did!

Yes, they loved their farm. But however much they lived and breathed their land, it would still be there when they had passed on, just as much as it had been there before they arrived. They were simply passing figures on a landscape. Yes, they had resonated with that piece of dirt over every season, resonated when others might not have done so, but the land was bigger than all of them, than all of humanity. No matter how humanity chose to exercise dominion over it, the land would end up as the final arbiter of human destiny. In their self-centred, self-indulgent world, in their arrogant pursuit of transitory wealth, far too many men and women failed to grasp how far they were only the guests of the land and all its resources. Meanwhile, their time on the land had taught Aubrey and Sabine so much in the abstract sense, let alone in the practical sense. They had learned a degree of humility that taught them they had a role rather than an entitlement. They had skirmished with birth and with death, and they understood the nuances of both; those same nuances connected them to the genesis of creation. They had learned when they needed to nurture, and when they needed to stand back, usually in awe, as Mother Nature conducted her business without them. Eventually then, their understanding of who they were came to be defined not at all by money, nor by status and recognition, because in the final analysis such things played such a minute part in what described true quality of life. To sum it up then, at that point in time when they made their decision, and thereafter too, the Hanlons remained perfectly comfortable in their own skins.

Oh yes, it is quite one thing to come to a momentous decision, it is quite another to suffer the prolonged pain required to implement it. The nuts and bolts of the decision were clear. They would sell the one quarter of land and keep the home quarter. That way they could still play at the farming they so loved, maybe keep twenty or so cows because cows had become so much a part of their identity. Yes, they would have to sell about eighty percent of the herd they had so painstakingly built up over the years, and yes, that would be painful in the extreme. But for once they had to think of themselves within the context of their own history, not so much in terms of their own comfort but in terms of their ability to manage as they aged. Better still, if they stayed where they were, they could remain a vital part of the community, the community that had become a part of them. The less they had to do on their own place, the more they could choose to go out and help their neighbours, those same neighbours who had willingly dropped what they had been doing to come and help them in times past. They could hang onto most of their machinery because most of it was worth not much more than a knave's ransom. They could even go out and do a bit of custom work if they got that ambitious. The crux of the decision though, was that by making it, they were giving themselves choices. Inasmuch as quality of life might amount to the company you keep, it also comes down to the luxury of being able to make your choices freely, however hard those choices might be to make.

So it was that Aubrey and Sabine Hanlon did not just navigate through the trials of that winter so much as they endured them. They locked themselves into their decision by talking to the boys down at Olds Auction Mart about conducting the dispersal sale of their cows and by choosing a date set in stone, the first week of February, February 7 to be precise. They even set the numbers, more or less, with the understanding that these numbers could be fluid up to three weeks before the sale. At that time, they agreed, the boom would be lowered and whatever numbers the Hanlons had decided upon would be advertised over the local radio and in the local press. And so the pressure began to build, and build some more as Christmas came and went, as New Year's Day breezed on through, as that day in February began to loom large on the calendar.

As always, both Hanlons internalized their feelings in their own way. Neither of them made the classic mistake of second-guessing their decision, while each of them relied on the comforting presence of their mate to bolster any flagging resolve. But it was hard. It was hard for both of them to see their bred heifers becoming more and more friendly every day; it was hard to keep up the pretence of loving them when, in the Hanlons' minds, they would never have the chance to have their first calf on the farm where they were born and had grown up. Aubrey and Sabine felt like frauds too when they greeted their cows and talked to them.

Worse yet, they still had to select which twenty-five they would keep back as their "retirement package". Aubrey kept telling Sabine to decide, but then he kept telling her to keep Petunia and Pansy and Rosebud. Unmentioned in all of this was what they would do with Nellie, now fifteen years old but a fellow traveller from the beginning of their adventure, and as much a part of that adventure as they were. Never had she lost a calf or calved late, never had she done what she was supposed to do either, but that was her nature; she had been as wacky and feisty as Aubrey at his best, as stubborn as Sabine at her worst.

The other thing that bothered the Hanlons was that sign, the one the real estate folks put up to show the land was for sale. It was like an eye irritation, however much it was a necessity. It seemed to signal demise, the fading of a dream, a recognition of their own mortality, even. But it did the job because it attracted the attention of a couple looking to abandon the frenetic city life they led in Calgary for their very own oasis in the country, a quarter section where they could build the house of their dreams on top of a hill with a view of the mountains, a place where they could keep a few horses. They got it all when the Hanlons accepted their offer to purchase, thereby reducing themselves down to the last quarter. Sadly in a way though, the transaction was in keeping with the dying out of the small family farm. To the new owners, the deal was a real estate coup; their own piece of paradise that they had always hankered after. The land was never conceived of as a farm to be worked and maintained as such, but an escape, a sanctuary away from the frenzy of human commerce. And so, in this respect it was hard for Aubrey and Sabine; they had to turn their backs on what had defined them as farmers, had to accept that someone else was going to do whatever they chose to "their" land, and they knew that never again would it be a going farm concern in their time.

Aubrey and Sabine knew they could never go back on their cattle deal either, when they heard that first radio announcement about the dispersal of their stock. Sabine was especially gratified by the statement "top quality cowherd, one of the best in Alberta". Aubrey just shut it all out of his mind. The ad in the weekly paper rammed the finality of it home; there was no turning back now. They booked two truckers rather than one because they wanted, needed, all of the cows trucked out in one shot. The day was going to be hard enough without having to say goodbye to their cows in two shifts. If they had hired only one trucker, he would have had to return for a second load. The sale was scheduled for noon on February 7, so the cattle would have to be moved out the day before. They would be held in pens overnight at the mart where food and water would be made available. They also had to be preg-tested by the auction mart vet with any open animals to be auctioned as cull cows. There was absolutely no room for sentiment now; what had to be done would be done.

Even with Pete and Jeannie and Steve Day to help, they would have their hands full on D-day, February 6, when they needed first to sort and then to ship. The plan was to bring all of the animals in, separate out the twenty-five cows Sabine had selected to retain at home and run them off to a far-off field where they could chew on a bale of hay; that would take them out of the picture. It would be a hard enough day without having them confusing the issue.

At this juncture, the issue becomes how to tell the rest of the story, whether to attempt a full description of those two days that rendered the Hanlons almost meaningless in their own eyes. But to tell it like it was with all of the gory details would be an invasion of their emotional privacy. When historians set out to piece together an event in the past, they seek anthropological evidence, artefacts and documents and such, that do much to tell it like it was. To show how the Hanlons got down to their last quarter, we are forced to rely on two "documents", writings penned by Mrs. Sabine Hanlon at the time. This was her way of both closing the book and venting her grief, for what the Hanlons had to do was akin to dealing with a death in the family, multiple deaths really. There were two such "documents", the first entitled "They're Gone!" and the second entitled "Sale Day".

THEY'RE GONE!
Yes, they're gone!
The statement is bald. Uncompromisingly bleak.
They're gone! This is a statement that amounts to betrayal, to abandonment.
The very moment we started to bring them in, they knew something was up. They always do, our girls. But like lambs to the slaughter they came anyway. For us. Our girls. And then came the sorting; it was as if we were called upon to decide which of our children we were going to keep and which to send off to the orphanage. Oh it was hard not to add extras to the ones we had chosen, but this was a decision that could not be tampered with. Snowflake and Petunia had to go. So too Matata and Mirabella. We had to keep back younger ones because these were they who would see us through. And of course we kept back our very own version of Nellie McClung, she who was as much a part of our own history as we were. We separated them and herded them out to a far field, our new aristocracy with their own King William, Willy Wonka.
Then we had to separate the bred heifers, for they had to go in a distinct package. They were still very much "our babies", the same who all year would come and beg for a skiff of chop because they knew we had a soft spot for them. Of them all, these were the ones who suddenly sensed the hardness of our hearts, and they were confounded, and rightly so. Somehow they knew we were about to betray them, and they stared back not with accusation but with hopeless resignation. That was what hurt, oh how that hurt!

As for the rest of the herd, the regular mamas almost all of whom had grown up on the farm, they knew too. This was the end of the story—not ours, nor theirs specifically but the story of our togetherness. Some of them acted as if they had expected it. Others, again because they still had faith in us, seemed to intimate that they wanted to believe something different. And they could and did until the liners showed up, those clattering iron monsters spilling their filthy diesel fumes into the cold winter's air. Now the message was unequivocal; for the girls knew all about cattle liners, how such monsters had sucked up all of their young the previous fall.

As we loaded them up, they looked at us beseechingly, only to be turned away, our connection severed. Forever. Worse yet, there is no dignity when it comes to loading cows into a liner. The prod is the law, forward momentum the only choice. No, not choice, for there was no alternative. The old-timers who had served us so long and so well dismissed us almost contemptuously as they accepted their fate; in our own way we had failed them. Betrayal has a completeness, a finality, no matter how gentle and how caring our neighbours were in coaxing our girls aboard, the same neighbours who ministered to our own distress.

Suddenly there was silence, the corrals were empty and the pastures deserted. That silence was not pleasing, but rather it was downright eerie: a tranquillity riddled with skeins of treason. There was no satisfaction for a job well done and our thanks for all the help seemed somehow insincere beside the huge sense of loss that we were experiencing. After all, it was as if we had been presiding over our own funeral, the demise of so much that we had come to live among and love.

SALE DAY!

If the day before was bad, the day of the sale was worse, far worse.

The auction mart down in Olds was already bustling with folk when we arrived.

"Go check your girls, just to make sure they're all okay," said Greg Sanderson, one of the auctioneer boys who greeted us. And we did, a way to kill some time.

So it was inevitable that we would come face to face, eye to eye with our girls. They turned away wearily. No matter how sweetly we talked to them, they turned away. They knew. We had abandoned them. "So go ahead," they seemed to be saying. "Say your last goodbyes if it makes you feel any better. What do we care?" We did; we said our last goodbyes, but they were whispered because we were so ashamed. We were almost weeping.

On our return trip through the maze of pens, we came across our bred heifers, "our babies". Like the cows, they had white stickers on their backs with the numbers of the month they were due to calve, 3: March, 4: April, 5: May. Like us, they were all but weeping. Some appeared to make a last-minute appeal, most just turned their backs on us. A couple almost made it clear that we should just go away. We had to; it was coming up sale time.

By now the place was teeming with people, an astonishing number of them our neighbours and friends. They knew all that we were going through and they cared enough to spend those hours in solidarity with us. That is the essence of true neighbourliness.

"You'd best come and sit up front with us," the sale auctioneer, Danny Rosehill told Aubrey. "So we can have you add a bit of colour and commentary where and when you need to." I was left in good hands though, for Marta and Hugo Hartford were there, as were Jim and Sonya Delamere, and of course Pete and Jeannie, Steve and Marie Day, Bill and Marie Stott, they were all there in support.

The boys of the auction knew our pain too. They had seen it before, done it before. From that fateful day when we had broached Greg Sanderson about selling, they had stayed in step with us all of the way. Oh, they were good! So professional! Better yet, they did not set out to milk the moment in order to make the biggest buck. They were not grasping, and for that they became instant family. They cared as much as the neighbours, which made them neighbours to all of us.

Finally it was time, and the realization for us that as much as it was all about money and how well or poorly we might do, it was also about "our girls" going to a good home.

As Aubrey climbed up into his seat alongside Danny, the main sale auctioneer for us, Greg endeavoured to reassure him that all would go well. There was no doubt these boys would do their very best, but even then, selling anything by auction is a gamble at the best of times. We had gambled on getting to this day, gambled the weather would cooperate, gambled there would be enough buyers interested in acquiring bred cows in the dead of winter, and here we were on the cusp of the greatest gamble we ever took. Aubrey looked up and had to turn aside to get control of his emotions. Then his eyes searched me out and found me in a lower section of the seating insulated by so many of our neighbours. Further up, there was the irrepressible Dick Conley, laughing with Quincy, and next to them Sig and Sybil. They had not come as voyeurs to our pain; they just knew how much their presence would mean to us.

The ring door clanged open and Tyler Rosehill, ring-man for the day, ushered in the first batch of five, and the sale was under way. Aubrey said his piece, and I listened as if I was on another planet as his voice boomed unnaturally over the speakers. I could not bring myself to look at those first cows, our cows; I was too busy fighting for composure while Jeannie, God bless her, held my hand. The bidding was brisk with Greg on the phone to some buyer who couldn't be there. And then that first batch was gone.

It was so hard to watch "our girls" go under the hammer like that, those same "girls" who had served us so faithfully all those years. In batches of two, three or five, they passed through that ring with style, a tribute to how we ourselves saw them and cared for them. They were, every one of them, as good as they looked, and they looked good!

Of course, I had to signal to Aubrey when Matata had come into the ring, that same Matata that would gladly have killed either one of us at calving time if we had given her the chance. We had agreed that in all good conscience, we could not sell her without warning any prospective buyer how great a danger she could be. Aubrey stopped the auctioneer and explained about Matata's disposition. It made not a blind bit of difference; the bidding just went up and up.

It was even harder to see the bred heifers, "our babies", sold; so hard to take their utter bewilderment at being bombarded by the alien sounds of this unfamiliar place, their very presence and all the work we had put into them condensed into one final bid.

In the end, I did not, nor could not, care. For inasmuch as we had sold our cows and our heifers, with every batch passing through that ring we peddled away a portion of our identity, of who and what we were…which in part is why we made it easy on ourselves by keeping back twenty-five.

Then came that moment when all of a sudden it was over; not the day's business, but our dispersal sale. Someone else's sale began, bred cows, the same as ours, and with it came the realization that inasmuch as our girls had done us proud, that sentiment went both ways; for the cows that now scrambled their way into the sale ring had clearly come from a different "ranching style", a hands-off, "money-is-where-it's-at" approach. These wide-eyed girls didn't have names, had probably never been seen as sentient beings, and that small illumination, that stark contrast gave us a small measure of closure. What gave us a far greater sense of closure, however, came from the unexpected attendance of so many from our own community, people who had come not to buy but to pay their last respects at the funeral of a lifestyle that we and they lived, a lifestyle they too would one day have to abandon. These were the ones who salved our wounds, who assuaged the deep feelings of loss and guilt, who made us appreciate what a privileged life all of us had led. We went home tired, exhausted, but nonetheless at peace. We had made that dread decision and we had lived up to it. Now it was time to move on, and to bring "our girls", the few that were left, back down to their corral. We were down to the last quarter!

Author Biography

Colin and Felicity Manuel were both born and raised on farms in Kenya, East Africa. In 1975, they made the move to Canada where Colin joined the teaching profession and Felicity worked in a bank. The couple's yearning for a piece of land to call their own led them to Dovercourt in the Rocky Mountain House area where they purchased **Shambani**, the Swahili word for "home farm". From there all manner of fun things unfolded. In essence then, these writings are a tribute to all our neighbours because it is those same neighbours who have so enriched our lives. And what better place to bring up our three boys! If quality of life resides in the company you keep, then truly we were blessed beyond words. Now down to a single quarter section, "the last quarter", we Manuels still play around with a few beloved cows because that defines so much of who and what we are. You may be able to scrub the dirt off the farmer, but you can never take the farmer from the dirt!

Illustrator Biography

In addition to illustrating numerous books, Ben's art is extensively published by Leanin' Tree. He has won many awards over the years, including the 2011 Moonbeam Award for children's books, 15 medals from Cowboy Cartoonists' International, and a very large spot on his mother's fridge. A family man with a wife and two daughters, he lives on top of Bizwanger's Hill, in west-central Alberta, where he can happily watch the world go by, grabbing what he can from life and living it to the fullest. When he's not making pictures, you can find him making music as he travels regularly throughout western Canada and the US to slather audiences with his twisted western wit. To add further dimension to Ben's art, visit his website at www.bencrane.com

A Debt of Gratitude

So much happens to a book in the final stages of publication. I would like to put on record my heartfelt thanks …

    …to Susan Chambers who makes editing into an art form.

    …to John Rempel who has worked magic with cover and book design.

    …to Kim Staflund who has steered the process with unqualified
        professionalism.